A Friend Request

Also by C. L. Gillmore

Of Roots, Shoes and Rhymes
A poetry book and accompanying CD

Winner of the 2011 Arizona Authors Association Literary Contest
in published nonfiction
Winner of the Sixth Annual National Indie Excellence Awards
in poetry

Uncommon Bond
Currently out of print, pending re-release with
added material and updates

Winner of the 2012 New Mexico-Arizona Book Awards for
Fiction-Romance
Finalist in the Indie Excellence Book Awards romance category
Nominated for the Global E-book Award for Best E-Book Trailer and
Best Romance Fiction

Uncommon Bond, aka **Love Whispers Softly** by Rose Richardson
Companion book to **A Friend Request**

Available in 2015

A Friend Request

A novel by
C. L. Gillmore

PLATINUM
POETRY & PROSE
PUBLISHING

A Friend Request
© 2014 by C.L. Gillmore

10-ISBN-10: 0692287655 First Edition Book
13-Digit ISBN: 978-0692287651 First Edition Book

Library of Congress Control Number: 2014952040

Published in the United States of America through:
Platinum Poetry & Prose Publishing, Surprise, AZ
www.clgillmore.com

Cover design by Terry Duffy
terry@glyphicsdesign.com
www.terryduffyartstudio.com

Cover Photograph by Todd Weinstein
todd@toddweinstein.com
www.toddweinstein.com

Editing and formatting by Ann Narcisian Videan
avidean@videanunlimited.com, http://ANVidean.com

Interior Photographs by © Jan Griesenbrock, 2014

Author Photograph by © Kelli Linn Martinez, 2014
kellilinnphotography.com

Publisher Trademark by Igor Brezhnev
igorbrezhnevdesign.com

Acknowledgments

I would like to thank the following people for their love and support along my journey to becoming a writer, and finally... a published author.

- My husband, Mike, and family – for your love, support, and understanding.
- Ann Narcisian Videan – for your professionalism, expertise, and patience as my editor.
- Alana Roberts – for your expert, virtual online assistance, positive disposition, friendship and love.
- Terry Duffy and Becky Ankeny – for your creative genius on the cover design.
- Todd Weinstein – for capturing such a lovely, haunting moment in the cover image.
- Jan Griesenbrock – for interpreting my words into the lovely, interior images.
- Jodie Wilson, Julianna Lyddon, Ann Videan – for taking time out of your busy lives to read and write the book reviews.
- My Reader's Circle—Beverly Belche, Deborah Summers, Randi Day—for reading and giving me honest input, while encouraging me to keep writing.
- Julianna Lyddon – for your intuitiveness in helping me... find me.
- Mary Holden – for your friendship, love, and honesty in making me a better writer.
- Bill True - for your friendship, honesty, and screenwriting/teaching expertise in allowing me to dig deeper into the components of this story.
- Carol McDaniels – for your friendship, expert advice, and steadfast encouragement.
- Tom and Cindi Kautz, Barb Woodstra, and Martha Walker – for always having a place for me to come home to.
- Cos Goldsberry and Sandi Strosnider – for a lifetime of memories, friendship, love and inspiration.
- Sharon Richardson – for being an amazing, inspiring, free spirit and forever friend.
- The Muscatine High School Class of 1967 – for remembering me with love and encouragement. You've filled my heart with fond memories, both past and present.

Each of you, in some way, filled my heart and soul with hopes, dreams, love, and memories. You gave me strength. You changed my life.

Now, you fuel my imagination, and inspire the words I write each day.

I dedicate this book to the guys in the band—Gary, Joey, Jake, Larry, Phil, and Randy—and to all those local bands of the late 1960s and early 1970s. Your music gave voice to an entire generation of dreamers. Dreamers, like me, who followed and loved you, and remembered.

A Friend Request

"Would our secrets be so secret if we were in each other's company or are we open because we can feel some private compassion? The secrets are an evolution. We evolved together, apart."

When Lightning Bugs Shimmered

by C. L. Gillmore

Heart memory stirs on shafts of moonglow
Releasing recollections from twilights long ago.

When lightning bugs shimmered in blue Mason jars
And flickered 'til daylight erased heaven's stars.

When field crickets chirped their rhythmic harmonies
And we played hide and seek among the maple trees.

When bare feet scampered over dew-covered grass
And lazy summer nights were so very slow to pass.

Endless possibilities, our lives had just begun.
Twilights long ago, when you and I were young.

[See the YouTube video at
http://www.youtube.com/watch?v=C6k5rKeR4QA]

Prologue

I remember as a child lying in bed at night
Covers over my head, listening to them fight.
And I always wondered when I heard my name
If I was the cause or if I was to blame.

The only real home I remember as a young child was the light-green house trimmed in white on East Carroll Street. My mom, older sister Carla, and I settled there after moving from one tiny Illinois town, Weldon, to another, Macomb, sometime during the summer of 1955 after my dad died. We lived there four years.

The street address and phone number there—1002 East Carroll Street, Amherst 2-7222—remain memorized.

My sister Carla, nine years older than I, knew a lot more about our life than I did at five and six. I learned from her, years later, that Mom spent months in bed—depressed—after my dad died. We lived in several apartments before the green house on East Carroll. I don't recall the other places well. I just remember the green house.

I recall the front porch swing, suspended on chains. On hot, muggy Midwest evenings, my sister and I swung there, listening to the buzzing of the cicadas, and the rhythmic clanking and creaking of those rusty chains.

The small, five-room house included a kitchen, living room, a dining room that served as my bedroom, two other bedrooms, and a bathroom. The living room's two southern-facing windows overlooked a graveled alley. My mom grew pink and purple lacy violets in clay pots on the southern-facing windowsills. I can still envision the brilliant yellow stamens in those violets popping against their velvety purple petals.

The narrow alley separated our single-story house from the brick, two-story directly across from us. I learned over the years the two-story served as a slaughterhouse and meat market, grocery store and finally, an apartment building, catering mostly to single men.

Carla and I used to scour the alley between our house and the apartment building on Saturday and Sunday mornings looking for money dropped by the drunks as they exited cabs late at night. We always managed to find something, mostly loose change, but sometimes dollar bills.

We took our newfound wealth, walked two blocks to a little neighborhood market and spent it all on things never allowed at home—Seven-Up candy bars, Topps baseball cards with gum, Hostess Cupcakes and Snowballs, giant dill pickles, slices of boiled ham, ice cream Drumsticks, and Dr. Pepper—depending on how much we found. We sometimes stuffed it all down as we walked back home, often making ourselves sick.

We never told anyone. It was our secret. A secret between sisters.

Once a week, very early, sometimes before the sun even came up, the city garbage truck rattled down that alley. Two ragtag men stood on the back bumper, holding onto a handle on each side. At each stop, the men jumped down, banging the dented metal garbage cans and lids to empty the smelly contents into the gaping truck. Then, they hopped back on, pounded the sides of the truck a couple times with their fists and shouted to the driver who then rumbled on to the next house down the alley. The sounds of those noisy men and the garbage truck always comforted me. Security in knowing the night and the darkness were over, the debris gone, and the morning light was beginning. Routine familiarity.

The sound of trash pick-up brought a sense of relief in knowing I made it safely through the night. Many of my nights were filled with fear, so I listened as other voices calmed me and soothed my heart. Voices of friends heard and seen by me alone.

It's interesting what a child remembers... and what a child forgets.

* * * * *

Summer 1955

At nearly bedtime, Mom occupied herself with putting away the supper dishes from the dish drainer. I sat at the table in my pajamas, eating a bowl of Corn Flakes and watching her. Carla was spending the night with her girlfriend, Nancy. She spent a lot of nights at Nancy's house. I wished I had a *real* friend like Nancy.

I loved to watch my pretty mom. She wore her dark hair short and curly, and she'd passed to me the same shade of green eyes. Short and rounded, she looked about the right size for a mom. She still wore the pretty blue-flowered dress and pearl necklace from earlier that morning, but she had abandoned her high heels for bare feet.

"Rose, I want you to go right to sleep after you brush your teeth. You hear me? No talking or whispering with your friends."

My *friends*? I couldn't believe she said that. I felt embarrassed, ashamed. Had she heard me talking with them? I wondered what she heard? Could she hear the voices, too? I thought I was the only one who heard the voices. They only talked to me.

Before I could answer, Glenn stormed in, slamming the front screen door behind him. He walked into the kitchen past me and grabbed my mom by her arm. He'd been drinking. I could smell it.

Glenn Williams was one of several men who passed in and out of our lives as my mom tried unsuccessfully to find happiness again. The kind of happiness she once shared with my dad.

Glenn towered over my mom, with strong, muscular arms from working odd jobs as a carpenter and handyman. He slicked back his gray-brown hair on the sides and combed it forward in the front. His steely blue eyes looked right through you, and his thin, narrow lips never formed a smile.

I was afraid of Glenn Williams. Carla feared him, too. She kept her bedroom door locked.

When sober, he spoke quietly. When drunk, his voice sounded like thunder. Very scary to a child like me. It probably made me a sinner, but I hated Glenn Williams. I wished everyday he wouldn't come back to the light-green house on Carroll Street.

"I told you what would happen if I found out you were talking to that insurance agent again when I wasn't home. Didn't I, Carolyn?"

Mom's hands shook as she tried to pull away from Glenn. I knew she was afraid. I saw it in her tear-filled eyes when she looked across the room at me and said, "Rose, leave your cereal and go to bed now. You don't have to brush your teeth and you can say your prayers on your own tonight."

Glenn glared at me as she spoke.

I did exactly what she said. Left my cereal bowl, went straight to my room and crawled under the covers. I wished I could close a door, but my room was open to the living room and kitchen. I had no doors to lock. Nothing to hide behind.

I could still hear Glenn yelling as I lay huddled on my side, knees drawn up beneath my blankets. I tried to block out his voice as I folded my hands and in silence, said my prayers.

Prayers. I don't remember when I began saying prayers, or when I realized someone might be listening to them... to me. I had prayed for as long as I could remember. And now I was afraid not to pray.

Dear Jesus,

It's me, Rose. I need your help again tonight. My mom needs your help. Please help us not to be afraid and keep us safe. If it's not a sin, maybe you could make Glenn pass out. I don't want him to live here anymore. But then you already know that. I guess you know everything. Carla doesn't want him here either.

Please help me not to do things that will make Glenn mad. I'm sorry for whatever I did wrong today. Help me to be good. Help me to not be afraid. And help me to find my friends tonight. I know you know about them.

Thank you for everything else, for my mom, my sister, my dog, and for my teacher at school. I love you. Amen.

"Carolyn, you'd better explain why you continue to lie to me."

"I'm telling the truth... nothing happened. I swear to you! Nothing happened."

I heard him drag her from the kitchen, through the bathroom and into their bedroom, next to mine. First, the door into the bathroom slammed, then the hallway door leading down to where I lay. The slamming doors rattled walls and pictures. Something fell to the floor and broke.

I remained huddled and hidden beneath my sheet, blanket, and chenille bedspread, even though I needed to get the plastic horse and rider from my nightstand. I always brought them to bed, but I'd forgotten them because I was in such a hurry to get away, to get under my covers.

As quietly as I could, I slipped my hand and my arm from under the covers and reached for them.

Oh, please don't let me knock them over onto the floor. Help me find them.

There. I felt a slender plastic leg, wrapped my hand around it, and pulled that horse with its attached rider under the covers next to me.

I heard a slap, and the dull thud of a fist as he hit her. After a muffled scream and a loud thump against the wall where my headboard rested, she started to cry.

I felt sick, like I was going to throw up. I always felt like I was going to throw up when the fighting started. It would pass. I needed to breathe, to catch my breath. I couldn't make a mess in my bed. That would make things even worse. Maybe he would hit me.

I kept swallowing and breathing and praying, *Dear Jesus, please don't let me throw up.*

I slipped farther down under the covers, clutching the horse and rider tighter and tighter. Tears. Trembling. I hated Glenn. I wished he was dead instead of my dad.

"Did you let him in? Did you pay him real good, Carolyn? Let him touch you, fuck you?"

Another dull thud. More crying.

I needed to get away from the sounds, the fighting, the hurting. I needed to go someplace safe. If I didn't, I would throw up. I would cry. I would make noise.

I needed to get to my *friends*. They would be there. They would help me. My *friends* would be waiting for me.

I clutched the plastic horse and rider tighter, closer to me. I closed my eyes and drifted away... away to my safe place.

The ride, bumpy and noisy, and I felt a little sick at my stomach. It would pass though, as soon as we stopped. Just a little farther now.

How pretty the western landscape looked with its blue sky and big, puffy clouds. A trickle of sweat ran down my temple, but I liked the constant warmth. It never turned cold here. It never rained here, either. Always perfect out west.

Closer to the ranch, I saw the horse trails, the big boulders, the tall, green, friendly cactus with arms that always seemed to wave. A couple of tumbleweeds drifted in the wind.

Off in the west, I saw the white buildings of the ranch. I was almost there... almost back... almost safe.

She begged him now, between sobs, but I could barely hear her.

"Please, Glenn... stop. Nothing happened. I opened the door just wide enough to give him the money you left. I swear I didn't let him in. He was only on the porch for a few minutes."

Drifting...

We drove through the entrance gate and I read the letters and words across the top... Double R Bar Ranch. Safe with my friends... Roy Rogers and Dale Evans

Their friend, Pat Brady, pulled up the Jeep he called Nellybelle in front of the main house. I climbed out and dusted myself off. Roy and Dale smiled, and waited on the front porch for me. They were always glad to see me.

They hugged me and kissed my forehead. Warmth and happiness radiated within me. Roy and Dale loved me. They said they wanted to adopt me someday.

"I know you're lying, Carolyn. You always lie about all the men you see when I'm at work. Who else stopped by after you took care of the insurance guy? Did you fuck the milkman and the paperboy, too?"

Just a blur of words so far away...

Roy spoke kindly to me. "We're so glad you came back to stay with us. We're always here for you. You're like part of the family."

"It's almost chow time! Hungry, Rose?"

"I'm hungry now that I'm here, Dale. You always have my favorites and I don't have to cook. "

"Of course not, you're a child. We'll take care of you. That's what adults do. That's their job."

"No, Glenn. I'm not lying to you. I didn't do anything with anyone I never have... only you. Why won't you believe me? Please, baby. Let me show you how much I love you... only you. No one else."

Only distant words.

Roy put his arm around my shoulder. "Sit down next to the other kids and fill your plate. Eat as much as you want. You won't ever go hungry here. "

Clothes tearing, and then someone hitting hard onto the bed. Two more hard slaps. More crying.

Breathe. Take a breath.

Dale sat down next to me and hugged me, "After you're settled in the bunkhouse, Roy and I will tuck you in for the night with our other kids. Would you like a bedtime story, Rose?"

"Oh, yes. I love stories... especially ones with happy endings. "

"We only read happy ending stories here, Rose. "

"Shut up! I don't want to hear you crying. You got what you deserved. I warned you, Carolyn. I won't take this shit, so you better get used to it."

Far away now.

"Can Bullet the dog sleep next to my bunk just in case there're any fights? Can he get under my blankets with me?"

"Of course he can, Rose. He can keep you warm, and be your friend. There is no fighting here, no reason to be afraid, no reason to hide under blankets. You're safe with us. Nothing bad can happen here Ever. "

The crying became softer and softer until I couldn't hear it anymore. It was quiet except for a bed creaking... rocking. Grunting noises and moans.

Safe until morning.

I saw Roy at the bunkhouse door. "No more jumping on the beds, little cowboys and cowgirls. It's time for a bedtime story, milk and cookies, and prayers."

"We're thankful Rose is here with us again." Dale sat next to me on my bed. "You've always been such a good girl. We look forward to your visits. You can always come to us."

"Even when I'm bigger... I mean, older?"

"Yes, you can come back for as long as you want or need, no matter how old."

"Dale, would you read the story about Prince Charming and the little princess? That's my favorite."

"Of course, Rose. That's my favorite, too."

Roy handed her the large, colorful storybook and she thumbed through the pages until she came to that particular story... "Once upon a time, a beautiful, lonely princess lived in a faraway land..."

* * * * *

I heard the garbage truck rattling down the alley. I pictured the ragtag men clinging to the back, emptying the dented metal cans into the truck as it pulled to a stop, and rumbled along to the next house.

Routine familiarity.

I pulled the covers from my head and peeked out. Home.

Shadowed streaks of sunlight poured through my window and danced across the tattered covers of my bed. The darkness and the noise of the night... gone.

I placed Roy and Trigger back onto the nightstand. The words of the happily ever after story resounded in my head.

Prince Charming knelt down beside the sleeping princess and brushed a gentle kiss across her scarlet lips. Her eyes fluttered, then opened. She looked up into his face, and saw love looking back. He took her small, soft hands in his, and helped her stand and steady herself. He easily mounted his graceful, white stallion, and lifted her up in front of him. Holding her tightly, they rode off as one, to find their hopes and dreams, to live happily ever after.

How would Prince Charming ever find me on Carroll Street? It would take a miracle. But I knew he was out there... searching for me. I wondered what he looked like... where he lived... when he would come into my life.

Day after day, I waited for him... for my happy ending... for love.

Please, don't wait too long to find me. Don't wait until it's too late.

Chapter One

Parallel tracks laid long ago
Beginning at a place called yesterday,
Where daydreams first began to grow
And tomorrow seemed so far away.

Rockton, Illinois
Fall 2007

I watched as Ben trekked from the idling school bus, across the graveled bus yard and headed in my direction, his breath trailing back and fading into the crisp, cold morning air. At six feet, he still stood taller than me, even if he was a year younger. He looked pretty damn commanding with his big frame covered in that faded green Army field jacket—the one he wore over everything. The Green Bay Packer's stocking hat added another couple inches. Nice touch. Ben Chapman *was* a classy dresser.

Not quite as classy as Jake Richardson though—my hair sticking out in every direction from underneath my faded and frayed Illinois Illini baseball hat. Classy. Yep, I looked like a real class act this morning, too.

Geez, Ben's field jacket had to be an antique by now. Hell, we were antiques.

I remember when Ben came back from Vietnam in 1971 after being discharged. He wore that U.S. Army Military field jacket when he stepped off the red and white Trailways bus from Chicago. The jacket looked old, worn and frayed even then... like it had been through a hell of lot... and so did Ben. He aged during those two years—not just physically—mentally he came back much older than everyone left behind.

Ben never talked much about Vietnam, what he'd seen or been through. I never asked.

He told me months later how strange he felt being in the jungle one day and home as a civilian a few days later... sitting on the front porch of the family farm. I think the jacket helped him during the transition period. He'd worn it nearly every winter since.

Hell, I still remember when he left for Vietnam. It was winter 1969 Ben was just twenty. I was twenty-one.

I'd moved with a couple of buddies—Jerry Parker and Max Reed—to Parkridge Apartments in Champaign. We took classes at U of I during the day and moonlighted in a band called Common Bond at night. Jerry played bass guitar, Max played keyboard and I served as the lighting and sound guy.

I think all the band members lived at Parkridge back then. Maybe. Hard to remember. That was a long time ago.

Ben and I go way back. Played together as kids. Both local boys who grew up fishing and hunting along the Rock River on adjoining farms our grandparents homesteaded.

Ben lived at home in Rockton when he called to say he'd been drafted. I hated hearing that word, *drafted.* I felt guilty for my Class 4F status—registrant not acceptable for military service. I flunked my physical due to a wool allergy. I never had to worry about being drafted or going to Vietnam. Lucky me. Not so lucky for Ben.

I wanted to see Ben before he left... in case he didn't come back. That was a real possibility during the Vietnam War. Even in the small towns surrounding Rockton, already several young men who left, didn't come home. They died young and alone in a country nearly 10,000 miles away. A country none of them knew, except for the morning headlines, until they stepped off the plane to defend it.

Ben hitched from Rockton to Champaign. Something only a twenty-year old would do in the dead of an Illinois winter. But hitching back then was different. It was relatively safe and you were pretty much assured of a ride. If they knew you were headed for Vietnam, it was almost a guaranteed ride to the front door of your destination and a hot meal along the way.

Ben turned up on our doorstep a couple of days following the phone call, suitcase in hand. A local farmer and his wife picked him up not too far out of Rockton and brought him all the way to Champaign, stopping only once for gas and cheeseburgers. Their son already served in Vietnam.

Ben stayed with my friends and me at Parkridge Apartments during those weeks before he shipped out for Basic and then Vietnam. God, what a great time we spent together.

Spent. Good descriptive word now that I think back on it.

With a phone call, Jerry fixed Ben up with this leggy redhead the first night. What was her name? Laurie? Gina? No. Gloria. Yes, that was it... like the song. *Gloria.* G-L-O-R-I-A.

That chick was just the ticket for a young man leaving for Vietnam, or so we thought. But sometime during the evening, he settled into a conversation with a lovely, tall, blonde named Karen.

Yep, I remember now. That's how it started. Jerry switched dates.

We partied from then on with Ben and Karen, Jerry and Gloria, the lead singer Cash and his wife Sam, and Max with somebody's sister. Can't remember whose sister.

And me.

And *Rose*.

Rose and Karen roomed together back then. Rose called her Ren for short.

We partied hard, non-stop, day and night—tripping on mescaline and acid, drinking beer and wine, eating pizza and cheeseburgers, and getting laid as much as possible. We slept only after we passed out, or from sheer exhaustion.

When you're young and in love, the possibilities are sweet. You figure your time is endless. That's what I figured anyway.

When it was finally time for Ben to leave, he was wiped out, hung over and—as he climbed on the chartered Greyhound bus heading for Basic Training at Fort Leonard Wood, Missouri—sported the biggest smile of his young life.

Eight of us huddled together for warmth that morning at the bus station: Cash, Sam, Jerry, Ren, Max, Gloria, Rose and I.

We watched through the fogged-over bus windows as Ben walked down the center aisle, situated himself next to a window and, despite the bitter cold, slid the glass open as far as it would go.

We shared a few last comments, jokes, and bits of advice with him, trying to keep the conversation light for as long as possible. Trying to delay the inevitable. He and Ren held hands through the window... she wearing Ben's big, clunky class ring on her left hand.

She promised to wait for Ben and write every day. And Ben promised the same. They believed one another because they were in love. Hell, that's just how easily it happens when you're young.

Could you actually be in love at that age? I knew the answer to that then, and now. Love can happen at any age. There are no rules when it comes to affairs of the heart. You can fall in love just as hard and as deep when you're young and inexperienced as you can when you're older and wiser. The capacity for the heart to love another shows no age preference. Love is timeless.

Our brief time together that morning passed in a blur of nervous laughter, forced smiles, fleeting promises, and freezing temperatures. And before we knew... it was time to go. Time to say good-bye.

Ben wiped tears from his cheeks with his free hand, clutching Ren's hand with the other, as we said—then waved—our final good-byes. There were no dry eyes that morning, only frozen tears on bright red cheeks.

Tears for the lost innocence of us all.

Ben reluctantly let go of Ren's hand, then her fingers, as the bus slowly edged away from the terminal and away from all of us... tires crunching in the snow, the smoky gray exhaust plume spiraling behind.

The open window framed Ben's smiling face as we watched his right hand and fingers form the peace sign. In turn, we smiled, raised our gloved hands and flashed the sign back to him. We could still see his hand, extended out the window, raised in peace, as the bus made the final turn at the end of the block.

Our friend, my childhood friend, Ben... was gone.

We returned to our apartments, our part-time jobs, our college classes and the band.

Ben went to war in the jungles of Vietnam and, over the next two years, saw and did things that would forever change him.

That winter day in 1969—the day he left—served as a reality check for us all.

Peace. Love. War.

By the time the Vietnam War ended in April 1975... 58,226 service men and support personnel never came back. One in ten were killed, 11,465 of those under the age of twenty. In the State of Illinois alone, 2,934 died.

Ben got lucky. He didn't become one of the statistics.

My childhood friend, Ben Chapman, came home. Home to begin his future.

* * * * *

Shit.

I hadn't thought about my years in Champaign for a very, long time. Don't know what triggered the thoughts this morning. Maybe seeing Ben in the Army field jacket. Maybe the time of year... getting close to another winter. Maybe my age. Can't say. I just know the thoughts, the feelings, the memories showed up strong this morning. Really strong.

The late 1960s and early 1970s... what a different era. A time of major changes and shifts... dress, music, sex, drugs, politics. Everything. It's hard to explain if you weren't part of it, a witness to it, there to experience it. And if you were, it stayed with you, got in your blood and became a part of you... who you are.

For me Champaign, Illinois, Parkridge Apartments, the band, and Rose happened a lifetime ago. I seldom let myself wander around in that lifetime I left behind nearly forty years ago. Now I lived in the real world. I was not a dreamer. I didn't let my practical ass get bogged down in what might have been. No point. Eventually I moved on. I had to.

Reality brought Ben banging on the bus-door window.

He placed his gloved, cupped hands against the glass and peered in at me—eyebrows raised—lips mouthing the words, "What the hell?"

I swung the door open just wide enough for him to slip in without letting too much heat out, and quickly slammed it behind him.

"Are you sacked out man? I've been banging on the damn bus door for at least five minutes. I froze my ass off out there!"

"Well, you're in now and your ass is still there. I was thinking."

"Thinking, huh? Never thought of you as much of a deep thinker. Must have been some pretty heavy shit."

I let the comment slide.

During this exchange, Ben climbed the bus steps and sat down in the front seat opposite me in the driver's seat, pulled his stocking hat off, and stuffed it into one of his many pockets. What hair he had left stuck up in all directions from static electricity. It looked more than a little thin on top. Damn. Ben was nearly bald.

"Nice hair," I said dryly.

"Smart ass!" he replied just as dryly, while unsuccessfully smoothing it down with his gloved hands. "You just haven't had all the worry and stress I've had."

"I'm sure that's it," I responded as I took my baseball hat off, ran my hand through my thick hair, and placed my baseball hat back squarely on my head. "Could be genetics, too. Maybe you just come from a recessive hair gene pool."

He flipped me off, removed his gloves and delved into the weather report, as if I wasn't familiar with it already.

"Shit, it's cold today... supposed to be cold all week. Windy, too. Feels like winter. I hate winter. What are we still doing here? I thought we had a plan to move out west?"

Ben. He had a mind like an elephant.

"It is and we did. And I'm pretty sure our time for heading west has run out, my friend."

"Well, you might be right about that, but it doesn't cost anything to still dream about warm places and fruity umbrella drinks, does it?"

"Nope. Doesn't cost a dime. As far as I know, dreams are still free, but the fruity, umbrella drinks I'm pretty sure you'll have to pay for out the ass. And since you're buying, make mine a beer. The last time

I drank anything with an umbrella hanging on the side, I woke up the next morning, married. I'm still paying on that tab."

"Okay. I'll give you a pass on that comment, even though I would love to get into your head about it."

"Thanks, and just stay out of my head. I try to keep the crowd shallow and thinned-out in there."

"Well, you're doing a damn fine job on the shallow part. Carry on!" He gave me a crisp, brief salute.

"Thanks. Will do."

Ben continued, "Hey, you want to meet at the Coffee Cup after you finish your run?"

"Nope. Can't today."

"Ah. Gotta work on the list, huh?"

"Yep. The list never ends. Lots of shit to do before the snow flies and I have to start scooping my way out. Probably put a diesel fuel blend in the tractor, so I'm ready to push snow. Furnace filters need changing, too."

"Maybe I'll get those out of the way, too. See you at the pub later? Will's having women's bikini Jell-O wrestling this week."

"Women's bikini Jell-O wrestling?" I repeated the words slowly. "Geez, how could any man pass that up? Yep, always got time for a beer or two. The boys have basketball practice until around eight thirty. I'll watch for a while, make sure they're headed home, then stop by."

Will's Place had been around since the early 1960s. Will's dad, *Will,* owned it back then. Never had to repaint the sign when young Will—a Grizzly Adams look alike—took over. Comfortable pub atmosphere—a long, dark wooden bar lined with stools on the left hand side, mirrored wall behind the bar—on the right side, ten or twelve table-and-chair set-ups. Lots of vintage neon beer signs and historical Rockton pictures hanging on the walls. Cold beer on tap, good wine list, and Will could concoct any mixed drink if you gave him a hint. He hired young, pretty waitresses. And now, women's Jell-O wrestling? The perfect man-cave.

"God, I'm glad I'm not herding kids anymore. Too old for that shit. What the hell were you and Beth thinking? Took you a while to get your shit together, I guess."

"Yep, we got a late start on getting our shit together, and thanks for reminding me of how old I am with two teenagers."

"You're welcome."

I looked at Ben. He looked at me. He knew why I got a late start and so did I. But neither of us went there.

Rose.

"I'll save you a seat close to the action. We'll pray for a wardrobe malfunction."

"Good reason to pray."

Ben stood and stretched, hands over his head, twisting at the waist a few times. I heard popping and cracking.

"Getting old's a bitch, ain't it?"

Ben slowly nodded his head, "Yep, it is."

He pulled the Viking's stocking hat from one of the pockets of his field jacket, covered his head and ears again, and slid his leather gloves back on. He headed back down the bus steps, muttering about women's bikini Jell-O wrestling and wardrobe malfunctions.

The cold air swooshed in as I opened the bus door just wide enough for Ben to squeeze back outside, and quickly closed it.

I watched him walk back into the shadowy, cold morning, toward his idling bus, breath trailing behind.

I wondered if anyone ever really got his or her shit together, that quintessential sixties term. I'd been trying for years and had a feeling mine was as together as it ever would be. I think my boys thought I had it pretty well together most of the time, though. That was important to me. Kids deserve to be kids for as long as they can, and not worry about adult things. There's plenty of time for that later.

I saw firsthand the damage done to a child when a parent can't get it together. The consequences of a child burdened by adult worries spill over onto everyone that child comes in contact with later down the line.

I stood in *her* line one day a long, long time ago.

What made me think of that... of her? It felt as if something, someone was tapping into my head, my thoughts today.

I turned the wipers on and off to clear the condensation. The sun was barely up, and the outline of the trees and farm buildings in the distance silhouetted darkly against the brilliant orange hues on the horizon. What a picture.

I took my Blackberry out, lined up the shot, clicked, and saved. Perfect. With another couple of clicks, I posted it on Facebook.

I consider taking a picture with a phone that fits inside a pocket a pretty damned amazing technology. Sending that shot to a computer for everyone to see was even more amazing. It reminded me of *Star Trek*.

Beam me up, Scottie!

Yes, indeed. Very cool.

Ben and I'd been doing this bus gig off and on for more than thirty years now. Driving a bus wasn't glamorous, but it provided extra money, and served as a good excuse for Ben and me to just be gone sometimes.

We both graduated from college in the seventies and, eventually married and raised families here in Rockton, Illinois. Population: 5,512 friendly people. According to the website, Rockton's an historic village with small-town charm and values, nestled on the northern edge of Winnebago County. Great schools, little-if-any crime, downtown shopping, and situated on some of the richest farmland in the Midwest. If you combine all of that with Walmart, The American Legion, Rockton Food & Spirits, Subway, Arby's, Will's Sports Bar and Grill... a funeral home and cemetery... it's damn near perfect.

Ben and his wife just celebrated their thirty-fifth wedding anniversary... Beth and I, our thirtieth. Their two girls made it through college, and married, while their divorced son and grandkids moved back home. I think the divorce contributed to Ben's hair loss. It's hard to watch your kid mess up.

Beth and I still had two sons in high school, but we got that late start. I was nearly thirty and Beth barely twenty-one when we got married. The boys didn't come along for several years after. That's just how things worked out.

Farming framed both Ben and my families. Our farms spanned a little less than two hundred acres each, which in the Midwest is considered *hobby farming*. Some hobby. Our so-called hobby involved growing corn and soybeans, and pretty much served as a full-time job year-round, with some seasons busier than others.

Hobby, my ass.

Ben, now a member of the school board, worked actively in local politics through the years. He ran for mayor once or twice. Hell, I voted for him even though he was a Republican. He lost anyway.

I began scratching my acting/directing itch at a local dinner theater thirty years ago. I enjoyed it, and it gave me an outlet. On stage, I could let go and be someone else, release all the responsibilities. I didn't have to be practical on stage. I just had to be convincing. Yep, the local dinner theater probably saved my marriage early on, simply by allowing me to live out a small part of my dream on a stage three or four times a year. Well, that and drinking.

Beth and I partied hard those first years of marriage... both mostly drunk or high for the first ten or fifteen years. I think part of it was because she was young, and I was a prick most of the time. When she was drunk or high, I ran around. Not a great marriage. It was fun... until it wasn't fun. When we started thinking about a family, Beth went to AA. She's been clean and sober for nearly fifteen years now.

And me? Don't do drugs anymore. Don't do the Jack Daniels or the tequila shooters much anymore—just beer. I stop by the pub a couple of times a week for a beer. On Saturday nights, when Beth's not working, we go to the pub together for dinner. I drink and she drives home. It works.

Back in the early seventies, Ben and I talked about heading west after we graduated from college. We read about and saw young people on television like us—living together in Haight-Ashbury, surfing off Venice Beach, smoking dope and playing music in Monterey—and we wanted to be a part of it. We wanted to live the California experience, especially since we were in a band.

When Ben came back from Vietnam, we swore to one another neither of us would end up like our parents. We still ended up there forty years later—Ben with a degree in political science, and me with degrees in English and cinematography—married... living in Rockton.. farming.

Life happens. Plans change. People you love come and go.

You move on.

You can never go back.

Overall, I liked my life. I was relatively happy. After all, happiness is a state of mind. Isn't that what they say?

Beth and I get along all right now. We're both well known and established in Rockton. People know her as an excellent cook, a good mother, and the first person at someone's door if help is needed. Our boys are almost launched. No major problems there. We all enjoy good health. Farm is paid for, and we can fall back on money in the bank. I have a good life with no reason to complain, so I don't. I get up every day, take care of my family and my responsibilities, and go about my life. That's what responsible men do who make commitments. That's how I was raised.

I just never thought twenty, thirty, or forty years would slip by so quickly, so quietly. Kids don't understand that. I didn't. One day you're twenty-something and—in a blink of an eye—you're sixty-something.

I finished my morning route around eight thirty, and parked the bus in the bus yard. I climbed into my truck and headed home to work on the list. On a farm, that list is never-ending, always stretching out before you with no way to catch up or finish. I just peck away at it, each day of each season of each year. It's what farmers do.

I find myself checking off less and less on the list as I get older, and not caring nearly as much as I did as a younger man. Christmas lights sometimes stay up from one year to the next, the house doesn't get painted nearly as often, and, for the past several years, I'm the last one to get my crops planted in the spring... the last to harvest in the fall. Things get done. They just get done on a different time schedule now.

My priorities changed. I like spending time at the lake I designed and built a few years ago. I don't mind working on anything associated with the lake: the dock, the shelter house, the trees and surroundings. I enjoy the solitude the lake affords me... fishing, skinny-dipping at night to cool off, drinking a few beers in the hammock, sitting around a fire at night and listening to Pandora radio. I enjoy just being there. It's quiet and peaceful, and I can be alone with my thoughts. I plan for my family to scatter my ashes at the lake. And since Beth is against cremation, I wrote it into my will. Nobody gets a dime until I'm scattered.

* * * * *

The tractor I used for snow removal stayed parked inside the barn. Good thing. No point in freezing my ass off if I didn't have to.

I looked around for the anti-freeze I'd left in the barn a few months back. Where the hell was it? There... partially hidden under the tarp I kept over the bike. I shoved the yellow, plastic jug over with my foot, and peeled the tarp back. There it was... my black 1971 Triumph Bonneville motorcycle. I grabbed an old shirt from the workbench and wiped somebody's butt print off... probably Dustin's. The bike still looked good. I kept the maintenance up and took it out now and then to blow the cobwebs out. Beth and I rode it a few times during our first years of marriage, but she never was too keen on motorcycles. She wanted me to sell it a long time ago, but I couldn't. The bike remained my last tangible reminder of a time and a place that would never come again.

I bought the bike after college graduation and headed west to California on a road trip to fulfill part of the dream we all shared back then. At first it felt so wild and free being out on my own, but, after a while, I was lonely with no one to share the adventure. After a couple of weeks, I drove back to Rockton, pulled the bike into the barn, and covered it with the tarp.

I started tending bar and a few years later, met a young, pretty waitress who thought the sun rose and set on my ass... Beth. I needed someone to think that. By then, I was nearly thirty years old and still alone... lonely. Time to move on with my life... so I did.

I rubbed the old shirt over the gas tank and seat one more time, and pulled the tarp back over the bike. Maybe Brian or Dustin might like to have it someday. I could never sell it.

An hour or so later, I finished with the tractor. The smell of coffee, a quiet house, and the dogs—Cooper, a black lab, and Teak, a rescued, brown and white, mixed mutt—greeted me.

I let out the dogs, washed up, poured a cup of coffee, and headed for the office and the computer. With Beth at work and the boys at school, I had the computer and the house all to myself. Perfect.

I slipped into the office chair, typed in my password, and pulled up Pandora. Crosby, Stills, Nash were singing "Lady of the Island" from the *Deja Vu* album. I listened. I drifted.

A sweet memory.

Rose.

For all I knew, Rose was fat and married with a bunch of kids and grandkids by now. Or maybe gone. I knew several people—friends and family—who had died over the years: my sister, my dad, my mom. There was a distinct possibility that Rose might be gone, too. That thought left me with a hollow, empty feeling inside as Crosby, Stills, Nash sang on.

I checked and answered a few emails, then moved on to Facebook.

I joined Facebook a few months back and sent and received occasional Friend requests, mostly from former high school classmates, some who still lived in Rockton and some who moved away.

It piqued my interest to see what went on with friends and family, read their posts, and throw in an occasional witty remark. It brought out my natural wit, so why not? And now I posted pictures taken with my phone. I posted two last week—one of the dog and one of the cornfield—and received several favorable comments.

This morning, I exchanged the picture of Cooper with the cornfield for my profile picture, after several comments about looking "dog tired."

The Internet, email, Facebook, chat boxes, Blackberries, and texting. Hell, I'd seen it all. I remembered when Beth and I bought our very first microwave and nuked a hot dog perfectly in fifteen seconds. I also remember blowing up a scrambled egg in forty-five seconds.

Today, I saw a new message *and* a Friend request. Cool.

I positioned the mouse over the message link and clicked. It opened a picture of a pretty blonde with dimples in each cheek. Next to the picture was her name—*Rose Allison Flynn.*

Damn.

I remembered that face. Remembered those dimples. And I would never forget that name... *Rose Allison, with two Ls.*

Rose Allison Flynn. Flynn must be her married name. Rose... married. Of course she was married by now. I was married.

I brought up the message.

It said simply, *"Are you the Jake Richardson who used to live at Parkridge Apartments in Champaign, Illinois, in the late 60s?"*

Damn.

I stared at the words and at the picture of the pretty blonde with the dimples. Silky, blond hair I once ran my fingers through... dimples I stroked softly with my thumbs.

It couldn't be her. After all these years—it couldn't be her.

But it was. It was *Rose.*

Should I reply? Did I want to go there? Shit.

What would it hurt to answer her, to let her know it was me? Hell, how long had it been? Nearly forty years? People change. Things change. Maybe she forgot everything.

I studied her picture.

She looked older. She was older. She wore her hair a little shorter, a little lighter. Her eyes, that pretty green.

She looked beautiful. She looked like *Rose.* My *Rose.*

I did. I did want to go there. I couldn't *not* go there.

I typed my reply into the message box and reread it a couple of times.

"Yep. That would be me. And you would be Rose Allison with '2lls,' right?"

Would she remember me calling her that? And my special spelling of "*2lls?*"

That was enough to say at this point. I couldn't think of anything more to say anyway. What do you say to someone you saw and spoke with nearly forty years ago, and never saw or spoke to again? How the hell does that happen? Neither of us knew it would be the last time. We were two young kids, barely in our twenties. How could we know?

We weren't kids anymore. And we weren't in our twenties anymore, either.

I positioned the mouse over the reply link and clicked. I accepted her Friend request.

A Friend request. Such a simple message.

My mind wandered back. I felt it going, with no way to stop it.

* * * * *

I met Rose through my friend, Jerry Parker, bass player for Common Bond. He and Rose met at Western Illinois University in Macomb the fall of 1968. I think they shared an early morning class together. Jerry talked about this cool chick he met at school, and how he was going to bring her to one of the band rehearsals so we could meet her.

I didn't really think much about it at the time. Jerry always met chicks and brought them to rehearsal. It was a band for Christ's sake. Pretty groupies always hung around. I figured Rose as just another starry-eyed chick. It happened all the time with members of the band. Chicks just dug being around them. It was a band thing.

Hell, it probably still is a band thing.

It even happened with lighting and sound guys like me. It didn't matter if I played an instrument or not. I was part of the band. That was part of the perks of the late nights and poor pay. After a gig, we indulged in booze, drugs, and chicks.

Rose was different. She didn't want the glamour and status of the band or its members. She looked for something else... a place to belong, to fit in. She looked for a family.

She was something—pretty, smart, witty—with pensive green eyes that seemed to look into your soul one minute, and roam a thousand miles away the next. We shared the same birthday, November 23rd, though I was one year older: she at twenty and I at twenty-one back then. We both fell under the sign of Scorpio—fire and gasoline—hot and dangerous.

Meeting her changed me.

I never forgot her. I thought I did. But seeing her face and reading the words—her words—on my computer screen today brought it all back.

After all the years, all the time, all the distance... the feelings remained.

I was right earlier today. Something, someone was tapping into my head, my thoughts.

Rose Allison with 2lls.

Chapter Two

Mrs. Roper kept a folder with pictures on a table.
Backed by beautiful colors on construction paper.
And when our work was done we'd look into that folder
Choose a picture, write a story that we could read for her.

Macomb, Illinois
Fall 1967

Saturday morning dawned. I didn't have to get up and go to school or work. No classes... no work for Rose Allison. Yea, for me!

I looked forward to the weekends—a time for me to regroup, to relax. A time for me to sit and think, dream and write.

Sometimes I wrote poetry, or added a page or two in my journal. Other times, I wrote stories, fantasies, about something or someone. All of these—my poetry, my journal entries, my stories—I kept in black, three-ring notebooks.

I carried my life around with me... in notebooks.

Writing my thoughts and feelings was something I'd done from a very young age. I needed to write, and I needed to read what I wrote. I could hardly explain it, even to myself.

Writing provided two outlets for me. One allowed me to fantasize and escape the realities of life. The other kept me in touch with the person deep inside... the person who knew the difference between fantasy and reality.

It helped me to stay in touch with me, with Rose. It helped me to stay in touch with reality.

Fantasy and reality. A constant battle I waged with myself.

I made up stories and poems for as long as I could remember. I recited them to myself, or to imaginary friends, late at night when I was supposed to be asleep.

A second-grade teacher encouraged me to actually put things down on paper. I excelled at it because of my vivid imagination. I frequently wandered off to places in my mind, and writing gave me the tools to bring the meanderings to life on paper. I wrote stories for my teacher.

As time went on... books, television, and movies further fueled my imagination, my writing... blurring the lines between fantasy and reality even more.

I loved books and made good use of school libraries. I looked at the pictures, read the words, and dreamed of riding dusty trails out west on *Black Beauty, Flicka, and Fury*. Nancy Drew and I joined forces with Ned Nickerson to solve mysteries, beginning with *Mystery of the Tolling Bell*. I read and reread books, taking note of the characters and how they fit into the storyline... and how the author devised each happy ending.

Saturday morning television provided hours of distraction. *Roy Rogers and Dale Evans, Sky King, Spin and Marty, Rin-Tin-Tin, The Lone Ranger, Annie Oakley, Fury* and *Flicka*. Imaginary friends I talked to, shared adventures and huddled under blankets with at night. Imaginary friends who took the place of real ones I never had.

Movies provided the ultimate escape. The vivid images of Herman Melville's *Moby Dick* remain in my mind to this day. Narrated words transported me across a vast, blue ocean on the whaling ship *Pequod* with Captain Ahab. I remember the blue water foaming red with whale blood, and watching as Captain Ahab's beckoning hand disappeared beneath the waves.

Days later, with my sister at the downtown library, I held that huge book in my small hands. I opened the cover, read the words on the first page, and marveled a writer dreamed all of this inside his head—the places, the characters, the storyline. Imagination flowed into words. The words formed images. The images framed a movie. A movie that transported me to another place and time.

I understood words and the power they held to transport *me*, but now, I understood how words could transport *others*, as well.

I opened the notebook, turned to the "poems" section, and jotted down the words formulated in my mind this morning when I woke up. If I wrote them down, the voice would stop repeating them over and over. I would be able to think of something else... and the voice would be still.

Bits and pieces of my life left both here and there.
Like segments of a jigsaw puzzle scattered everywhere.

I established a nice Saturday morning routine since moving into my first apartment several months ago. I got up, dressed, walked a block to the neighborhood grocery store, and bought two glazed twist donuts and a small carton of chocolate milk. A treat I looked forward to weekly.

As I walked back, I shuffled my sandaled feet through the brown, orange, and yellow leaves strewn along the cracked sidewalk, scattering them here and there. The sky shone a brilliant blue. Autumn in Illinois was my favorite time of year... cool weather, fall colors, football games, sweaters, and jeans.

I climbed the steps leading to the small side porch and flipped open the top of the metal mailbox hanging outside the apartment door. I thumbed through the pieces of mail... the phone bill, the gas bill, an events flyer from the college... and this month's Social Security check. I tucked the mail under my arm, unlocked the door, and climbed the steps to my second-floor apartment.

As a freshman at Western Illinois University, I carried a full load of classes in the mornings, and worked in the registrar's office in the afternoons. I tried to keep myself on a tight budget so I could stay in school. I knew early on, education was my ticket up and out.

I was only five when my forty-six-year-old dad died of a heart attack. My mom spent the next sixteen years trying to recreate the life she shared with him by dating and marrying an odd assortment of flawed men. During the process of trying to find her life—dragging me from town to town, school to school, and apartment to apartment—my childhood and my innocence disappeared into stress and responsibility.

I worried about everyone and everything—desperately trying to maintain order in a world constantly spinning out of control.

Over time, I learned to leave things behind: schools, teachers, friends, loved ones, pets, and homes. I learned to keep my emotions in check. I learned to detach. Without realizing it, I stopped forming meaningful relationships... friendship or otherwise. I lost trust in those around me. I pretended to participate in relationships but, instead, remained distant. I became so practiced no one realized my talent for creating distance. I used my smarts, and compensated nicely with a quick wit and keen sense of humor. I didn't realize then how this would affect my ability to form relationships the rest of my life: friends, lovers, husband, children, grandchildren—every relationship.

The crazy life with my mother came to a screeching halt two years ago when she took her own life at age forty-six. I was just seventeen.

Once again, I left the life I knew behind, gathered the scattered pieces, and started over. But this time... I started alone, happy to finally be on my own, to call a place mine.

I lived alone in a furnished, upstairs, three-bedroom and one-bath apartment on a quiet residential street in my hometown of Macomb. Small, but comfortable, it met my needs, as I was used to living in apartments.

My mom fixed up the apartments we rented over the years, making them more livable, more like a home. If the floors were bad, she bought inexpensive linoleum to cover them. Our kitchen floors always featured some sort of large checkered pattern, the bedrooms a more subdued floral or neutral design.

As a child, the shiny new linoleum in those simple upstairs rooms, became imaginary ballrooms where I pretended to be a famous dancer or movie actress. I framed my arms around an imaginary partner—waltzed, glided and twirled across the slick new floors—then stopped and delivered dramatic one-liners to the handsome leading man, my Prince Charming.

I spent a great deal of time living in an imaginary world, talking with the voice in my head. A constant voice who listened to me... who understood me... who protected me.

To fix up our apartments, Mom also bought rolls of wallpaper with matching borders for each room. I watched her measure, cut, paste, and hang each piece, then climb onto a kitchen chair to carefully attach the pasted border along the top, finishing each room. Sometimes she let me cut along the penciled lines or help spread the wallpaper paste with a big brush. I loved to help. When we finished wallpapering, she painted the woodwork bright white enamel. I don't know how she found extra money to buy the linoleum, wallpaper or paint. I can only imagine.

Finally, she cleaned and arranged the sparse furniture and began adding personal touches to make it our home—personal pictures on the walls and tables, Grandma's crocheted doilies on the backs of chairs and couches, my school crafts and artwork placed strategically around the apartment. As a finishing touch, we would make a trip to the nearest variety store, Kresge's or Woolworth's maybe, and buy one or two clay pots filled with lovely pink or purple African violets.

One time I asked her how she learned to do all of this... lay and cut the linoleum, wallpaper, and paint. She looked at me with tears in her eyes and said, "Your daddy and I did this together. He showed me how."

I don't remember her talking about him other than that one time, but I knew when I looked into her face how much she missed him... how much she still loved him.

To this day, I remember the scent of new linoleum, freshly hung wallpaper and enamel paint that made those old, well-worn apartments seem fresh and new. I think it was my mom's way of starting over each time, trying to find that same fresh and new beginning with someone else besides my dad.

This process, again and again, made an apartment a home, our home. I learned it well from my mother. Children pattern from what they see... good or bad... the brain connections are made, the pathways followed.

Now, I patterned after her. I wallpapered, painted woodwork, cleaned and arranged furniture, organized, and added personal touches to my apartment... to my home.

I ran my hand over the red, Formica tabletop and remembered all the Saturday mornings as a child that started out exactly this same way... mom sitting across the table from me sipping her coffee. She wouldn't let me drink coffee, but she let me dunk my doughnut in her cup. Sometimes, I still smell the coffee and taste the sweet-bitter soaked doughnut.

It's interesting the selective things you remember.

I washed the pink Howdy Doody glass, and placed it back on the cabinet shelf next to the yellow one. The glasses once belonged to Grandma and Grandpa Allison, and now were treasured possessions I kept close to me.

I acted a little compulsively when it came to a clean, orderly apartment. I liked everything neat, in straight lines... shoes, clothes, books, pictures, window shades, pillows, and even canned goods. If anything looked out of order or crooked, I took care of it as soon as possible. I had to.

More childhood baggage. Keeping my room, my immediate environment straight and orderly, in some small way gave me control and brought order into a chaotic life, over which I had little control.

That was how the OCD began... obsessive-compulsive disorder. I embraced it in spades.

All of the Saturday routine—cleaning, laundry and grocery shopping—I watched my mother do for as long as I could remember. I wondered how many other habits and patterns I inadvertently picked up from her. The question always lingered in the back of my mind. It worried me.

My mother suffered terrible mood swings and battled depression to the end. I tended toward these same things, and wondered if it ran in our family. I knew she was lonely. A type of loneliness a child can't fill. I felt lonely and depressed at times, too.

Living with my mother before her death became increasingly stressful and difficult. I endured her previous suicide attempts and many days and nights of being left alone.

All things considered, I thought I did pretty well dealing with all of it.

Though I did spend many nights, feeling afraid... isolated... lonely. Honestly, I found it hard to understand the concept of *aloneness*. I *wanted* to be alone. I was used to being alone. I loved my apartment and the independence it afforded me.

I did long for company—to share with someone, to talk with someone—a friend, a lover maybe. Yet, I purposely chose to feel alone. Even when surrounded by people, I felt alone. I felt alone in a crowd. How could that be? Though I knew all of this must relate in some way to my childhood, I never could make sense of it.

I didn't look for help in figuring it out, either. I wasn't comfortable talking with anyone. Who would I talk to?

I didn't discuss my feelings with anyone other than the child inside me—the one who protected me, who helped me write, who shared my fantasies but reminded me of reality—the one I talked with continually.

I sucked it up like I thought everyone else did, and continued on with my life. My life... alone.

What else was there to do? Only rich or crazy people went to shrinks, and I was neither.

* * * * *

Macomb, Illinois
Fall 1968

A lot of kids from high school attended Western Illinois University, along with a lot of new kids I didn't know from surrounding Illinois and out-of-state towns. That was one of the reasons I planned to attend the Battle of the Bands "mixer" at the Student Union later.

But the main reason was Jerry Parker.

I met Jerry the first day of classes in late August. He was one of those *new* kids. We both had Psych 101 at seven twenty in the morning in the tiered lecture hall of the Social Science Building. He came strolling in the first day of classes fifteen minutes late. The professor already had taken roll and was explaining the syllabus when Jerry stopped by his desk, pointed to his name on the roster, and headed for the nearest empty seat. The chair right next to me.

Tall and thin, with long, dark hair to his shoulders, and sporting dark-rimmed glasses, Jerry didn't fit the mold of the clean cut, all-American preppy kid typical to Macomb. Instead, he dressed in faded bell-bottom jeans, an army fatigue jacket with a black T-shirt underneath, and sandals. Somehow it all worked for him, that hippie look. Whatever he had working for him, worked on me. I liked him the minute I saw him. Jerry was nineteen back then.

He appeared a bit disheveled and disorganized as he slid into the desk chair next to mine. He shoved all but the psych book underneath the chair, picked up several cigarettes he'd dropped, and shoved them back into a pocket of the army jacket. Once settled, he looked over and checked the page number I was on, turned to the page, and flashed a wide, gummy grin at me. In a whisper, he introduced himself.

"Hi, I'm Jerry Parker... and you are?"

And with those few words, my friendship with Jerry Parker began.

"Rose. Rose Allison. Nice to meet you, Jerry." I smiled, picked up another cigarette he'd dropped on the floor, and handed it to him.

He slid that one behind his ear, and I watched it disappear in the mop of dark hair. "Thanks. Got up late today. Long drive from Mason City. "

"That is a ways. You'll have to get up earlier or drive faster!"

Mason City mapped out about seventy-five miles east of Champaign, so he did make quite a drive every day. I later learned Jerry flew down the highway in a 1967 gold Plymouth Barracuda fastback. Flew!

Jerry nodded and continued to flash the grin. I wondered how many girls he had flashed the grin at since hitting puberty. For some reason, I immediately wanted to help with the disheveled look, take him home, and cook him dinner.

Yes, he'd worked that grin for quite some time.

Over the next few weeks, Jerry and I became good friends and often met for coffee in the Student Union before I left for work in the Registrar's Office... before he headed back to Mason City. He said he played bass guitar in a band called *Common Bond* that kept him busy most evenings and weekends. I had heard of the band, but never saw them perform. They played mainly in the Champaign area, easily 130 miles from Macomb. Jerry invited me to sit in on a couple of rehearsals, but the long drive on a weeknight was too far. That was the closest we ever came to actually dating. Meeting him at the dance was kind of a date, I guess.

Common Bond was one of the bands battling at the mixer along with two others... *St. John and the Disciples* and *Children of Darkness*. Finally, I would get to watch and listen to Jerry's band... put faces with the names he talked about.

The Battle of the Bands was kind of a new thing that started a year or so earlier. Each band played a forty- to forty-five-minute set, and those at the dance determined the best band by their level of applause at the end of the evening. With no prize or anything, they earned just the bragging rights.

* * * * *

I loved music, all kinds of music, and knew that love came from my mother. She sang and played the piano, and encouraged me to sing and take piano lessons whenever we lived somewhere long enough. It was one of the few things we did together. She played the piano, and I sat next to her and sang along with her beautiful alto voice.

I loved to watch her pretty hands glide over the black and white keys, with her long, graceful "piano" fingers, as she called them. By stretching her thumb and pinky, she could easily span an octave or more on the keys.

I looked down at my hands and stretched my thumb and pinky. I inherited her piano fingers, along with her voice, except I sang soprano. I sang and played in high school, and now did so even more in college.

I cherished this memory of my mother, and held gratitude for my abilities to play and sing. Grateful to her for doing whatever she had to do, so I could take music lessons.

Through the years, we always filled our apartments with sounds of the latest hits on the radio, or with the vinyl voices of Frank Sinatra, Nat King Cole, Tony Bennett, or maybe Jim Reeves drifting from the record player. My mom saved up money over the months from her checks as a waitress, and later as a secretary, to buy a stereophonic record player. Stereophonic sound and records, specifically recorded in stereo, were quite innovative back in the day.

The first stereo record album we listened to was *Nice 'N Easy* by Frank Sinatra. Frank sounded like he was performing right in our living room. Over time, I knew the words to every song on that album.

I kept only a few things after Mom's death, but they included her radio, and stereo record player and records. So, now I filled my apartment with lovely music as well. The music I listened to differed greatly from her favorites. I loved The Beach Boys, The Beatles, Simon and Garfunkel, Bob Dylan, The Doors, Janis Joplin, and James Taylor. I read all about the members of each group, what instruments they played, and I memorized the words of the songs,

I loved to read and hear the pattern of the words as someone's thoughts blended with the notes to become songs. Songwriters dared to share the most intimate details of their lives, their souls, for the sake of the music. Every poem a song, every song a piece of someone's life. Songwriters truly did 'lay it between the lines.'

I wrote poems that lent themselves to song lyrics, but never shared them with anyone. The words remained for me alone. I recited, discussed, and edited them within my head. The words helped me find a voice for my feelings, my frustrations, my sadness, my loneliness. I found, early on, that writing took me places I could only hope and dream to go. Most of all, writing allowed me to create happy endings. I was driven to create happy endings. The child within could take no more sad endings.

* * * * *

Concertgoers thronged the Student Union when I arrived that evening. Jerry suggested I arrive a little early so I could meet the band members, but this was the best I could do. Even though my Volkswagen Bug seemed to run forever on a buck's worth of gas, the indicator light came on as I pulled away from my apartment.

Inside, most of the fluorescent overhead lights were switched off, softening the cavernous Student Union Hall and creating a more intimate dance atmosphere. Standard brown, metal-folding chairs lined the walls... the observational fringe area. An area familiar to me.

I saw three bands setting up in various locations within the room. I studied each band, looking for Jerry. Evidently he was watching for me, too, because when my eyes focused on the band at the far right, I saw him waving and walking toward me.

Not only did I sort of have a date with Jerry, but I was going to meet the band members, too. I had never met a band before. Never been close to an actual band. Excitement and nerves threatened to overwhelm me as this took me way outside my comfort zone. My inner voice and I held quite the conversation.

Over the years, I became used to meeting new people and making new friends, but still suffered with childhood insecurities of fitting in. I worried about how I looked, my dress, and what I would say. I found it hard to make conversation, and wasn't good at small talk. I felt most comfortable when I observed from a distance... from the fringe area.

Jerry flashed the grin... walked over, and hugged me... closing the distance.

He dressed much differently than when I'd seen him that morning. No bell-bottomed jeans, green fatigue jacket, T-shirt or sandals. Instead, he wore a purple Nehru shirt over black, pinstriped bell-bottomed dress pants, and black leather boots.

Oh, my. He looked very nice and very tall. And I was very happy to stand next to him.

"Hey, Rose. I was beginning to think you ditched the dance."

We talked as we walked toward the other band members.

"Are you kidding? I wouldn't miss this. I had to stop for gas. Even a VW runs out once in awhile."

"Well, if you would put more than fifty cents in at a time. You know, fill it up once in awhile?"

"Actually, I splurged and put in three dollars."

"Holy shit! What the fuck, Rose? Check must have come in."

The word "fuck" or the expression "what the fuck" fell out of Jerry's mouth quite regularly. At first it bothered me, and reminded me of my childhood... the men, the step-dads. After awhile, though, I got over that association. Now, when I heard either of them, they reminded me of Jerry. A sad memory replaced with a new one... a process that would happen again and again in my life... a process to help old wounds heal.

"Yes, check came in." I paused, and asked, "So when do you play?"

"We're last... which is good. After everyone hears the other two bands and then we play... Well, let's just say there won't be anyone wondering who the best band is at the end of the night." He flashed that grin at me.

Well, he oozed confidence. I'd give him that.

We joined the other four band members, chatting, tuning, and doing whatever it is bands do before they play.

"Time to meet the guys in the band, Rose." And the introductions began.

"Rose... Cash McGraw."

"Cash... Rose Allison."

"Cash sings lead and is married to Sam, who's not here. She's home taking care of their two little kids, Emma and Tucker.

"It's nice to meet you, Cash. Jerry's been telling me about the band for weeks now."

"So *this* is Rose. Hi, ya', honey." He looked me over, smiled, and gave me a hug. Cash's voice sounded a bit gravelly, and I wondered what he sounded like when he sang.

Oh, my.

His smile made his entire face light up and crinkle when he laughed. He had the most beautiful brown eyes and long lashes. I wondered why guys always got the long lashes. He stood about 5'7" with curly light-brown hair that fell below his ears. He was very tan, very well built, and very handsome. He dressed in a dark-brown, wide-collared shirt with several buttons undone, exposing brown curly chest hair. His shirt tucked neatly inside tan bell-bottomed pants with a wide brown leather belt and brown leather boots. Cash was twenty-six.

I thought to myself... *if he sings even half as good as he looks, they absolutely will win!*

Next, Jerry introduced me to twenty-three-year-old Max Reed, who stood behind a Hammond organ with a Leslie speaker.

"Rose, this is Max Reed... keyboard and vocals. Not married."

Max was tall and slender, fair-skinned, blue eyed, and handsome. His light-brown hair reached nearly shoulder length, and he sported a full mustache. He wore black, pinstriped bell-bottoms, a white peasant shirt with a red scarf, a wide black leather belt, and black leather boots.

He took the cigarette from his mouth. "Hi, Rose... I play guitar and write music, too," he added in a low soft, smooth-as-silk voice. "I hear you write poetry. I'd like to read some of your poems."

Without giving me a chance to respond, Max returned to smoking his cigarette and practicing a particular set of notes over and over. Notes I recognized as the infamous opening to *Light My Fire* by the *Doors.* Sounded perfect to me. He never missed a note.

Gesturing over at the tall, thin guy sporting the curly blond, white-boy afro— whose fingers were expertly running up and down the neck of his Stratocaster—Jerry continued the introductions. "Rose, Chuck Mills, lead guitar and vocals."

Chuck looked over at me with steel blue eyes and, in a quiet voice, said, "Hey, Rose." He smiled at Jerry and back at me, and added, "I'm not married, either."

Chuck wore black bell-bottoms, black boots, and a blue and black brocade Nehru jacket. He wasn't exactly handsome, but something about his look, with that quiet voice, and his mannerism just appealed to me in a rugged sort of way. I doubted he ever lacked for dates, but then, like Jerry, he was probably too busy with the band for dating. Chuck was twenty-two.

Finally, Jerry introduced me to Zach Watters, the drummer. Zach looked young, cute, and innocent, just as Jerry described him. Small, compared to the others, he sported a short brown crew cut and big brown eyes. He dressed in khakis with a yellow button-down Gant shirt, sleeves rolled up... and Weejuns on his bare feet! He *did* look like the poster boy for the all-American, clean-cut kid, just like Jerry said.

"Rose, this is our drummer, Zach Watters."

"Zach... Rose."

Zach twirled his drumsticks in my direction.

"Hi, Zach." At barely fifteen, he seemed a little shy in contrast to the others.

Just as I finished saying "Hi" to Zach, the first band began to play, and it got really loud, really fast. The guys stopped playing and joined Jerry and me. We moved together as a group among the dancers and found a better location to watch the bands perform.

I never enjoyed an event as much as this one, so it didn't matter if I danced a single dance or not.

Most of the evening I listened as the guys talked among themselves, discussing the other two bands... the types/brands of guitars, drums, keyboards they played, their expertise or lack of, the song choices and difficulty, the pitch and timing of the songs, stage presence, and how they were dressed.

They talked about the *sound* of each band. The individual sound of a band became their trademark. For a band to make it—really make it—they must create a unique sound that set them apart from other bands.

I never realized before how guys talked about other guys in such detail. Then I realized it was a "band" thing, not so much a guy thing. Their conversation fascinated me, and I surprised myself with how much I actually understood. I commented appropriately regarding the pitch being flat or sharp, rhythm being on or off, or the missed words in a particular song. Maybe I had more in common with this group than I realized. Maybe I wasn't such an outsider after all.

All of them made me feel comfortable, like I belonged. They loved music and they knew I loved music. It was nice to share something with these new... friends.

Friends. Was that possible?

After the second band finished, and everyone took a fifteen-minute break, *Common Bond* played. I watched as Jerry, Cash, Max, Chuck and Zach took their places and began last-minute sound and mic checks, guitar tuning, lighting adjustments and song order. I learned I hadn't met *everyone* in the band. Their sound mixer and lighting person wasn't with them. One of his brothers was involved in a car accident a couple of days earlier, so he'd driven back home to Rockton and his family.

I knew only his name... Jake.

I noticed Cash and Jerry off to one side talking. Jerry motioned me over.

"Rose, we've got a job for you," Cash announced.

"A job?" I was starting to get nervous.

Jerry continued, "We want you to do our lights tonight since Jake's not here."

"Oh, Jerry... I don't know anything about lighting. I don't..." Cash immediately cut me off.

"Rose, this will not be a hassle. I promise. See this switch?" He asked pointing to a black, light switch on a large square wooden box. Two other rows of buttons lined up underneath it.

"Yes. But what are all those other buttons underneath it?"

Clearly amused at my question, Cash continued with, "Fuck those other buttons, Rose. I have it set. All you have to do is turn the black switch on when you hear the first note of the first song... and turn it off when we finish the last note of the final song. That's it." Cash and Jerry both nodded and smiled confidently at me.

Jerry added, "Just so you know, the first song is 'Magic Carpet Ride' and the last song is 'Light My Fire.'"

I knew those songs. "Okay. I'm your lighting guy!"

I sat down and waited for that first note to play.

As we discussed light switches versus buttons, a crowd steadily gathered in front of the band. There was quite a buzz on campus this week about *Common Bond* playing there in Macomb, at WIU. Evidently they were well known, well liked, and enjoyed a following.

I noticed several girls at the front of the crowd talking and flirting with the band members, especially Cash. I wondered how Sam, Cash's wife, handled all of this? I laughed at myself when I thought earlier about how poor Jerry, Chuck, Zach and Max were too busy with the band to get dates. What was I thinking? They could pick and choose every night they had a booking, probably on rehearsal nights as well.

I really needed to get out more. I needed to get a life.

Student Body President Tom Larson stepped up to the center mic. "And now, our final band of the night... all the way from Champaign. Give it up for *Common Bond*!"

The crowd clapped. The girls screamed. And Max worked his magic on the keyboard playing the distinctive sustained beginning of "Magic Carpet Ride" by Steppenwolf.

I hit the lights.

The other band members watched Cash as he stepped to the front of the stage, and in his gravelly, Joplin-like voice, he belted out those first few words, "Well, you don't know what..."

They followed the opening number with several other popular songs. I marveled at how easily they played and sang at the same time, making it look easy. It wasn't. I knew from personal experience playing the piano and singing was difficult. I'd never mastered it. Yet they did both with ease.

After the last note of "Light My Fire" ended, I switched the lights off. Right on cue.

Jerry was right. The other two bands didn't stand a chance. The thunderous applause at the end of the evening indicated *Common Bond* easily won the Battle of the Bands, complete with bragging rights and groupies. This was so fun, so exciting, so unlike anything I'd ever experienced.

Somehow I managed to fall in with this group. It was nothing short of a miracle. I couldn't help but think there was a reason our paths crossed.

* * * * *

C.L. Gillmore

Journal Entry—September 1968

Common Bond won the battle of the bands tonight! I met Cash, Max, Chuck, and Zach. They are all so cool. They smoke grass and say fuck a lot. Getting used to hearing it. I ran the lights tonight since the lighting guy was gone. I'm so glad I met Jerry... so glad I met the band.

Chapter Three

Lost in thoughts this Christmas Eve
I pray that I may still believe
In all that's tender, good and right
Within my heart this Christmas night.

Macomb, Illinois
Fall 1967

The following week, we had a two-day class break on Thursday and Friday. The band planned to practice Thursday night, and Jerry invited me to rehearsal again. Sam and the kids would be there, and he wanted me to meet them.

This forced me to step even further outside my comfort zone.

During psych class on Wednesday morning, in between note taking Jerry managed to draw a map for me so I could find the rehearsal barn. His drawing came complete with farmhouse, barn, silo, tractor, cornfields, and a large brown cow. Clever. When class ended, he tore the map out of his notebook, handed it to me, and I tucked it into my purse.

Later, in the Student Union, I ordered my usual coffee, grilled cheese and fries and waited for Jerry. I typically arrived first, and knew he was there when I heard "Light My Fire" by The Doors playing on the jukebox.

Jerry dressed in his usual bell-bottom jeans, black T-shirt, and green army jacket. Since Illinois temperatures blew in a little cooler in October, he'd switched from sandals to boots.

He sat down, finished his cigarette, and grabbed one of my fries. He noticed his map unfolded on the table in front of me. He grinned and asked, "So, what do you think?"

"I think you should change your major from business to art, or architecture maybe."

"Nah, probably not. I'd get stoned and caught up in the colored pencils and shit, and never get anything else done but the coloring part. Then, they'd fire my ass and I'd have to pawn my guitars to buy cigarettes and weed."

Weed. Drugs. I learned after many long conversations with Jerry— mostly over coffee, grilled cheese sandwiches and fries—that everyone in the band, except Zach, smoked pot and did other drugs as well... hash, acid, Mescaline. That didn't really come as much of a shock to me. Drugs were everywhere. I didn't do drugs, but I never had the opportunity... until now.

"So, can you find this place or not?"

"Yes, I'm pretty sure I can follow the map if I remember to turn at the big brown cow, and stop before I hit the green John Deere in the cornfield. If either of them moves though, I'm screwed!"

"You can't miss it. Is Ren going to drive up with you?"

Ren was the nickname of my high school friend Karen... Karen Anderson. Her name came up frequently during noontime, grilled cheese chats.

"Depends on whether her mom can watch Jack or not. Different priorities now."

"I know," he said reaching over and grabbing another French fry. "I just hope I see you both tonight." He then asked, "Are you finished with your grilled cheese?"

"Me, too. And yes, my grilled cheese is now *your* grilled cheese." I slid my plate in his direction, and watched him happily munch away.

We talked about the band, a new song Max was working on, and about the Martin D12-35 twelve-string acoustic guitar he just bought. Although he played bass guitar in the band, he could easily switch to lead or rhythm as well, and had quite a collection of guitars... the Martin twelve-string his latest acquisition.

I always liked sharing lunch with Jerry. I enjoyed listening to his fun, animated talk about the band, the music, and his life in general. A life so different from mine. He still technically called Mason City home, where he lived with his parents and three sisters, but spent more and more time in Champaign because of his commitment to the band. I learned Max shared an apartment with Jake, and now Jerry was thinking about moving in with them.

We walked out to the parking lot together and stopped next to Jerry's car. The Registrar's Office sat just one building over. He pulled me close and gave me the sweetest kiss. He'd kissed me after the dance Saturday night, too.

"See you later, Rose. Don't hit any cows!"

With that, he climbed into the gold Barracuda and pulled out of the parking lot.

I held such mixed feelings about Jerry. He was sweet and uncomplicated, and I enjoyed his company. He made me laugh. Made me forget about how alone I felt sometimes. The band was just an extra bonus. Still, even though the kisses were lovely, that spark, that magic I knew happened between people, didn't happen with Jerry and me. I liked him very much, but only as a friend.

I dated a few boys in high school, but no one on a regular basis. For the most part, I kept them at a distance, like everyone else. I didn't have friends. I had people I talked with occasionally. Ren probably came the closest to a real friend I had up to this point. I don't think I did this consciously. It was just my way of not getting too close. If I didn't get too close or too attached, it wouldn't be as difficult when the friendship ended... when one of us left.

I was anxious to see and hear the band play again, and to meet Sam and the kids. I also developed a curiosity about Jake. His name always seemed to come up in conversation when Jerry and I talked. I knew they were good friends, and now Jerry spent most weekends at Jake and Max's shared apartment in Champaign. I think he called it Parkridge Apartments. Cash and Sam and their two little kids lived there, too. How fun would that be... to live somewhere close to the band members?

It all depended on the call from Ren.

Karen Anderson and I became friends in grade school. My mom and I were always moving, either away from Macomb or back to Macomb, so Ren and I found ourselves attending the same schools off and on over the years. Now, we both attended classes at Illinois State. I carried a full load, while Ren took two night classes. Her priorities differed from mine.

Ren looked like a model to me, tall and thin, with long blonde hair, and blue eyes. She and her mother sewed most of her clothes, and she wore them well. I wanted to look and dress just like her.

Ren thought she was too tall, too thin, and hated her homemade clothes.

She came from a large Catholic family with three younger sisters and two older brothers. Her mom worked as a secretary at the college, her dad worked as a yardmaster for the local railroad. I thought she had the perfect family.

Ren couldn't wait to move out and get away from them.

I had to laugh at how differently we saw one another. Before this past year, I often found myself looking at her and thinking how perfect her life must be... beautiful clothes, a nice house, and a great family always involved in her life. She, in turn, thought my life was perfect... always on my own with no one to set any rules, only a three-room apartment to clean, and clothes purchased from J. C. Penney's or Montgomery Ward's.

But now I knew we both struggled every day with our own insecurities and loneliness... just in different ways.

Ren—a talented artist, even in high school—worked as the student art director for the yearbook and school newspaper, and designed the scenery for school musicals and plays. Individually, you could not call either of us extroverted but, together, we gave each other confidence.

We shared some great times those last two years of high school. I spent the night at her house once in awhile, but she was never allowed to stay at my house. She never said why, but I figured it out eventually. My mom was never home. I lived alone and unsupervised almost every weekend. What responsible parent would want their daughter unsupervised all weekend long?

I was one of the few high school girls with access to a car on a regular basis, and Ren and I made the most of it. We shopped, attended dances, and regularly toilet-papered the homes and yards of guys we were afraid to talk to at school, and girls we didn't particularly like.

Ren understood the situation between my mom and me. She never asked questions and went with the flow. She was there for me... no demands, no expectations.

* * * * *

Three years ago, on Christmas night, my mom and I opened presents together. I remember it started out as such a nice evening, gathered around the new funky aluminum tree with the rotating spotlight Mom insisted on buying. I hated it, and missed the smell of a real tree.

I wanted Mom to open her package first. I saved enough money from my job at the grocery store to buy a matching wool skirt and sweater set in light mint green. She tried it on and it fit perfectly. I thought she looked beautiful and she seemed so pleased.

Mom always looked beautiful. She stood a couple of inches taller than me—5'4"—and had a nice figure for a mom. She wore her dark-brown hair short and curled. A dimple in each cheek accentuated her full lips, pretty smile, and green eyes. I got her dimples and her eye color. She dressed smartly, and smelled of Tabu perfume.

I unwrapped my present from Mom next, and found a lovely powder blue, wool sweater and slacks set. The color complemented my blonde hair, and it fit perfectly, too. We both hugged and exchanged a few fond words. We so seldom exchanged any kind of verbal or physical affection.

I thought we would spend Christmas night together that Friday evening. Mom made chili and cornbread. We arranged freshly baked frosted sugar cookies on a holly-trimmed Christmas plate. "Have

Yourself A Merry Little Christmas" from Andy Williams' *Merry Christmas* album played in the background. Outside, huge, lacy snowflakes silently floated past the living room window framing the color-changing aluminum tree. A perfect evening.

A knock at the door.

Vic.

I hated Vic.

Tall, handsome Vic was one of my mom's ex-husbands, and now a boyfriend again. His dark auburn hair contrasted with piercing blue eyes. Eyes I never trusted. He always smelled of Bay Rum cologne and wore expensive dark suits, a dark overcoat, and shiny Florsheim wingtips. Vic had money, and he used it to manipulate people. He manipulated my mother.

Mom changed into an entirely different person when Vic showed up, and that evening was no exception. Her face lit up immediately upon opening the door... happy, smiling, almost giddy, like a teenager. It made me sick to watch. How could she not see the real man? I knew exactly who and what he was... what he was capable of doing. She was an adult, my mother. Why couldn't she see?

There was no way I was going to share Christmas night with Vic and my mother, but I soon found out I wouldn't have to worry about that. He came to pick her up for the weekend. I should have guessed. She always left on Friday night for the weekend. It didn't matter that it was Christmas.

After returning from the bedroom with her overnight tote, Vic helped Mom with her coat. She turned to me, hugged and thanked me again for her skirt and sweater, and wished me Merry Christmas.

Vic smiled a sickening grin at me, and tried to press a five-dollar bill into my hand. I let it fall to the floor. Just the sight of him, let alone him touching my hand, made me nauseous. I walked into the bedroom Mom and I shared, closed the door, and waited for them to leave.

I heard my mother apologizing to Vic for my rudeness, assuring him she'd raised me better. As the front door closed, he said something about taking the car away so I wouldn't have anything to drive on the weekends.

I hated him. I hated her when she was with him. I hated them both. They deserved one another.

I waited five or ten minutes... until I knew they were gone, and it was safe to come out. I was alone. Sometimes, most of the time, it was much better to be alone.

The house fell quiet except for Andy Williams.

I fixed myself a bowl of chili, cut a piece of cornbread and slathered it with lots of butter, and poured a glass of milk. But first, I ate two decorated sugar cookies. I could eat my dessert first. I could do whatever I wanted.

I called Ren and wished her Merry Christmas. She told me about her gifts and her family activity, and listened as I told her about my gifts and my evening.

Snow blanketed everything, and I didn't like driving on slick roads So, Ren and I agreed to walk and meet each other halfway to model our new clothes. I liked walking in the snow much more than driving in it.

Big fluffy snowflakes fell in the light of the moon as I walked to meet her. The cold and quiet made it beautiful outside. In the distance the bell from the big Catholic Church on the hill pealed nine times, then began to chime "Silent Night." I sang the words to myself as I walked alone silently, my boots swishing through the glistening snow.

The night reflected a silent night, a calm night, a bright night, but I wasn't sure about it as a holy night. I wondered if anyone really slept in heavenly peace.

Ren and I met halfway and used the sidewalk as a runway to model our new Christmas outfits. We munched on sugar cookies I'd wrapped in a paper towel and stuck into my pocket, talked about what we got for Christmas, and listened to "Turn, Turn, Turn" by The Byrds on Ren's new pocket-size, transistor radio. It included earphones, too, so we took turns listening. What a cool present.

Later, we hugged and wished each other Merry Christmas, and walked back home... Ren to her big family, and I to Andy Williams and my dog Dottie.

She never asked questions. We never talked about it. We didn't have to.

That was the last Christmas with my mother.

A few months later, Ren was with me the afternoon I came home from school and found the suicide note from my mom, propped up against the sugar bowl on the red Formica kitchen table. The same table gracing my apartment. How thankful I felt that Ren stayed by my side.

She was there for me, and I would be there for her a few months later.

Ren didn't date much until her senior year, until she fell in love with tall, blond, hunky Jesse... her first real boyfriend. He was older by three years and she wasn't prepared for his level of experience. By December, she was pregnant, and her life, her plans, her hopes, and dreams all changed. In August, she brought into the world a sweet, little baby boy named Jack.

Ren told me first when she suspected she was pregnant. I supported her through her morning sickness, and when she tearfully outgrew her jeans. I anxiously waited at the hospital during labor and delivery.

I never asked any questions. We never talked about it. Again, we didn't have to. I was there for her.

* * * * *

The phone rang as I unlocked the apartment door and hurried up the stairs and into the kitchen.

"Hello!" I said, totally out of breath.

"You must have just gotten home." It was Ren.

"I did. So... can you go? Can your mom watch Jack?"

"Yes! Mom's going to watch Jack. I'm so excited. What are you wearing, and what time are you picking me up?"

"Bell-bottoms and my flowered empire blouse. I have to get gas... so probably around five, or a little after. I figure it will take us a couple of hours."

"Perfect. I'm back in my bell-bottoms as of this morning and I'm wearing those with my blue button-down shirt and burgundy sweater. See you around five."

"Okay. See you then!"

It would be good for Ren to get out. Good for her to meet some new friends... some new guy friends. I knew she still loved Jesse, but he'd moved on shortly after she told him of her pregnancy. Why did she have to get mixed up with him, of all people? Her life was forever changed, while his life just moved along as if nothing happened.

A little after five, I pulled up in front of the big white Queen Anne-style house where Ren, Jack, and her family lived. I loved that house. Loved spending the night there. The big, two-story reminded me of a princess's beautiful castle. It featured a big wrap-around front porch, stained glass inserts on both sides of the double front doors, and a round, two-story library room. I loved going into that round room. It truly felt like a castle inside, or at least I thought it did. The huge, twelve-room house included five bedrooms and three bathrooms. When Jack came along, Ren's mom and dad moved the family crib down from the attic into her room, and life went on.

Life went on, but it would never be the same. She lost her innocence in more ways than one that year. Life was no longer carefree. Life was serious business. She became responsible for another person's life. Ren was a mother now.

I knew she wanted her own apartment, but no way could she manage it financially at that time. She stayed with Jack during the day and took classes at night. To move out, she would need to drop out of school, get a job, and find someone to watch Jack. That was a lot to think about, a lot to make happen. With only one bedroom, my place couldn't accommodate her and Jack. Just the same, we talked about sharing an apartment sometime in the future. It was a hope, a dream... for me and Ren and Jack.

Ren stood in the doorway holding the little guy. She gave him a kiss and hug, handed him off to her mother, and bounded down the front steps. To look at her, you'd never know she had a two-month-old baby boy, and all the responsibility that comes with him. She looked young, carefree, and beautiful.

I so wanted her life to have a happy ending.

Sliding in next to me she began... "You're right on time. How do I look? You look great. I wonder if Jack will be okay. I need to call when we get to Champaign or where ever it is we're going. Have you eaten?"

"Holy shit... take a breath! Still on the Dexedrine, I see!"

Dexedrine served as the diet drug of choice for both of us when we wanted to shed a quick ten pounds. She'd shed twenty-five, and was still losing.

Intentionally talking at a much slower, exaggerated pace, I responded. "You look great. Jack will be okay and, yes, we can call later. No, I haven't eaten. Do you want me to drive through Henri's on the way out of town?"

She laughed. "I guess I am speeding just a little, huh? I'm just so happy to be out, and Henri's sounds fab!"

"Yes, you are speeding, just a little." I continued. "Hey, grab that folded up notebook paper out of my purse. It's a map Jerry drew to help us get to the rehearsal barn."

"Cool map," she remarked as she unfolded it. I especially like the big brown cow on the corner of Gravel Road A and Gravel Road B."

Since Ren took classes at night and missed the mixer, she had yet to meet Jerry. She heard about him and the rest of the band from me. I talked about her with Jerry, too, so he knew her through our conversations. He knew she was tall, blonde and pretty. He knew she was single and had a baby. I figured the rest of the band knew her story by now, as well.

"Yes, I kind of liked the green John Deere tractor, parked in the cornfield, the best. It's right down Gravel Road B from the brown cow."

"Yes. Nice detail."

We laughed as I shifted into first gear, pulled away in the little black Volkswagen Beetle, and headed for Henri's. Forget the diet.

Thirty minutes later we were screaming down the highway toward Champaign— "Born To Be Wild" blaring from the radio—wolfing cheeseburgers and fries, and sharing a Dr. Pepper.

It felt like old times again.

The drive went by quickly. We listened to and sang along to favorite songs on the radio, and talked... about Jack, clothes, hair, the band, guys. Chick chat. Before we knew it, we needed to turn our attention to Map Reading 101. Ren served as navigator.

Twilight fell as we turned off the main highway about eight miles outside of Champaign, and followed Gravel Road A north for three miles exactly. We turned left and headed west for another mile on Gravel Road B. So far, the map had been right on, but if we couldn't see the cows or tractor we might be in trouble. We came to an intersection edged by a field holding several black cows and one very large *brown* cow. "Hey, there's the big brown cow!" Ren announced and pointed. "This is where we turn and start looking for cornfields and a green John Deere tractor."

We drove down the gravel road, following along the cornfields, and came to a green John Deere tractor. Perfect. I made the final turn and saw the farmhouse, silo, and barn. Several cars parked by the barn and, as we got closer, we heard the band playing. We definitely found the right place.

I pulled in between a red Rambler and a brown Ford Falcon station wagon.

"Ready?" I asked.

"Yes, Ma'am. Let's do this!"

We climbed out of the VW and walked up the graveled driveway toward the barn... toward the music... toward the band. The closer we got to the building, the louder the music.

We stepped through the doors onto a gray concrete floor. Round fluorescent lights hanging from the tall ceiling lit the space well. The band set up toward the back, between two tractors: an orange Allis Chalmers and a green Oliver. I laughed at myself for identifying tractor brands. How Midwest was that?

As the band played "Gimme Some Lovin'" by The Spencer Davis Group, Jerry gave a smiling head nod in our direction. Cash raised his eyebrows. While Max, Chuck and Zach—focused on the music—missed our entrance.

A pretty, dark-haired young woman sat to the side on an old wooden chair. A sleepy little boy straddled her lap, his face snuggled against her breast. Surely Sam, Cash's wife, and their little boy, Tucker. A short distance away, a blonde, curly-haired little girl sprawled on her tummy on the floor, coloring book and crayons spread in front of her. Emma. She looked just like Cash, curly hair and all.

Ren leaned closer, to speak over the music. "Is it just me, or are all those guys major hunks?"

"No, it's *not* just you. I thought the same thing the first time I saw them together."

We continued taking everything and everyone in.... earthy scent, huge barn, farm stuff hanging on the walls, fluorescent lights, tractors, old chairs, Sam and the kids, hunky band members and...

I saw him.

Next to Sam stood a really cute guy—watching, talking, laughing and helping to entertain Tucker and Emma. He reached Cash's height, about 5'7", with straight sandy-brown hair skimming his ears. He wore a tight black T-shirt accentuating his broad shoulders and muscular well-tanned arms. He tucked that tight T-shirt inside tight bell-bottom jeans with tapered orange, white and navy blue paisley inserts running up each side just below his knee. And sandals. Even in October, he still wore sandals on his golden-brown feet.

He had a good build... and a really nice butt.

"Oh my," I said out loud to no one in particular.

Just as those two words left my lips, he looked right at me. He didn't smile. He just looked at me... all of me. Slowly. Up and down.

"Oh my, is right." Ren repeated. "Don't look now, but there's a really cute guy checking you out. Who *is* he?"

"I'm not sure, but I think it might be their sound and lighting guy. You know, the one who missed the mixer because his brother was in a car accident?"

"Oh, right. I remember you telling me about him. Well, he's major cute, and I hope his brother recovered from the accident and looks just like him, only in a taller version."

Cute Guy's eyes and mine met once again. This time he smiled and walked back toward the band. I thought about what Ren said, about him checking me out. I wondered if he knew I had just checked him out as well.

We walked over to the pretty brown-haired young woman with the two children and introduced ourselves.

"Hi, I'm Rose Allison and this is my friend Ren Anderson."

"Nice to meet you both. I'm Sam McGraw and this is Tucker and Emma."

Almost in unison, Ren and I responded, "Nice to finally meet you, Sam."

Ren bent down and asked Emma if she could color with her. Delighted at the suggestion, she immediately scooted over to make room.

In the meantime, the band finished one song and transitioned into the next. They hadn't played this new one at the mixer.

I watched as Cute Guy walked over. He knelt down next to where Ren and Emma were coloring, and talked with them. I couldn't hear or see much of what they said because of the music and their positions, but I figured it involved introductions and small talk.

He stood up, and looked as if he was about ready to say something to me when Sam interjected, "Cash sounds better now. Harmonies are better, too. What did you do?"

"I pumped up the volume on the front speakers and turned them in. Sounds better, huh?"

"Yes, much better, and Cash doesn't have that 'what the hell?' look on his face anymore. I just hate that look, don't you?" Sam asked, smiling.

"Yes. We all hate that look."

He and Sam had a connection. They were friends. Good friends.

I watched and listened as they continued the conversation. He was so animated... gesturing with his hands, his arms, his face, his entire body. He reminded me of an actor on stage. I was mesmerized.

He had the deepest blue eyes. They twinkled when he smiled, and when he laughed. His voice sounded steady and deep. I found myself watching his mouth, his lips, as he talked.

Oh God... he had it all working... just like the rest of them.

Of course he did.

"Hey. You still with us?"

I suddenly realized he was talking to me. He looked into my face... looked through me, and I was lost. Lost in his voice, his words, his lips his eyes. My mind wandered off somewhere into a cornfield with the large brown cow and green John Deere tractor.

He said something else... maybe his name. I didn't catch it. With the loud music, I couldn't hear.

I kept looking at his lips. Maybe I should introduce myself. Of course I should.

Now let's see... who was I?

Returning from my daydreams, I gazed back at him and managed to remember my name.

"My name is Rose... Rose Allison."

He shook his head and said a little louder, "Rose, what?"

I knew I hadn't spoken loudly enough. He hadn't caught my last name, so I spelled it, nearly shouting the letters out this time. "A-l-l-i-s-o-n. Rose Allison with two Ls. And are you Jake, Jake Richardson?"

He leaned in toward me, placed his hand on my shoulder and in a deep, steady voice spoke slowly and clearly into my ear.

"Yep, that would be me. And you would be Rose Allison with two Ls, right?"

I felt his breath against my ear as he spoke. His voice sent shivers to my core. His touch on my shoulder, firm and warm, made me tremble.

I pulled back and looked into his face, into those blue eyes, and answered into his ear in as steady a voice as I could manage.

"Yes, Rose Allison... with two Ls."

For just a few seconds the words hung in the air between us as we looked at one another. Something happened. I saw something in his face, his expression.

Electricity.

Did he feel it, or was it just me? Was I imagining this?

Slowly his gaze trailed from my face down to my feet. He grinned and said,

"Nice sandals."

"Thanks. Nice bell-bottoms. I like the paisley inserts."

"My mom sews. Have some fabric left... enough for a headband. Interested?"

"Headband?"

"Yep... it goes around your head... hence, headband."

"Oh, sure. Yes."

Brilliant conversation on my part.

I couldn't breathe. Couldn't catch my breath.

He leaned in closer—his hand still resting on my shoulder—and whispered, "Take a breath."

He smiled ever so slightly, and let his hand, his fingers, trail over my shoulder and down my arm as he walked back over to the band.

Oh, my. I did need to take a breath. Suddenly no oxygen remained in the entire barn.

Shit. Shit. Shit. What just happened?

I looked down at Ren who was finishing a page with Emma, and realized she'd watched this entire exchange.

Slowly she mouthed the words, "What the hell?"

I just shook my head and looked over at the band, first at a grinning Jerry Parker, and then at Jake Richardson, who was busy, once again, tinkering with the sound.

What the hell was going on?

Nothing like this ever happened to me. No one got through. I didn't let them. Yet somehow with just a smile, a touch, and a few well-chosen words, he managed to cruise in under the radar and back out, without detection.

Oh, my God. I let him in.

When rehearsal ended, I introduced Ren to the rest of the band members. They laughed and joked with her just like they'd done with me early on. They made her feel at ease... a part of things. I watched her smile, laugh, and interact with everyone, and I knew in my heart this was a good thing. A good thing for her... a good thing for me.

We listened as the guys discussed how the rehearsal went, and firmed up plans for an upcoming booking at The Library in Champaign. It was fun to listen and watch everyone interact. The band reminded me of a big family, with Cash and Sam serving as parents to the rowdy, talented, opinionated bunch of kids.

After rehearsal... Zach, Cash, Sam, and the two kids piled into the Ford Falcon station wagon and drove back to Champaign. The rest of us headed to Dixie's Truck Stop—about fifteen minutes down Highway 150—for coffee and conversation.

Jake and Max drove in the red Rambler, Jerry and Chuck in the Barracuda, and Ren and I in the VW.

Jake and Max strategically maneuvered everyone into the horseshoe-shaped booth at the truck stop. Somehow Max and Chuck ended up in the middle with Jake and me on the left... Ren and Jerry on the right. As we all picked up our menus, I noticed Jake smiling into his.

Leaning against his shoulder, I looked into his face and asked, "How did you manage to pull that off?"

He turned that smile on me. "It's a gift." In the next breath, he said, "I recommend the tenderloins. They're especially good with lots of yellow mustard."

And then, pausing, he said just loudly enough for me to hear, "Trust me."

The expression on his face changed with those two words. He wasn't smiling anymore. He was searching my eyes, my heart, for a connection. Did I understand what he was saying? He wasn't talking about tenderloins anymore.

I did understand.

Something happened between us, even though we just met. I felt like I knew him, that he knew me. Kindred spirits. Kindred souls. Was that what this was?

I looked into his face, his eyes.

"Tenderloins are good, huh? I should trust you?"

"Yep and yep."

"Okay then. I just might."

Looking from Jake to the waitress, I said, "I'll have the tenderloin with pickles and lots of yellow mustard."

Jake smiled. "Good answer. I like pickles, too." He turned to the waitress, "Make that two."

* * * * *

I sat in bed, snuggled under the covers, my back cushioned against two feather pillows, a black notebook resting on my lap. I placed

Jerry's wrinkled map into the binder and jotted down my thoughts from the evening.

Journal Entry—October 1968

Tonight, I finally met the lighting and sound guy, Jake Richardson. I barely know him and yet I feel comfortable with him. He's a farm boy... cute, witty, funny, and gentle... prone to answering questions with "yep" and "nope." Yet, he's smart, easy to talk to, and a good listener. I like his voice... low, steady, and calm. Jake, Jerry, Max, Ren and I went to Dixie's Truck Stop after rehearsal. I sat next to Jake. Our shoulders touched. We talked about tenderloins and mustard and trust. I don't think we were talking about tenderloins or mustard though. We were really talking more about trust.

What is it about him? When I look into his eyes, I see something different. I can't explain it. I just know something extraordinary happened tonight. It's like a connection with someone I already knew. But that can't be, can it? I just want him to hold me. I want to listen to his voice forever. When I look at his lips I want him to kiss me. He makes me ache inside. I can't wait to see him again. I like the words to the song the band played—"I'll Be There," by The Four Tops. That's how Jake makes me feel... like I want to reach out... that he'll be there for me.

Out on the edges of the notebook I wrote Jake's name several times, trying different types of cursive "Js." I'd never written that letter of the alphabet much. Didn't know any "J" people. After practicing his name, I wrote Jake + Rose and drew a heart around it.

Geez, how corny was that? How high school was that? I didn't care.

Then I wrote... Rose Allison Richardson... closed the notebook, fluffed my pillows, and turned out the light.

* * * * *

Several good things happened after that Wednesday night when Ren and I found our way along the graveled roads, the cornfields, the cows, and tractors to the rehearsal barn near Champaign.

After the truck stop, the tenderloins, and the trust.

It started with a long conversation the following Monday between Jerry and I over another split grilled cheese sandwich and fries lunch. We realized what developed between us amounted to a really great friendship and nothing more. No violins played or sparks flew between us during the kisses we'd exchanged. We didn't do it for one another. But we had a good laugh over it, and the friendship continued.

Jerry said Jake asked about me after Ren and I left Dixie's last Wednesday night. I tried to act nonchalant, but Jerry knew I was interested.

"So, what do you think, Rose? Would you go out with Jake?"

"Of course. Are you supposed to report back or something?"

"Yea, or something."

"I thought only girls did stuff like this."

"Cut me some slack, Rose."

"Sorry. Tell Jake I'd like to go out with him. Not sure what that means exactly, since the only places you guys ever go is to rehearsal, a gig, or a truck stop."

"Good point. But Jake doesn't play in the band, so you could actually dance with him when he's not busy fixing shit with the sound or lighting. He's pretty creative. I'm thinking he'll figure something out for you two to do."

With that last remark, Jerry gave me that huge, gummy grin of his, and raised his eyebrows up and down a couple of times.

"Is that all you guys ever think about?"

"No, we think about music and food, too—but not nearly as often."

I slugged him in the arm.

It was an easy next step for Jerry to ask about Ren. It thrilled me that he asked. Jerry was kind, patient and accepting... and he was tall. Perfect.

Not long after this, Ren and I decided to put our education on hold in favor of following a band. At the time, the band was much more exciting than any classes offered at the university. Both nearly twenty, we had a lifetime to finish college. The band was happening now.

Chapter Four

My grandma stood in front of the stove and lovingly cooked for me.
Wiping well-worn hands on her apron, and lifting me up to see.
Now, as I hold her delicate china, that image remains in my mind
Standing close, feeling her touch, remembering a face so kind.

Champaign, Illinois
Winter 1968–1969

*R*en and I brought the signed lease to Mr. Cody and picked up the keys to our apartment one cold Saturday morning in November. On our way out of the clubhouse, we stopped by the mail area. I skimmed my fingers over the wall of metal mailboxes until I came to ours—1216. Ren slipped the address label for our apartment into the front ID window of our mailbox.

Rose Allison
Karen Anderson
1216 Parkridge Apartments
Champaign, Illinois 61821

We now officially lived at Parkridge Apartments, and moving day was tomorrow. Holy shit!!
With keys in hand and bundled up—I in my navy pea coat, white stocking hat, and mittens, and Ren in her grey wool maxi-coat, wide-

brimmed floppy black hat, and gloves—we gingerly walked down the snowy, partially-cleared sidewalk to the parking lot.

We had packed both cars—Karen's family station wagon and my Volkswagen Bug—floor to ceiling with as many boxes as we could fit in and still see to drive. We squeezed back into our cars and drove the short distance across the apartment complex to Building 12. Our townhouse sat at the end.

Ren unlatched the tall, wooden patio gate, and we plodded up to the red, metal front door. I slipped the key from inside my mitten, unlocked the door, and we stepped inside... shedding mittens, hats, coats, and boots.

The front door of the townhouse opened to an L-shaped living, dining and galley-style kitchen. A stairway off the living area, led to two bedrooms, and a bathroom on the second floor.

We stood side-by-side, taking in our new apartment.

"This is so far out, I can hardly believe it, Rose. We made this happen... you and I."

"We did. We talked about it, dreamed of it, made plans, and now it's reality."

Ren breathed deeply. "Smell the new?"

"Yes. Always a favorite scent of mine."

Everything smelled new—carpet, linoleum, paint. The kitchen appliances still had the factory tags attached. We wouldn't have to do a thing except move in. I wondered what my mom would think of this. I often thought of her when new things, good things, happened in my life. High school graduation, my first apartment, buying the Volkswagon, college... and now my life here in Champaign. All these things she'd missed. Did she not realize suicide was permanent... a fatal decision one can't come back from?

"Hey... Earth calling Rose. Come in."

"Sorry. I got caught up in the *newness* moment! What did you say?"

"I said, I'm glad we decided on the fireplace."

"Oh, me, too. It's beautiful. I never thought I'd live anywhere with a fireplace."

That was the absolute truth. Ren's big family home had two, so this probably was no big deal for her. It was a very big deal for me.

All the townhouses at Parkridge were the same, except for the color scheme. Our townhouse featured avocado-green carpeting, drapes, and appliances. The featured color in Cash and Sam's apartment... harvest gold. Jake, Jerry and Max's place came with blue carpeting and drapes, and white appliances. All the apartments sported dark kitchen cabinets, white bathroom fixtures, white-flecked kitchen and bath linoleum, and white paint throughout.

We walked into the kitchen, across the shiny white linoleum, and explored. Though small, the galley layout was efficient with plenty of storage. Having new appliances—stove, dishwasher, and refrigerator—was a treat. My familiarity with appliances involved well-worn equipment that came with the three-room and bath apartments my mom rented, or used appliances she purchased at local auctions. This was the first time I'd seen new appliances other than on Sears' showroom floor.

"I can't wait to get our things in here and unpacked, and settled in."

"Me, either. I'm looking forward to the day I can bring Jack here permanently, too. Then, it will really feel like home to me."

She turned around slowly, arms outstretched. "I love this place already. It feels like a new start for me. You know what I mean, Rose?"

I knew exactly what she meant.

"I do. It's a new start for me, too. No old memories here, only new ones."

We walked up the short flight of steps to the second floor. The bathroom sat at the top of the stairs, across a small hallway. Next to the bathroom, a linen closet, and two bedrooms at the end of the hall.

"Ren, you and Jack take the larger bedroom on the right. I'll take the smaller room. It's the perfect size for me."

"Okay, thanks. He does have a lot of stuff, and once I bring him up on a permanent basis, we'll definitely need the extra room."

For the time being, her family offered to watch Jack during the week, and she would drive back to Macomb on the weekends to be with him. The plan was to bring Jack to the apartment permanently after we fully settled. That would require finding a sitter she trusted and could afford. All of this would take some time to work out. She was lucky to have a family who loved her enough to help her become independent.

We walked back downstairs and sat on the floor in the corner of the living room. We discussed the apartment, our new jobs, the band, and planned for the upcoming summer, the future. I think we even dreamed a little that morning about possibilities. It's a good thing to have possibilities.

I'd never lived in a nicer place, not counting the foster homes in high school. But those didn't really belong to me. This was mine. My name was on the lease. Rose Allison. Well, Rose Allison and Karen Anderson. It was ours, I guess. But that was okay, too.

Ren seemed like herself again. Bubbly. Happy. I saw something in her face, her blue eyes, this morning that wasn't there a few months back. I saw hope. Hope for a future again, for her and for Jack.

Maybe this was finally my chance. My chance to be happy. My chance to leave the memories and baggage behind, and start fresh. I needed to keep hope alive in my life, too.

Everyone needs hope. Without hope, you're never free to dream. And without dreams, there's no reason to move forward with your life. I had been a dreamer for as long as I could remember. Hope and dreams brought me this far, through many dark and difficult times, alone. Maybe they would bring me a little farther.

* * * * *

Luckily, we found my radio near the top of one large box on the first trip. We spent the next two hours listening, singing, and dancing to the songs from Chicago's WLS Silver Dollar Survey with Clark Weber, while unloading both cars.

These were the most enjoyable hours of unpacking I could remember because, this time, my move was different. I made the choice to move. I moved somewhere I wanted, with people I wanted to be near. What a difference it made to have a choice, a voice, a say.

After stacking the empty boxes in a corner of the living room, we climbed into the VW to run errands. We stopped at Illinois Power, and both the water and gas companies, to transfer the accounts into our names, and arranged for phone installation on Monday from Bell Telephone.

After a quick drive-through at McDonald's, we drove back to Parkridge. Ren needed to drive back to Macomb to finish packing and to be a mama again. I planned to follow her shortly.

"I'll call you when I get back to Macomb, Ren. Maybe I can help you finish packing. I won't be much longer. Just wanted to look around a few more minutes."

"I totally understand. And, yes, call me. You can help me finish packing, and we can plan out where we want everything to go tomorrow."

* * * * *

Moving day was the next day. For the first time in my life I actually looked forward to moving. Up until now, moving was anything but a pleasant experience for me. I silently counted all the moves I could remember after my dad's death when my mom, my sister Carla, and I moved back to Macomb.

Nineteen. And those were just the ones I remembered. Carla remembered ones I didn't. Who really knows how many times we moved?

I remembered nineteen different places to try to fall asleep at night without fearing unfamiliar sounds and unidentified shadows on the walls and windows of a strange bedroom. Nineteen new neighborhoods to find safe places to play, and make new friends. Nineteen new schools and teachers to adjust to.

Nineteen apartments, bedrooms, neighborhoods, friends, schools, and teachers to eventually leave behind.

I hoped and prayed that this move, number twenty, would be the best move of my life. I said a silent prayer, "Please... let this move bring good changes. Let it bring someone into my life who will always remember me... always love me... and never leave me behind."

I walked into the kitchen, turned on the clock radio, and opened the cabinet door above the sink. On the bottom shelf, sat my Grandpa and Grandma Allison's Howdy Doody glasses, a pink one and a yellow one, once filled with Welch's grape jelly. Of all the things left me, I considered these two glasses the most precious. My milk and donut, Saturday morning glasses always brought a smile to my face no matter how difficult the day.

Both glasses overflowed with memories—of my grandpa and grandma, my sister, my dad, my mom—of my childhood.

My grandpa and grandma told me at a young age how special my dad was to them. They believed God sent him to them when they couldn't have children of their own. They told the story about how one spring morning, long ago, Dad's biological parents abandoned him and his two older brothers—left them behind in their farmhouse to fend for themselves. I don't recall hearing an explanation for why the parents abandoned their children, I just remember Grandma and Grandpa saying they found them the next day. My dad was just a toddler, his brothers maybe four and five.

Grandpa explained how times were difficult back then and money scarce. He and Grandma could only care for one child, not three—so they adopted the youngest, my dad. They placed his brothers in an orphanage.

I always thought the story sad, and wondered what happened to his brothers. No one seemed to know or talk about it. Grandma and Grandpa loved my dad, and as part of him, they loved me, their only grandchild. When my dad died, I think they loved me even more.

My mom often left me with my grandparents on the weekends or during extended vacation times. I was happy to stay with them... to be away. With Grandpa and Grandma Allison I felt safe and loved and wanted. For a time, their home became a sanctuary from everything beyond my understanding and control.

I walked back to my living room and sat on the floor in the corner. I needed just a few minutes rest before driving back to Macomb. I closed my eyes and drifted away... floated into that ethereal place between dreams and wakefulness.

I dreamed I walked through a cool, quiet, and peaceful yard smelling of green and springtime. I recognized the yard, the flowers, in Grandma and Grandpa Allison's yard—the one that surrounded the big, two-story, brown-shingled house overlooking the LeMoine River in Macomb.

I climbed the steps to the small front porch where Grandpa's weathered wooden bench nestled off to one side. The bench creaked as I sat and settled back against the armrest with my legs out-stretched along the length of the well-worn seat. Planted next to the porch, just behind the bench, grew a climbing rose bush enclosing everything in bright crimson flowers. Opposite the bench, a stained glass window caught the sunlight to cast shimmering bands of red, purple, yellow, and green light over the entire porch. This was one of my very favorite places—shady, quiet and secluded. I sometimes imagined it as the bunkhouse of the Double RR Bar Ranch where the little cowgirl rode horses with Roy Rogers. I dreamed up a castle where the beautiful princess lived and waited for handsome Prince Charming to sweep her up onto his white horse and carry her far away to live happily ever after.

This place, only dreamers could find.

* * * * *

I don't know how long I slept, but I awoke to a knock at the door. Maybe Mr. Cody, the apartment manager, bringing the extra key we requested.

I got up—opened the door a few inches— to see who was there.

"You know, Rose... you might want to look through the peep hole, or keep the chain lock on, or ask who's at the door before you open it. Could be an ax murderer."

Jake.

I quickly closed the door and waited.

Another knock.

"Who's there?"

"An ax murderer. May I come in?"

I opened the door. "Yes. Come in. I've been expecting you!"

I'd last seen Jake a couple of weeks ago. We had seen each other at two more rehearsals in the past month, sharing tenderloins and conversation at Dixie's afterwards. Lots of conversation.

I found it easy to talk with him. Maybe because he listened well. I never thought much about being a good listener. But, there is a difference in looking and nodding at someone, and really listening to what they say.

Jake listened.

Jake remembered.

He walked through the door and announced, "I come bearing gifts." He held a small, white, bakery sack in one hand and a quart of chocolate milk in the other. "Figured with all the stuff you and Ren had going on, you missed donut day this morning."

Donut Day.

Yes. He listened. He remembered. Amazing.

"You figured right." I took the sack from his hand and peaked inside. "Oh my, glazed twists, my favorite!" I gave him a quick hug... embracing Jake, the donut bag and the chocolate milk. "Thank you for remembering."

"Does this cancel out the ax under my jacket?"

"Absolutely! But I may have to frisk you from now on before I let you in."

"I have no problem with being frisked. Please... frisk at will."

Jake crammed his Illinois Illini stocking hat and leather gloves into the pockets of his jacket and toed his shoes off. He pretended to hang the jacket on an imaginary hook beside the door and let it fall to the ground.

"Thanks for hanging up your jacket. I'll find us a couple of glasses."

"Welcome."

Jake eyed the empty boxes in the corner of the living room.

"You've been busy this morning."

"We have. Packed the cars last night and drove up around seven this morning. Ren drove back a couple of hours ago to finish packing. I fell asleep, or I'd be on my way back, too."

"Well, I'm glad you fell asleep. Or I'd have been forced to eat all of these damn donuts, plus drink all the chocolate milk, and then I'd be sick. And it would be your fault."

"Yes, well, I can see where that would be totally my fault. So... pull up some carpet and make yourself comfortable. I'll get those glasses."

"You know—we could just share germs and drink out of the carton—save washing glasses later."

"No can do. I'm a donut dunker."

"Should have guessed. You look like a dunker."

I smiled, shook my head, and headed to the kitchen.

I loved this—this dance, this electricity—whatever was going on between us. It started that first night at the rehearsal barn with Jake asking me, "Hey, you still with us?" and leaving me with, "Take a breath." It was still going on.

He made me smile, made me laugh, made me want to trust.

I returned from the kitchen with one pink and one yellow Howdy Doody glass in each hand. I found Jake seated on the rug in one corner of the living room, donuts and napkins spread out picnic style. I guessed the two glazed twist donuts were for me and the two chocolate sprinkle donuts were his.

I sat down next to him and handed him the yellow Howdy Doody glass.

"Chocolate sprinkles, huh?"

"Yep. I've always been a chocolate sprinkle man."

"Good to know. I'll file that away for later."

"Nice glasses." Jake said as he turned and inspected the yellow characters and writing on his glass. "Haven't seen these in awhile. Used to come with grape jelly in them. I forgot about the embossed characters on the bottom of the glasses. Clarabelle's on mine." I held mine up for him to check. "You've got Howdy Doody... cool."

"I think my mom stashed a couple away somewhere. Won't let me or my brothers touch them. She says we broke all the rest. Used to have six or eight, I think."

"Oh, that's hard to believe. I can't imagine why she would hide them away," I said sarcastically.

"Because my mother is a cruel woman. That's why."

"I'm sure she is. You probably come from a long line of cruel women."

"As a matter of fact, I do. My grandmother was a cruel woman as well."

I set my glass down, opened the chocolate milk and began pouring. I looked at Jake. "Say when."

I poured until the glass was nearly full and about to spill over the top, and thought, *I'll play your silly game. I've got plenty of napkins.*

At the very last second, Jake grinned and calmly said, "When."

I'll bet he and his brothers gave his mother a fit when they were little. The words "ornery shit" immediately came to mind.

Three ornery shit sons. His poor mother. No wonder she hides things.

Jake sipped just enough milk off the top to keep it from running down the sides of the glass. He picked up the other glass and held it as I filled it, but only halfway.

"Chicken," he said, handing the glass back to me.

"Ornery shit," I said in return.

We munched on the donuts, sipped our chocolate milk, and settled back against the wall, next to one another. It felt—comfortable. Yes, that was the word. Comfortable.

I held my pink Howdy Doody glass up and inspected it.

"These glasses belonged to my Grandma Allison. She died a few years ago. Left a cardboard box behind with my name on it. These glasses and a few other items were inside it, all carefully wrapped in old newspapers. I love drinking out of them. Reminds me of staying at Grandma and Grandpa's house on the weekends when my mom was gone."

Maybe one day I would share that part of my life with Jake. Tell him about my grandparents and the childhood place I went to find solace when things got too crazy.

Maybe.

Jake carefully touched his glass to mine and looked at me. "Here's to your Grandma Allison. I'm sure she's happy knowing you're using her glasses and remembering her, Rose."

For some reason, Jake's comment overcame me—his simple, heartfelt words. Maybe it was because I was tired. Maybe it was that time of month.

I pursed my lips and swallowed, but the tears rushed to my eyes anyway, blurring my vision, and finally spilling down my cheeks. I tried wiping them away and turning away so Jake wouldn't see, but it was too late. They fell too quickly. My body, my heart betrayed me.

Jake took both glasses and set them off to one side. He gently wrapped me in his arms, turning me just enough so my leg rested on top of his, and my head nestled against his chest.

He felt so solid, so warm beneath me. I felt his breath against my cheek, the steady rhythm of his heartbeat beneath my head. He smelled of soap and spicy cologne.

I tried to control my tears, swallow my sobs, and remain silent. I had years of practice doing this. But Jake was having none of that. He massaged the back of my neck, and ran his fingers through my hair with one hand, while kneading the small of my back with the other. He whispered in my ear.

"It's okay, Rose. Let me hold you. I've got you."

Once again, his simple words, his sincerity somehow gave me permission to be held—to be comforted—to rest and to let go. It was okay if the tears fell. It was okay if someone heard me cry. It was okay because Jake said so.

So, for no reason—other than maybe hormones, lack of sleep, and sentimentality over a Howdy Doody glass of my grandma's—I cried, quietly sheltered within Jake's arms.

A few minutes passed, the tears subsided, and Jake handed me a napkin.

"Blow," he softly commanded, still holding me in his arms.

I managed a "thank you" and blew as discreetly as I could. I placed the soggy napkin back into his out-stretched palm.

"Good girl," he said, tossing the napkin next to the glasses.

Jake leaned closer, thumbed a few lingering tears from my cheeks, and hooked his finger under my chin to lift my face. Everything felt so right, and I knew at that moment, he would kiss me.

I thought about closing my eyes and just letting it happen, but I couldn't. I wanted to see. I wanted to watch him.

I looked into his eyes, those beautiful blue eyes, and saw something I hadn't seen before. Something different, something more. More than friendship. He couldn't hide it. He didn't try to hide it.

I watched his mouth come closer and closer to mine until finally his lips brushed softly across mine—so softly, back and forth, nibbling and coaxing—his hand curled over the back of my head controlling just the right amount of pressure and direction. My eyes closed from sheer pleasure, and I let my brain shift to the other senses: the touch of his lips on mine, his hands entwined in my hair, the other caressing my back, while his chest pressed tightly against my breasts. I heard the sensual sounds of the kisses, his breathing, his heartbeat. I savored the smell of his cologne, his scent, the taste of his lips, his mouth touching mine.

Jake traced the outline of my lips with the tip of his tongue, and repeated the action once again. I let my tongue glide over his pouty, bottom lip and sucked on it ever so slightly. His tongue, his lips felt like velvet. I parted my lips and Jake deepened the kiss, taking control, sweeping deeply in and out, then flicking my lips lightly with the tip of his tongue, over and over. Each kiss, deeper than the one before, intensified those deep achy, sensual feelings.

No one ever kissed me like this. No one ever made me feel like this. His kisses intoxicated me. They made me tipsy, drunk with them. How could an act so simple feel so good in so many different places at once?

It prickled like hundreds of tiny little sparks igniting and exploding Like rounding the top of a Ferris wheel over and over, and never quite reaching the bottom. Like two bodies moving as one in a beautiful, sensual dance.

I never wanted this moment—these feelings, the kisses—to end.

He kissed me one more time so softly and tenderly, and pulled me into his arms in front of him, my back resting against his chest. His heart pounded. My heart pounded. Together they beat a single rhythm.

I didn't know what to think, what to say, what to do. I closed my eyes, leaned against his chest, and held onto his arms wrapped tightly around me.

Minutes passed in silence.

I waited for him to say something, anything. But still he said nothing and continued to hold me. We shared a lovely silence.

Finally, his words began.

"Geez. I don't know what's going on, but something is."

"I know. I felt it that first night at the rehearsal barn. I'm not sure either, and it scares me sometimes."

"Did I scare you just now? I didn't mean to."

"No, you didn't scare me. I think I scared myself. I'm usually in control of everything, everyone... and I wasn't. It scared me that I didn't care. I just wanted you to kiss me." I paused, and said, "I wanted to be with you, Jake. And I'm not sure if that's right or wrong."

My voice trembled as the words spilled out. Maybe I shouldn't have said that. Oh God, too late. The words came so easily when I didn't have to look into his face.

He pulled me closer and ran his lips over my ear. "Rose, you don't have to be in control with me, or ever feel afraid with me. I'll never do anything you don't want me to."

"Jake, I'm not what you think I am. I talk like I know so much about all of this, but I don't. I've never let anyone kiss me like that. I'm not a virgin, but I'm not... I don't... " The words, the explanation, just wouldn't come.

He rested his chin on the top of my head. "I know that, Rose. I get it. You don't need to explain anything to me. I don't know what has gone on in your life and I don't need to know right now."

He turned me in his arms and I looked into his face, his eyes.

"I'm not in any hurry. I don't want anything to happen until you're ready, okay?" he asked quietly.

I nodded. "Okay."

He kissed me again, tracing my lips so softly with the tip of his tongue, then kissed the tip of my nose. He drew back, grinned, and asked, "Can I have the rest of your donut then?"

Oh my. I was in serious trouble here. Serious trouble.

Jake was handsome, smart, sexy as hell, and had a sense of humor that totally disarmed me. I had no defenses in place to protect myself from him, and it didn't seem to matter. Shit.

"Yes, please feel free to eat the rest of my donut and drink all the chocolate milk, too. You might want to check the refrigerator. You know, see if there's anything else that looks good to you."

"Thanks. I think I will. Want me to bring you anything?"

I slugged him in the arm.

"No. But after you check out the refrigerator, you could help me take all the boxes to the dumpster before I head back to Macomb."

"I could—I will—on one condition." He smiled that wicked little smile of his.

I looked at him through squinted eyes. "I'm afraid to ask. What condition?"

"Rose, stay here tonight. Come to the dance with me instead of driving back to Macomb. You're packed and ready to move tomorrow. I'll drive back with you in the morning."

Oh, shit. If I stayed here, I wasn't so sure how the evening would end. Jake said he wasn't in a hurry, but could I trust myself? His kisses made me want to throw caution to the wind. They made me wonder how it would feel to make love with Jake.

I thought about it a lot. Some days it filled my mind completely.

Jake made me feel things I'd never felt before... desire things I'd never wanted before. I wanted to hear his voice... watch him as he talked, as he moved. I wanted my body close to his, to feel his body brushing mine. I wanted that achy feeling deep inside me to linger.

Would he be patient with me? Would he be gentle? Would I know what to do? Would he stay or leave?

I knew I would have the answers to my questions soon—if not then another night. As much as I wanted Jake, something... someone inside me was afraid. That someone told me to keep my distance. Distance meant safety.

And so I fenced.

"Oh, Jake, I'd love to, but I can't. I told Ren I'd help her finish packing. And besides, I don't have any clothes other than what I've got on, and they're pretty grubby for The Library."

Jake studied me slowly, and countered.

"We can solve this, Rose." He finished my donut in one bite and drank the rest of the chocolate milk from the container. "First of all, we both know Ren has plenty of family to help her pack. Let's walk over and talk with Sam and Cash. I know they won't care if you crash at their place. The chaise lounge is really comfy. I've slept there a few nights myself. And as far as clothes, Sam probably has something that will fit you. You're about the same size."

As the words left his mouth, we both looked down at my chest. Sam was probably a 38D while I, on the other hand, was considerably smaller.

Our eyes met again, and we both smiled.

"Okay, Rose, so you're not quite the same size everywhere. Close enough."

Damn. He was good.

"I don't know, Jake."

Weak, very weak. Once again, he countered.

"Well, I do. Bundle up, baby! We'll deep-six the boxes, and head over to Cash and Sam's."

He took me in his arms, kissed me one more time until I was breathless, and whispered in my ear, "Trust me, Rose. Please."

Game over.

Jake, one. Rose, zip. Inner voice, quiet.

Oh my, yes. I was in serious, serious trouble.

I looked at Jake, cupped his face in my right hand, and trailed my fingertips down his cheek. His skin was so soft, warm, and it flushed the prettiest pink. I wondered if I made his cheeks flush, and wondered if mine matched his.

I brought my mouth next to his ear and whispered softly, "Alright. You win, Jake."

We kissed one more time. He pulled me close and held me in his arms. Once again I felt the hardness of his body against my hips. It seemed so natural with Jake, not like when I'd been held before. It didn't scare me. Quite the opposite, in fact. I liked having that affect on him.

Jake had a way about him. That's all I could say. He had a way about him.

A few minutes later, after discarding the boxes, we discussed the upcoming evening with Cash and Sam. Problem solved. Champaign for the dance, borrow one of Sam's outfits, and tomorrow morning Jake and I would drive to Macomb for the move.

Later, I called Ren and told her my plans. I heard the excitement in her voice when we talked. She understood everything. I knew she would.

"I'll be thinking about you while I'm here packing... alone." Then she whispered, "Have the best time ever with Jake tonight. Don't overthink it... just let it happen."

She knew me too well.

"I'll see you in the morning, Ren."

"You will. I'll be the one waiting by the curb with my bags and boxes packed."

C.L. Gillmore

Chapter Five

In my youth I was a dreamer... imagination my best friend.
My mind could safely take me places and bring me back again.
Now all those places of my youth have become sweet memories.
I hold them close within my heart and cherish each one tenderly.

Champaign, Illinois
Winter 1968-69

That evening, after dropping Emma and Tucker off at the sitter—Sam, Cash, Jake and I met up with the rest of the band. It took four cars and a small trailer to transport all of us, plus the equipment, to The Library ballroom booking, thirty minutes northwest of Champaign.

At exactly eight that evening, the crowd noise died down, and the band began the soulful, super introductory beat to "Gimme Some Lovin'" by The Spencer Davis Group. Jake hit the lights and began sound adjustments.

Longhaired, young men and women filled the dance floor... dressed in bell-bottoms, Nehru jackets, peasant shirts, tie-dyed dresses and skirts. Many sported wide-brimmed hats or headbands, and wove colorful beads and feathers through their hair. The movement of the bodies and colorful clothes, hats and hair—undulating like a giant wave on the dance floor—hypnotized me.

I wore Sam's black bell-bottoms; a black and white flowered, empire top; and black, T-strap suede shoes. My sun-streaked hair fell loose with strands of black-beaded ribbons braided through it in the back. I used a little of Sam's makeup, and a dab of Ambush perfume behind each ear lobe.

Sam wore brown bell-bottoms with an orange, yellow and tan peasant blouse, and brown leather boots. Her straight, dark brown hair was teased on the top and angled toward her face on the sides. I thought she looked like Barbara Streisand.

The lingering aroma of patchouli oil and marijuana hung like a low cloud suspended over the dance floor. I never actually saw anyone light up or smoke inside the building, but I knew everyone did. It was an unspoken presence. Any kind of acid you wanted to drop, or anything you wanted to smoke... you just had to ask.

Sam and I took a couple of hits from joints the guys rolled and smoked before unloading, so we were good to go.

At that dance, you didn't need to smoke or drop to get high, you just breathed deep, held and exhaled a few times, and you were there.

I couldn't take my eyes off Jake. And whenever I looked at him, he seemed to be looking back at me. I was so glad he asked me to stay the night in Champaign and come to the dance. I was surprised at how many girls stopped to talk and flirt with him, even with Sam and I sitting next to him. They did the same thing in front of the stage to Cash and the other band members. I wondered how Sam handled that week after week. I knew they all wanted to be in our place. They wanted to associate with the band. How well I understood that. Now, though, I saw them differently. I saw them only as friends who happened to play in a band. Spending time with them, with Jake, made me happy inside.

Maybe the music and the crowd transported me somewhere else. Or, maybe the closeness of the band members and the sense of belonging I felt when I hung with them. Maybe Jake awakened feelings deep inside me I thought I would never feel. Maybe all of that contributed to it.

Whatever it was, it felt good, it felt right, and I was very glad to be me.

Jake danced the first slow dance with Sam. He set the lights, and led her to the dance floor. He placed his right hand in the middle of her back and held her hand. They moved effortlessly around the dance floor, talking and laughing as they danced. As the song ended, Jake twirled and dipped Sam in front of the stage.

Cash and Sam started out as high school sweethearts, and were still very much in love. It was visible, tangible. That's how she handled the pretty girls week after week. Cash found *his* pretty girl years back, and no one would ever take her place.

The next slow song the band played was "Baby I Need Your Lovin'" by Johnny Rivers. Jake set the sound and the lights, and led me out onto the dance floor for the first time.

I was a terrible slow dancer, I never felt comfortable. There had been no one to teach me. I didn't know how to follow. I felt awkward and invariably stepped on my partner's foot, or missed a beat and tripped. Slow dancing was stressful—and it was too close, too intimate for me.

That was before Jake.

We stopped in the middle of the dance floor. Jake put his arm around me and held my hand in his.

"What's wrong? You're shaking, Rose."

"Jake, I can't slow dance—can't follow anyone. I'll step all over your feet and—"

I didn't get a chance to finish my sentence. Jake pulled me closer, gazed into my eyes, and whispered in that low, steady voice, "Shh. Hush now. Take a breath and relax. I'm a strong lead. Close your eyes and move with me. Just move with me, Rose."

I listened to his voice and did exactly what he said—took a deep breath, closed my eyes, and moved with him.

Magic. The only word that described what happened when Jake held me in his arms and we danced. Simply... magic.

All my fear, all my apprehension, faded away.

I heard the music. I felt Jake's arms around me. I clasped both hands over his shoulders and around his neck and rested my head against the side of his face. I felt him spread the fingers of each hand across my hips and pull me closer against him as we moved. Our bodies fit perfectly. I felt the slightest nuance of movement as we danced, and it was easy for me to follow him.

Jake led—I followed.

Slow dancing with Jake... very different than anything I'd experienced before. I felt safe in his arms. He whispered softly in my ear and no matter what the words, when he spoke them—they became sensual, erotic. In between the words, he lightly brushed his lips over my cheek and ear, and I felt his breath against my skin. I felt his chest move against my breasts as he breathed in and out. Something ached deep inside me.

Jake took my breath away. He made me tremble. Made me long for him. And when I looked into his eyes, I saw that same longing for me. No one ever made me feel like this, and I wondered if anyone made him feel this way. I hoped not. I wanted to be the only one. I wanted him to always remember how he felt with me.

Jake Richardson was the most sensual young man. Something about him... I felt it from the moment we met—his manner, his touch, his sureness, the way he looked into my face. He knew what to do with a woman's body when he danced with her—with me. It was lovely, more than lovely.

I never wanted the song to end. I never wanted the dance to end. I wanted to stay in Jake Richardson's arms forever.

* * * * *

After loading out, we caravanned back to Parkridge.

The miles clicked away outside through the cold and darkness, while the green dash lights glowed, and the radio softly played "Daydream Believer" by the Monkees. Inside the little Volkswagen Bug, we stayed warm and cozy.

I was the daydream believer and, more and more, I thought of Jake as my white knight... my Prince Charming.

He talked about his family as he drove. I listened.

He told me his mother taught slow dance basics to him and his brothers, but his dad actually showed them how to hold and dance with a woman. I thought about what he said. What would it feel like if your parents taught you and your brothers to dance? I found it hard to even visualize that scene... hard to imagine. I had no idea. None.

I looked over at Jake. We sat so close to one another and yet were so far apart in so many ways. Jake had no idea, either. No idea where I came from, or what I brought with me. I was truly a stranger in a strange land, and wondered if transformation was possible.

After unloading at Parkridge, we all met at Cash and Sam's, pooled our money, and ordered pizza. Everyone brought drinks. Everyone brought marijuana.

I learned a lot about marijuana that night. For one thing, if you smoked it, you didn't call it marijuana. You referred to it as weed, grass, dope, reefer, or pot. Marijuana cigarettes were rolled in Zig-Zag papers, lit with Bic lighters, and were called joints, numbers, doobies or Js. Knowing how to roll a nice, tight, uniform joint was considered a good skill to have.

This was my first experience smoking grass and everyone, especially Jake, eagerly taught me the basics of inhaling, holding, exhaling, and passing to the next person. By the end of the night the words *puff, puff, pass* rang in my ears. I learned the technique of inhaling the smoke, holding it, then rolling the joint off my index finger and thumb as I passed it to someone else. When the joint got too small to pass, they placed the remaining part in a roach clip and passed it along.

Good to know. Up until then, the only thing I knew about roaches was to spray or stomp them.

I decided I preferred being stoned or high on grass, rather than tipsy or drunk on alcohol. The words that came to mind to describe my state of being? Happy and mellow. Yes, I much preferred happy and mellow over dizzy and sick.

Over the next couple of hours we drank, smoked, laughed, sang and talked. I couldn't remember ever having such fun, or feeling so relaxed and comfortable. They caught me up in this magical, mesmerizing, and wonderful experience... all of it: the band, the music, the drugs, the times.

And I was caught up in Jake. Oh, how I was caught up in Jake.

I would always remember—the voices, the laughter, the feelings, the closeness—and these friends. Always, as a part of me now. Still, I tucked this memory away... just in case.

In case I woke up one morning and it was all gone.

Getting together after rehearsals and bookings had become a familiar routine, one I looked forward to. I liked routine. I liked being in the same place with the same people. Routine familiarity... a good thing.

I especially liked the routine starting between Jake and me.

We sat together on the mauve, velour, chaise lounge in Sam and Cash's living room, legs outstretched, his resting over mine. I leaned back against his chest and he wrapped his arms around mine. "With A Little Help From My Friends" from the *Sgt. Pepper's Lonely Hearts Club Band* album played on the turntable.

With a little help from our friends, Jake and I were full of pizza, stoned, and neither of us could stop smiling. Everything Jake said or did to me was amplified. This must be another reason people liked to get high, I thought.

He brushed his lips softly back and forth against the side of my cheek and whispered in my ear, "Want to stay here on the chaise lounge or borrow a couple of sleeping bags and try out the new fireplace?"

I turned my head toward his lips, his voice, and closed my eyes. I pictured the two of us cuddled up in sleeping bags in front of the glowing fireplace, wrapped in one another's arms.

Cuddled up in sleeping bags? Where did that come from? Did I care? No. I didn't.

"I don't have firewood, Jake... but I have a bag of marshmallows."

Jake continued to brush the side of my face with his lips. "Firewood is no problem. I'm a thief."

He placed a soft kiss on my earlobe and tugged on it just a bit with his lips. "And I love marshmallows, especially hot, sticky toasted ones."

Another kiss on my cheek.

"So, is that a 'yes,' Rose?"

Oh, my. Dear Jesus, help me.

"Yes, Jake. That's a yes."

He kissed the tip of my nose. "Okay then, Rose. We have a plan."

83

He kissed my lips, my cheek, and continued on toward my ear again as we finished the conversation.

"Rose?"

"What."

"I love when a plan comes together."

"Me, too. You have to have a plan."

He helped me bundle up and we drove to his apartment first. We grabbed a couple of sleeping bags from the closet, took the two pillows from his bed, and drove to my apartment.

Since the Volkswagen heater depended upon the engine to generate warmth, my teeth chattered as we drove the short distance from his Building 24 to my Building 12. Despite the cold, the smiles remained plastered on our faces. I couldn't decide if it was the result of the pot, or simply our happiness because we were about to share marshmallows and sleeping bags. I chalked it up to a probable combination.

I studied Jake... sweet, sweet Jake.

Did he know this was the nicest place I ever lived?

Did he know how much living here at Parkridge and being close to him and the others meant to me?

Did he know how much his friendship meant? How much I enjoyed listening to him talk about his family?

Did he know how much I appreciated his kindness, his gentleness, his sense of humor?

Did he know how much it meant to me that he was willing to take a chance on me—to get to know me better—to maybe even fall in love with me?

I wanted to share all these ideas with him. Maybe later.

But, maybe he already knew. He knew a lot of things about me already, and I wondered how that was possible.

It was becoming easier for me to talk to Jake. He listened and his comments made me laugh, made me think, and made me care more and more about him.

We talked a little about our childhoods and how differently we grew up. I didn't go into much detail, but he knew I moved around a lot. Jake grew up on a farm near the small town of Rockton with his dad and mom, sister, and two brothers. He lived in the same farmhouse and went to the same school his entire life.

Rockton, Illinois sounded like a made-up TV town, a Mayberry RFD, where Andy Taylor, Aunt Bee, Opie and Barney Fife lived alongside other families in lovely homes instead of apartments—a pretend place.

Now I began to think such a place might exist after all, and Jake lived there. Maybe I could live there someday... with him.

Yet, listening to him over the past few weeks, I realized he wanted something else. His goals didn't include farming. He didn't care to live in Rockton—in Mayberry, RFD. He wanted something entirely different.

Jake loved everything associated with film and theatre, and was working toward a degree in English and cinematography. He loved to both act and direct, and excelled at both. His creative gifts extended to photography, too. He captured the most beautiful, thought-provoking pictures with his Nikon. I noticed several of his pictures hanging on the walls in his apartment—photos of friends, of strangers, interesting buildings, the band... slice of life images.

Jake had plans. He wanted to finish his degree and move somewhere in the west, maybe New Mexico, Arizona, or California, to pursue acting, directing, or maybe photography. I could see excitement about his future when I looked into his eyes. I saw the dreamer, too. Just like me.

Would he find a place for me in his plans, his dreams?

All of us—Cash, Sam, Jerry, Max, Chuck, Zach, Ren, Jake and I— held hopes, dreams, and plans for the future. All in our twenties, with our lives yet ahead of us, anything was possible. Anything.

Later, Jake unlocked my apartment, flipped the light switch on, and tossed the sleeping bags and the pillows over near the fireplace.

"Be back. I'm off to steal firewood."

"Okay then. I'm off to find a bag of marshmallows."

Teamwork.

I slipped off my shoes and headed for the kitchen.

A few minutes later, I heard a bump against the door and looked out the window. There stood Jake cradling several logs in his arms and clutching a rolled newspaper in his left hand. I opened the door for him.

"Geez... you *are* a thief!"

"I am, and you forgot to ask who was at the door before you opened it again, Rose."

"Oh, you are so wrong. I looked out the window first and saw it was the ax murderer from this morning."

"Okay... good to know."

"Where did you find the firewood and newspapers?"

"From your new neighbors next door, of course. They had more than enough wood. They'll never miss it. I took it from the bottom of the pile and fluffed it back up. I found newspapers stacked up nicely in a box next to the firewood. I figured it was a no brainer. One-stop stealing."

"Yes, a no brainer." I paused. "Exactly how does one fluff up firewood?"

He grinned, toed his shoes off next to mine, and walked past me. "Just go with it It's a trade secret among thieves. If I told you, I'd have to kill you."

"Of course you would. I'd expect nothing less from an ax murderer."

I looked over at Jake's shoes next to mine. I liked seeing them next to one another. "By the way, I hope you have matches, because I don't."

He set the firewood and papers down on the tiled hearth and pulled something from his pocket. "No, but I have a BIC!"

He proudly displayed the small lighter between the thumb and index finger of his left hand... and flicked. Instant flame.

"Of course you do."

I suspected we could toss one-liners back and forth all night.

Jake proceeded to arrange the firewood and papers inside the fireplace, while I went upstairs to change clothes. I was glad I brought a few personal items with me this morning, so I could change clothes and freshen up a bit.

I washed my hands and face, and brushed my teeth. I walked into my empty, dark bedroom—lit only by the hallway light—and dug through a couple of boxes until I found my black sweatpants and Jake's U of I sweatshirt, which I'd borrowed a week or so ago. I slipped comfortably into both, and rummaged through another box for my perfume.

Down near the bottom of the box I found my mother's *Tabu* perfume. I picked up the rectangular glass bottle and daintily traced the letters *Tabu* with my fingers. I remembered the pitch words from a magazine: *When you get this far into Tabu, there's no turning back.*

Appropriate words for my mother, I thought.

I removed the sleek, black lid and breathed in. I could just see her there in the room with me. I was a little girl again, watching her put on a beautiful evening dress and dab perfume behind each earlobe before she left for the evening, for the weekend. Before she left me.

Once again, I felt like that little insecure girl of the past, doubting my self-worth, second-guessing my decisions, afraid to connect, to trust or to love anything or anyone for fear of being left behind.

Carefully, I put the lid on the perfume bottle and placed it back into the box.

Now I wasn't so sure about going downstairs to Jake. I wasn't sure if spending the night with him was the right thing to do. I wasn't even sure being friends with him was such a great idea now.

I walked over to the window and stared out into the darkness. I saw a reflection looking back from the windowpane at me—the reflection of a little, blonde, green-eyed girl with dimples. She looked so serious.

She whispered, "Stay upstairs where it's safe, Rose. You can tell him you're tired and he will understand. He will leave, and you and I will be alone. It's safer when there's just the two of us. You and me, Rose."

I didn't want this conversation. The child's soft voice was persuasive. She had waged and won many debates between us over the years. I didn't want her to win this one.

I listened—waited— then found my voice and countered.

"I don't want to be alone with only you for comfort, for companionship, for love. I want to be with Jake. He's a good person, a good man. I can trust him. He won't hurt me. I know he won't."

She countered.

"You don't know him. He's a man, and they are all alike. You know that. He will use you and betray your trust. He will hurt you. He will leave you for someone else. It's better if you leave him first."

"No. You're wrong about him. You heard him say he didn't want me to be alone anymore. Jake loves me. I can see it in his eyes even though he hasn't said it yet. He loves me."

"He's lying to you. He's using you, Rose. Listen to me. I'm the only one who can protect you. I'm the only one who really cares about you, loves you. I'm the only one who never left you. I've always been here for you."

"No. I can't listen to you. I won't listen to you. Please go away. Please stop talking to me. I'm not listening anymore."

I stood in front of the window. Waiting. But I heard only silence. Blessed silence. The other voice fell quiet now. I was alone.

I turned and walked back to the box. This time I reached for a different bottle... *Ambush.* I shook the bottle a couple of times and removed the glass stopper. I dabbed a little perfume behind my ear lobes, and in the crease of each arm, replaced the stopper, and returned the bottle to the box. I left the darkness of the bedroom, walked toward the light of the hallway, and stood at the top of the stairs. I took a deep breath—then another—and walked down the steps to Jake.

It certainly didn't feel like an ambush.

The apartment was dark except for the golden red glow from the fireplace. The logs popped and cracked and sizzled, filling the room with the scent of burning wood. The flickering flames sent graceful shadow-dancers up the stairway wall and across the ceiling. The apartment felt warm and full of promise, despite the lack of furniture.

Softly in the background the sounds of radio drifted to me. Jake had tuned in KAAY, Little Rock, The Mighty 1090. The familiar voice of Clyde Clifford and Beaker Street introduced "Will You Love Me Tomorrow?" by Carole King.

Jake sat cross-legged on the sleeping bags he'd zipped together. The pillows lay side by side to his right. He'd taken off his sweater, and was down to his black T-shirt, bell-bottoms and socks. His left hand held a straightened metal coat hanger with two flaming marshmallows dangling precariously at the end, ready to fall into the fire.

"I hope you like your marshmallows well done. It's the only way I know to cook them."

"They look a little more than well done. I think they're burned, Jake."

"Oh, I can assure you they are."

He scooted to the left and patted the area next to him with his right hand while attempting to blow out the flames on the skewered marshmallows.

"Come, sit and enjoy a sticky, burned marshmallow with me."

I sat down next to him on the sleeping bag palette. It was very comfy. Very cozy. He slid one of the gooey marshmallows off and brought it to my mouth.

"Open wide."

I did, and he popped it in.

I closed my eyes and slowly savored, chewed, and swallowed the sweet morsel. I couldn't remember toasted marshmallows ever tasting that good or being that chewy or gooey.

"Oh my. Toasted marshmallows were never like this."

"No... it's the grass. Everything tastes better, feels better... usually lasts longer, too."

Were we still talking about marshmallows?

Jake continued. "And why is it when someone else opens their mouth for a bite of something, you feel compelled to automatically open yours, too?"

Maybe we were still talking about marshmallows.

"I don't know. Why is that?"

I reached toward the second marshmallow, slid it off, and held it out.

"Here you go. Open wide."

He opened his mouth and I dropped it in.

"See, your mouth opened, too," he said, pointing, and talking through a mouthful of sticky marshmallow.

I hadn't realized my mouth automatically opened with his.

"You know, it's not polite to point or chew with your mouth full."

Jake caught my hand in his and, one by one, gently and carefully sucked and licked the sticky marshmallow remnants from my fingers.

Did he know how sensual, how erotic that simple action was? Did he?

Oh, he most assuredly did.

When he finished, he held his fingers up for me and said with eyebrows raised "Mine are sticky, too."

"I see that."

I took Jake's hand and one by one, tentatively licked the marshmallow remnants from his fingers.

I never did anything like this before, but it seemed like the right thing to do at the moment. Everything with Jake seemed like the right thing.

"Mm-m-m. That was nice. Very nice." His words purred.

Yes, it was. I had to agree.

He leaned closer and kissed me, cradling the back of my head with his hand. First one kiss, then another. So sweet. So gentle.

He never seemed in a hurry. He took his time with me. He always took time to find the right words. Now he took time to find just the right touch.

He kissed me again... first my lips, then brushing across my cheek to my ear. He sniffed my ear, my neck. It tickled.

"Mm-m-m. You smell good."

"Marshmallows?"

He took my arm and sniffed the crease of my inner elbow.

"Nope. Smells more like... *Ambush*."

"Yes. *Ambush*."

My mind wandered.

How could he know my perfume? Did he smell a lot of women's perfumes... while they wore it? And how did he know where to sniff?

He sensed my concern.

"My sister, Michelle, wore that perfume. My brothers and I snuck into her room when she was on a date to smell her perfume. I liked *Ambush* and *Wind Song*. They liked *Chantilly* and *Emeraude*.

I pictured the three of them sneaking into her room and sniffing perfume on the sly. They probably watched her put it on, too, which would explain why he knew where to sniff. The words "ornery shits" came to mind again.

"So, does your sister hide her perfume now, like your mom does the Howdy Doody glasses?"

Jake's smile nearly disappeared. He hesitated a bit and looked away from me and into the fire.

My comment hit a wrong chord. I could feel it.

"Michelle was killed in a car accident coming home from college one weekend a few years back. A drunk driver. He was okay, the drunk driver. Not a scratch. My sister and her roommate, not so lucky. He crossed the centerline and hit them head on. They were both killed instantly."

So, bad things do happen to good people, even in places like Mayberry, RFD.

I placed my hand on top of Jake's. "I'm so sorry. That must have been hard for you... for your family."

"Yep. It's been hard on all of us. Still is. There's not a day goes by that I don't think about her. Just now your perfume reminded me, but in a good way, a sweet way. Smelling *Ambush* is a good memory."

He stopped, seemingly lost in thought, and started again.

"It was especially hard on my mom and dad. I overheard a conversation between them one night a few months after it happened. They were talking about how people expect children to lose and bury their parents, but no parent expects to lose and bury their child. That's just not the order of things. Not how things in life are supposed to happen."

"No, I guess it isn't."

He was right about the order of things. But even in Jake's world, sometimes life didn't follow the rules, the correct order. At that moment, I wanted to break the rules. I wanted to fix the order in Jake's life, but I couldn't.

91

I thought about my own life. I never had experienced order in my life, and didn't know any other way. I never thought about the parent/child thing like that before. Never thought about my sister or me dying, or my mom missing either of us. I experienced the opposite position, though I lost my parents in different ways, at different times. I was still dealing with my feelings. Sometimes I felt abandoned, or alone. Betrayed. Angry. But most of the time, I felt ambivalent. I wondered if that was wrong.

Jake wouldn't feel that way, I'm sure. But, I wasn't Jake... and his parents weren't mine... not even close.

The room fell quiet now. We sat next to one another—shoulders, arms, knees, and legs touching—and watched the fire, listened to the music.

This silence wasn't awkward—the type when you wish someone would speak. Instead, it soothed, comforted, and connected the two of us.

The silence became anticipatory... as though he waited for me. Waited for me to trust him, to share an intimate moment from my out-of-order life.

Could I do that? I looked straight ahead into the fire and began to talk.

I talked. He listened.

I talked about my childhood—my dad, my sister, my mom, the moves—about my chaotic life, about all the broken rules.

Now and then, he commented, but mostly, he listened.

I told him about my love of writing—about my poetry, my stories, my journals—and how I dreamed of being an author someday.

"You can do that. You know that, don't you? Go after that dream, Rose."

"Maybe I will someday."

"Remember all of this... write about it someday in a book. I'll look for it."

"Okay... yes... look for it."

Even my fantasy about being adopted by Roy Rogers slipped out. I figured he would laugh... but he didn't.

"Will you read to me something you've written?"

I thought about his request.

"I've never read anything to anyone except my second-grade teacher."

Silence. He waited me out.

"I wrote a poem a few years back about Roy Rogers. Wanna hear that?"

"Yep. I love a good Western."

"Figures. Must be a guy thing. I'll get my notebook from upstairs."

"I'll wait."

"If you're not here when I get back, I'll figure you changed your mind about westerns."

"I'll be here. Count on it."

Jake used levity to ease me in and out of conversations, of situations. He did it so easily.

I came back down with the notebook and found Jake poking at the fire with the coat hanger skewer.

"See? Still here. Ready for the cowboys."

He laid the skewer on the hearth, folded his legs Indian-style, and rested his hands in his lap. It reminded me of a second-grader ready for story time in the library.

"Yes, I can see that."

I thumbed through the black, three-ring notebook until I came to the poem. Jake still sat attentively and smiling. Maybe he still felt the effects of the grass... or maybe being with me made him happy.

I began to read.

Adopted by Roy Rogers

I remember as a child lying in bed at night
Covers over my head, listening to them fight.
And I always wondered when I heard my name
If I was the cause, or if I was to blame?
Had I played too loud and made them mad?
Forgotten my chores and made them sad?

I had to do something that was for sure.
I needed to be adopted by Roy Rogers!
Praying he'd hurry and find me each night,
Hiding under my covers 'til the time was right.
Then off into the sunset we would both ride
Adopted by Roy Rogers, partners side by side.

I always knew that Roy adopted kids like me.
He only wanted special ones for his family.
I'd have to like horses and ridin' the range.
Could I wear chaps or would I look strange?
Was my head too small for a ten-gallon hat?
And if I wore boots would I fall down flat?

I had to do something that was for sure.
I needed to be adopted by Roy Rogers!
Praying he'd hurry and find me each night
Hiding under my covers 'til the time was right.
Then off into the sunset we would both ride
Adopted by Roy Rogers, partners side by side.

I didn't ever give up even though he never came.
And hiding under blankets became a nightly game.
My westward imagination helped tune out all the fights.
And pretending Roy was on his way got me through those nights.

I had to do something that was for sure.
I needed to be adopted by Roy Rogers!
Praying he'd hurry and find me each night
Hiding under my covers 'til the time was right.
Then off into the sunset we would both ride
Adopted by Roy Rogers, partners side by side.

~ Rose Allison~

I finished reading, closed the notebook and looked at Jake. I'd glanced at him a couple of times while reading. Once he stared right at me, and the other time his gaze fell on the ground, apparently in thought.

He looked down now, and I waited for his response.

After a few seconds, he looked at me—just a slight smile across his face—and shook his head slowly back and forth.

My thoughts traveled back to earlier that evening—*he never seemed to be in a hurry. He took his time with me. He always took time to find the right words.*

That was exactly what he was doing now. Taking his time to find the right words I needed to hear.

"Wow. What an imagination. You *are* a writer. I pictured your words. That's a gift, Rose."

My eyes welled with tears.

"Thank you... about it being a gift. I feel that way, too... that my writing is a gift. I see a picture in my mind... and the words just come to me.

Even as a young child I wanted to write. I found out early on that writing and imagination could take me much farther away from any of the small Midwest towns where I lived. I could be someone else, go back to places I remembered, or travel to new ones. Plus, I could go alone or take with me whoever I wanted.

Every day I dreamed of new adventures in faraway places... adventures I tucked away inside my heart. When they overflowed with too many to hold inside, I took a breath, and let my words flow onto paper.

I often hear the words in my head, as if someone is talking to me and I'm talking back to them. A voice. It makes me wonder sometimes if I'm crazy."

I stopped after those words spilled from my mouth. Did I say too much?

Silence.

He gently placed his hands around my shoulders, leaned forward, and brought his lips close to my ear.

"You're not crazy, Rose. And I'm here. I'm real. You don't have to be alone anymore."

He meant those words. I could feel it. He didn't want me to be alone.

I didn't want to be alone. I wanted—no, I needed—someone real in my life.

Could a childhood fantasy actually come true? Was Jake Richardson my Prince Charming? Could he rescue me?

Maybe... just maybe, he was... he could.

He held the sleeping bag open and we climbed in next to one another. The fire flickered—the shadows danced—we lay wrapped within one another's arms. He kissed me softly, he kissed me passionately, he kissed me until my eyes wouldn't open anymore. I drifted in and out of the loveliest dreams until morning, dreams of faraway places in the West, dreams of Jake Richardson and me.

* * * * *

Journal Entry—November 1968

Today is moving day and soon Jake and I will be headed for Macomb. I can hardly wait! I never thought I would say that, but then I never thought I would meet anyone like Jake Richardson either.

I woke up next to him, and watched him sleep. He takes my breath away and my stomach is fluttery all the time. God, I wonder if this is what it feels like to be in love. I feel like I have the flu... Jakefluenza.

Oh, my. I hope there is no cure.
Rose Richardson.
R. A. Richardson.

Looks like an author's name. Sounds like an author's name.
High on Love *by Rose Richardson.*
Love Whispers Softly *by R. A. Richardson.*

Chapter Six

Again we are caught up in time... youthful, wild and free.
Together we laugh, we dare, we love... unafraid to simply be.
It might have been just circumstance... the music, or just the time.
Whatever it was, it has become a most lovely memory of mine.

Champaign, Illinois
Winter 1968-1969

Within a few weeks of moving into Parkridge, Ren and I settled into a nice routine of shared apartment living, shift work, and a budding social life.

On lazy Monday mornings—following a busy weekend—we slept later, stayed in our pajamas longer, girl talked and listened to music until we left for work at two thirty in the afternoon for our three-to-eleven shift at a local manufacturing company.

Tuesday through Friday mornings we got up around nine and cleaned, did laundry at the clubhouse, grocery shopped, and rummaged local thrift and antique stores... refurbishing and painting our finds for the apartment.

Life in Champaign for Ren and me was a shared adventure to embrace and enjoy. Two independent young women out on our own.

I especially liked sharing an apartment with Ren—having someone to talk with, to listen, to bounce ideas back and forth—and to not be alone.

A few times a week, Jake and Jerry stopped by the apartment after our shifts finished late in the day around eleven thirty. Some nights both Jake and Jerry visited. Other nights, only Jake. How they managed to fit us in between classwork, part-time jobs, and band rehearsals was a mystery, but we never questioned it. We were always glad to see them.

Most nights, Jerry brought his latest album purchase, along with his twelve-string acoustic guitar, while Jake arrived with a bag of four-for-a-dollar hamburgers and fries from Henri's. One or both of them brought joints rolled and ready. The four of us would spend the next several hours talking, listening to music, getting stoned, eating hamburgers and fries, and making out.

Perfect... simple evenings together.

On nights when only Jake showed up, he and I often drove around the residential areas of Champaign looking at houses... houses where families lived.

I collected favorite pictures of houses, rooms, and furniture I liked from *Better Homes and Garden* magazines. I taped them inside my notebooks and journals. All of this became part of the dream, the fantasy life I carried with me in my notebooks.

Jake picked up on this, and enjoyed playing out the fantasy with me.

When Jake described his family home, it sounded like one I'd dreamed of, with a living room, dining room, kitchen, den, sunroom and bathroom downstairs, plus five bedrooms and two bathrooms upstairs. His home sounded like a mansion.

I found myself lost in daydreams, and I fantasized walking around inside Jake's big farmhouse: watching television in his living room, warming myself in the sunroom, cooking breakfast in the kitchen, climbing the steps and walking down the hall to his bedroom... taking a bubble bath in the tub.

I wondered if I would ever have the opportunity to drive the streets of Rockton, to see Jake's farm or meet his family. Could any of this be reality, or was it only a young girl's daydreams and fantasies? Time would tell and, until then, I tucked them away—snugged them away in my head and in my heart—with the others.

On Saturday nights, I went with Jake and the band to bookings. Once in awhile, Ren and I would both call in sick on Friday nights and go together. This didn't happen very often, though, because of Jack.

Ren's family looked after him during the week while she worked. Ren returned to Macomb and cared for him over the weekend. That was the arrangement until we got our first raise and found close suitable care for Jack.

Ren's fantasy included the band. Her reality involved Jack.

In my fantasy world, anything was possible. My reality had always involved something else. In the past, my life always teetered like a carefully balanced tight-wire act. I tried to maintain balance perfectly on the wire. But the wire swayed, people shook it and bounced on it, and every so often I lost my footing and fell. Falling... failing was my reality. After awhile I put a safety net in place... a safety net of fantasy. I placed that safe net of fantasy to catch me until I could climb back onto the wire again, until I could continue on with my balancing act.

In the past year or so, my reality changed and the balancing act—though still firm in my memory—temporarily suspended. I wanted to believe anything was possible, but then, that's what dreamers do.

Jake dreamed and fantasized, too. But he knew what was real... how to make things real. I began to think Jake could make almost anything happen.

Neither of us mentioned *love*. No words. But we shared an unspoken thing between us. Love was there. It grew stronger every day. In only a matter of time, one of us would express the feeling.

I didn't know if I could say those words out loud... to Jake or to anyone.

I hardly remember the last time someone said, "I love you" to me. I couldn't remember my mom ever saying it to me, or me to her. Yet, I heard Ren's mom say it to her almost every time she left the house.

"I love you, Ren. Drive careful."

"Love you too, Mom. I will."

Such a simple exchange between two people, between a mother and daughter. How easily they spoke the words. How could something so commonplace seem so foreign? How does this happen?

When I lost my mother, I lost my home—the furniture, dishes, pictures and all the other familiar, personal items that belong in a house—including my mother's clothes, shoes, jewelry, and most of her perfume. Everything was sold, given away, or put into storage.

I had no choice.

When I lost my mother and my home... I lost my dog Dottie, too. In foster homes—no matter how nice the people—I couldn't take a dog. I had to give her up.

Again, I had no choice.

I found a home for her with a friend from high school. I knew she would take good care of Dottie and love her, but it was hard to leave her behind, to let her go. All that day I held her against my chest, hugging her, crying, and trying to explain the situation. I poured my heart and soul out to Dottie hoping it would help her or me, or both. Later that day my friend came to take her. I held her close one more time.

"I love you. I hope you understand, Dottie. I love you, but I have to let you go."

With Dottie gone, I was alone. We both went to a new home, a new life.

I felt as though I lost my identity—whatever it was that made me, *me*. That part of me was sold, given away or stored somewhere—a piece here, a piece there. The apartment we shared sat empty until rented within two weeks after her death. Everything familiar, everything that grounded me, was gone. I felt scattered, splintered... with no control over my life. Would I ever be able to gather up the pieces?

As dysfunctional as my life was through the years, my mother still provided a physical presence. Good or bad, she was there. She was my mother.

Most of my childhood, I lived in fear of losing her, being separated from her. No child should have this stress, this worry. I constantly played out worst-case scenarios in my mind. She would choose a boyfriend or stepdad over me and walk out. She might injure or kill a boyfriend or stepdad during an argument and be locked up in prison. She would die of a disease or be killed in a car accident. Later on, as I grew older, I worried she might commit suicide. Each of these scenarios left me alone.

Suddenly, circumstances forced me to live my worst childhood fear. My mother took her life... left me behind... alone.

Telling Dottie I loved her was the last time I remembered saying those words... *I love you.* That happened more than two years ago.

Saying it to a dog who loved me back unconditionally—where there was no risk—was a lot different than saying it to a person, to Jake. I'd learned loving came with conditions, consequences, and risks

People leave, they die, they don't always love you back, and they expect things, and set conditions, in return for that love. I found it easier not to love, not to become attached or emotionally involved. Unfortunately, keeping myself isolated also had its drawbacks. When you don't love or become attached or show emotional involvement, you disassociate yourself from everything and everyone. Eventually nothing is reciprocated, and you find yourself alone. There is no one to say "I love you" to, and there is no one to say it back to you.

I thought about my mother. Did no one say those words to her either? Her mother? Her father? Was that why she couldn't say them to me? How long and how far did this inability to express affection go back? I could only speculate.

I didn't want to follow or even stand in that generational line. I wanted to start a new line, to follow a different path.

Right now I wondered if I could love Jake. I really didn't know if I was capable of loving anyone. I wanted to love him—with all my heart I wanted to love him. But a constant battle waged within me, between me and a voice. Who was this voice? Was it a voice from the past? The past was over... Or was it? Was I capable of winning this battle? I didn't even clearly understand my opponent.

I felt distant even with people around me... a kind of detachment I couldn't explain or understand. People remained distant... the voice inside me stayed close.

I needed to talk with someone. Someone who could help me make sense of it all, help me understand. Someone I trusted.

Jake. Maybe I would talk to Jake about it. Maybe he could help me work through this... help me understand.

I prayed God would help me... that He would help Jake help me.

* * * * *

December 1968

Christmas Eve. The first major winter storm began the day before with falling temperatures and freezing rain. During the night, a glistening white blanket of snow quietly covered Champaign and most of Illinois, Iowa, Wisconsin and Indiana. The snow did look beautiful, but didn't bode well if your plans included driving.

Luckily, everyone but Jake left early the previous morning before the storm set in. Jake unfortunately had an eleven-thirty class exam given by an I-make-no-exceptions-for-weather professor.

Ren went home to Jack and her family in Macomb. Cash, Sam, Emma, and Tucker packed up the station wagon and left for Christmas in Chicago with Sam's mom and dad. Jerry, Max, Chuck, and Zach drove home to their families, scattered in Iowa, Illinois, and Wisconsin.

Jake now gained a legitimate excuse to spend Christmas with me instead of going home to his family... the weather. We were snowed in together. Merry Christmas!

I sat on the countertop with Jake leaning back between my legs. We shared a cup of coffee as he dialed his family in Rockton. He held the receiver out from his ear so I could listen.

"Hello. This is Eddie."

"Hey, Dad... it's Jake."

"Good to hear from you, son. I'm holding the phone out so your mother and brothers can hear the conversation, too. How's the weather there? Not worth a toot here."

I tried to picture faces as I listened to the voices.

"Awful, Dad. The roads aren't plowed, and the ice underneath is slicker than fresh cow shit! Plus, the Triumph wouldn't start this morning again, and I borrowed a friend's VW so I wouldn't miss any classes or exams."

Jake glanced back at me and raised his eyebrows when he mentioned a friend's VW.

"Well, that was certainly nice of your friend to loan you his car."

"I'm afraid I'm not going to make it home for Christmas, but I'll be home in February and might bring that friend with me. *Her* name is Rose." Jake rubbed the side of my knee with his hand.

I heard his brothers, Keith and Pete, in the background, "Hey, Jake... are you bringing home a hippie chick?"

"At least I'm bringing *someone* home." Jake looked at me, shook his head, and mouthed the word "brothers" as he rolled his eyes.

"You bring home whoever you want, Jake. Your friends are welcome here anytime."

"I know, Mom. Thanks. I'll let you know." Jake covered the receiver and whispered to me, "My mom, Anna."

"Well, it won't be the same without you here, but Dad and I understand. We don't want you to take chances on the roads." She paused a moment, then asked, "How's the money situation, honey?"

"I'm good, Mom."

"Just the same, we'll get a card in the mail with a twenty in it. Be looking for it."

"Okay. I will... and thanks,"

After one more discussion about the weather with his dad, and a preview of the missed Christmas dinner menu from his mom, they finished the conversation with a group good-bye.

"Good-bye and Merry Christmas! We love you, Jake."

"I love you, too. See you in February."

He hung up the phone and took a cigarette from the pack in his pocket. He lit it with the BIC lighter, also in his pocket, and took a couple of long drags.

I hadn't seen him smoke in a long time. Well, not cigarettes anyway. He was trying to quit.

"First time away from my family at Christmas since I had my tonsils out. Think I was six or seven. They waited for presents and dinner until Dad brought me home the next day."

"Nice of them to wait."

"Yep."

"I'm sorry you couldn't go home. Shitty Illinois weather."

"It's okay. I'm kind of glad it snowed. Nice to be together in shitty weather."

"It is. Wonder if McDonald's is open tomorrow? I have no groceries. Didn't shop much this week."

"No problem. I think we might have two Swanson TV dinners in the freezer at my apartment... turkey, dressing, and mashed potatoes."

"Perfect! And we have leftover donuts for dessert."

"No, we don't. I ate them while you were in the shower."

"You are such a little pig!"

"Thank you."

"Welcome."

He missed being home for Christmas, no matter what he said or how he joked. I saw it on his face when he talked to his family. He missed them, and they missed him... and I could not relate. There wasn't a soul I missed. Jake would be the only one.

He took one more drag on the cigarette, ran water over it in the sink, and let it drop into the garbage disposal.

"I wanted you to come home for Christmas with me... meet my family... see where I live. I just never got around to asking you. What about February? Wanna go with me then?"

I thought about it. Thought about the family I just listened to... Eddie and Anna, Keith and Pete. I wanted to meet them. Yes, I did want to go even though it was way outside my comfort zone.

"You want me to meet your family? Are you sure about this?"

He turned to face me and kissed me firmly on my lips. "I'm sure."

"Okay then, road trip in February. Hope the weather's better."

"I've driven in snow before. I'll get us there."

I slid off the countertop into his arms. He kissed me again—longer, harder—flicking my bottom lip with his tongue.

"Want to go upstairs and look at the Christmas tree with me?"

I rolled his question over in my mind, along with all the implications that went with it. Did I want to go upstairs in my dark bedroom and look at the Christmas tree with Jake? Just the thought of what might follow made me breathe harder.

"Yes. I'd like to see how the room looks with the tree lit."

He took my hand and switched the kitchen light off and walked out into the living room. He flipped over the Dave Brubeck album on the turntable, and added the Beatles' *Sgt. Pepper's Lonely Hearts Club Band.*

We walked upstairs. Jake led. I followed.

The small Christmas tree nestled in the corner on my nightstand lighted the room. Jake surprised me with the little evergreen this morning, along with donuts and chocolate milk. He'd gotten both on his way home from classes yesterday, despite the weather, and trudged through the snow and ice this morning from his apartment to mine.

After some searching, we found strings of lights, a box of glass ornaments, and a package of tinsel tucked inside a small box in the hallway closet... leftovers from my tree in Macomb last year.

Together we decorated the tree, shared donuts and hot chocolate milk, and listened to Jake's *Time Out* album by Dave Brubeck. When we finished, we carefully carried the tree upstairs and placed it on the nightstand next to my bed.

The little tree looked more beautiful than ever. The multi-colored lights cast shadowed pine branch patterns across the ceiling and down the walls. They blinked rhythmically on and off to the faint jazz sounds of Dave Brubeck, side two, drifting up the stairs.

Besides the music, I heard only our breathing in the room. I felt the strong, steady beat of his heart against me. The chilly room smelled of pine, and shimmered in the darkness. The room felt *magical*... like a setting in a fairytale. But this was *real*.

We stood facing one another beside the bed, with only a breath separating us. I watched Jake and wondered if my cheeks glowed rosy pink like his—if my eyes radiated anticipation and desire like his? If his heart beat as fast and hard as mine? Was he nervous, too?

I felt his hands glide over my arms, up and down, finally coming to rest on my shoulders. He leaned in and brushed his lips softly over mine... once, twice... and kissed me. His mouth, firm... his lips soft, determined.

My questions, my concerns, drifted away on the waves of pleasure from those kisses.

"You're trembling, baby. Are you cold?"

Baby... he called me *baby*. Oh, my God. No one ever called me anything but Rose, not even my mother.

I replied so softly I could barely hear my own voice. "No... I'm not cold. I'm not sure why I'm trembling. I think it's you... you make me tremble."

"Mm-m-m... good to know."

"It is?"

"Yep. Very good to know."

He cradled me against his warm, firm chest. I snuggled closer toward the heat of his body and rested my head on his soft burgundy flannel shirt. The scent of him—his skin, his hair, his clothes—was wonderfully familiar to me now. He smelled of soap, shampoo, spicy aftershave, and that unique Jake scent. Collectively, their potency awakened sensual places deep inside me.

He felt solid and strong, and I felt safe and secure within his arms.

His deep, soft voice whispered against my cheek, my ear. "I want to make love to you."

His breath, his words—against my skin—made me shudder. I could barely breathe, and I think my heart actually skipped a beat. My legs felt as wobbly as Jell-O, and I held on tightly to that lovely, flannel shirt.

All of this was too much... and yet not enough... not nearly enough.

"I want that, too. Very much."

The next several minutes we spent leisurely undressing one another... something else I'd never experienced. Not like this.

We slowly unbuttoned... my blouse, his shirt... then slowly slipped them over shoulders and arms. We unzipped bell-bottoms—mine, then his—and eased them down hips, legs, and over feet.

Only his black briefs and my pink, flowered panties and bra remained.

"So pretty."

"I bought them last week, I wanted... " I stopped. Did I dare tell him my fantasies of him?

"Did you buy them for me... to wear for me?"

I let my thoughts, my fantasies, become my words to him.

"Yes, I thought about you... about you seeing me in them... what you would think. I wanted to look pretty for you... special.

"You look beautiful." He brushed another kiss along the side of my cheek. "I knew you were special the first night I saw you at rehearsal... the first time I heard your voice."

My mind floated back to that first night. I remembered my inability to breathe... that spark of electricity between us... that feeling of knowing him before.

Dear Jesus, did all men use words the way he did? Lovely words I knew would stay in my heart... replay in my mind... forever?

I wanted to tell him how handsome and sensual he looked in those black briefs. How soft the fabric felt against my fingertips... how solid his hips felt beneath my hands... how hard his body felt through the thin, knit fabric. Did he wear them especially for me?

I wanted to say all of these things, but I didn't. I didn't say anything. I didn't want him to think I was looking there, thinking about that, even though I was. Oh, my. It was difficult not to look there not to think about it. He was beautiful. He felt so good against me.

He skimmed his hands down my arms and cupped my hips, drawing them tightly against his. I followed his motions, running my hands down his arms and cupping his hips to mine. He bent his knees slightly and pushed into me—finding that most sensitive place on my body—the place only I knew.

I discovered I was wrong, Jake knew about it, too.

Every kiss, caress, and whispered word sent the most exquisite pain to that secret place deep within me.

Whatever he said, whatever he did... I wanted him to say it again, to do it again.

Murmured love words... like raindrops sliding down a windowpane... saturated every sense of my being. The actual words mattered little compared to how he said them... the tone, the rhythm, the intensity. Love words... soothing, tender, coaxing. Love words... sensual, suggestive, erotic.

I never wanted him to stop. I never wanted the night to end.

He brought his left hand up my back and unfastened my bra. I felt the release and held my breath as he slipped it over my shoulders and let it fall to the floor. His chest grazed my breasts... my nipples suddenly grew achy and taut.

He massaged the small of my back in a circular motion, applying firm pressure with the palm of his hand. His other hand slipped between my legs. Gently he drew his fingers back and forth over that little bundle of nerves. I thought my knees would buckle at any moment.

Everything he did and said, felt so good. I could no longer contain my feelings, and a soft moan escaped from deep inside. He covered the moan with a firm, warm kiss, sweeping his tongue deep inside my mouth. He tasted of coffee and donuts.

He hooked his thumbs in the waistband of my panties and eased them down... trailing kisses over my neck, breasts and tummy... as he pushed them lower and lower until finally I slipped out of them.

Softly he whispered, "Touch me. Don't be afraid. Whatever you are thinking, fantasizing... I'm thinking that, too."

I took a deep breath—replayed those last four words in my head, *I'm thinking that, too*—and moved my hands over his hips, massaged them with my fingertips. They felt different from mine, soft but muscular. I remember looking at his butt that first night in the rehearsal barn and thinking how perfect it was. Later, alone, I fantasized how it would feel if I could touch it, run my hands over it. Now I knew it felt strong and warm, and its lines curved nicely into my hands.

My right hand moved along his ribs and onto his stomach, coming to rest on his erection. I let my fingertips trail over the black, knit fabric and feel the hardness, the heat, beneath. He was long and thick.

I touched him and heard the same moan of pleasure that escaped my lips earlier. The touch of my hand on his body, the touch of his on mine, brought such indescribable pleasure. How could something so simple as touching one another evoke such pure joy?

Until then, I never realized the importance of human contact one to another—loving, mutual human touch. I could barely remember a loving touch from anyone. How could that be? How could that happen?

Jake let me look, let me explore, let me touch him... without making me feel embarrassed or self-conscious. He did the same with me... looked, explored, and touched. I had never done this before. I found myself saying things to him I never thought I would say... doing things with him I never thought I would do.

"I want to make you feel good... like you make me feel. Show me.. help me."

"I will, baby. I will."

Using his tongue, he pressed little sucking kisses along my neck, my cheek, my lips, then placed his hands over mine and moved them to the waistband of his briefs, one on each side.

I moaned into his mouth and he plunged his tongue deeper, filling me with his heat. I wanted him. I wanted his hands on me, touching me, every part of me.

"Oh, Jake... " The only two words that floated into my brain and out my mouth.

"Shh... easy. I'll help you." The soothing whisper tickled against my temple.

Again, his voice sent shivers down my spine. My hands trembled under his as I hooked my fingers into the waistband. Slowly, with his hands guiding mine, I slid the black briefs over his erection and down his thighs. He stepped out of them, and they joined my flowered panties and bra.

Every article of clothing he and I wore—jeans, shirts, bra and panties, briefs and socks—now lay scattered on the carpeting between the bed and the dresser.

We stood facing one another, holding hands like little children. I watched Jake's eyes travel slowly up and down my body. I found myself doing the same. I couldn't stop looking. His body was beautiful... muscular, lean, and tan.

"You're so beautiful, so soft, Rose. You take my breath away."

I said what was in my head, my heart, as I looked at Jake standing in front of me.

"You're beautiful to me, too. I never thought of a man's body as beautiful."

Jake cupped my breasts in his hands. I dug my fingers into his shoulders and held on. Just when I thought my legs would no longer support me, he wedged his knee between my legs. I eased down onto it for relief... but found myself filled with even more urgency. I needed a release from this.

Jake thumbed my nipples into hard little distended darts, then leaned forward drawing first one and then the other into his mouth, sucking and swirling the tips with his tongue. I thought nothing could feel better than the touch of his hands on me, but I was wrong. Oh, God... I was so wrong.

Sheer delight zinged through me and I whimpered against his cheek. I clutched at his shoulders and trailed my hands up his neck and into his hair, tightening my fists in it.

He brought his mouth to my lips, wedged his knee deeper between my legs, and drew me closer to him. I felt the hardness of his body tuck within the soft folds of mine. I closed my eyes and followed his lead, much like when we danced together for the first time.

He cradled me in his arms and laid me gently down onto the bed, pulling back the comforter and sheet. He settled next to me on his right side, his left leg angled and resting over me, my tummy, my hips, my legs.

He smoothed his hand over my stomach and down my legs, stroking the inside of one thigh and then the other, moving back and forth over my pubic bone. After several passes, he pressed his hand between my legs and moved it in a circular motion over my vagina, his fingertips delving between the folds.

The pressure from his hand, the movement of his clever fingers made me ache, made me shiver, made me wet. Everything he did took my breath away. Everything he did felt so good.

Each kiss grew more intense than the last... hot and passionate. He plunged his tongue deep inside my mouth, in and out. His fingers mimicked the movement. I felt my careful control slipping away... slipping away on wave after wave of sheer pleasure.

I didn't want him to stop, and yet something inside my head—the voice—urged me to make him stop.

I closed my eyes—tried to relax—tried to quiet the voice. I wanted to hear only Jake's voice.

He nipped and sucked the tip of my tongue... trailed kisses to my ear, and whispered, "Bring your knees up for me, Rose."

I heard his voice, but my body would not respond. My legs trembled and felt like jelly. I wanted to bring my knees up—I tried—but they wouldn't budge.

Jesus, help me.

"I can't. They won't move. I'm sorry... I'm trying. Oh, Jake, I'm trying. Please don't hurt me. Please... don't hurt me."

Oh my God! What did I just say?

Please don't hurt me...

I could not pull the words back. It was too late. They hung over us in the air like an impending storm.

The kisses stopped. His hands stilled. The room, oh so silent... except for our breathing and the faint sounds of "Yesterday" by the Beatles.

Please don't hurt me. My inner voice blurted out what I'd tried to keep quiet for so long.

Chapter Seven

I can close my eyes, clear my mind of all the collective clutter,
Then let my weary soul lift up on wings that quietly flutter
Back through time so effortlessly to nearly forgotten places
To treasured friends and bittersweet lovers, now cherished
ageless faces.

Rockton, Illinois
Fall 2007

After the initial message and Friend request, I spent some time perusing Rose's Facebook page—reading her information and posts—looking at pictures.

All of this still seemed unreal—the flashbacks, hearing the old songs, feeling someone tapping into my thoughts lately—and now, actual contact with someone lost to me for more than forty years.

And not just *any* someone, but *the someone* lurking in nearly every person's past. Their first love. The one they gave their heart. The one they never really got over.

That someone.

For me, that someone was Rose Allison. And now, by some quirk of fate, she showed up in my life again.

Unreal.

Rose lived in Albuquerque, New Mexico. She was married to Paul Flynn, with two grown children—a boy, Joe and a girl, Jenna—and grandchildren. She graduated from college with a BS in Elementary

Education and an MS in Special Education. She served as a special education teacher for more than twenty years.

Yep. I could see Rose working with special needs children. She always had a soft spot for little kids and animals. Adults, not so much. I guess she figured they knew enough to make choices. Kids and animals, at the mercy of adults, had few, if any, choices.

She had been a busy girl the past forty years.

Reading her accomplishments made me happy. If anyone deserved a good life, she did.

I remembered the words to something she wrote and read to me late one night, years ago... a story about a little girl who dreamed of living happily ever after somewhere in the West.

Albuquerque, New Mexico, definitely fit somewhere in the West. That made me smile.

I did a quick Google search on Paul Flynn. Among several, only one popped up in Albuquerque. That must be him—Flynn and Madison Law Firm, LLC—attorneys specializing in business and franchise law.

So, Rose Allison—former band groupie, pot smoking, hippie poet—married a lawyer. Interesting. I never pictured Prince Charming as a lawyer.

She still wrote poetry. She posted several on her page—about teaching, her students, her family—about life, in general. One particular verse from a poem caught my attention.

A place where wheelchairs can come and go,
And fragile friends can swing to and fro.
A place to explore on hand and knee,
With things to touch when eyes cannot see.
Where trickling waters and fine white sands
Sift and flow over stiff, small hands.

She still had the gift, the ability to visualize a picture in her mind, find the well-chosen word and perfect turn of phrase to evoke emotion, and to form the picture in the reader's mind, as well. I could easily imagine the students referred to in the poem.

Reading her words again brought back a sweet memory of two young people cuddled in a sleeping bag in front of a cozy fire. I remember telling her writing was a true gift.

I liked reading the comments from others on her posts, and I liked her responses. They came across as witty, observant and truthful... a part of Rose that remained the same.

I noticed no responses, no comments, from Paul.

Interesting.

I moved on to photos.

They included pictures with her children and grandchildren, with her students and co-workers. I found images of her dogs, her home, her office, her yard, the flowers on her patio, but saw no pictures of Paul. No pictures of her and Paul together.

Again, interesting... but then I didn't post pictures of Beth and me either, so that wasn't too unusual. Hell, most of my pictures captured dogs, cornfields, farm machinery, or weeds posing as wildflowers.

But, hey, my pictures were good... damn good.

I liked what I saw in the photos of Rose. I was a visual kind of guy, like most guys, I guess. She looked good in her pictures—older—but still very pretty.

I saw the young girl I first met at the rehearsal barn in the fall of 1968. The girl who spelled out her name for me—"A-l-l-i-s-o-n. Rose Allison with two Ls"—and asked, "Are you Jake, Jake Richardson?"

I saw the young girl whose words hung with mine in the air between us as we looked into one another's faces and felt that initial electricity.

I saw the young girl I fell in love with back then, and I remembered her.

I remembered Rose Allison with 2lls.

* * * * *

I would describe Rose as a free spirit who danced to a different drum—to a beat, a rhythm that at times only she could hear. I couldn't line her up alongside anyone I knew from my small hometown of Rockton. She was pretty and smart, and quick-witted with a sense of humor I liked right away. Someone who made me think, made me dream, made me long for more of everything life had to offer back then.

Rose filled my life with color... with possibilities... with love.

She loved music—all types of music—classical, jazz, blues and rock. One chilly Saturday morning we hung pictures, arranged furniture and ate donuts to the mellow sounds of Frank Sinatra, Nat King Cole and Tony Bennett... albums she saved from her mother's collection. At Christmas, we watched the tree lights blink on and off rhythmically to Dave Brubeck's *Time Out* album.

And for two unforgettable years we danced, smoked, got high, and made love to the music of Janis Joplin; Jim Morrison; Eric Clapton; The Beatles; Crosby, Stills, Nash and Young; Santana; and Jimi Hendrix.

Rose knew every word to every song, and quickly learned the words to new ones. She understood words. She loved words.

Inside Rose lurked a writer and a poet who communicated her observations, her inner thoughts and feelings, her insecurities, through writing. She found escape from her demons and comfort from loneliness through writing. And she kept everything she wrote in black three-ringed notebooks or in a little black, leather diary she carried in her purse.

As time went by, we grew closer and I learned more about her... about her past.

Her mother continually tried to get her shit together, to make a life for Rose and herself, after her sister married and moved away. She never quite succeeded. Rose basically took over out of necessity.

She did a lot of things for herself from a young age... cooking, cleaning, caring for herself. She learned to stay busy, stay out of the way, and stay quiet by entertaining herself, by using her imagination.

She worked at becoming the perfect child... a perfectly silent child who learned by observing on the fringes, and created an alternative reality within. A perfect child doesn't cause problems for her mother, for step-dads or boyfriends, for teachers... for anyone.
They become invisible.

Becoming the perfect child is a heavy and impossible responsibility. The inability to reach perfection often leaves a child stressed, insecure, with low self-esteem, and strapped with obsessive behaviors. Rose exhibited them all.

Somehow she managed to hide them from most by keeping her distance and dictating the terms of a relationship to friends... to lovers. If the terms weren't met or she felt threatened, the relationship ended. Rose ended it by walking away... by leaving.

Her complicated psyche became layered from the everyday worry and stress of dealing with adult situations and adult problems. She implemented all kinds of coping mechanisms to get by, to get through life. Hers had been in place for a very long time, and she carefully avoided allowing anyone close enough to see. But I saw them. I got closer than most.

She felt uncomfortable with people she didn't know, or in crowds. She once told me it was difficult for her to breathe in a crowd, and they made her feel dizzy and disoriented. Consequently, she withdrew, and hung on the fringes. Sometimes I found myself standing next to her on the fringes looking at life through her eyes. Observing. Constantly taking mental notes.

She seemed so together, but I gradually discovered her deep insecurities, and how hard it was for her to step outside the comfort zone she created for herself. I was glad Jerry reached out to her and brought her to the band... and eventually to me.

Rose possessed an uncanny ability when it came to reading others. She pretty well had their number, figured them out, just by watching and listening.

For the most part, Rose kept people at bay. Out of self-preservation, I imagine. Even those friends who considered themselves close to her, really weren't. She created the illusion. I wondered how many people along the way thought themselves best friends with Rose, but really never knew her at all. I wondered how many people mistook her caution, her fear, for aloofness.

All her childhood drama, the emotional baggage, would crush most people, but Rose wasn't most people. She kept moving forward, kept reinventing herself as the years ticked by. Unfortunately, that came with a heavy price. She didn't trust or allow herself to connect with people. Now that I think back on things, I'm not sure Rose realized she didn't make connections—ones that lasted anyway. When you stop trusting, stop connecting with people—you lose the ability to recognize affection or love when it comes along. If you can't recognize it, it's nearly impossible to give or receive love either.

How to love and show affection is learned, patterned... usually from parents. Rose's mother gave her a skewed outlook on love and affection. And even though she knew what she *didn't* want out of love, life, and relationships— she never met a role model for what she *did* want.

All of this seemed so basic, so simple, so taken for granted by most... by me. But none of it was simple for her. Relationships, in general, were complicated and difficult. Not so much in initiating, but in maintaining them.

I managed to get close—to get under her radar—and we began a relationship.

Yep, I had all the answers back then... had it all figured out. I knew I could fix everything. I wanted to fix everything. I wanted her to be happy. I wanted her to be happy with me.

I loved Rose. She was my first love, and I loved her as only a young man loves. And using a young man's logic, I thought if I loved her enough, I could fix whatever was broken.

That was the plan—basic and simple. An idealistic young man who hadn't yet learned that even innocent, heart-driven plans don't always work out the way we picture them.

* * * * *

A day passed with no response from Rose.

Ben and I drove the football team, cheerleading squad, and pep club to an away game in Belvidere—followed by a caravan of parents and loyal hometown supporters.

We lost 42 to 3. I anticipated a very, long football season this year.

Most small Midwest towns revolve around school activities, with the high school sports program at the center. The entire town comes out to support the kids and their events—good or bad, win or lose—and Rockton, Illinois, exemplified this.

Small-town Rockton is the place where everyone knows your name and your business—and they remember both—and some are slow to forgive or forget that business. They remember the divorcee who ran off with the town's married veterinarian. They remember the town bad boy who got the head cheerleader pregnant senior year. They remember the farmer's son who went off to college and came back a marijuana smoking, long-haired, hippie freak, war activist.

And who in the hell gives a flying fuck, years later? Well, apparently quite a few. Since I was that marijuana smoking, longhaired, hippie freak, war activist—my mom and dad got an earful of parenting advice from the locals. That's a small town, for you. That's where we lived back then and that's where I live now... where Beth and I raise our family.

Who would have thought that forty years ago? Not me. That's for damn sure.

I got home around ten thirty. Walked the dogs, sent a text to the boys to remind them it was a school night, and grabbed a couple beers from the refrigerator. I headed into the office.

I brought up Pandora. Stevie Ray Vaughn soulfully sang "Ain't Gone 'n' Give Up on Love." Appropriate, considering my thoughts.

I started to turn up the volume, but remembered I wasn't alone, as Beth already went to bed for the night. High volume... not a good idea. I liked to keep things peaceful, calm, and on an even keel with Beth. Life for everyone—including the boys—stayed better that way.

Beth was always high-strung and emotional, but after menopause and turning fifty, the emotional outbursts and mood-swings intensified. As the peacekeeper in the family, I ran interference on behalf of the boys.

Over time, I became the Secretary General of my own United Nations.

In direct proportion to the mood swings and emotions running amuck—our sex life became non-existent. Now, Beth didn't want me to touch her or even bring up sex. She finalized her feelings on the subject by moving me upstairs. I came home from my route one morning and found all of my things neatly arranged in the upstairs bedroom—my childhood bedroom with the solar system wallpaper border—complete with spindle twin bed and matching dresser.

Beth said she made the change because I snored. She couldn't sleep. If she couldn't sleep, she felt depressed and cranky the next day.

Bullshit. I never snored before and, if I did, it never bothered her before.

I am not sure how sound her logic was either. She remained depressed and cranky even after I moved back upstairs.

Again, bullshit. Total bullshit.

That was five years ago.

The first few weeks of the arrangement, I tried showing up in Beth's room at bedtime, thinking she would cave. She ran my ass out. Since then, an unspoken rule between us keeps me from entering her room after sundown. She never ventures into mine, either. I do my own laundry. She doesn't even have to put clothes away in my room.

I never thought Beth would stop wanting sex. When things got rocky between us those first few years of our marriage—we always fell back on great make-up sex. She was passionate, spontaneous, and could wear my ass out, but she was younger than I.

The passion simply died... quietly replaced over time with the minutia of daily life, daily routine. We didn't kiss anymore. We didn't touch anymore. We just lived in the same house.

Shit happens.

I wondered if this happened to other couples in long-term marriages. Maybe that's why so many guys my age and Ben's visited the pub night after night. Maybe they slept solo in twin beds, too.

If a guy knew on the day he said "I do" that he would work most every day of his life from sunrise to sunset, hand the paycheck to his wife and kids, and find out after twenty-five or thirty years of marriage there would be no more sex, what man in his right mind would say "I do" to that? I mean, what the hell?

Maybe this is why men have mid-life crises. Why they buy convertibles, motorcycles, four-wheelers, and other shit, then leave their wives for younger women.

They want sex.

They need sex.

Shallow, even for me.

I didn't only miss the sex. I missed the intimacy, the closeness that sex brings to a couple like nothing else can. It's the mutual trust the intimacy brings, which keeps the love alive and the passion in the marriage. Without passion, it's kind of like being married to your sister. Well, kind of.

I missed being touched, being held. It didn't seem to bother Beth. She continued to pull away, to grow more distant. Her focus shifted to Brian and Dustin, to her family and her work. Mine shifted to the farm and finances, problem solving, bus driving, the lake... and drinking.

Geez. I should write a book or something. I can do a hell of a job pointing out what's wrong in a marriage. I just can't seem to fix it in my experience. That's probably the case with most doctors and psychiatrists. They write best sellers and get rich from theories they create a platform on and lecture about, but can't put a damn bit of the practicum into their own marriages. Sounds about right.

Things were definitely different between Beth and me now. We were close because of the boys, our family, and mutual friends. We were close because of the farm and finances. We were close because of our thirty-year marriage investment... the shared history between us.

I loved Beth. I knew she loved me. For Christ's sake, we established a home and family together. We'd been friends for over half our adult lives. But the love we shared now was quite different than when it began. The love remained out of respect, obligation, responsibility... and routine.

Maybe that's as good as it gets after a certain point. Maybe I shouldn't expect anymore than that. I had a great life—family, friends, a free and clear farm, four vehicles and two dogs—and my own damn room! What more could I ask for? What the hell did I have to complain about? So what if I didn't have a sex life? I had two good hands that still worked just fine.

Some days I wondered about the situation at Ben's house. Did he sleep alone in an upstairs bedroom, too? Did I dare broach that subject with him? Hell no. No way could I go there with Ben. I had an idea where the conversation might end up. It might end up in the past... my past. I couldn't change the past. No one could change the past. I moved on. Everyone moved on. That's why it's called the *past*.

Maybe I would Google the topic later. See what the "experts" had to say on sex and long-term marriages. I spent a lot of time Googling by myself. I excelled at it. A natural Googler. Most men are.

Still, I wondered if this was the way it was supposed to be—the way all marriages ended up? At this point, I didn't know, and really hadn't thought much about it until the Friend request... the *Friend request* from Rose.

That wasn't the only thing I found myself wondering about. A lot of things crossed my mind lately. Things I hadn't thought about for more than forty years.

The music, the words of The Beatles, "In My Life" drifted in my ears. I closed my eyes and let the words wander around inside my head—places, friends, lovers—and I remembered.

No one wrote words like The Beatles... no one.

And no one made me remember like Rose... no one.

I checked email first. I found reminders from the vet for Cooper's shots, an Amazon local deal notice, and prescriptions ready to pick up at Schnucks Pharmacy. More shit to add to the list for tomorrow.

Routine minutia. I did it well. Had it down.

I moved on to Facebook and typed in my email and password.

I had a message. Nice.

I centered the hand over the icon and clicked. There it was— a response from Rose.

I clicked on her name and read the reply.

"Yes, Rose Allison with 2lls."

I smiled at the reference, and read the next line.

"Have you seen or heard from Sam at all in the past several years?"

There it was. The reason she sent the Friend request—why she made contact with me. She wanted to find Sam.

Of course. That made sense.

She wasn't searching for me after all. Her memories and mine were probably quite different. Understandable.

I typed in my message.

"I had coffee with Sam about ten years ago. She was with her daughter, Emma. Said she was living in Springfield now. That's the last time I heard from her."

And pushed reply.

I remembered five or six years earlier than that—before we had coffee together—Sam called late one night. She sounded tired... her voice soft... and her words rocked me to the core. "Cash is gone, Jake. He died a few hours ago of congestive heart failure. I wanted you to know."

Jesus. What a thing. I didn't know what to say other than how sorry I was. Cash was always bigger than life. They had such big plans when I visited them in California. How could this happen? I hung up the phone and felt older... out of touch... sad. Another part of the dream we all had back then, died.

* * * * *

A couple of days later, Rose messaged back.

"Thank you for sharing that information with me. I'd really like to get in touch with her. She's not on Facebook and I haven't had much luck with a telephone number either. If you should happen to get any information on her, could you message it to me, Jake? I would appreciate that so much. Thanks."

I didn't have any more information to give her. I wished I did.

"Will do."

I pushed send and watched her drift back out of my life again... much like she did forty years ago.

That was the last message between us.

Time passed.

Football season came to an end and, after its rough start, Rockton somehow ended up in the play-offs, losing in the third round.

Brian and Dustin both made the varsity basketball team again.

Beth planned and perfectly executed another delicious Thanksgiving dinner, after I scooped a parking area and path through the snow for twenty-eight family and friends. Good thing I'd weatherized the tractor and attached the snow scoop a few weeks before.

The day after Thanksgiving—Friday, November 23rd—I turned sixty years old. How the hell did that happen? Unbelievable. You never think you'll be sixty-something, especially when you're twenty-something.

That evening I found myself alone.

Beth, her two sisters, and her mother decided to do a little Black Friday and Saturday shopping in Chicago. They strategically planned this yearly event and eagerly awaited it. Early this morning, I gassed up the van, checked tire pressures, added a quart of oil, filled the wiper fluid, and sent them on their way.

Dustin and Brian both had dates and, despite having jobs, hit me up for twenty-five bucks each. I think I remember trying that same tactic with my dad, but never even got the requested ten bucks. Instead I got a lecture on frugality starting out with "when I was your age," that went downhill from there. Where the hell did I go wrong?

Finding myself home alone in the winter was a fairly rare occurrence. The cold kept me from doing anything productive outside, other than puttering around, pretending to be busy. And since we didn't heat either the shop or the basement, I pretty much resigned myself to indoor activities. Most years by February I perched on the edge of going stir crazy. Even ice fishing—at ten below zero on a frozen lakebed with a steady north headwind blowing—looked good.

Later, I had the computer all to myself, I brought up Facebook and Pandora.

What should I listen to? Birthday music, of course. I typed in The Beatles' "Birthday," turned up the volume until the windows in the office rattled, and sang along.

Head bobbing.

Foot tapping.

I programmed Pandora with enough birthday songs, Beatles songs, blues and jazz and other late 1960s and early 1970s songs to play for hours, or until I went to bed or passed out, whichever happened first. It didn't really matter. I established the pattern long ago.

I went back to Facebook, typed in a few witty comments on my friends' posts, and responded to a Friend request from an old high-school buddy who now lived in Florida. I was up to seventy-seven friends.

Impressive.

I brought my friend's page up and looked at his pictures. Geez. Did I look like that? I wasn't old, fat, or bald. Okay... one out of three. According to his information, he was four months older. Well, that would account for why he looked the way he did... and I didn't.

Birthdays and their significance as time markers tend to change with age, along with the need to celebrate. I enjoyed my share of birthday celebrations and surprises over the years. I now preferred to skip any formalities or plans associated with my birthday.

This afternoon, I met Ben at Will's Place for lunch—greasy cheeseburgers, sweet potato fries, and beer—since we weren't driving bus today. I was fortunate to celebrate birthdays with a friend like Ben. We'd celebrated our annual days since he came back from Vietnam. Today, he kidded me about my graying hair and salt 'n pepper moustache. I returned the jabs by reminding him I still *had* hair to turn gray. Hard to believe Ben's thick, Beach Boy blond hair remained no more than a memory.

The evening was uneventful and yet perfect. I could play my music as loud as I wanted, and drink beer until I was ready to head up to bed, or I passed out, or both.

Yep. Happy Birthday to me!

Over the years, my birthday often reminded me of *her* birthday. Rose turned fifty-nine today. I found that even harder to comprehend than me turning sixty. I wondered if, over the years, she remembered my birthday.

I wondered if she remembered anything at all about me, about us.

I logged onto Facebook and I brought up her page... something I did now on a regular basis. Her feed showed numerous birthday wishes from friends and family... maybe seventy or eighty. Wow, so many remembered her birthday.

I wondered how her day went... how she celebrated. Did someone take her out to dinner, buy her flowers?

I saw nothing from her husband. Not unusual, I guess. I didn't comment on Beth's pages as a rule either, but I think I did make a comment on her birthday last year. Don't remember now. Must have been something memorable on my part.

I wanted to wish Rose happy birthday. What would it hurt... one friend wishing another friend a happy birthday?

I pulled up the message box and typed her name in along with my message.

"Happy Birthday to you! Happy Birthday to you! Happy Birthday, Dear Rose! Happy Birthday to you! (Sung to the tune of Happy Birthday)."

Original.

I finished another beer, pushed send, and went back to her page. Read all the recent posts and looked through her pictures... again. As I looked at her current pictures, at the woman she was now, I saw only a girl of twenty-something looking back at me. In my mind, Rose remained the same. It was as if time stopped. I guess in many ways it did.

One album showed a picture of Rose from the early 1970s, only a few years after she left Champaign... after she left me. She sat next to a swimming pool in a bathing suit—her skin tan, hair wind-blown, a faraway look in her eyes—like her mind floated somewhere else.

I studied the picture. I remembered that faraway look. It took me back to another place, another time.

* * * * *

It was after a gig at The Library, I think. Rose and Ren were moving into Parkridge Apartments that weekend. Rose stayed in Champaign and went to the dance with me.

All of us came back to Cash and Sam's after the dance for pizza and to get stoned.

Rose and I stretched out on the chaise lounge.

I remembered our amazement when she and Cash sang "Leavin' On A Jet Plane" as Chuck and Jerry accompanied them on guitar. They sounded great together and, up until then, no one knew Rose could sing. It was another one of those things she kept to herself. Maybe the weed made her let her guard down. Maybe she got caught up in the music.

She went somewhere else as she and Cash sang. Words had a way of doing that to her—of transporting her somewhere else. I saw a faraway look in her eyes, and watched her drift away.

I wondered how many times she found herself left behind, left alone. I suspected way too may times.

Looking at the picture—I saw that same faraway look on her face. Was she still drifting away? Did anyone in the crowd notice she was gone? I wondered.

* * * * *

The next afternoon I finished my route and found another reply.

"Thank you for the song, the sentiments, and for the hint on the tune. Never would have recognized it otherwise."

She kept her sense of humor.

I messaged back.

"Do you know when my birthday is?"

I'll see how much she remembers, or wants to remember. My birthday was not in any personal information on Facebook.

On Rose's twenty-first birthday, I took her to Little Phil's in downtown Champaign, a local bar where the band played occasionally. I watched as they carded her at the front door and she proudly presented her driver's license. We walked to a booth in the back, sat down next to one another, and she ordered both of us a beer.

The next day I received more words... more words from Rose.

"Happy belated birthday, Jake. I did remember we have the same birthday. My first legal beer at Little Phil's. You drove."

I responded.

"Yep, Little Phil's and I drove."

Rose remembered my birthday. She remembered spending it with me. These were personal things between Rose and me. Things that had nothing to do with Sam.

She remembered us.

Was the connection still there? Did it matter?

There really was no point. We'd both moved on. The proof of that appeared on my computer screen—on the Facebook pages—her page and mine.

Realistically, logically—what I thought about when alone—I knew could never happen. It was wrong of me to think about it at all.

I wouldn't think about it.

Right.

Damn it. I couldn't stop thinking about it.

Eventually, I made a decision. Right or wrong, I was going to find a way to quietly creep back into her life.

I needed to find out if anything remained... anything remained at all between Rose Allison and Jake Richardson.

If anything did?

Well, I had no clue what I was going to do. Not a damn clue.

Chapter Eight

Intimate moments remembered,
Down to the smallest detail.
Whispered fantasies softly stirred.
Gently he pulled back the veil.

Rockton, Illinois
Fall/Winter 2007

*I*knew it was after the fact. We were well into fall and sliding into winter, but a couple of events in the news this past summer had taken me back, made me think of Rose even before the Friend request. I wanted to remind her... wanted to give her something else to think about, to remember.

I had a beer—I had another—and I Googled *Apollo 11 Moon Landing*.

When the page came up, I scanned down and clicked on *First Moon Landing 1969—YouTube.* I watched and listened to the video several times. It was in black and white, grainy, and the commentary sounded dated.

Hell, it was dated... a little over thirty-eight-years-ago dated. But still the events of July 20, 1969, lingered.

The evening brought little relief from the Midwest summer's heat. Even at around ten in the evening it was still hot and muggy. We had gathered in Cash and Sam's air-conditioned apartment. We all sat huddled in front of the small television set—smoking grass and getting stoned—and watched the Apollo 11 crew prepare to land on the moon.

All of us, at one point or another during the evening, walked out of the apartment and gazed up at the moon. I think the general consensus was if we squinted hard enough. Or looked long enough. We would be able to catch a glimpse of the spacecraft, or see a tiny astronaut walking around. But, of course, we were all stoned.

We listened to CBS anchorman Walter Cronkite's commentary, and hung on every word of the transmission between NASA officials and the astronauts as they approached and landed on the moon. Finally we watched Neil Armstrong hop down the ladder of the lunar module and take "one small step for [a] man and one giant leap for mankind."

It was as though the entire world stopped—held a collective breath—and uttered the words "far out" in the exhale.

The moon landing blew your mind if you were straight—let alone if you were stoned—and one of those experiences you never, ever forget. One of those moments in time that defines you... that becomes part of your identity forever.

The Apollo 11 moon landing became a defining moment in the identity of an entire generation... my generation... the baby boomers.

Rose and I shared that moment in time. I never forgot the events of that evening, and I never forgot I shared them with her. I doubt she did either.

I copied and pasted the link in a Facebook message, hovered the mouse over *send...* and clicked.

How simple and easy to reconnect.

My life to her life.

How simple and easy to complicate lives in the same way.

My life to her life.

I stared into the monitor and saw my reflection in the screen. It wasn't the reflection of a footloose, twenty something kid. It was an older, responsible man—a man I barely recognized.

What the hell was I doing?

I told my kids daily to make good decisions and good things would follow. Here I was about to make decisions maybe not so good for good things to follow.

I knew exactly what I was doing. I didn't care.

I finished my beer, logged off the computer, and continued on with my days, my routine.

A couple of days passed with no response from Rose. Maybe I read too much into the birthday thing. Maybe I shouldn't have sent the Apollo 11 connection. That's what happens late at night after too many beers. You don't make good decisions.

You think stupid shit. You do stupid shit. You say stupid shit.

But, then again, maybe she was afraid to reply... afraid of complicating her life with mine.

I had no idea what her life was like now. All I knew about Rose was what I read on Facebook—from what showed up in front of me. The things not there, the things I wondered about, I filled in with my imagination.

Early one morning, I fixed a cup of coffee, let the dogs out, and sat down at the computer to check emails and Facebook before I left to drive my route.

First, I checked Hotmail. Nothing important. Junk. Miscellaneous shit.

I logged into Facebook. I had another message.

"Each year when the anniversary of Apollo 11 makes headlines... I remember. It's hard for me to realize so much time has passed. I thought about us looking up at the moon... thinking we might spot an astronaut walking around. We were so wrecked. We were so young. Thanks for sharing, Jake."

I read through the message a couple more times, logged out, and walked into the crisp, cold air to begin a day that didn't seem quite so routine anymore.

I thought about her words... and *I remembered.*

The words made me smile... quickened my pace. The words brought warmth and color to an otherwise cold, gray day. The words gave me something to look forward to. What that something was, I wasn't quite sure of yet. But just having a reason to anticipate—something unfamiliar, yet so familiar—seemed extraordinary.

Up until now, my life *was* routine. Typical. Ordinary. Predictable.

Not now. A simple message changed everything... *a Friend request*.

* * * * *

Ben and I drove the boys' and girls' basketball teams to Machesney Park that evening... our Indians against their Huskies. They split the games. The girls lost both the JV and varsity games, while both the JV and varsity boys' teams remained undefeated.

Ben and I flipped a coin before we left Rockton to see who would drive the girls. We did this frequently during basketball season. Fortunately for me, Ben lost. I knew from experience exactly how bad the trip home would be. Teenage girls are emotional. They turn even more emotional when they lose basketball games. Ben would share a long, sad, tear-filled ride back to Rockton with the girls.

Yep. Win or lose... give me the boys' bus every time. I can deal with the swearing, boasting, bragging, and a few fists hitting the side of the bus, because I know they will soon follow it all up with silence. Guys get over things and move on. Guys are spent. They need sleep, and the rocking movement of the bus works like a charm every time... all the way home.

Guys. Simple. Predictable. Easily satisfied.

God, I was thankful to have sons. Every once in a while you get lucky. If Beth had given birth to girls, I'm sure I would have drowned in a raging sea of heated, hyper-active hormones by now.

Yep, damn lucky.

* * * * *

Late before heading upstairs to bed, I logged onto Facebook. I wanted to send Rose one more message—a picture this time—of a country road in northeast Iowa leading back to a rock fest site. Rose and I, and 50,000 other young people, camped out in sleeping bags on

131

the hard ground for the three-day event, July 31 through August 2, 1970, in Wadena, Iowa.

I copied and pasted the picture in a message. No words were necessary. The picture conjured up more words than I could ever write.

I finished my beer and pressed send.

I pulled up a YouTube video of the Chambers Brothers singing "Time Has Come Today" and listened. I moved on to the blues with "Oh, Pretty Woman" by Albert King, and finished the night with Luther Allison singing "Love Me Mama."

I'd watched and listened to those men perform them that weekend in 1970.

As the last song played, I closed my eyes—saw Luther on the stage in the middle of Clarence Schmitt's oat field—and pictured myself dancing, drinking, smoking and tripping out to the music. The whole while, I watched Rose from a distance—across a sea of faces—slipping farther and farther away from me. I remember feeling helpless... wanting her so badly I ached... and not knowing what to do.

In the end, I did nothing. I let her go. I let her walk away.

To this day, I'm not sure what happened... what went wrong.

* * * * *

The next morning I woke up in my bed and had no clue how I got there. That happened on occasion... actually, more than I liked to admit.

Did I shut the computer down? Hell, I couldn't remember.

I walked downstairs. Quiet. No one up yet but me. Good deal.

I continued into the den, sat down at the desk and pressed the space bar on the computer. Facebook message page came up... with the messages Rose and I sent back and forth. Shit.

I refreshed the page and waited.

This could have been really bad. Beth, Dustin, or Brian might have been sitting in the computer chair this morning wondering who Rose was and why were we sending messages and pictures back and forth.

Beth made a joke the other night to Dustin about getting off the computer so Dad could chat with his old girlfriend. Wasn't funny then... even less funny this morning.

I deleted the messages and logged off. Next, I pulled up the computer history, deleted everything, and logged off. Paranoia was setting in. Good. I needed a damn wake-up call.

This could not happen again. It wouldn't happen again.

I needed to be more careful from now on. If the messages continued, I would need to type some precautions out to Rose. We needed to be on the same page.

* * * * *

The weekend passed... filled with routine activities.

Early Saturday morning, Ben and I drove both the boys JV and varsity teams to a basketball tournament in North Chicago, returning late that afternoon. Ben and his wife joined Beth and me for dinner and drinks at Will's Place in the evening. Outside of family dinners, going to Will's and seeing an occasional movie were the few things Beth and I still did together... in close proximity to one another.

I drank a lot of beer Saturday night. Beth drove home.

Routine activity.

Snow fell early Sunday morning, bringing the total to ten inches for the winter. I spent most of the morning on the tractor plowing our driveway and the neighbor's. The rest of the day I stayed in the basement rearranging my collective clutter under the guise of cleaning, straightening up. I did this a lot, especially during the winter. The basement, though not heated, was the only semi-warm place, besides the main floors of the house, where I could be alone with my music, my beer, and my thoughts. The workshop in the barn wasn't heated, and the shelter house by the lake was a distant memory until spring. I claimed the basement or nothing.

If I looked long enough, I always managed to find something really cool stashed inside the cardboard boxes—overflowing with years and years of family accumulations and memories we'd moved to the basement and basically forgotten. Today was no exception.

I spotted a worn, dog-eared box on a bottom shelf in the corner, a box of Beth's canning jars on top. Across the side of the box... Eisner Grocery... the store we shopped and *shoplifted* while living at Parkridge Apartments back in the day.

Jerry and I used to stop at Eisner's after classes. We'd pay for a couple of items, like bread and milk, but walk out with several packages of hamburger, steak or hot dogs shoved under our jackets or down our pants.

Justification for the shoplifting? We only did it when we were flat broke and/or out of food... or both. Government commodities—cheese, rice, oatmeal, and butter—only went so far.

I dug the Eisner box out, and carried it over to the wooden bench in front of the canning shelves. Shelves neatly lined with Beth's canning. Mason jars filled with tomatoes, green beans, pickles and peaches.

I sat down, placed the box on the floor in front of me, and peeled off the silver duct tape still in place after nearly forty years. Inside the box—carefully wrapped in sheets of crumpled newspapers—I found all my drug paraphernalia. Oh, my God.

One by one, I unwrapped the items from my past and placed them on the bench beside me—the dark blue, glass hookah water pipe, two metal hash pipes with the filter screens still intact, several different types of roach clips, and two partially used booklets of Zig-Zag rolling papers, one blue free-burning booklet and one orange slow-burning booklet. Back then, it was all about freedom of choice... even in Zig-Zag papers.

I arranged them, inspected them and brought each to my nose— closing my eyes—inhaling deeply. The smell of hash and grass residue lingered after all these years. Talk about a flashback. Scent triggers memories quicker than any other sense. Immediately I was transported back to Champaign, to Parkridge Apartments, the band, the music, the clothes, the drugs, the rock fest, the university, the war, the protests.

Plus, the one person I associated all of this with... Rose.

I looked back into the box and lifted the last layer of newspaper to make sure everything was out. There nestled in the bottom of the box was a faded, slightly flattened, red burlap rose on a wrapped metal stem with two green burlap leaves attached.

Unreal.

I gave the rose to her the night she tripped on acid for the first time Probably ripped it off from a flower arrangement in the clubhouse. Too long ago to remember. What I do remember... she trusted me enough to trip for the first time, and carried the rose with her for sixteen hours. Something concrete to hold when things got heavy. Something besides me.

I pictured her, dipping the rose into the clubhouse fountain, and explaining how it changed into colored strands of dripping plastic. Trippy. Sunshine-acid trippy.

Another night I never forgot.

I picked it up and ran my fingers over the rough fabric—the flower the leaves, the stem. What a picture. A grown man, sitting on a wooden bench in the basement, holding a damn, dilapidated rose. Geez I couldn't help it. Something tangible traveled through time—a reminder that those days happened—and I was there.

The scent of drugs lingered. The memories lingered. And now a piece of reality lingered as well. Something concrete for me to hold on to in case things got too heavy.

A real possibility.

I rewrapped the pieces, placed them back in the cardboard box and laid the rose on top. I closed the box with new duct tape and placed it with other items of mine... items found on previous winter days digging through the collective clutter of my life.

* * * * *

That evening, after waiting in the computer line behind Beth, Dustin and Brian, I finally sat down and checked my email and Facebook pages. We really needed another computer, maybe a laptop. Patience. I learned to wait for things. Made my family wait for things.

Nothing but junk mail and a class reunion update in my Hotmail account. My forty-year class reunion happened last year, and now the reunion committee sent me sporadic updates on who died. Great. Something to look forward to.

Why is it after a certain age, obituaries rank right up there with the weather?

I logged onto Facebook and read another message.

"The summer heat; the hard, trampled field beneath my bare feet; the smell of grass; the sea of faces; and the sound of the music. Music that filled my senses and my soul to overflowing. I remember it all, as if it was yesterday. I remember you and me."

That was the response I was waiting for. The words were telling. The connection still there.

We began messaging regularly. Soon the messages started to flow back and forth daily, usually in the evenings.

I looked forward to reading her messages. Sometimes she wrote only a sentence or two, while other times she shared several paragraphs. We talked to each other in these messages as one friend to another.

Sometimes she talked about the weather. Sometimes she told me about something that happened in her day. Whatever she shared... I liked it... I wanted to read it. It was good to be in touch again, no matter what the reason.

After a couple of weeks of messaging, we figured out Facebook's chat line feature through trial and error one night.

I brought up the list of friends on chat, clicked her name, and typed.

"Good evening."

After several minutes, Rose responded.

"Hey, you. I wasn't quite sure where to type."

"I figured that. Not exactly user friendly."

"No, it isn't."

I stared at the screen, marveled at the technology, and replied.

"Geez, I almost feel giddy about this. Like a first date or something."

She typed back.

"I feel the same way. I'm kind of nervous. Crazy, huh?"

Not crazy at all. More like amazing. After all the time, the friendship between us remained. Chatting with her again through messages seemed so natural, so easy. It was like closing a door yesterday and opening it again the next day, except forty years passed in that one day. There was so much to catch up on, so much we both wanted to know.

At first, most of what Rose shared with me I already knew from her Facebook page—where she lived, who she married, about her kids and grandkids, her education and teaching career. Gradually, she filled in the details Facebook left out.

She lived in a tan, stucco, four-bedroom home with a pool, and enjoyed gardening.

She had two married children, Joe and Jenna, and five grandchildren. Joe worked as a detective with the Albuquerque Police Department... Jenna, a pharmacist in Santa Fe. Rose thought about retiring at the end of the school year, after twenty-five years of teaching. She owned two dogs, Fritz and Stanley... and drove a truck. I found that amusing. Maybe she still retained a little Midwest farm girl inside.

She obviously loved her kids and grandkids, and dogs, enjoyed working with the special needs children, and took pride in her home. She shared and wrote about these topics the most.

What she wrote about least was Paul. She mentioned, as a lawyer, he traveled a great deal, and was eight years her senior. She didn't offer any more information. I didn't ask.

I recapped the past forty years of my life for Rose.

I began by telling her I finished my degree in English and cinematography, and participated for the past thirty years in a local dinner theatre group, both acting and directing.

I told her Beth and I married in 1978—had two sons, Dustin, seventeen and Brian, eighteen—and that Beth was nine years younger than I. I wondered how and if she would compare the age differences between Beth and me... with her and Paul.

I told her I took over the family farm in Rockton after my dad and mom passed, drove a school bus part-time, and had two dogs, too. That was my life the past forty-plus years.

Rose typed she was sorry to hear about my parents. She remembered I had my mother's eyes. I thought that remarkable. She commented about the dinner theater, about acting and directing, and said how glad she was I continued doing something related to my degree, something I enjoyed. She was happy about my marriage, about my sons.

I typed much the same thing back to her—that I was proud of her accomplishments, her marriage and family—that she was able to realize her childhood dream of living out West. Finally, I told her how glad I was she still wrote.

"I meant what I said back then. You do have a gift... still have it. I've read your poetry on Facebook. You still see the picture in your mind and find the words so others can see it as well. I remember your words. I remember you. I've never forgotten either."

Her response... sweet, sincere.

"Thank you for your words. They mean so much coming from you. Writing is still a wonderful outlet for me. Something I stayed with over the years. A sweet young man once told me I had a gift. I never forgot his words. I never forgot him, either. I hope to see you perform on stage someday, Jake."

I hope to see you perform on stage someday... Now wouldn't that be something?

After all the basic information was typed out and discussed, our conversations took on an entirely different rhythm... a familiar past rhythm. It dissolved those forty years and brought us back to Champaign, conversing with the band members in someone's apartment.

I threw things out on the chat line to test the waters, using my usual dry sense of humor... frequently punctuating the conversation with my two favorite words: *fuck* and *bullshit*. I loved teasing, getting a reaction from her. I loved it back then. I loved it now.

Most nights as we chatted back and forth, I laced my words with subtle sexual innuendos. I was fishing. I wanted to know if Rose still had feelings for me... those feelings... the ones that sparked between us so many years ago.

I teased her about my big tractor. She and I both knew we weren't talking about tractors. I think she knew I was fishing, and only nibbled at the bait on occasion to keep my hopes up of maybe reeling her in.

One night she responded with, *"I no longer ride on farm equipment no matter the size."*

"You don't know what you're missing... and size matters."

"Jake, you are not a nice man."

"You already knew that."

Each time we chatted, the words erased a difficult day, a routine day, just like a smile, a hug, or a kiss on the cheek.

I don't think Beth or the boys wondered or even gave a shit what I did on the computer. After all, I was just dad, a husband, a bus driver and farmer. Who would be chatting me? Who the hell would be interested?

Who the hell, indeed.

Some nights I felt Rose guarded some of her answers—told me things up to a point and then stopped—often changing the subject or signing off for the night. When she paused during chats, I would ask, "Thinking, typing, deleting?" She sometimes answered "Thinking," but many times the answer was "deleting." I wondered what she felt she had to delete... what she couldn't share with me.

I found myself doing the same some nights. I wanted to say things to her, ask her about something, but stopped in mid-sentence— deleted—went in another direction.

Maybe it was time to share the subtle details both of us so carefully left out. I didn't know if Rose would go there with me or not. But I wanted to find out.

"Let's not delete anymore. There shouldn't be anything we can't say to one another... ask one another."

After a pause, she responded.

"Okay."

From then on, nothing was off limits or out of bounds.

It was as though I was back driving the red, Triumph TR-3 convertible down an open road, and saw her in the distance, walking along the side. I stopped, leaned over and opened the door—she remembered me—smiled, climbed in and closed the door. We took a breath and sped down the open road together again, the music playing on the radio, our hair trailing in the wind, her hand resting on my knee.

One evening Rose was telling me about her day at school... with her students, her assistants. I read her words and wondered how connected she really was to those around her. I wondered if that part of her changed. Did she connect or did she still feel alone and isolated at times?

"Do you feel alone in a crowd, Rose?"

Minutes passed without a response.

"Yes."

Bingo.

"I'm familiar with that feeling. I'm surrounded by family and friends every day, but still I feel lonely sometimes, just like you. I don't want you feel alone anymore. Even though we're miles and miles apart. I'm here."

"Tears."

"Take a breath."

"I'm here for you, too, Jake."

"I know."

It was easy to feel alone in a crowd. I didn't understand it as well back then, but I understood it now. Only my brothers and I remained from our close-knit family.

The death of my sister by that drunk driver devastated our family, especially my parents. For them, time stopped the day of her death. Every event that took place afterward was marked from the date Michelle died.

We put a new roof on the house four years after Michelle's accident. We bought the new tractor six years after Michelle was gone. Beth and I were married ten years after Michelle's death.

That's how our family reckoned time from then on. I wondered if all parents marked time in this manner after the loss of a child—or if a husband or wife mourned the loss of a soul mate in the same way. I imagined so.

Fifteen years from Michelle's death, after Beth and I married, Dad died of cancer. Since my brothers didn't farm, and lived away, I took over and did the best I could.

Those first few weeks and months without him were terrible. I felt lost. The man I went to with questions could no longer supply answers.

I was on my own, with only memories to remind me of my father's teachings about farming over the years. The years I swore I would never be a farmer like him. The years I tuned him out because I knew all the answers.

I remember buying seed corn alone for the first time—bringing it home in the truck and stacking it under the lean-to—with the intent of planting it before the day's end.

Spring was rainy and the fields wet that year. Finally a week passed and the rain let up. The fields dried out just enough for a tractor to get in without getting stuck. Time to plant.

I stood with paper and pencil in hand, leaning against the sacks of seed corn—thinking, planning, and writing out exactly how I was going to do everything—when I heard raindrops slowly plink, one by one, against the tin roof.

More rain. Exactly what I didn't need.

Discouraged, depressed, and overwhelmed, I crawled up and sat on top of the bags of seed—elbows propped on my knees, head in my hands—and sobbed. I felt like I was drowning in a mix of tears and raindrops. Drowning in the responsibility left me.

I held my own little pity party.

I wanted to quit. I wanted to sell the farm. I wanted out from under the responsibility.

None of that happened.

It was time for a reality check. I couldn't go back. I couldn't stay in my present state, either. It was time to move on, move forward, with the life lying in front of me.

I looked back on that year, that particular spring, and recognized my stubborn streak could help me to do most anything. I embraced "stubborn" like my dad, who taught a *know-it-all* son everything he needed. I just never realized how deep he'd sown those seeds within me.

A few years after Dad passed—Mother died during routine gall bladder surgery. I remember holding her hand, kissing her cheek, and telling her not to worry, and I would see her in an hour or so. That never happened.

Since then, the word *routine* means something different.

Nothing in this life is routine.

Family holidays look different now than when I was younger and our family was together. Once in a while we all gather here at the farm, but not very often.

Alone in a crowd? Yep, I got it.

Chapter Nine

You once said I had saved you, but the truth is you saved me,
By waking me up from years on end of details and complacency.
You found that girl who once was filled with dreams and desires.
Gave her the strength to strike the match that finally lit the fire.

Rockton, Illinois
Winter/Spring 2007-2008

Rose and I chatted about the weather, bus routes, rowdy kids... about me having cabin fever and stopping by the local pub more often than usual. I told her about Brian and Dustin excelling in basketball. She told me how beautiful it was in New Mexico this time of year and suggested I buy a retirement home there to take advantage of the low interest rates.

"Describe your office, Rose. Need a visual when we chat."

"Okay... I can do that. Decided to convert the back bedroom into my office a year or so ago, mainly for the view. Situated the black, L-shaped desk next to the window and have a beautiful view of the backyard flowers, the pool, and the mountains in the distance. Opposite the desk, is a brown leather loveseat where the dogs sometimes nap. In the opposite corner are two bookshelves, filled with romance novels I've read and collected over the years."

"Nice. What's on your desk... besides your computer?"

"On the corner, next to the window, are four clay pots filled with pink and purple violets. Next to them, an antique pewter desk lamp,

and two old books of poetry I found at garage sales. There's an OfficeMax desk calendar next the computer where I keep appointments, and doodle... a box of Kleenex, and a black plaque with the word IMAGINE printed on it.

"Suits you."

"Oh, almost forgot two things you might remember. I framed my Sgt. Pepper's Lonely Hearts Club Band *and* Abby Road *album covers and hung them opposite my desk, above the loveseat."*

"Yep. I remember listening to them at the apartment."

"Me, too. I think about those times whenever I look across my desk."

"What are you wearing?"

"Jeans and a light-blue T-shirt."

"From now on when we chat, I'll picture you in your office, wearing jeans and a T-shirt, surrounded by things you remember, you love."

Was I still part of those things she remembered, she loved?

Each time we chatted, we talked around our feelings. On that particular night, I couldn't talk around them anymore.

"You saved me, Rose. I have a reason to get up in the morning. Hard to explain."

Well, hell. That slipped right out.

"You don't have to explain. I know. You've done the same for me. Given me hope. Brought color back into my life. I can't wait to get up each day. I never thought I'd feel like this again."

"I get it. Same here."

"I have so much inside me I want to say... things that have been there for so long."

"Okay. Listening."

"I know it's been a long time, but I want to tell you how sorry I am for hurting you. I remember the night you stood outside my bedroom window, so close to tears, apologizing to me for whatever you thought you did. I can't get the picture out of my mind even after all these years. I was so messed up and we were so young. When I said it was me, not you... that was true. I think I was afraid of my feelings for you... afraid of loving you. Something inside me just shut everything down.

All I could think to do was leave... run away. I left you and a life I wanted more than anything. And, if I could take back that night or change those events, I would. I never meant to hurt you. You were the last person I ever wanted to hurt. I'm so sorry, Jake."

I was immediately struck by the fact she thought the break-up was all her fault. She remembered things differently, or didn't remember them at all. I never knew what happened... what went wrong.

"It was a long time ago and we were kids. There's nothing to forgive."

"I know, but I'm still sorry... for hurting you... for causing you pain."

"It's over. In the past. Time to move on."

She obviously didn't know all the facts and, even after all these years, I still didn't either. She thought it was her fault... I thought it was mine. I couldn't undo the past. Neither could she. But maybe we could piece together what happened all those years ago and both find some type of resolution... absolution... for both of us.

I was pretty sure it had something to do with Ricky Wheeler. I wondered if Rose even remembered him. Time to fish.

"Rose, think back. Do you remember anything about those couple of weeks before all that happened... before the break-up? Anything at all? I remember Jerry, Max, and I got a new roommate... Ricky Wheeler? Do you remember anything about him? The little prick stole money from me."

"Ricky Wheeler? I don't think I remember him. He stole money from you? He must have been a real loser. I'll rummage around in my head and see if he's in there hiding. In the meantime, I need to get some sleep or my kiddos will be running my classroom tomorrow."

"Okay. We'll talk tomorrow. Night, Rose."

"Good night, Jake."

Early the next day, before I left for my morning bus run, I checked Facebook messages. There was a message from Rose.

C.L. Gillmore

"I couldn't sleep last night... thoughts and words swirling in my head. I got up and wrote them down. The first poem in a long time not related to school. See what you think."

Wondrous Days

Fingers quieted on the keyboard, her eyes were immediately drawn
To the brilliant blue horizon, heightened by the morning sun.
Sapphire skies etched and framed the rugged, layered mountains
That tower, stretch, and silently soar just beyond her closed front door.
How could she not have noticed these wondrous days before?

Drifting through life's ebbs and flows, somehow she'd gotten lost
To the simple, timeless beauty of the things that had mattered most.
An innocent touch that soothed and urged her lost and damaged soul
With unselfish love he had to know, she'd find her wings and go.
How could she not have noticed these wondrous days before?

Defying time and explanation, her closed front door has opened
To the past, the present, the future where dreams
have the chance to mend.
Dreams that help the heart to heal and allow her soul to soar
By allowing time to temper, to bend and grant her hope again.
How could she not have noticed these wondrous days before?

~ By Rose Allison ~

The poem was about forgiveness, about hopes and dreams, lost and found. It was about feeling alive again. I could relate.

Later, Rose and I chatted.

"Damned if I don't know a poet. Very nice."

"You do. Glad you liked it. Unfortunately, I didn't get much sleep and my kiddos took charge. It wasn't pretty. I lost my glasses after morning circle and didn't find them until nearly lunch time."

"Where were they?"

"On Nique's nose! She wheeled up to the lunch table wearing them."

"Lost control, indeed."

"You have no idea. My assistants will never let me live this down. I see blackmail in my future."

"Understandable. Easy mark."

"Thanks."

"Welcome."

I finished my beer and opened another one.

"I didn't finish what I wanted to tell you last night."

"Still listening."

"Paul doesn't live here much anymore. He has a condo... stays there most of the time. Comes home for family dinners and holiday stuff. We're separated, but never use the word. It's been nearly a year now."

There it was. That explains the absence of Paul in Facebook pictures and comments. He must have something going on besides Rose. Men don't move out to get in touch with themselves, their feelings... they move out to get in touch with someone else. What an idiot.

"So what do your kids think of this arrangement?"

"They haven't really said much. Paul always traveled, so him not being here, except for family dinners and holiday get-togethers, is pretty normal. They're too busy with their lives, their kids, to get involved in ours."

"I'm still parenting, so can't relate. They'd miss my wallet... and the empty beer cans. They'd know I was gone for sure."

"They would."

"So... Paul have extra-curricular activities?"

"I don't know. Maybe. Probably."

"How long?"

"Years, I think."

Years? That's bullshit.

"You don't know, or you know and haven't caught him, or haven't asked?"

"Just suspect and would never ask him. Afraid."

Son-of-a-bitch... afraid?

"Why are you afraid?"

"Afraid of confrontation. Don't want to deal with it. Doesn't matter anymore. Kids are grown and gone."

"Divorce?"

"Probably not. I'm married to a lawyer. He'd figure out a way for it to be my fault and I would end up fucked... so to speak."

I laughed as I read the word *fucked*. She probably hadn't used that word in awhile.

"You're not fucked, Rose. Does he still pay for things?"

"Yes. We kind of split things. The house and vehicles are paid off. So it's just utilities and credit card bills mostly... life insurance. It's okay and I'm still teaching, so I have a paycheck coming in. Have my own money and will have a retirement income. Won't be rich, but will be okay, I think. Have been saving money in an account over the years, too."

"That's good. Smart."

"When I retire at the end of the year, I want to write again. What do you think of that?"

"A good thing. What do you want to write?"

"Not sure. More poetry. More short stories. If I find a good editor, maybe I can sell to magazines or something. Haven't thought it through yet."

"Stop thinking it to death. Write some vampire shit, get rich, and hire your own damn lawyer!"

"LOL! Don't do vampire shit."

"How about a novel? Vampire shit novel?"

"Actually started a romance novel when the kids were little, but never finished it. I'll think about it. But no vampires. You suck!"

"Oh, you have no idea."

"Are we still talking about writing a novel?"

"You are, apparently."

This seemed like a good time to wade into my shit.

"Beth and I are kind of separated, too. Separate bedrooms for nearly 5 years."

"Well, that sucks. What happened?"

"Not sure. I snored. She lost interest... in me, in sex... both, I guess."

"Sounds like menopause. Hormones dry up. Hot flashes start. Sex stops. GPs tell you it's a natural process you'll get through, prescribe Prozac, and send you on your way."

"Sounds about right... the age thing, hot flashes, and no sex. Bingo on the Prozac, too."

"Maybe that's why men have affairs... why they look for younger women. Their wives aren't interested in them anymore... other than to bring home a paycheck and fix things."

"I can relate. I bring home an occasional paycheck and occasionally fix things. Haven't had any affairs though... not yet."

No witty response from Rose after that remark. I continued.

"Is that what happened with you and Paul? You lost interest?"

Fishing expedition.

"No. When that started happening to me, I went to a specialist. Didn't matter much, though. I think Paul always had someone else. I never really knew for sure. Still don't. Just always had my suspicions. It doesn't matter. He probably felt trapped from day one."

Interesting take on things. More fishing.

"Why would he feel trapped? He made the choice to marry you."

There was a very, very long pause on the chat line. Shit. Maybe I should have left my pole on the bank.

"Jake, a lot of things happened after I left you, left Champaign... some good, some not so good. I'm going to give you a Cliff Notes version and maybe we'll talk about it more another time. Okay?"

"Sure. Let's have it."

"I left Champaign and started classes in Indiana. You know all of that. After a semester, I planned to come back over spring break... to see if things had changed... to see if we could work things out. Anyway, my car broke down and I couldn't get back."

"Jesus, Rose. Why didn't you call me?"

"I wanted to. I even dialed your number late one night and let it ring a couple of times before I hung up."

"Shit."

"Don't be mad."

"*Not mad. Just frustrated thinking about the near miss.*"

"*I know. It's hard for me, too.*"

"*So...*"

"*I was lonely, depressed, and turned to a friend for comfort. Something I rarely did. Anyway, he didn't use protection and I didn't notice. Stupid young girl. Two months later I was pregnant. I didn't bother to tell him. No point.*"

"*Son-of-a-bitch.*"

"*Paul and I were friends back then. He sensed something was wrong one night when we were talking. I told him my predicament. He asked me what I wanted to do... what he could do to help.*"

"*Again... why didn't you call me?*"

"*I wasn't thinking clearly and made a decision... alone. I felt I had no other options at the time. I figured you wouldn't want me anymore.*"

"*I would have married you and never asked questions.*"

A very long pause on the chat line. I waited.

"*Jake, I had no way of knowing that. For me the door closed on us when I became pregnant. Emotionally, physically... I knew I wasn't capable of caring for a child. I made the decision, right or wrong, to terminate the pregnancy. Paul made the arrangements and helped me through that difficult time. He was kind and gentle. Never judgmental. For the first time I could remember, someone took care of me. That experience increased the trauma and guilt I already carried from the suicide death of my mother. A few months after that, we married and my life began. I really never looked back. I couldn't.*"

I didn't know what to say. I always wondered what happened. Now I knew. It was almost better not knowing... not knowing how close we came. Two unanswered rings on my phone all those years ago.

I managed the words, "*Jesus. You had a lot on your plate, Rose. I'm glad Paul was kind and gentle to you... that he took care of you.*"

"*Me, too.*" She paused, and began again. "*Do you remember seeing Paul and I a couple of years later—with Cash and Sam—at a restaurant in Champaign?*"

"Yes. I remember. Sam called to let me know you were coming that weekend. That's why I showed up at the restaurant."

"I never knew that. I thought it just coincidence you were there."

"No. Sam and I planned it. She knew I wanted to see you. The meeting didn't exactly go as planned."

"No... I guess not."

"You came to the bar."

"Yes. I remember brushing your shoulder as I sat down next to you I didn't know what to say... but you did, Jake."

"I figured I'd go for broke. I told you I wasn't over you. I couldn't move on. I don't know what I thought would happen. That you'd leave Paul and come back to me, I guess. Instead, you told me I needed to move on... that it was over between us."

"Yes. That's pretty much what I said. I wanted you to move on with your life and stop waiting for me. I wanted you to find someone and be happy. I said that because..."

She stopped in mid-sentence and I filled in the rest with what I wanted to read... *I still loved you.*

I waited.

"You didn't know and I couldn't tell you... but what I wanted more than anything that day... for you to take me in your arms and not let me go. But, instead, I walked away."

"And I let you go."

"Yes. You let me go because of what I said... because of my words."

"Thanks for explaining. Answers questions I've had for a long time."

Another pause. She messaged again.

"Jake, I'm glad you found someone."

"I never found that someone... I just finally had to move on."

No response came from her.

I knew exactly what I wanted to say—the words stayed locked inside me for nearly forty years. Time to let them out.

I typed—held my breath—pushed return.

"I love you, Rose. I loved you then... I love you now... I'll always love you."

Shit. Nothing like going for broke. I waited—and read her words back to me.

"I love you, too, Jake. Never stopped loving you over the years. Just tucked you away in my heart. It was the only way I could move on."

When we closed our chat, the routine salutations changed.

"Night, night, Rose. LU2lls."

"Night, night, Jake. LUJ2lls."

As I typed the words and letters in, watching them appear on the screen—and watched them come back to me—I couldn't keep from grinning at the damn monitor.

The odds of finding the person you loved at twenty something... again at sixty something? Astronomical, probably. But here we were.

Different place. Different time. Same two people.

Together, yet separate. She, in her office, surrounded by the mountains of New Mexico. I, in my office, surrounded by the farmlands of Illinois. It didn't matter where we were on the globe. Not one damn bit. Separately, I continued on with my life and she with hers. Both playing the hands dealt.

We gave each other purpose, without strings, conditions, or timeframe. We loved one another purely for who we were and for what we brought with us. We added another dimension to each other's lives. Together, we renewed a friendship, a love affair we walked away from years ago.

* * * * *

Over the next several months, life went on. I continued to farm, drive bus, and act and direct in productions at the local dinner theater. Our roles as parents continued. Our roles as husband and wife continued. Our friendship continued. Our love continued.

The love and friendship—via chats, texts, and emails—bridged the gap of nearly forty years. Our love affair began again, but this time... much differently.

We figured a way to pick up and go on. We didn't try to define it or put it in a neat little box, or label it... we just went on. Like love affairs throughout time, I think we both realized the words between us might be all we ever shared. Again together, yet separate.

I wondered... would our secrets be so secret if we were in each other's company, or were we open because we felt some private compassion? The secrets contributed to our evolution. We evolved together, apart.

* * * * *

One evening, the familiar exchange between us began with Rose asking about my day.

"How's your day, dear? Puttering down the list again?"

"Good day, actually. And puttering—while piddling, pecking, and drinking—can be productive when you're an expert. How about you? Writing, or straightening canned goods?"

"Working on a poem... in between straightening canned goods and picture frames.

We're pathetic. You do know that, don't you?"

"Yep. Don't give a shit."

"Me either."

Neither of us contended with the day-to-day routine minutia, tedious habits, or established addictions of the other. We brought only the best part to one another. She wasn't a part of that other life with me... and I wasn't a part of hers. These belonged to a life lived with someone else, somewhere else. Our life together was separate... something we'd created in the lingering space between *then* and *now*, and the *what next.*

"What's the poem about?"

"Old friends... memories."

"I like both. Will you write a poem for me sometime... something they can read after I'm gone?"

"Gone where... gone fishing? Gone for beer?"

"Funny girl."

"Loved that movie. Nicky Arnstein and the ruffled shirts."

"I got your ruffled shirts, baby."

"Yes, tractors and ruffled shirts. I have a visual on that."

Familiar banter, comfortable rhythm. Old friends, memories.

"I was going through some boxes in the back of my closet last night and found my old journals. I think they might be a good starting place for my writing."

"Nice. Good idea. Find anything else?"

"I did. I found a couple of things in the bottom of the box. I found the lease Ren and I signed when we moved into Parkridge. I forgot we were both underage. When I looked at the signatures, one was Ren's mom and the other was my sister. Both signatures were forged by Ren and me. OMG! Mr. Cody probably didn't even bother to check. He was just happy to take our money."

"He was a letch. Glad to take your money, and hoping to get in your panties later."

"You're probably right, and Ren and I were too naïve to get it. Know what else I found?"

"What?"

"I found the black leather diary I kept during the two years Ren and I shared the apartment at Parkridge. It's on my desk now, along with the two poetry books. I'd almost forgotten about it. I wrote nearly every day—mostly about Ren and me—then later about you and me. Some of it near the end was hard to read... hard to remember... but most of it was beautiful, sweet. We were so young, so in love back then."

"Yes, all of those."

"I took pictures of a few pages from the diary I thought you might like to see. I'll text them to you."

"Please. I'd like to see them, read them."

Rose sent several pictures to me via texts of entries from the diary. The pages opened discussions, and triggered memories for both of us.

Later, when I was alone, the memories played out on the stage in my mind like a movie.

Journal Entry—December 1968

Jake. I've never felt like this about anyone before. He's cute and funny, kind and gentle. He listens. Each day, more and more, he makes beautiful things happen for me. Having him in my life makes everything beautiful. Tonight, we made love for the first time. He took me to a place I've never been. A place I felt safe and loved and cherished. It's hard for me to understand these feelings... overwhelming to feel so deeply for him or for him to care so deeply for me. My inner voice is afraid. I need to talk to someone, maybe Jake. He tries so hard to understand.

I read those last three sentences over. *My inner voice is afraid. I need to talk to someone, maybe to Jake. He tries so hard to understand*

I remembered the pleading words... *please don't hurt me.*

I had no idea at the time why she said that, and wondered if I'd hurt her in some way without realizing it. Later on, I found the answer.

I closed my eyes and remembered so clearly. Once again, I heard her trembling voice, pleading with me...

"I'm sorry... I'm trying. Oh, Jake, I'm trying. Please don't hurt me."

Warm tears ran down her cheeks.

"Shh... easy, baby. Everything's okay." I interspersed my words with soothing kisses... on her cheek and brow.

Gently, I pulled her into the crook of my arm and rocked her against my body—stroking her head, her hair, with my hand. She nestled into me, resting her head against my shoulder. She suppressed the tears... swallowed the sobs.

I thumbed the tears from her cheeks... and slowly, deliberately—in a deep, steady voice—said, "I would never hurt you, Rose."

I continued stroking her head, brushing my lips over her hair, rocking her in my arms.

A few more minutes passed in silence. I stopped rocking.

I rested my head on hers.

"Did someone hurt you?"

Though directed at her, the question floated into the cool, darkness of the bedroom.

Silence.

I wanted to look into her eyes—to see if I could catch a glimpse of something, anything that might help me know what to do, what to say—but she kept her eyes closed.

"Can you shake your head "yes" or "no?" And then we won't talk about it again... unless you want to."

She waited—thinking about what I said—and slowly nodded once in the affirmative.

"Shit."

The word slipped out quietly under my breath.

The wheels inside my head churned now—searching for the right thing to do, the right words to say—to bring her back, back to me.

I moved my lips to her ear and quietly said, "I love you, Rose."

I brushed my lips over her ear and stroked her arms with my hands, as if to warm her, to comfort her.

"I would never hurt you... ever. That's something that's not in me, has never been a part of me. I wasn't raised that way. And it's hard for me to understand or forgive it in others."

Soft, warm, gentle kisses on her temple, her cheek.

"I don't know what happened, who hurt you. but I think you need to talk to somebody. Somebody you trust."

She turned and looked into my face, directly into my eyes. I wanted her to see all the love I felt for her.

"I trust you, Jake, more than anyone I've ever known. And I'll try. That's all I can promise you. I'll try."

"That's a start. We'll work on this together. I'll be here for you... no matter how long it takes. Okay?"

"Okay."

Then she said the words to me I wondered if I'd ever hear from her.

"I love you too, Jake."

With Rose... I learned the difference between sex and love. Up until then—having sex, balling, fucking, screwing—were all interchangeable man terms for what most women referred to as making love. Simple semantics.

After that—having sex, making love—I knew the difference. I felt the difference. I never forgot the difference.

We made love the first time on her twin bed, intimately exploring one another for the first time, nestled under a cozy red corduroy comforter. The second time we made love on the floor... on top of the red corduroy comforter.

"God, you feel so good, so soft," I told her as I settled my hand over hers and guided it down between us, to the place where my body flowed into hers.

"Touch me. Feel how I move in and out of your body. How slick and wet and warm we both are. Feel how hard you make me."

I don't think either of us ever touched another person so intimately.

Our bodies fit perfectly and moved in sync with one another—my hardness flowing into her softness. Moving in and out of her body created the most wonderful sensations... sensations causing both of us to moan from sheer pleasure.

Making love with Rose felt good... felt right. Whatever she wanted from me... I gave her. I took her wherever she was willing to go. I wanted all of the beautiful feelings, the beautiful happenings between us, to continue. I never wanted it to end.

I loved her, and knew she loved me.

After Rose fell asleep, I rummaged through our scattered clothes on the floor—looking for my smokes—and saw her black notebooks stacked on the floor beside the dresser. I took one, maybe two of the notebooks—along with my cigarettes and lighter—and padded naked into the bathroom, closing the door behind me. I knew it was wrong, an invasion of her privacy, but justified the action under the pretense of wanting to read more poetry.

Right. That was bullshit and I knew it. I wanted to know about her... what made her tick... and if she wouldn't tell me? Well, all bets were off now. I needed information.

I don't remember how long I read. Quite a while. When I finished, I felt like someone hit me in the gut.

Over the past few months, she shared some of the past with me, probably as much as she felt comfortable sharing. Now I realized how little I actually knew.

After reading most of one journal and a bit of another, I understood why she acted so guarded and kept people at a distance—why and how she read people so easily—why she kept all of her coping mechanisms in place.

Each was a safeguard.

Her entire childhood was filled with people she couldn't trust... including her own mother. What became very clear was her reason for not trusting men. The reason for those whispered, haunting words to me... *Please don't hurt me.*

Someone hurt her.

In one of the journals, she wrote a letter to her mother a few months after her death, the suicide. In the letter, she told the truth about Vic—the last stepdad for Rose—her mother's final lover. Reading her words made me sick... made me furious.

She described how late one night, Vic left her mother sleeping on the couch in the living room and came into the bedroom Rose and her mother shared. She awoke in the darkness—panties down below her knees with him straddling her—his huge hand covering her mouth.

"Keep your fucking mouth shut, Rose. Your mother will never believe you over me anyway. She knows what a little bitch you are. It's time you find out what you're missing... but then you're such a little slut, you probably already know."

He took her control away. Made her feel worthless... not to be believed. And then he took her innocence.

She remembered every ugly word he said, and wrote them down verbatim in the notebook... followed by her words... her thoughts.

"I closed my eyes and went far away... until it was safe to come back... until I heard the bedroom door close... until he was gone."

She never used the word rape—probably couldn't say it—but I knew that's exactly what happened. Son-of-a-bitch.

She said in the letter, she never mentioned anything because she didn't think her mother would believe her... would assume it was her fault and not his. Exactly the words he said to Rose as he held her down.

All of this was in the letter in the notebook. A notebook no one would ever read other than Rose... and now me.

I remembered thinking to myself... *Jesus. Has anyone touched her since? Has she let anyone get close enough, or was I the first?*

I felt a weight of responsibility like I'd never felt before and from then on, Rose lived in my head, in my heart.

* * * * *

The next night, Beth and I had dinner and drinks at the Eagle's Club, and watched a double win by the boys' basketball teams at the high school. We drove home and went our separate ways. She went to bed. I waited up for the boys while chatting Rose on Facebook. I easily worked her into my routine.

"Did you get a chance to read any of the pages I sent you?"

"Yep. Read the entry about our first night. Sweet."

"Yes, very. You made it special. I never forgot."

Rose typed, and I read her memories on the chat line. Our memories were the same... up to a point... the point where she asked me not to hurt her. She never mentioned that in the journal entry.

Interesting. Was it an intentional omission or something else, something she blocked out?

"That's pretty much how I remember it, too," I said.

There was a pause in the chat.

"I was young, inexperienced with men, and you picked up on that. I know in my heart that's why I never forgot you. You were patient and kind and gentle with me."

Another pause.

"I'm thankful to this day that with all the men in my mother's life—the stepdads and boyfriends—none of them ever took advantage of my sister or me. It could have been much worse for both of us."

Damn. I was right. She blocked out that bastard and what he did as if it never happened. In her mind, she wrote her way out of it, an alternative twist, a happy ending to the story.

Son-of-a-bitch. I hated that bastard all over again.

She carried that baggage and I wondered how much more. Had no one in her life over the past forty years helped her unpack? No one ever suggested she talk with someone... get help? Where the hell was her husband?

Then I answered my own questions.

Of course not. She never changed.

No one really knew her—she never let them know her—not even Paul. Probably not even her kids. And since no one knew her, no one knew she needed help, and no one reached out.

Now I knew. I knew she was still alone in the crowd. I knew she still needed help.

We needed to talk, and this time it would be different. This time I would do what I said. I would *reach out and be there*.

I would help her finally unpack.

Chapter Ten

The shadowed streaks of twilight slip silently away
And tuck behind the mountains to mark another day.
Now leaving just the night sounds to whisper and remind
Of magical trips and trusted friends, lost and left behind.

Rockton, Illinois
Winter/Spring 2007-2008

The next night, Ben and I sipped beer and watched Drake beat the shit out of Illinois State on the new big screen TV at Will's—now officially known as Will's Sports Bar and Grill.

After nearly forty years, Rockton now had an Arby's, Walmart, Subway, Food and Spirits, and its own sports bar and grill. Progress, baby, progress.

A text swooshed in from Rose.

I discreetly turned from Ben, read the text from Rose and replied.

"Home? FB?"

"Pub. FB later."

"K"

"Beth checking up on you?" Ben asked.

Geez, if he only knew. Not happening.

"Nope. Beth knows where I am. Pretty hard to hide in this town."

"That's true enough. I noticed you're pretty good at that texting shit. Must get a lot of practice... with the boys, I guess."

Fishing. Ben was fishing. He'd have to troll alone. I ignored his comments and moved the conversation along.

"Think I'll finish this beer and head home. Not much point in watching the end of this sorry ass game."

"Well, I think I'll have one more and finish the abuse. Later, buddy."

"Yep, later."

I got home and grabbed a beer, pulled up Facebook chat, and found Rose waiting.

"Good evening."

"Hello, my friend. Good day? Looked warm there."

"Yep... nice day, but wind was a bitch. This time of year the sun is getting some strength so, hopefully, the snow won't be on the ground long... the days lengthen/the cold strengthens."

"Well, aren't you Mr. Almanac? LOL! May I quote you?"

"Please, feel free to quote at will. I meant to tell you before we signed off last night you weren't the only one finding shit from Parkridge days."

"Oh? What did you find?"

"Was doing my weekly reshuffling of shit in the basement... to get away... when I came across an Eisner's grocery box. Remember that store?"

"Yes, I remember you and Jerry shoplifted there. What was in the box?"

"We were starving."

"You were not starving. You were thieves. What was in the damn box?"

"All my drug paraphernalia... the dark blue glass hookah, hash pipes, roach clips, Zig-Zags."

"OMG! Did you try to snort it, light it, lick it?"

"Close. Still smelled and tasted exactly like the day I packed it away. Guess what was at the bottom of the box?"

"What?"

"A red, burlap rose."

"OMG! That's the rose you gave me... the one I carried around and dipped in the fountain the night Sam and I tripped. How did you get it?"

"No clue. Then, last night, I read the diary text you sent about that night. Geez. Talk about a flashback."

"I know. I flashed back, too, when I read it. Good thing you were there. I would have freaked. Another first for us."

"Yep..."

"Would you ever blow dope or trip again?"

"Yep, planning on it when I retire. Won't have to take the random drug tests."

"I'd love to smoke again with you. Wouldn't be the same with someone else. Don't think I could ever trip again. Too heavy for me now. Would freak. Think we'll ever get the chance?"

"I don't know. Maybe. Nice to think about though."

"It is. Keep the rose for me. Maybe someday you can give it back... okay?"

"Okay. Will do."

I thought about the other rose I had from back then... the one she knew nothing about. Maybe someday I would find the chance to show her.

I figured, about now, we'd started thinking similar thoughts... seeing each other, being together again. And then what? Still no clue. No plan.

I knew Beth and I were still parenting two sons who weren't quite launched. They remained my priority... my commitment... no matter what.

I wasn't sure about Rose... her priorities or her commitments.

As much as I wanted things to be different, I couldn't change the timing and our current circumstances. I couldn't go there, and didn't want to take her there either, but that's exactly what I was doing.

I should care... but I didn't. I didn't want the contact to stop, and some days I felt like a selfish prick for it. The kind of selfish prick I drilled into my sons not to be to anyone they cared about it... they loved.

So... do as I say, not as I do. Great role model.

* * * * *

Weekends were busy. Sometimes Rose and I didn't have time for much more than a *good morning* or a quick *good night*. We understood that. We led separate lives. The time factor for us differed from others'. We didn't confine what we shared to a time schedule like most people use as a reference for the days, weeks, and months. Time happened for us when we communicated through texts, Facebook messages, or emails. Phone calls still remained complicated for me and, so far, we hadn't figured them out.

Saturday afternoon—in between a morning bus run with the show choir and supper with Beth's sister and brother-in-law—I stretched out for a quick nap. It was my first chance to read a text Rose sent earlier while I was driving.

"Morning. Beautiful here. Walking dogs. Hoping to avoid death by falling space junk. Maybe text/chat later. Be safe. LU2lls"

I smiled at the space junk comment. A few days earlier, we saw a post on Facebook about the odds of being struck and killed by falling space junk, which now littered the atmosphere above the earth. She joked about being an easy target while walking the dogs on the desert trail near her home. I said I was at greater risk while driving the fields on my huge tractor. I got back an *"LOL... get over yourself!"*

"Hey, Dad." Brian stepped into my bedroom. "I'm thinking about spending the weekend in Champaign with friends. You okay with that?"

"Yep. I'm okay with that. What did your mother say?"

"Not good with it."

"I'll talk to her. No drinking or texting while driving... whoever you're with... got it?"

"Got it. Thanks."

"Welcome. Drive careful. Use your head. Keep your phone close and expect contact."

"Okay. Will do. Be home Sunday night."

"I'll count on it. Close the door on your way out."

Brian would turn nineteen this summer—Dustin, seventeen. I remember thinking what a man I was at that age. I had all the answers. Now, when I looked at Brian and Dustin at the same age, I only saw kids with no clue. Parenting changes your perspective.

I saw them as my dad probably saw me. What goes around comes around, indeed. Time. What a leveler.

I pulled out my phone and brought up Rose's diary texts. Usually, I deleted as soon as I read—Rose did the same—but the diary pages were different. I saved every one of them.

Each time I read an entry—saw my name or that of a friend in print from nearly forty years ago—it was as though my life was validated. I was young once. I was there in a time both remarkable and turbulent. A time that changed me... changed an entire generation... changed America forever.

Journal Entry—Spring 1970

Things are scary here in Champaign since the killing of the students at Kent State. The demonstrations stepped up on campus and the National Guard mobilized again after the ROTC lounge was fire bombed a couple of weeks ago. Protests against the war happen nearly every day now. Ren and I called in sick at work so we could join the protesters on campus. Jake, Jerry, Max and Cash are going... not sure who else. I keep thinking about what Chuck told us a few months back after his Uncle Bill, a high-ranking Army dude, stopped by to see him. As he was leaving, Chuck asked him when he thought we would get out of Nam. He answered, "Chuck, we can get out of there any time, but they are making so much money."

It made us all sick hearing those words but we knew they were true War makes money. I thought about Ben. How much money was his life worth? I'm scared about being on campus, but I want my voice heard for Ben.

* * * * *

That afternoon I napped and drifted in and out of memories from those turbulent days and weeks following Kent State. Now there was a real cluster fuck.

On the afternoon of Monday, May 4th, 1970 at twelve twenty-four on the campus of Kent State University in Kent, Ohio, seventy-seven national guardsmen fired sixty-seven rounds over a period of thirteen seconds, killing four students and wounding nine others.

The dead included Allison Krause, nineteen... nearly the same age as my son Brian; Jeffrey Miller, twenty; William Schroeder, twenty and Sandra Scheuer, twenty-one... the same age as Rose and Jerry back then.

Children. This was the day America killed her children: for asking questions and expecting answers, for demanding accountability, for exercising their right to free speech in asking why.

All of us were caught up in the student demonstrations and protests that spread to college campuses across the United States. Swept along by the winds of social change... the winds of a new freedom.

It was as though it happened yesterday...

I remembered the crowd on the U of I campus steadily growing that afternoon until it became one entity with its own purpose and energy... serious and specific in the cause... contemplative as we waited together. Waiting for what, we didn't know. We only knew the comfort in being together... comfort in our numbers.

The mood was somber. No one exchanged smiles that day.

Earlier in the week, random acts of violence and vandalism broke out in the local business district. Protestors hurled rocks, bricks and cinder blocks, and shattered every window of Follett's Book Store. They also vandalized other stores, set fires, and spray-painted anti-war slogans on buildings and signs.

It didn't matter *who* was responsible—student demonstrators or outside agitators—the students were blamed and labeled as "bums"—a term President Nixon saddled all of us with after Kent State.

I held Rose's hand and pulled her close as the eight of us huddled behind bushes and buildings near the Quad, along with four- or five-hundred other students. We watched as the state police rolled up Green Street—squad car windows rolled down, rifles visible—helmeted officers beating billy clubs against the sides of the patrol cars. Officers barked out instructions with bullhorns... telling us to clear out or be arrested. Some left, but most stayed. We stayed.

Intimidating. Frightening. Surrealistic.

City buses lined up in front of the Quad... buses that became mobile jails for those later arrested and transported to Memorial Stadium for processing.

Helicopters hovered above as the National Guard arrived in full riot gear carrying M-1 rifles.

The Guard or County Deputy Sheriff's officers surrounded the Quad on all four sides. Again, an officer blurted instructions from a bullhorn ordering the crowd to disperse or be arrested.

He said, if arrested, we would carry criminal records for the rest of our lives. We would not be able to hold public office, or pursue careers connected with law or law enforcement.

Intimidation.

A few more demonstrators left, but the majority stayed. We stayed.

After about five minutes... all hell broke loose as police and National Guard herded us into a smaller and smaller area within the Quad. I looked into Rose's face and saw the fear... and wondered if she saw mine.

I pulled her close, kissed her cheek, and whispered, "We'll be okay. Stay close."

But the truth was, I didn't know if we would be okay or not.

She didn't answer... just seemed kind of dazed. I squeezed her hand.

Screaming and yelling students were shoved and pushed to the ground by officers and guardsman. A student a few feet away from us was clubbed in the back of the head, and blood spurted everywhere. I pulled Rose into my chest so she couldn't see.

Just as we turned to change our position... a tall, hulking state trooper grabbed the back of my shirt and jerked me around to face him. He raised the billy club in his hand above me. Rose scrambled out of the way, and I instinctively dropped to the ground, shielding my face with my arms and hands. I waited for the club to hit... and hoped Rose was with Cash or Jerry.

I peered up at the trooper, through my arms, and saw his raised hand holding the club. He released his grip on my collar, looked into my face and said in a calm, low voice, "I won't hurt you, son. My boy's in Vietnam... wouldn't want anything to happen to him either. I'm just doing my job."

I lowered my arms and sat there on the grass, amid the chaos, looking up at the trooper. Stunned. Evidently he raised the hand with the billy club to scratch his head, not to club me.

Unreal.

He held his hand out. I grabbed hold, and he pulled me up and we walked side-by-side toward the buses. We'd walked only a few feet when I felt Rose's hand slip back into mine. The deputy escorted both of us to an awaiting bus. We climbed the steps, sat down together, and watched as they systematically filled each bus with student demonstrators... including Cash, Max, Chuck, and Ren.

They transported all of us to Memorial Stadium, where we sat for two hours on the concrete floor discussing the day's events until released.

Jerry and Zach managed to slip through the crowd, climb the fire escape at the back of Davenport Hall, and enter through an unlocked window. They watched the events unfold from the third floor, and later walked to Jerry's car on Mathews Street. They waited for us outside Memorial Stadium in the gold Barracuda.

No one filed charges against any student that day, and all were released either the same day or the next.

I don't remember the deputy's name or what he looked like, but I will always remember him calling me... *son.*

* * * * *

Sunday morning I woke up to the smell of coffee drifting up the stairway from the kitchen. A programmable coffee pot—what an invention—ranks right up there with the remote control.

I checked the cell phone and retrieved a text from Rose.

"Big Sunday dinner with both kids' families today & Paul. Will text/chat later. Sent you a poem on FB. This one's for you. LU2lls."

168

Cool. A poem for me.

I thought about her... about me. I did a lot of thinking.

Wonder if we would have made it, if things had been different? Somehow she didn't seem cut out to be a farmer's wife, then or now. Yet, I probably wouldn't have been a farmer. I pictured us out west somewhere, in Arizona or California, or maybe even New Mexico. I think I might have found more opportunities for a lot of things out west rather than in the Midwest.

I stumbled into the bathroom. Took care of morning business, washed my face, wet my hands, and finger-combed my hair. Close enough for government work.

Jesus.

I looked at myself in the mirror. Some mornings I found it harder to look than others. Today, well... Too many beers last night and not nearly enough sleep. After a certain age, there was no such thing as "catch up" sleep. Dark circles ringed my eyes, which glared back, glassy, and bloodshot. I knew what I looked like and I wasn't going there this morning.

Jesus.

I had some wild-ass hair going on, too... in every direction but down. The longer it got, the more gray. Hell, if I was going to smoke and trip... might as well look the part. Let's just say Tom Selleck and I wouldn't be mistaken for twins this morning. Then again, I could give him a run for his money with the mustache. Yep, me and Tom... bro's all the way. Right.

I let the dogs out, poured a cup of coffee, and sat down at the computer. Quiet house. Either everyone was gone, or no one was up... or perhaps I died in the night. Didn't matter. Quiet house.

I typed in my password and pulled up my Facebook messages.

"Just for you. 2lls."

Listen, Look, and Remember

Weep not, cry not, do not grieve for me—my soul at last runs free.
My immortal spirit, unbound soul, forever young will be.

Scattered, wind-blown ashes now faded and unseen
Gently dance across well-worn paths and mark where I have been.
Imprints faintly left in place, that help recall to heart and mind
A lifetime of hopes, dreams, and clutter now stilled and left behind.

Listen for me on those quiet early mornings as waves lap and fall
Upon the shores, while a hawk glides and soars gracefully over all.
Look for me in the whispered glow of a sultry summer night
As the waning light of a brilliant sunset fades quietly out of sight.
Remember me as winter's laced, gray fingers secret away the sun
And sprinkle icy snowflakes on an eager, outstretched tongue.

As ageless winds gently sweep the passing of time and season,
You'll feel my touch upon your face and know beyond all reason
That every life, yours and mine, becomes a unique, entwined endeavor.
Leaving precious memories as eternal reminders
that life goes on forever.

Weep not, cry not, do not grieve for me—my soul at last runs free.
My immortal spirit, unbound soul, forever young will be.

~ Rose Allison ~

I read through the poem and replied in my usual wordy fashion.
"Oh, my."
Later, we chatted on Facebook.
"Good evening."
"Oh, my? Does that mean you liked the poem?"
"Very much."
"Glad."

"Snowflakes on an out-stretched tongue. Geez, made me tear up. Reminded me of my brothers, my sister... a long time ago. A good memory... very personal to me... a good poem to read when I pass. Thank you."

"You're welcome. Not planning to pass any time soon, are you?"

"Nope. Shit happens, though."

There was a pause in the chat, before Rose continued.

"I've pictured the lake in my mind so many times. I hope we get the chance to be there together someday."

If she only knew all the times I'd kept her close to me at the lake. Maybe that's why she pictured it so clearly... why it was so familiar to her... so easy to write the words.

I finished a beer and opened another one. My words poured out as easily as the liquid slid down my throat. Good or bad. That's how a lot of these conversations happened.

"Me, too. I've thought about spending time there with you... of holding you in my arms and whispering all the love words to you I've typed out in chats and texts over the months. I've fantasized dancing with you... making love to you under the moonlight. But most of all, I've dreamed of us being there together."

"I dream of that every night... of being together again. I always felt I knew you... that we were kindred spirits. It helps my heart to know you dream about the same things I do, Jake."

"I've always liked the term kindred spirits and felt that with you early on. I've never felt it with anyone else."

I thought about the power of written words between two people in love when words were all they could share. It reminded me of lovers in the past.

"I'm going to wax poetic... ready?"

"Please do... right up my alley. Never been poetically waxed by a farmer."

"You'll like it. Trust me."

"I do trust you, Jake."

"I thought about how powerful the words between us are... in our chats and texts... loving, passionate, erotic messages that keep us close."

"Yes. We never would have connected without the texts or chats... without the words between us."

"We're like distant lovers of the past who wrote and sent paper letters—filled with their love, passion, and devotion, year after year—often never meeting or sharing a physical relationship. Yet devoted and in love with one another. Sometimes families found a packet of letters, bundled together and tied with ribbons, after their deaths. It was the only tangible proof of love, of relationship, or the power of the written word. It reminds me of the love affair—the shared words—between John Keats and Fanny Brawne. May I share a part of a letter John wrote to Fanny in 1819?"

"Please."

"My sweet Fanny, will your heart never change? My love, will it? My Creed is Love and you are its only tenet - You have ravish'd me away by a Power I cannot resist: and yet I could resist till I saw you; and even since I have seen you I have endeavoured often 'to reason against the reasons of my Love.' I can do that no more - the pain would be too great - My Love is selfish - I cannot breathe without you. Yours for ever, John Keats"

"Oh, my... you had me at 'hello.' Thank you for sharing."

"Welcome. You still make me smile, Rose."

We paused in the chat. That usually allowed one of us to think a little deeper.

"Sometimes it's as if you search inside my head, my heart, Jake, until you discover something I've kept hidden away... a secret."

"You can trust me with your secrets."

"I know. You can trust me with yours. In time you'll know this secret... just not now, not yet."

"Okay. I'll wait."

"There seemed to be so much time...once upon a time. I never thought about dying, about death, but I do now. Do you, Jake?

"Yep, on occasion. I think it must have been that space junk article."

"You're never serious for very long, huh?"

"Nope. No point. You need to start wearing a helmet when you walk the dogs."

"Okay... will look for a purple one."

"Have a visual on that... sexy."

"Only you would think a purple helmet sexy."

The chat line fell quiet. Must be thinking again.

"Seriously, Jake... if something happened to you or me, how would we know? Who would tell us?"

"There isn't anyone who knows about us... no one we can share this with. You know that."

"I know. I guess we would find out about it on Facebook or maybe read about it online in our local news."

"Yep. That would be my guess."

The prospect of either of us finding out about the death of the other that way was more than I could think about. Neither she nor I had any one to share our heartbreak. We would mourn the other's passing alone, both enduring in silence.

Both of us knew at some point in time this would become reality. Reality sucked sometimes. It really sucked.

* * * * *

One evening, we discussed the diary pages again. I shared my campus riot memories with her from Saturday's nap and she responded

"My memories are different from yours. I remember the motion of the crowd of students and feeling closed in, like I was trapped. I couldn't breathe and had this feeling of dread or fear in the pit of my stomach. I felt dizzy, off balance, almost trippy. It was as if the whole scenario was an out-of-body experience—something I watched from above—that played out before me like a newsreel or movie. Holding your hand, feeling you next to me, was the only thing that kept me together. Kind of like the night I tripped. You were my reality in the middle of a delusion. I don't remember the incident with the state trooper, or being arrested and loaded onto the buses. I remember Jerry and Zach picking us up in front of Memorial Stadium. I barely remembered any of that until reading your messages tonight. Kind of scary. Like I blocked all of it out."

Shit. Here was the perfect opportunity to bring up another blocked out time in her life... but I didn't. I needed to bide my time until I felt she was ready to go there with me. I would know when the time was right. I would feel it.

* * * * *

The bitter cold days and nights eased a bit. The lake began to thaw.

Like distant lovers of the past... our words continued on... we continued on. Sharing friendship, intimacy and love—from the most mundane topics to our most private secrets—using only our words.

"Wassup?"

"Nothing much here. One of my little students stuck a bean up his nose today. I had to call the nurse for an extraction."

"Messy. Where'd he get the bean?"

"We were counting with them during Math."

"Ahh. Moved right from addition to subtraction, huh?"

"Yes. Exactly. If Carlos has 5 beans and sticks one up his nose... how many beans does he have left?"

"Way to think on your feet."

"It's a gift."

"It is. I wanted to say it's SNOT funny, but I didn't."

"Thanks. Glad you held back."

"Welcome."

"How was your day?"

How was *my day*? Well, lets see... my shitty day started off with a flat tire on the bus in the mud, followed by a verbal battle at lunch with Beth over Brian's new girlfriend. The day ended with a puking dog under the supper table—all distant memories once Rose and I began chatting.

I pictured her at home in the office, in jeans and T-shirt, sitting at the desk by the window, typing words to me and reading my responses on her computer. All I wanted was to pop some corn, curl up next to her on the loveseat, and listen to the Beatles. I wanted to be close to her. I wanted to see her smile. I wanted to hear her voice.

How was my day?

"*Perfect. I had a great day.*"

"*Good to know.*"

"*Have you had a chance to look through any of your notebooks yet... read anything?*"

"*Kind of... skimmed through most of them... read a little. I noticed pages torn out of some of those earlier notebooks. Strange. I don't remember tearing pages out. Don't know who else might have torn pages out.*"

Shit. Pages torn out? What the hell?

"*Can't help you there, Rose.*"

Soon, though. Very soon... I'm going to help you.

"*A little unsettling... not remembering things. I did read through the diary again about the rock fest. Remember? I texted that page to you, didn't I?*"

"*Yep. Downloaded them from my phone and saved all the pages in an email folder awhile back.*"

"*I don't remember a lot of that weekend... just flashes. How about you?*"

"*The same... flashes... but then I'm sure I was drunk, tripping, and stoned the entire weekend. I was hung over and without sleep for thirty-six hours when I drove home. What the hell were you thinking... riding with me?*"

"*I was judgment impaired and probably stoned... maybe a little tipsy from wine, too. I don't think I tripped that weekend though.*"

"*No, I don't think you tripped again after the acid episode with Sam... maybe once on mescaline with me... but not that weekend.*"

"*What do you remember about the weekend, Jake?*"

"*I remember it was the end of August... unbearably hot. And you were hot. Tight bell-bottoms, a skimpy, little halter-top with no bra, and sandals. You had woven beads and ribbons through your long, blonde hair, and it spilled over your shoulders and down your back. Jesus... you were hot.*"

"*Pretty good for not remembering anything but flashes. I remember how sexy you looked with no shirt and those tight bell-bottoms and sandals. Your hair windblown and free. You were so fine.*"

"Yep... we were a couple of hotties back then."

I pictured Rose. God. She made me hard back then and had the same affect on me now... 1,346 miles away... but then who counted miles?

"I remember driving there. Every time your arm touched mine, or your leg brushed against me... I wanted to pull the car off the road and make love to you. Being that close and not touching was awful."

"Well, why didn't you?"

"I should have. I realize that now."

She didn't remember. I knew she didn't. Just like she didn't remember going back to the apartment alone after the demonstrations and the arrests. Damn. How much had she blocked out?

"I don't remember much about the weekend. Don't remember eating, sleeping or peeing... any of that. I remember the constant reverberation of the music and looking across a sea of undulating bodies, faces... and finding you in that crowd... looking back at me. You were beautiful... tan and... arms raised above your head, body moving rhythmically to the music. You were mesmerizing. I loved you, Jake. I loved you so very much."

Jesus. It was hard to read those words. I would have given anything to hear them back then, but instead, she stayed silent, distant from me. Yep, should have made love to her and married her that weekend. Things would have been different for both of us.

"I wish things could be different, Jake. I wish we could go back and change things... have a do over, you know? Just one time out, one 'kings-x'... a do-over."

"I know. But we can't. We can never go back. All we can do is move on."

What did move on mean? How could we move on?

"When I think about moving on... I want to see you... be with you again. I try not to think about it, but I can't stop it. Some days that's all I think about. Maybe I shouldn't tell you this, Jake."

"You should... I think about you, too. Scares the shit out of me some of the things I think about."

"I know. It scares the shit out of me, too. I never meant for this to happen. Never planned it, never gave it a thought when I sent the Friend request."

"I know. It just happened."

We said our good nights, deleted our conversation and logged off Facebook... and the texts began.

I never thought two people could make love with words alone, but I was wrong.

Some nights I wondered what the hell happened to that practical man... the one who insisted on living in the real world... the one who'd moved on. I knew no one on God's green earth would understand this. It defied logical explanation. Only those who lived it would understand—to others it would seem flat-ass crazy—maybe even perverted. Well, fuck them.

I thought about all the words in the scripts of plays I'd acted in, the movies I watched, and the books I read over the years. The written word was powerful... especially when the words were all you had.

We shared only words. No physical contact, so far, not even the whisper of a voice... only the words inside our heads, our minds, as we read one another. I was an actor and she was a writer, so we knew about fantasy. We knew about imagination. We knew how to pretend.

So, our thoughts and fantasies inspired the words for the script our imaginations performed on the stages of our minds. Without boundaries or limits, the thoughts, fantasies, and words reached places much deeper than anything physical.

Several days later, I came home from my morning run and checked email and Facebook. I didn't much care about the emails anymore, unless it was a bill needing to be paid, but I did care very much about the messages.

I pulled up the message from Rose and found another poem waiting. No explanation... just the poem.

Beautiful Bell-Bottomed Boy

Shirtless, bronzed, bell-bottomed boy,
Beautiful, young, and lean.
Soft, silken coffee-brown hair,
Wind-swept, wild, and free.

Graceful, fluid, outstretched arms,
Expressive, gentle hands.
Lovely, curved, sensuous hips,
Legs strong, slender and tan.

Rocked by the gods of music and freedom,
Swaying in rhythmic jubilation.
High on life and love's sweet passion,
He danced for her in celebration.

One girl alone was hypnotized,
In the midst of a thousand faces.
Her eyes linked to his piercing blue eyes,
And put her own feet in his paces.

Gone are the days of the young summer sultan,
And the girl who watched him with joy.
He dances forever within her heart,
Beautiful bell-bottomed boy.

~ Rose Allison ~

She wrote about the one thing she remembered from that weekend. And what she remembered was me.

I read the poem, and read it again... repeating the last two lines... *He dances forever within her heart, beautiful bell-bottomed boy.*

I was the beautiful bell-bottomed boy she remembered that weekend so long ago... better than I remembered myself. She closed her eyes and saw me... the way I looked back then... at my best, in my prime. She captured that moment in words... for herself, for me, for whoever read the poem. No matter how old I got or after I was gone... I would forever be the beautiful bell-bottomed boy in the poem.

How many men had poems written for them... about them... by a woman who loved them? Not many I suspect. Not many at all.

No matter what became of Rose or me or of the relationship... now there were words to mark our passing... our space and place in time. Much like the words in Rose's diary... they validated us both.

Once we lived. Once we were here. Once we were young and in love. For one moment in time, we found a place to be together in one another's hearts.

Chapter Eleven

A story recalled...rhyming words spin.
Texted chats ebb and flow.
Kindred spirits coupled again.
From once upon a time ago.

Rockton, Illinois
Spring/Summer 2008

I drove down by the lake after the morning bus run and pulled the truck next to the shelter house, facing the dock. With the ice finally melted, the water stretched out smooth as glass... blue sky and slowly drifting white clouds reflected on the surface. Two pair of Northern Shovelers, aka Smiling Mallards, paddled near the shore.

I rolled the window down. The temperature only reached the forties, but today felt like spring... smelled like spring. The sun shone with a toasty warmth. Planting time.

Past winters seemed longer, colder, than I remembered. But this one was different, the days not as long, the cold not as bitter. I knew the reason. *An old man in love is a flower in winter*—Carl Sandberg, American Lit 101 class.

Yep. Carl knew. New love at my age was rare... precious.

I slid the seat back, unzipped my sweatshirt, closed my eyes, and napped—in the sunshine—like an old dog.

I woke up several minutes later—don't know how long I napped—didn't matter. I checked my cell phone. Forgot a text Rose sent earlier during my drive.

"Out of shower, heading for hair, make-up, and wardrobe. Program at 10. Wish us luck!"

I texted back, *"Luck."*

Rose wrote a program for the special needs students at her school a few weeks back and today was show time. Over the years, she'd written many programs, but this one would be the last.

Hair, make-up and wardrobe—a term coined years back by theater friends we watched perform, and later partied with—was now a daily, self-motivating routine. I understood that all too well.

Another text. Beth this time.

"Pick up Rx and drop off $20 to Dustin at school. Thx."

"K."

I took a deep breath, rolled up the window, adjusted my seat and blinked back to reality.

Crazy. While a farmer in Illinois napped in his truck—a teacher in New Mexico directed a school program—1,346 miles apart, yet so close.

Only the two knew, or cared.

Later, the farmer and the teacher chatted about the day, about lost years, addictions, and finally shared a conversation forty years overdue

"Good eve."

"Hey, you."

"How'd the program go?"

"Great! Kids were super and no one did anything inappropriate. Well, Charlie, from Mrs. Grassle's class, stepped forward during the curtain call and exclaimed rather loudly, 'Thank you, Jesus! Praise the Lord!' and took a bow."

"Nice touch."

"I thought so. I think it had something to do with him standing next to me before the program when I whispered, 'Dear Jesus, help us all.'"

"Well, there you go. Good listening skills on his part."

"Yes. We had the bases covered in the 'help' department. Oh, and I met an editor today—Kathryn Harmon.

"How did you know she was an editor?"

"She had that editor look."

"Editor look?"

"Yes. The NOT teacher look. No Kleenex or drool or snot anywhere on her person. Not dressed for crawling on the floor, running or hurdling obstacles to retrieve stray students. Pretty, petite, and thin. Probably never lets Doritos or Twinkies cross her lips. Really nice, thick, shoulder-length, silvery gray hair. Would kill for her hair."

"Nice description. You'd kill for hair? Geez. Did you happen to get her number? Think she'd go for flannel, or maybe a tractor ride?"

"No, I did not get her number... but I have yours... flannel Tractor Boy."

"Yep, you do."

"She took pictures for a magazine article she's writing, and we talked briefly after the program. She asked me about the script—how long I'd been writing—and wanted to know if I wrote other things. I told her I wrote mostly short stories and poetry. She said she'd like to read more and asked me to send her some samples of my work"

"Good deal."

"I attached a couple of poems and a short story with the 'thank you' email. Who knows? Throwing it out into the Universe."

"Hey, I say, go for it."

"Me, too."

"Thought about you when I was napping at the lake this morning."

"Nice place to think about me."

"Lake is thawed. Spring is here. Time for fishing and copious amounts of alcohol."

"What about farmer things? You know—plowing, planting—driving your big tractor around?"

"Farmer things begin this week. Will be busy, busy soon... working ground, getting ready to plant."

"Good to hear you can work the farmer things in with the fishing and copious amounts of alcohol."

"Practice, practice..."

There was a pause in the conversation. Better check.

"What doin'?"

"Thinking."

"About?"

"So... been drinking a long time then, huh? Wondered about that."

Yep. I was right. Wondered how long she'd been mulling that over. No point in lying.

"What's a long time? Like forever? Then, yes."

"I guess that is a long time then. I thought about you the other night... about those years in between... after I left and before you got married."

"What about?"

"I wondered what happened. More years I don't know anything about. I guess it doesn't matter now. I just wondered."

"Lots of pot... some acid. Heroin once... made me sick. Cocaine twice—never saw the excitement—compared to hallucinogens."

"Oh, geez, Jake... glad you didn't get hooked on heroin or coke... but drinking a lot, huh?"

"Yep. Dodged a couple of huge bullets there. Didn't drink much in Champaign... more after I got back to Rockton and started tending bar. That's where I met Beth. You know, the much older, experienced bartender meets the much younger, naive waitress."

No point in telling her about my exceptionally lost years after we broke up. The drug and alcohol use increased proportionately to the distance and time between us. The drugs tapered off, and finally stopped with Brian's birth. The alcohol never stopped, just tapered a bit. Mostly beer now.

Rose was my reason—my excuse—for escape. Not her fault. Mine. I made the choice.

"I can see how that might happen."

"Jerry and I used to sit around the coffee table and do shots of tequila, then smoke a bunch of pot so we could go downtown and stay high all night. Only have to buy one or two beers that way."

"You and Jerry, huh? Was there anyone, a girl, you were involved with then?"

"Yeah, but the girl wasn't a smoker, not into anything. A pretty straight arrow. She fell in love with me when I ordered milk with my Henry's burgers. Thought I was healthy, I guess."

"Serious about her?"

"Kinda. Didn't have much in common though."

"Broke her heart, huh? Ever see her? Hear from her?"

"No, no, and no. Guess she moved on. Don't think I was as healthy as she thought."

"No, I guess not. It's hard to make people understand who they see on the outside is not always who you are on the inside."

"Nope."

"Sometimes life looks perfect from the outside... but reality isn't always the once-a-year Christmas newsletter."

"Nope, it isn't."

"Just life, I guess."

"Yep. I suspect."

This retro conversation seemed like a good starting place to plow into Rose's memories or lack thereof. I wasn't sure how far to go—how hard to push—but I had to try. No one else could do it, only me.

"Rose, do you remember when we chatted about the student protests and rock fest... how we had different memories?"

"Yes. Not sure why they were different."

"I know. Do you remember going back to the apartment after the demonstrations? Was I with you?"

"I don't remember. Ren and Jerry were there. You must have been. We were practically living together then."

"What about the rock fest? Do you remember being with me... doing anything with me... other than riding in the car?"

"No. I just remembered watching you dance from a distance. I don't remember anything else. We must have slept together, made love. You'd think I'd remember that."

I typed the next words carefully—read them over—held my breath and pressed return.

"Rose, you don't remember being with me because we weren't a couple then... not during the demonstrations... not during the rock fest. We were just friends then... not lovers."

"What do you mean we weren't a couple... that we were just friends? Of course we were."

"Do you recall when we split?"

"I don't know exactly... but it was after that."

"No. It was before... months before. I recall we were a couple for a year or so. Then we split. We were together, but not lovers that spring or summer. Not lovers during the protests... not lovers at Wadena. That's why I said I should have made love to you then. That maybe things would have been different."

No response.

I knew this would be hard, but there was no going back now.

"Do you remember me asking you about Ricky Wheeler—the roommate that moved in with Max and Jerry and me—the little prick that stole money? Think back, Rose."

Still no response. Shit. Maybe this wasn't such a great idea after all

"Still there?"

I waited—five minutes—ten minutes. Finally, a response. Her words floated onto my screen.

"Oh, God. Oh, God. I remember."

Son-of-a-bitch. Here we go. Ready or not.

"Take a breath. I'm right here. What do you remember?"

"You came over to the apartment with Ricky one night late, after work. It must have been on a Friday because Ren was gone, back in Macomb with the baby for the weekend. Just you, Ricky, and me. You sat there and didn't say a word. Ricky did all the talking. He said all of you got stoned and drunk, and screwed this girl at your apartment the night before. He said I shouldn't blame you... it wasn't your fault. I couldn't believe you would do that to me, Jake. I didn't understand... couldn't handle another betrayal, another loss. I loved you. I trusted you."

Her typing stopped for a moment, then resumed.

"I always thought my feelings for you just stopped, turned off like a faucet because we were getting too serious. Now I know it was because you cheated on me. You lied to me."

Another pause in the typing before she continued.

"After we broke up, I remember not really giving a shit about anything... my friendships, the apartment, my plans... our plans. I just wanted to leave all the pain behind and move away. I was used to moving away, used to leaving things behind, used to detaching from my surroundings. That's when I decided to go back to school somewhere other than Champaign."

I felt like I'd been kicked in the gut.

"Rose, that wasn't me with Ricky. He either came over with someone else, or he was alone. Do you think I would sit there and say nothing while he lied? That doesn't make sense. Think about it."

"It was you."

"No. It wasn't me. I wasn't there."

"But why would I think that? Why would I remember you being with him that night?"

"I don't know, but I suspect Ricky came up with that story to cover his ass, to get back at me. Little prick. Jerry and I confronted him about the money and told him to pack up his shit and get out. I was at the apartment the night that girl showed up only because I was sick. Otherwise, I would have been with you, at your apartment."

A few minutes passed in silence, and then her words began.

"Yes. You called me the night before and said you were sick and couldn't come over, and were going to the infirmary the next day. I do remember that."

"That's right. I was sick. I think I tested positive for mono. I heard them with her in the other room, but I wasn't with her. I was never with anyone else when we were a couple. I never cheated on you, Rose."

"There's an entry in the diary about you having mono. BRB."

"Okay."

A few minutes later Rose responded with the long-ago written words from her diary.

"March 1969—Jake thinks he has mono. He called to tell me he wasn't coming over tonight. Shit... maybe I have mono, too. I don't care if I get sick. I miss him. I love him so much I ache inside."

"I never caught mono from you, Jake."

"No. We weren't together anymore. I never really knew what happened. I tried calling you, and you wouldn't answer, wouldn't talk to me. I came over late one night, stood on the patio and threw rocks at your bedroom window to get your attention."

"Oh, God. I remember. You wanted to talk things over. Wanted to know what you'd done. You were crying. Asked me what was wrong, what happened. I wouldn't listen, didn't want to talk to you or see you."

"Oh, Jesus. So forty-three years later I find out I broke up with you because of a lie. I wouldn't let you explain? Oh, Jesus, Jake."

I couldn't say anything. I sat there staring into the computer screen How could this happen? Why didn't I make her listen? Why did I give up so easily and let her walk out of my life?

I messaged back.

"Who knows, maybe I would have screwed her if I hadn't been sick I was twenty."

"No you wouldn't. You're just saying that now. That's not who you were back then, and I knew that down deep inside. The years have hardened you and changed your outlook on things, but you weren't that way then. You weren't raised that way. That's why I trusted you... why I fell in love with you. Now I know I was right about that, about the kind of person you were. God, I'm sorry, Jake... so sorry for what I did to both of us. It wasn't your fault. I know now it was mine, and mine alone."

"Life happens. It wasn't anyone's fault... not mine, not yours. If it was anyone's, it was that lying little prick's fault... Ricky Wheeler. That's probably why I still hate the bastard after all this time."

"I changed the course of both our lives because I believed a liar— someone I barely knew—instead of you. I shut my feelings off and ran away. The two things I knew how to do best. I need you to forgive me, Jake. Please say you forgive me."

"It was a long time ago. We were kids. There's nothing to forgive now."

"Please. I need to read it. I need to see it."

"I forgive you."

"Thank you. This is hard for me."

"I know it is, Rose. But better to know the truth than keep a lie buried or suppressed. Until tonight, I had no idea what happened. At least we know the truth now. We know what happened. This is how you move on, how you heal."

I waited. I knew she needed time to let all this new information settle. A few minutes later, another message.

"Why do I remember you being there when you weren't?"

"Don't know. I can only play armchair psychologist."

"Please play."

"Okay, but it's gonna' cost you five cents."

"Seems only fair, considering."

I thought about what she remembered, what I already knew, and began to type my theory out on the chat line.

"I think part of you was scared about how serious things were getting between us. Part of you wanted to bail. I think you intentionally put me in the room. Your subconscious putting me there, made me aware of what happened, and gave you an out. You saw no reason to talk to me or hear my side because, in your mind, I knew everything. You avoided confrontation. I think that's why, when you remember the night, I was in the background and didn't say anything. I was there in your mind, but not actually there in body. Make any sense?"

"Maybe. Yes. Why would my mind do that? I loved you. I don't remember wanting out of the relationship. I was thinking marriage."

"I don't know. Maybe something inside your mind tried to protect you, give you an out, an escape."

Damn. She was thinking marriage? This is messed up.

"I was thinking marriage, too. Was going to ask you to marry me that winter weekend we drove home to Rockton... find a justice of the peace. I planned to do the same thing the weekend of the rock fest. Lost my nerve both times. Afraid you'd say no. I was a procrastinator... still am."

"I had no idea. You never said anything, never let on you wanted to marry me."

"I know. But maybe some part of you picked up on what I couldn't say, and that part of you talked the rest into running away."

There was another pause. I waited.

"As crazy as that sounds, you might be right. Do you think this happened before or since? Is there something wrong with me? Do you think I am crazy?"

"No, I don't think you're crazy, but I think you went through enough trauma as a child that your mind started protecting you. Maybe you're not even aware of it."

"Okay. Can I ask you something?"

"Certainly. Not all questions have answers though."

"I know." She paused, then asked, *"Do you talk to yourself?"*

"Yep. I think everyone does. It's part of the thinking, reasoning process maybe. Not sure."

"Do you hear voices? Do voices talk to you in your head? Talk back to you?"

"Have to think about that. Maybe."

"Jake, I've heard a voice inside my head since I was a child. I don't just talk to myself. I talk to a voice. I hear the voice inside my head and she talks back. It's like there're two of us. I am crazy, aren't I?"

Shit. We just tested out of Armchair Psychology 101 and moved into Advanced Psychotherapy Shit 680. I now wondered if I heard voices and if they talked back to me. Time to pass this football off.

"You're not crazy. Don't think that shit. But maybe you need to talk to someone... someone who actually knows something about this stuff. My only real expertise is corn, tractors, and bullshit."

"I've thought about it. Just never made a decision to actually do anything. Hard for me."

"I know. Sucks being a grown-up. Sometimes you have to do hard things."

"Yes, it sucks and it's scary too. Really scary. Maybe that's why I've never grown up."

"Well, at least you have an excuse. I'll be here for you as much as I can be. But you have to take that first step."

"I know. Maybe I can now. Thank you for being there... for not thinking I'm crazy... for plowing through this with me."

"Welcome. I do know a thing or two about plowing."

"You do.

The clock struck one a.m.

Any further words or solutions dried up... or floated away on too many beers. So, instead, I typed, *"Late. We both need sleep."*

"I know, but it's hard for me to let go of you... to let you drift away into the night."

"I'm never far away. Night night. LU2lls."

"Night night. LUJ2lls."

Alone in my twin bed, surrounded by moon and stars wallpaper, I dreamed something so real, as if she was with me and I with her. An experience more than a dream.

It was late in the day and I was tired, worn out. I walked into a large room and saw Rose sitting in a big, overstuffed chair, watching... waiting for me. I came over, sat down on the floor next to her, and rested my head in her lap. She stroked my hair with her hand, over and over, sometimes running her hand up the back of my neck. Her touch comforted, soothed. I moved closer and wrapped my arms around her. Her body felt soft and warm beneath me.

She stroked my head, and whispered, "My sweet, sweet baby."

Others in the room didn't seem to notice us. No one spoke. I heard a woman crying.

Rose and I looked at one another, searching for answers neither of us had. The clock continued to tick along and our time ran short.

I wanted to take her somewhere private... somewhere we could be alone. I wanted to love her again, but we saw no place to go. I took her hand and pulled her up.

We walked out of the room and onto a porch. A young boy there spoke with Rose, asking her things about life, about love.

I knew the boy, remembered him, but he didn't know me.

* * * * *

A few weeks later, Ben and I sat at Will's one evening, drinking beer and trading lies. Well, I was drinking... and Ben, fishing, again.

I finished my beer, glanced over at him, and checked for texts. Nothing. He watched my cell phone disappear into my pocket.

190

" So... you seem to get a lot of texts. I hardly get any, but then, I don't send any."

"Well, there you go... that probably explains it."

Would he let this pass? I wondered. Maybe a subject change would do the trick.

"Thinking about fishing at the lake tomorrow. You up for that?"

"Maybe." He paused. "'J' gets lots of texts... but he's looking for a new woman, so I guess he's got a reason."

Not going to let it pass. I'll try deflection.

"Good that he's looking. Means he might get married and move out. Just you and the little woman then."

I raised my eyebrows up and down a couple times in Ben's direction.

He grinned. "That would be nice. Hard to play slap and tickle with your grandkids around twenty-four/seven... you know, like little Klingons?"

"No shit. Kind of cuts down on the spontaneity, I'd guess. You need Scotty to beam them up and away."

"Yep. I'll tell her you referred to her as 'the little woman.' She'll love that!"

"I'm sure."

The cell phone vibrated in my pocket. Bingo. I discreetly read the message.

"Good meeting. FB later?"

I texted my reply. *"Yep. Pubbing."*

I slid the phone back in my jacket pocket and met Ben's eyes... again. Oh, shit. Here it comes.

"We've been friends a long time. Shared a lot of things over the years... good and bad."

"Indeed we have."

I sipped my beer and looked straight ahead.

Ben looked away and talked to the bar space in front of him.

"I know things aren't the same with you and Beth. Women visit... you know how that goes down. None of my business. But if you ever want to talk... you know, about anything... it would be between you and me."

Time to go.

I finished the beer in two huge gulps, set the bottle down, and looked Ben squarely on.

"I'll keep that in mind. Headed home for now. Let me know about the fishing."

"Will do. Headed home myself soon. G'night, Jake."

"Night, buddy."

I started the truck and stared out the window into the night... thinking about what he said. Geez. If he only knew how much I wanted to share this with him sometimes... but I couldn't. Whatever Rose and I had going must stay between us. Hell, the "whatever" we were having was an affair. It didn't matter that we hadn't touched one another physically... we touched one another emotionally, intimately... daily. I didn't see that setting well with Ben's right-wing Christian, Bible-belt ethics. Nope. This was private, a secret between Rose and me. For now, that's how we needed to play it out.

I wondered why Rose never asked more about Ben. Why she never asked about Ren or Jack. Why she never connected the dots.

Maybe I should have said something early on, but that's not how this relationship between Rose and I evolved. For the most part, I let her bring things up first. That way I knew exactly where I needed to take the conversation.

I knew she and I didn't remember things the same, and some things she didn't remember at all. She and Ren acted like best friends, but with Rose, you never knew. Ren went home nearly every weekend to Macomb, even after she brought Jack to stay at the apartment. I suspect Ren lived another life on the weekends. And Ben was in Vietnam.

Rose spent her weekends with me, with the band, and with Sam. She and Sam grew close, and they must have stayed in touch for a while. Otherwise, how would Sam know Rose and Paul were coming to visit the weekend I confronted her in the restaurant? Maybe that's why Rose asked about Sam in that second Facebook message, not Ren. Who knows why someone does or doesn't do something? My guess is, eventually, she lost touch with everyone. Probably, she'd also take some time to reconnect with everyone, as well.

I turned the truck lights on, shifted into drive, and followed the back roads home.

* * * * *

Later that evening we chatted on Facebook.

"How'd the editor meeting go? Fancy office? Snacks and wine?"

"Good meeting. No, we met at a bakery and discussed everything over coffee and bagels."

"Sounds Jewish."

"Catholic, actually. I had a feeling she related to me, to my writing because she might be in a similar situation."

"You mean with a rekindled romance or something?"

"Maybe... not sure what... just a feeling."

"Well, there's probably a lot of that going on."

"Yes, I'm sure there is. She suggested I try my hand at writing a novel."

"Good idea. Think that came up in conversation before."

"Yes, I think it did. Still don't know anything about writing novels."

"Write about what you know. Think of it as a really long play, a really long poem."

"That's what Kathryn said. Write, write, write... and let her edit."

"Well, there you go."

"In the meantime, she's going to edit and help me publish a book of poetry and short stories. Kind of hard to believe."

"Why?"

"Too fast... haven't paid my dues or sung the blues."

"Trust me... you've done plenty of both over the years. Write. I have faith in you."

"Thanks. Makes me feel like I can do this... be a writer, an author."

"Absolutely."

"Oh."

"What?"

"*Kathryn's friend, Molly Roberts joined us later. Tall, pretty and blonde, in her forties—liked my poetry, easy to talk to.*"
"*Another editor?*"
"*No—a therapist.*"
"*No way.*"
"*Yes, way. Has a degree in Marriage, Family, and Child Counseling.*"
 "*And?*"
"*I figure she was placed in my path for a reason, so I'm going to make an appointment with her.*"
"*Good girl. Any other fortuitous happenings?*"
"*I love when you use big words. Actually, I had a prodigious dream about you the other night.*"
"*Prodigious... huge, sizable, immense, enormous? Had to be about me. Send, please.*"
"*Prodigious... extraordinary, phenomenal, remarkable, amazing. Obviously, about me. Will send later.*"

We typed our good nights and I shut down the computer. In the silent, moonlit office, I finished my beer and thought about Rose, Kathryn, Molly... and dreams. Sometimes shit happens in the universe you can't explain.

* * * * *

After finishing the morning route the next day, I brought up my email and found a poem and Rose's dream waiting for me.

Common Bond

The shadowed streaks of twilight slip silently away
And tuck behind the mountains to mark another day.
Now leaving just the night sounds to whisper and remind
Of magical trips and trusted friends, lost and left behind.

A Friend Request

To a time when only dreams had the power to transcend
And bring us together, beyond the unrest, one by one as friends.
Kindred souls, sharing a moment, bound by love and freedom.
Moved by the words and music... we danced to a different drum.

Those days and nights are forever etched deep within my heart.
I see their faces, hear their voices, though so many years apart.
Their love and friendship, counsel and humor, are a part of what I say.
And nudge me now so gently with thoughts I write each day.

I wish I would have realized those many years ago
Our moment was just an instant in the lives we were to know.
I could have brushed a farewell kiss as I gazed into each face.
But one by one, we left not knowing we had shared our last embrace.

~ Rose Allison ~

A time never to come again—Parkridge Apartments, the band, the music, the drugs, the intensity of finding and losing a first love—resurfaced in the words of the poem.

The poem told of a time of freedom with few limitations, when belief in yourself—your talents and abilities—fueled your dreams. You never gave a thought to not being able to do something. Life hadn't filled you with doubt or negativity yet. That gig belonged to a past generation's philosophy... your parent's.

Back then, you answered to no one besides yourself or your friends You were free to simply *be*—to share your thoughts, your dreams, your beliefs, and your disillusions about the times—and listen to the music that pricked your imagination and pierced your soul.

It allowed you freedom to experience and suffer through that first intense, passionate love affair. The one leaving the indelible imprint on your heart and your soul. The one lingering through decades of space and time. The one sometimes arriving intact on the other side of life's continuum.

All that... delivered through the words of the poem.

Finally... I read the words of the dream... a dream feeling all too familiar.

Jake, this dream seemed real. I felt so close to you, like I was touching you, hearing your voice. Not sure any of it will make sense, but I wanted to share it. I love you all over again. How could this happen twice? LUJ2lls.

The dream:

I was inside a farmhouse. Someplace I'd been, but couldn't quite remember. It wasn't here in New Mexico. It was far away.

I sat in a big chair. You came to me and put your head on my lap, as if for comfort, like a child comes to a parent.

You seemed tired, overwhelmed, as if you didn't care what was going on around us. You rested your head in my lap and I stroked your head and face... like a sweet baby. We both apparently needed to feel the other close.

After a short time, several people came into the room. Everyone and everything seemed drab, colorless. The room dimly lit. The mood, subdued. People filed in and sat in chairs arranged in a semi-circle. You and I were off to the side, away from them in the big chair, maybe a chaise lounge. You continued to sit on the floor and rest your head in my lap.

I remember feeling nervous at first. Afraid the people would see us—wouldn't like me being there—and you would be in trouble. We could see them and I think they could see us, but there was no interaction. They didn't speak, but most smiled.

I found it odd, their smiling.

Paul walked into the room and looked at us, but didn't react. Like he saw us, but it didn't matter... and he walked back out of the room. He didn't stay with the rest of the people, and I sensed he didn't know them. He felt like he didn't belong there.

I felt so close to you. Like you were real. I could sense your presence. I felt the texture of your hair beneath my fingertips as I stroked your head, the softness of the skin on your flushed cheeks. You looked so tired, with dark circles under your eyes. I felt the weight of your head in my lap. I swear it was real.

You seemed sad, yet filled with love. There was no way for you to express it other than to lay your head on my lap and wrap your arms around my hips, my waist, and hold me. I felt your hands and fingers tighten and draw me closer.

You looked up at me and our eyes met, as if we were both searching for some sort of answer.

I asked, "Where's Beth?"

You answered, "She's crying."

After awhile, we got up and walked into another room, an enclosed porch, or maybe a barn. You held my hand as we walked and stayed close to me, touching me, brushing against me.

A young boy waited in that other room. I knew him, recognized him but you didn't seem to know him. I let go of your hand and walked over to the boy. He took my hand and started asking me questions about love.

"How do you know it's love? What is love? How does it feel?"

I replied, "You know when it's love. You can feel love. I feel love."

The young boy said, "But sometimes it doesn't always happen."

And then I heard you say from a distance to the young boy, "It can happen. It is love."

You took my hand and we walked away, outside, I think. You wanted to take me somewhere, but couldn't figure out where to go, what to do. We felt an urgency to be alone. You wanted to love me. You knew I wanted you to love me again. We needed a place. We needed time.

I kept wondering how we were doing this—how we were together—how we were in this place without texting or chatting. Somehow we communicated with one another and appeared there together.

I worried about how I could contact you again if I needed you to be close.

I experienced it as much more than a dream.

How the hell could I explain that? Like she read my mind, stepped into my dream, walked around inside my head.

Kindred souls, kindred spirits? No other explanation. None.

Chapter Twelve

If someone would have told me just how quickly life slides by
I might have chosen differently, giving other paths a try.
But life is born of endless details, and dreams just simply die
A painless and unnoticed death... no time to mourn or cry.

Rockton, Illinois
Summer/Fall 2008

Summer months seem to pass more quickly than any other time of year. Maybe because summer on a farm is flat-ass busy from dawn 'til dusk. I woke up tired and came in at the end of the day with my ass dragging. I showered, and went to the pub most nights for a few beers... to relax, to unwind, to think... or try not to.

I remembered Dad saying some people shower in the morning to greet their peers, others shower at night to wash the dirt of the day away, whatever the dirt might be. He was right about that. But then, he was right about a lot of things. Just took me awhile to realize it.

I leaned against the shower stall, and let the hot, soapy water spill over my head and cascade down my tired, aching body. The steam floated toward the ceiling as all the dirt of the day spiraled down the drain.

My thoughts turned to Rose. I pictured her standing in the shower... hot, soapy water trailing down her soft, naked body... trickling over her breasts, her stomach, her hips, between her legs. Just the thought made me hard... something that happened less and less.

My libido, like the years, fleeting now. I could easily see how once passionate couples changed to platonic friends.

Use it or lose it... a truism for sure. That *time* thing again... over the years it slowly chipped away layer after layer of the person I used to be. Soon that person would be gone... would become just another distant memory... like the summer.

* * * * *

Brian left for college, while Dustin officially reached his senior year. He planned to graduate early at the end of first semester. The corn and soybeans, finally in the rearview mirror. Beth changed jobs and seemed happier. I began rehearsal for another play at the dinner theater. We continued our responsible marriage.

Rose retired from teaching and began writing full time. With Kathryn's help, she published her first book of poetry and short stories. As part of the ongoing therapy with Molly, she began writing her thoughts and memories, dreams and fantasies... in a novel. She and Paul continued their unofficial separation.

With each passing day—the desire and longing to be together—intensified between Rose and I.

One late night after returning from Will's... Rose and I chatted.

"Wassup?"

"Tired eyes. I've been writing most of the day... working on that really long poem. You know... the novel?"

"Ah, yes. How's the novel business?"

"Pretty good. Trying not to think... just releasing the thoughts... letting the words flow. Like Molly said."

"Surrender. Make no excuses or apologies. Take no prisoners."

"Pretty much, Jake. I have to let go, and stop being afraid... of myself, of others... of what I might find, or of what they might think."

"Let go of some childhood baggage?"

"Yes. Unpacking a little at a time. Seeing what's there—what I can live with, and what needs to be discarded. Writing it out helps me see things more clearly. I do this through the characters... using both

fantasy and reality. I let them discover the dreams, the nightmares. Some days it's a real mess inside that novel."

"I'm sure."

"So, what's the storyline, Rose?"

"It's about two ordinary people who meet on Facebook and rekindle a romance after years of being apart. That meeting sets everything in motion."

"Oh, geez. Sounds vaguely familiar."

"Yes. I thought it might. But it actually happens to people every day, not just you and me. I researched it. Besides... surrender, let go, stop being afraid. Remember?"

"Yep. I do. What else?"

"I've written about childhood memories, about people who walked in and out of my life over the years—family, friends, teachers, the band—and you. The characters, the memories, some are real, some imagined. It's hard to tell the difference. But the more I write, the clearer it becomes for me. Some of the people, the experiences, are like an out of focus lens slowly coming into focus. Not everything is clear. Lots of things are still fuzzy. Does that make sense?"

"Yes, it makes sense to me."

"That's good to know. I'm glad you're there, Jake."

"I'm here... just a text, a chat, away."

The messages stopped for a few moments. I sent another one.

"Don't stop fantasizing though, or dreaming. I've always loved that in you, Rose."

"I won't. That's what I do best. In fact, the female lead fantasizes about becoming a published romance writer and making lots of money."

"Nice."

"Yes, I thought so."

"Killed anybody off? Authors have been known to kill people off in their books."

"Not yet, but real close. I may kill off the husband or the mistress or both before the end of the book."

"Seems appropriate."

"Who knows? I may kill off a lead character before I'm finished with the story."

"Geez. Which one... male or female?"

"Don't know. I wouldn't tell you anyway... spoil the ending."

"I guess it's not a good idea to piss the author off."

"No, probably not."

"I'll keep that in mind, Rose."

"Think I'll get the band back together."

"Might as well. They're probably not doing anything."

"Probably not."

"I'm constantly thinking of ways to bring our love-struck, time-traveling, Facebook lovers back together. Any ideas on that?"

"Maybe they get together at a reunion thingy with the band?"

"That's good, Jake... that might work... a perfect scenario."

"Tell me more about your two lead characters. I think I recognize them."

"You might. Both characters are flawed."

"Well, of course they are. Normal people are boring."

"Exactly. No one wants to read a novel about normal people."

"Nope. Please continue about characters."

"One lives in a fantasy, the other lives in denial."

"Perfect couple to ride off into the sunset together. More, please."

I knew where Rose lived. That left me living in denial. I had a feeling this conversation was about to get *real* real.

"Okay, you asked."

"I did."

"The female lead has unresolved childhood issues. She has obsessive-compulsive disorder, hears and talks to a voice inside her head, and suffers detachment syndrome. It's as if she's spent her life as a passenger in her body, rather than the driver. She can easily maintain an online relationship, but might find it difficult to connect in real time, in person. She lives and writes somewhere in the gap between reality and fantasy, waiting for Prince Charming and the 'happily ever after' ending she read about as a child. Did I mention, she's in therapy?"

"No, but that's a good thing."

"Yes. It means there's still hope for her... for Prince Charming... for the happy ending... for all of it."

"I like that. What about the guy? Prince Charming, right?"

"Yes. Years of disappointment and loss have taken their toll on Prince Charming. He spent most of his life in crisis mode, and never fully realized his potential. Somewhere along the way, he stopped believing in hopes and dreams, and forgot about love and passion. Over the years, he numbed the pain with drugs, alcohol, and complacency. After the rekindled romance began, he catches a glimpse of what might have been, and sees a glimmer of future hope."

I took a deep breath, exhaled slowly, and typed.

"Jesus. Surrender and take no prisoners, I guess. No point in walking around the elephant in the room anymore."

"No. No point."

I took another deep breath and continued the chat. What else could I do?

"So, an escape for both of them, huh?"

"Pretty much."

"Does she blame herself for his drinking, for what happened all those years ago?"

"Yes... sometimes."

"Well, for what it's worth, Prince Charming is responsible for his own actions. In the end, it's his choice. There's no one else to blame. She needs to understand this so she can get her shit together. Let him deal with his own shit."

"Maybe she does understand, and wonders if he'll ever get his shit together."

"Trust me, Rose, he either will or he won't. She can't do it for him. What she can do for him is focus on healing herself."

"That's good to know, Jake. I'll tuck that away for future reference."

The messages stopped. Probably both rereading and thinking about that last exchange. It was good she and I could talk to one another. There were no secrets between us. Well, none she was aware of yet.

I tried lightening the mood.

"Happy ending?"

"You know I believe in happy endings. Besides, it's not a true romance novel unless it has a happy ending."

"Well, hell. That settles it. We need a happy ending for Prince Charming and his Princess."

"Yes, we do. I could use some help figuring that out."

"Okay. Will give it some thought."

Another pause. She messaged back.

"How do you like walking around in my fantasy world, Jake?"

"Nice place to visit. Don't think I could live there, though."

"Why is that? Haven't you ever wanted something so badly you dreamed about it—put your heart and soul into making it happen—and it happened?"

I read what she typed, thought it over, and answered.

"Nope."

"Never?"

"Nope."

"Think back when you were young. Did you dream of me walking back into your life... dream of me loving you again?"

Shit. I dreamed both scenarios for years. Finally one day, I gave up the fantasy— the dream—and moved on.

I typed back.

"Yep, I dreamed about both. Been so long ago, I forgot."

"Welcome to fantasyland... the place where dreams come true. Never give up your dreams, Jake. Wait for them... just wait for them."

How practical and reasonable I was when this first began. Maybe she was right, and happy endings were still possible. Maybe I just needed to think outside the box, way outside the box in fantasyland, where Rose lived.

* * * * *

One evening a few weeks later, I found myself alone again, sipping a beer, and listening to "The Long and Winding Road" by Lennon and McCartney playing softly on Pandora.

I pulled up Rose's Facebook page and looked at the new book cover... *Seasons of Rhyme and Reason.*

As a child, she dreamed of living in the West. As an adult, she dreamed of becoming an author and writing a book. Tonight, the small-town girl from Illinois would share her stories and poems, and sign her book, with the Mountain View Road Runners Book Club. Proof dreams come true... with perseverance, creativity, and a little luck thrown in for good measure.

I thought to myself... *you've come a long way down the road, baby... a long way, indeed.*

A text from Rose.

"Almost show time. Nervous. Excited. Hope I don't throw up."

"Hope you don't either. Pen won't write on soggy book pages."

"Thanks. I knew I could count on your support."

"Proud of you. You're one strong woman."

"I am. Thanks. Wish me luck."

"Don't need luck. You have a gift, remember?"

"Yes, I remember."

"Text later."

"Will do."

With the two-hour time difference, it was well after midnight when Rose texted back. I was in bed, and barely heard the text come in.

"Hey... still awake?"

"Kind of. How'd it go?"

"Great, once I got over the urge to vomit."

"Good thing. Sell a lot of books?"

"Define, a lot."

"More than 5?"

"Yep, 11! Pretty good, huh?"

"Indeed."

"Not even a fraction of the printing costs, LOL!"

"People have no idea, do they?"

"None. Think of it as a really expensive hobby and you'll feel better about yourself."

"Thanks. I feel better already. Late. Sweet dreams."

"U2. Night night, Rose. LU2lls."
Night night, Jake. LUJ2lls.

* * * * *

The next night, we continued the conversation on Facebook chat.

"Wassup? In your office, or in bed with the laptop? What wearing? Need lots of visuals tonight. Very needy."

"Well, that's because you're a needy guy."

"Guilty."

"I'm lying in my king-size bed, with three feather pillows behind me, laptop resting on a pillow across my bare thighs."

"Bare thighs? Naked chatting?"

"No, are you? Wearing my blue and orange Illinois State T-shirt and blue knit boxers."

"Not naked. Don't know exactly when Beth is coming home. Would be hard pressed to explain sitting in front of the computer, naked, drinking a beer. On second thought, ... maybe not."

"That's exactly what I was thinking. What wearing?"

"Wife-beater T-shirt, cut-offs, and sandals. Commando. Hot out today."

"Oh, my. Now I have a visual and would like to see that up close and personal sometime."

"Me, too... on the T-shirt and boxers. Commando?"

"No. What's new on the farm report?"

"Mm. Here's the farm report. Brian wants to transfer out of state after this semester. Beth's pissed. Dustin sprained his ankle at last night's game and is on crutches for two weeks. Beth's pissed. The dogs rolled in something dead then napped in my recliner. I'm pissed."

"All that happened since we chatted last?"

"Yep, the boring life of a farmer. Oh, and the female lead at the dinner theater has strep throat."

"Geez. Hope you're practicing safe sex during the clutch scenes."

"Funny. No clutch scenes, and all I do is practice."

"You know what they say about practice?"

"Yep, and I'm damn near close to perfection."

"Smiling."

"Me, too. Forgot something in the farm report. Ben's son and grandkids moved out. J's living with a gal he met at a school board meeting a few months ago... widow with two kids."

"Ah, she's the result of all the texting he did before?"

"Bingo!"

"I'll bet Ben's house is a happy place."

"Understatement. Smile on his face since the moving van pulled out."

"I'm sure."

"Wassup with you?"

"Well, my life is boring in comparison. Might as well say good night."

"Doubtful. Tell me more about the book thingy? Didn't sell enough copies to pay for printing or to move to Tahiti?"

"The book thingy was very fun. Felt like an actual author, reading excerpts from my book, and writing cool stuff to those who bought copies. And that would be a 'no' on printing costs and Tahiti."

"Glad it was fun and you didn't puke on anyone. Too bad about Tahiti. Have a visual of you naked under a palm tree—both of us sipping fruity umbrella drinks—while you read poetry to me, and I rub suntan oil all over your naked body."

"You said naked twice."

"That's because I think about you naked twice as much as I think about anything else."

"Figures. You're such a shallow guy."

"Ben's accused me of being shallow, too. It must be true."

"Must be."

The conversation stopped, and then another message came from Rose.

"Whenever you mention Ben... I can't help but think of Karen, of Ren. I've wondered about her over the years. We lost track of one another after Jack got sick and they moved back home to Macomb. She's not on Facebook... I've checked off and on. But neither is Ben."

Shit. I knew it was just a matter of time before my friendship with Ben churned up memories and questions about Karen. Actually, I was surprised she'd never made the connection between Ben and his son—his stepson—Jack. I guess it was time to help her fill in a few more puzzle pieces.

"No, Ben likes his privacy and can barely manage texting. What are your last memories of Ren, of Jack?"

"Everything went well the first few months after Jack moved in with us. The sitter was close, reasonable, and good with him. Ren and I earned raises at work. She continued writing Ben, though he wrote less frequently. We both pictured him as her Prince Charming... and a great future daddy for Jack. But all that changed. First, there was the letter from Ben. He suggested she date other guys, and asked for his ring back. She tried hiding her disappointment, but his words left her heartbroken. A few days later she mailed his class ring back home to Rockton in care of his parents."

"Yep. Ben wrote me... told me about the letter. He said things were bad in Vietnam. None of us knew how bad. But that's why he wanted Ren to date around, why he asked for his ring back. He didn't want her left behind, grieving for him, if something happened. He loved her. Writing that letter wasn't easy."

"Oh, poor Ben. It all makes sense now. It didn't back then."

"No, a lot of things didn't make sense back then, but they do now."

"Shortly after the letter, Jack got sick. Do you remember? We took him into emergency. I think you and Jerry went with us, maybe Cash and Sam, too."

"I do remember. Jerry drove. Cash and Sam met us at the hospital. Ren's family drove from Macomb. We sat there most of the night while they ran tests on him. Found a heart murmur, a valve problem. Something congenital."

"Yes. No one had any idea. He seemed so healthy. The doctors told Ren he needed surgery—probably more than one—and that's when she left Parkridge and moved back to Macomb. Too much for a young mother to face alone. She needed her family around her."

The messages stopped. I figured Rose and I'd both drifted back to Parkridge days. After a few minutes, I typed another message.

"Still there?"

"Yes... thinking... remembering."

"Yep... me, too."

"I waited with Ren and her family during the first surgery. It was rough, but Jack came through it. It was during this time... in the shuffle of surgeries, moving, and new roommates... we lost track of one another. A few months later, I left."

"We all left eventually, and most of us lost track of one another, except for Ben and me."

"I'm glad you and Ben are still close. I wonder if he and Ren ever got together after he came home from Vietnam, or if he's heard from her. You should know, Jake."

"I do know. I've been waiting for you to ask. Would you like to know the rest of the story?"

"Yes, Jake... very much."

"Ben returned from Vietnam in winter, 1971. Jerry and I picked him up at the bus depot. He stayed with us awhile before heading home to Rockton and his family. Several months later, Ben drove through the night, in blizzard conditions, to bring a pretty blonde and her son home to meet his family. That spring, I stood beside him as best man at their wedding. Little Jack was the ring bearer."

"Oh, my God! He came back for Ren and Jack?"

"Yep. They've been married for thirty-five years and have three kids, Jack and two girls. Ren owns and operates a little antique store on the square in Rockton. She's the set designer for the dinner theater."

"So, Jack is J, the divorced son, the one you and Ben discuss over beers at Will's Sports Bar, the texter?"

"Yep. Healthy and all grown up with three kids of his own. I thought for sure you'd make that connection."

"No. It never occurred to me.

The messages stopped. This time, I waited for her.

"Tears. Overwhelmed with joy for my friend. I couldn't write a happier ending than this for her, or Jack, or Ben. I'm glad you were there for both of us, Jake. I only wish we..."

She never finished the sentence. She didn't need to. I knew we shared the same wish... that we could have stood, hand-in-hand, and been married by the local justice of the peace like I'd planned. Planned, but never carried out. I wanted to tell her how sorry I was but, again, no point. It wouldn't change things now.

"*Thank you for the bedtime story, for the lovely happy ending. I know what you're thinking, and I want you to stop. I love you, Jake... still love you. That's all that matters now... all we can control.*"

"*Welcome. And I know you're right. Night night, Rose. LU2lls.*"

"*Night night, Jake. LUJ2lls.*"

* * * * *

The next day, I finished spraying weeds around noon and drove back to an empty house for lunch. Forgot to look at Beth's schedule this week... she must be working. I washed up, fixed a peanut butter and jelly sandwich, grabbed a beer, and sat down at the computer. I pulled up Facebook chat. No Rose. I sent her a text.

"*FB?*"

"*Walking dogs. Be there in 10.*"

"*K.*"

A few minutes later, she joined me on the chat line.

"*What doin'?*"

"*Finished spraying weeds, eating PBJ, drinking beer, chatting you.*"

"*Writing, walking dogs, and still thinking about Ben and Ren... Karen Chapman. I love the sound of that. Jack Chapman... even better.*"

"*Yep. I referred to her as 'the little woman' a few weeks ago and Ben told her. Karen called and said she knew a little woman who wanted to whip my ass!*"

"*I love it. Guess she hasn't changed much over the years.*"

"*No... still feisty, pretty, and crazy in love with Ben.*"

"*All good things.*"

"*Indeed. Anything new in the wild West today?*"

"*I finished Chapter Sixteen early this morning.*"

"*Geez. For not knowing how to write a novel, you're writing one pretty damn fast.*"

"Yes, well... we'll see if speed correlates with quality after I'm finished."

"Will you send me a copy of the manuscript when you finish?"

"Yes. You're probably the only one who will ever read the novel, besides Kathryn and Molly. Speaking of Kathryn, she called late last night, and I might have a book thingy in Chicago, not sure when. She's working on it. A friend of hers has connections with several book clubs in the Chicago area. We're waiting to hear back with a tentative date and place."

Jesus. Rockton to Chicago... ninety-five miles. Two hours travel time in traffic. Close. Much closer than New Mexico, for damn sure.

"That's close."

"Yes, it is. My mind is working overtime, along with the voice. I can visualize us there together so easily. Can you?"

"Yes, I can, Rose. What I can't visualize... is a reason for me to be in Chicago."

"There must be something you can think of. Some reason to leave."

"I know it seems like B and I are independent of one another... that we do our own thing... and that's true to a certain extent. But the reality is we're in business together within the confines of the farm. That's farm life. My office is the farm and we live in my office. We are always in close proximity... except when she's at work. That's why I go to the lake, the shop, the basement... for privacy, to be alone. She goes places independent of me, but I seldom pull out of the driveway without her. Again, that's farm life... togetherness. Not much 'doing your own thing' goes on."

"You don't go anywhere alone?"

"Not much. I go to the pub for a beer with Ben, the lake to fish, or to take a leak. But then the dogs watch and I get performance anxiety and can't pee. Unless it's school-bus related, which involves local kids and families who would know what's legit, I have no reason to leave for extended time periods."

A silent chat line, until she typed again.

"Can you tell her you need some time alone?"

"Nope. Why would I need time alone? That's totally out of character for me... to leave the farm... to go off by myself. I don't play golf, so I wouldn't fly anywhere to play for a weekend. Never mind that I haven't gone anywhere alone in forty years. Whatever the reason, red flags would fly before the last word left my lips. Trust me, I've played every possible scenario in my mind. I have no plausible excuse to go anywhere alone."

"Did you ever have a plan... ever think you might need a plan when this first started between us?"

"No. I didn't have a plan then, and felt like a prick... and still don't have a plan, and feel like an even bigger prick."

"Well, stop being a prick and try to come up with one. How difficult can that be?"

She had no idea.

"Okay, think about this, Rose. How difficult would it be for you to get away for a weekend if Paul still lived at home, if you didn't have the writing gigs What would your excuse be?"

A few moments of silence passed.

"Maybe I wouldn't have a plan right away, but eventually, I'd come up with something. I'd figure it out. If you want something bad enough, you figure a way. You never give up, especially for your dreams, Jake."

"I haven't given up. It's complicated. I don't do complicated very well."

"Life is complicated. None of us do that well. It was complicated forty years ago, and here we are again. No plan then. No plan now. Maybe it's time for a fucking plan."

Rose seldom used the word "fuck" unless really frustrated or pissed. She stopped typing.

I walked to the kitchen, grabbed another beer from the fridge, and headed back to the office. Still nothing.

Maybe I needed to lighten the mood. I typed a message back.

"Are we having our first fight?"

"Maybe."

"Thought so. Feel like throwing something?"

"Already did. Kleenex box from my desk is out in the hallway. Sharpened all my pencils, too."

"Good for a writer to have sharp pencils on hand."

Another pause.

"Will you do something for me, Jake?"

"If I can."

"Will you visualize the two of us together? That's all. Just visualize it happening."

"Yes. I do that every night anyway."

"Thank you."

"Welcome. Can I visualize us together naked?"

"Damn it, Jake!"

"Does that mean we're still fighting?"

"Yes. I'll let you know when we're done."

"Okay. You're sexy when you're mad, when you swear at me."

"Shit. You don't fight fair, Jake. You never did."

"I know. It's a childhood thingy. Don't fight much at all... not very competitive either. Used to play with mini-cars out on second base when I was supposed to be catching fly balls and sending them home. Never too concerned with crossing home plate or finishing first either... more fun just playing around... checking out the scenery."

"Yes, I can see that. Are we still talking about baseball?"

"Probably not."

* * * * *

I walked a few steps down the hall, and picked up the Kleenex box I'd thrown from my desk a few minutes earlier. A good excuse to take a breath and step away from the conversation with Jake.

Maddening. Exasperating. Annoying. And, no, he didn't fight fair. And yes, I loved him partly because of that. Like unwrapping a lovely present, I never knew exactly what to expect, or what awaited me. Jake still held mystery, still surprised me.

I walked back to my office, sat down in my comfy chair, and placed all the newly sharpened pencils—scattered across my desk— back in the desk caddy.

I thought about his choice of words—about finishing first—and smiled into the computer screen. Something I had done quite frequently since Jake and I first began chatting.

Here in New Mexico, I looked out my office window, and listened to children's voices as they played on the greenbelt—beyond the backyard pool—just beyond the sprawling peach tree. I pictured Jake and his competitive older brothers, as young boys on a baseball field in Illinois, and wondered if the noncompetitive little boys made better lovers later on?

The little boys who skipped stones, played in sandboxes, and drove mini-cars over second base. The ones who listened to music, played guitars, and joined bands. Were their heads filled with dreams and far away places instead of rules for first-place finishes?

Were the competitive boys, with all the right equipment, so obsessed with attaining first they missed the scenery rounding the bases in favor of a quick slide home?

Based solely on Jake, I pictured the stone skipping, band boys digging mini-cars out of their pockets—driving them back and forth over second base—while fly balls flew into the wild blue yonder. Eventually they meandered toward home, sometimes sitting on home plate to look around.

As a young man—a young lover—I remembered how much Jake enjoyed touching, playing, and checking things out. He loved looking at the scenery, and never acted in a hurry. He never missed touching a base before heading home... and never crossed home plate first. Ever.

I wanted him to touch all the bases again, but most of all, I wanted to cross home plate together... again.

* * * * *

"Still there, Rose? Find more pencils to sharpen... pitch another Kleenex box down the hall?"

"Still here. No and no. I wandered off to a baseball field in Illinois Pictured you with your mini-cars on second base, driving your brothers crazy."

"Yep. Probably still pissed at me."

"Probably." She paused, and began again. *"Thanks for letting me cross home plate first."*

"Welcome. Smiling into the computer screen from that comment."

"Me, too. I remember the incredible pleasure you brought me each time we made love, Jake."

"It was the same for me, a total rush watching your face... feeling those lovely contractions deep inside. And each time, you returned that same pleasure to me. Something I never forgot."

"No, me either. When we see each other, Jake, will you hold me in your arms, just hold me close so I can feel your heart?"

"Yep."

"I can feel your arms around me. Close your eyes. Feel mine?"

"Yep. I'm holding you close, baby."

"I've never been able to let my guard down, Jake. I've always been on the defensive, always in control. I don't want to be in that position anymore. I need to feel vulnerable, yet safe. Do you understand that?"

"Yes. I understand. I can do that. You'll be safe with me... safe in my arms. And I need to feel that way with you, too. That I can let my guard down... be vulnerable... feel safe."

"You can, Jake. You'll always be safe with me. We'll keep each other safe. I love you... so very much."

"I know. And I love you."

Jesus. I could see this happening. I pictured her in my arms... her head against my chest... her heart beating with mine. I saw us together.

Rose... me... and the universe.

Later, in the quiet darkness of our distant rooms, we texted our fantasies to one another. The words scripted the scene of an intimate, sensual play. And always the same play... that first time together... after all the years apart.

Chapter Thirteen

Dim the lights, raise the curtain... let the action begin.
The one act play is about to spin... again and again and again.
Intimate moments remembered,
Down to the smallest detail.
Whispered fantasies softly stirred.
Gently he pulled back the veil.

Rockton, Illinois
Fall 2008

I finished play rehearsal around nine-thirty in the evening and stopped by Will's on my way home. The place sat empty except for big, burly Will, who'd always reminded me of Grizzly Adams, and the new, perky, young brunette waitress, Heather. Will had a knack for finding perky, young waitresses over the years.

Yep, only three of us closed out the evening. Small town. Gotta love it. Sidewalks roll up at nine on weekdays. Ten-thirty on weekends

I sat at the bar, finished a second beer, and sent Rose a text.

"Pub. Headed home. FB?"

By the time I paid my tab and climbed into my truck, she returned the text.

"Yes. Take care, honey."

Nice. I liked being referred to as *honey* and having her voice concern over my safety. Small, yet meaningful, occurrences since Rose stepped back into my life. We both appreciated the small things—the endearments and concerns for the other—no longer expressed in our marriages.

"*Good evening.*"

"*Hey, you... always good to close out the day with my best friend.*"

"*Indeed it is. And your day?*"

"*Good. Nearly finished with the book... one more chapter.*"

"*You've been busy, busy. Do I get to read the finished manuscript first?*"

"*Yes. But only if you promise to cut me some slack. Wrote another poem, too.*"

"*I promise. Send the poem, please.*"

"*I will. How's rehearsal going?*"

"*Rehearsal at this point is disconnected and involves a lot of waiting around. Nature of the beast. Used to it.*"

"*Do you have the performance schedule?*"

"*Yep. Got it... Thursday, Nov. 20th–Sunday, Nov. 23rd. Dinner's at 6 and the performance starts at 7:30 p.m., except Sunday matinee— dinner at 12, performance at 1:30.*"

"*Sunday's our birthday. Matinee birthday dinner, maybe?*"

"*Maybe. I could light up the onion rings.*"

"*Nice. I'll sing you a voice memo. Beth and her family coming Saturday night?*"

"*You know, it's the damnedest thing. Beth's mom is scheduled for medical tests Saturday at St. Francis Medical Center in Peoria, where she lives. Since that's a two and a half hour drive from Rockton, Beth's leaving Saturday morning and coming back Tuesday. Wants to spend some time with her. She and her family are coming to the Friday night performance since she works Thursday night.*"

"*That is crazy... of all weekends for medical tests. Good she can be there Friday night. Ben and Karen coming?*"

"*Probably Thursday night. Ben's always liked opening nights because things go wrong... actors forget lines, miss cues, occasionally fall off the stage. He loves shit like that.*"

"*Oh, my. I now have a mental picture of you falling off the stage.*"

"*I'll tell Ben and Karen to sit close... break the fall... catch the beer before it spills.*"

"Good plan. I had a phone session with Molly late this afternoon.
"How'd that go?"
"Good. Started the discussion with childhood and ended at long-term marriage relationships. How they shift and change over the years You don't know if you're happy or not... you're just there... with lots of history between you."

I could relate. Long-term marriage... plenty of history. At this point in time, I wasn't happy or unhappy... just *there*. Figured that's where most marriages ended up. Love and passion replaced by companionship and security. And as time ticked by... you forgot how either felt.

I forgot.

Rose forgot.

Until the *Friend request*—brought it all back—for both of us.

It might be possible to have it all... companionship, security, love and passion. I knew marriages like that existed. Ben and Karen's marriage was like that. Back in the day, I figured it would be the four of us. I figured wrong.

I wondered if I still had the strength and tenacity to make major changes. How much was I willing to give up for what I wanted?

I stared at the Miller High Life can in my hand—at the numerous empties in the wastebasket from previous nights—then closed my eyes and took several long swallows.

I could do almost anything after a few beers... except make a decision. That hadn't changed one bit over the years.

Damn. Where did they hide that big, red *easy* button?

"Yep. I can relate."

"I know you can, Jake. I kept telling myself whatever was wrong was my fault, and I was the only one who could fix it or make it right. I think that's part of the reason I never thought about a divorce. Now I realize I was wrong on both counts. It takes two to break things... two to mend them."

"Yep. And you both have to realize there's a problem. I'm sure Beth thinks things between us are fine. I guess they are. Depends on your definition of fine. It's all perspective. And then there's the shared history together. I have that with Beth. You have it with Paul."

"Yes. Perspective and shared history. Some days I feel relief, and other days, sadness. It's not an easy thing ending a marriage, no matter the condition."

"Nope. Like you said, you feel the need to fix things, to make things right, and sometimes that's not possible."

"No, it isn't. BRB. I need to change into T-shirt and boxers, and move to my laptop in the bedroom. Pour a glass of wine."

"OK... will wait."

I leaned back in the computer chair, closed my eyes, and fantasized Rose and I enjoying a glass of wine, discussing the days events, while lounging in as few clothes as possible.

A few minutes later, the computer beeped, indicating another message.

"Back. T-shirt and boxers, snuggled in bed with laptop and wine."

"Perfect. Have a visual. Flanneled up. Cold here in Illinois. Sending a pic."

"K... waiting. Want one back?"

"Yep. Scorpio. Always want it."

"I know... me, too. What is it about Scorpios?"

"Fire and gasoline. HOT! Remember the first pic I sent? Wasn't sure whether to send it or not. How you would react. Took a chance... held my breath, pressed send, and hoped for the best."

"I remember the pic. So glad you sent it."

"Me, too. I remember the one you sent back. Mm."

Within a few seconds, we exchanged bedtime pictures, me in my plaid flannel, she in her T-shirt and boxers.

"Thanks. The T and boxers are hot. Not hot here... colder all the time. Winter soon."

"Yes, winter. Is Dustin still on track for graduating at the semester?"

"Yep. Enrolled in college classes starting in January. Empty nesters soon."

"Time passes. Makes you think. I've been doing a lot of thinking since Paul moved out."

"About?"

"What I've missed from the relationship after things changed."

"Tell me."

"Human contact. Touch. I miss being held... feeling skin against skin... hearing another heart beating with mine. I miss cuddling."

"Understand. Miss those, too. Cuddling's medicinal, you know?"

"It is? According to Dr. Jake?"

"No. I read something. Cuddling kills depression, relieves anxiety, and strengthens the immune system. I think we're both suffering from a severe case of NCS."

"NCS?"

"No Cuddling Syndrome."

"We most definitely are."

Our chatting paused for a bit. Probably both thinking about cuddling. I typed another message to her.

"It's not just sex I miss. I miss the intimacy that happens during sex... the deep connection... the soul-to-soul connection. I guess that's part of that human contact thingy."

Geez... that sounded pretty damn good.

I thought about the past thirty-some years with Beth. We never discussed things like that. Not once. It would make us both uncomfortable. And we never shared a soul-to-soul connection between us either. Pretty pathetic, considering she's my wife... the woman I spent the better part of my life with.

Rose typed back.

"Yes, it is. I miss the sex sometimes, too. But Paul and I never shared that kind of intimacy... that kind of closeness. That was the only time he held me, but we never talked. I used to blame myself for something I was or wasn't doing—but I don't look at it that way anymore. Talking with Molly helped."

"A good thing. Beth and I never had that kind of intimacy either. I don't think it's anyone's fault. It just happens or it doesn't."

"You and I talk about anything... everything."

"We do."

"Why is that?"

"Not sure. Might have to do with not being judgmental or having an agenda, probably a lot to do with trust."

"I trust you, Jake."

"And I trust you."

"We know things about one another no one else knows... sweet secrets between just you and me. I say and do things with you I've never done with anyone else, or ever will. Do you think it would be that way if we were together?"

"Yep, I suspect it would. Whatever we chat or text... we can do."

"I remember some kind of a connection with Paul in the beginning. I tried to love him, be close to him, the best I could. I always thought he loved me on some level. But over the years, the love and relationship changed, replaced with careers and children and responsibilities. We made no time for anything else. We didn't bother. Didn't seem to matter."

"It happens probably more than we know. You don't realize it until one morning you wake up in separate bedrooms and meet in the kitchen to discuss prescriptions, paint color for the house, and dental insurance for the kids' braces. Kind of like your marriage turned into a business merger... and you lost out on the fringe benefits."

"Yes, or the fringe benefits were so few, you found you could live without them."

"Kind of makes you lose your company loyalty."

"Especially after your kids leave the firm."

"Jake?"

"What, baby?"

"I'm glad we found each other again. It's as though you took my hand in yours and pulled me through time, back to your side. And I don't want to miss a single day of being in touch with you, of loving you."

"I understand that. I can love you... will love you. I just have to figure out how to love you. The way things are, I can't love you the way you need to be loved, Rose."

"The way you're loving me is fine... beautiful. We'll figure this out. Just don't let go of me, Jake."

"No, I won't. We won't let each other go again."

* * * * *

A Friend Request

Woodstock's Town Square Dinner Theater posted a publicity flyer for *The Odd Couple* on their Facebook page... a page I now regularly checked. Jake and his fellow actors beamed back at me. The play opened in two weeks and he rehearsed nearly every night, seriously curtailing our text and chat time. His acting... a love/hate thing with me at this point.

I loved the picture, loved seeing his face, seeing him happy doing what he loved. Something in his smile made me remember the young man who sent lovely shivers up my spine with only the touch of his hand. Now, the man he became affected me in a much deeper way—creating a constant craving—with only his words, his imagination, his fantasies to touch me.

How crazy that must sound to most people, Yet, I knew others understood perfectly about the words, the fantasy, the craving.

Each day I wrote, I thought about those others in the universe. I reached out to them.

I stepped into the pages and walked around inside the novel, using ideas he and I often created. I wrote the words that moved the characters along in the storyline... their fate resting sometimes in imagination, sometimes in reality. Until I finished the novel, they remained suspended in time, waiting for me to come back.

The process mimicked exactly what I did as a child. I lived in a make-believe world I created within my imagination. I filled that world with characters who became familiar friends. Friends I loved, who were always there for me. Friends who kept me company when I was alone.

I crossed back and forth... between the fantasy of an alternative world and the reality of a tumultuous childhood.

Now, as I wrote each day... I found the perfect outlet for my fantasy and reality... fiction and fact. I knew first-hand of both places.

Jake and I lived our own novel, based on fantasy and reality, fiction and fact. As the storyline played out... I added new pages to the novel. Sometimes the storyline and what happened in our lives were the same... reality. Sometimes they were different... fantasy.

No one knew where fantasy ended and reality began. No one, except me... not even Jake.

I shared this during my sessions with Molly. Each time we talked, I understood myself better... the inward me, the outward me. Gradually my years of avoidance and pretending made sense. I understood why I did things a certain way... or didn't do some things at all. I understood my deep feelings for some, and total lack for others. I recognized the voice, the little girl within, and her purpose in protecting me.

I learned the past influences the present... and time doesn't heal all wounds. But time helps manage the intensity—the pain—of living with the wounds. Simple. Complicated. A universal truism for most people.

I continued to study Jake's face on the monitor... tracing his mouth, that smile, with my finger. I wanted to see him on stage, acting again. I'd visualized it happening over and over.

This morning Kathryn called and told me the book club event in Chicago would take place on Sunday evening, November 23rd, the same weekend as Jake's play. I would be two hours—ninety-five miles—from Rockton.

Coincidence? Not in my world. Today the universe set things in motion.

* * * * *

Rockton, Illinois
Same morning

I finished the morning route and came home to find a couple of Post-its from Beth stuck to the cabinet door above the coffee pot. She must be working. I read the first: *Pick up Rx at vet for Cooper.* Then the second: *Take clothes on chair to cleaners.*

Husband, father, referee, counselor, cheerleader, farmer, fisherman, handyman, mechanic, chauffeur, dog walker, director, actor, tightwad, asshole, and gopher. Over time, the list grew.

A Friend Request

Hot coffee. That's what I needed. Lots of hot coffee. I poured a cup, headed to the office, and pulled up Facebook. No Rose. Checked email and found a poem waiting. An appropriate title for those of us living our final season.

One Final Season

Lay me down and let your love wash gently over me.
Soothe me softly with that low, steady voice of reason.
Strip all the craziness away and let me just float free.
Heart to heart, soul to soul... if only for one final season.

You rocked me once in innocence with young, trembling hands,
And gave me a reason to trust again by making no demands.
Now let me sink slowly under your soul... warm, close, and tight.
Hold me within your arms through this long, wondrous night.

You once said I saved you, but the truth is you saved me,
By waking me up from years on end of details and complacency.
You found that girl who once was filled with dreams and desires.
Gave her the strength to strike the match that finally lit the fire.

So, lay me down and let your love wash gently over me.
And soothe me softly with that low, steady voice of reason.
Strip all the craziness away and let me just float free.
Heart to heart, soul to soul... if only for one final season.

~ Rose Allison ~

Jesus. The words, emotions, and memories of our love affair resounded within the poem. *You rocked me once in innocence... the truth is you saved me.* Did she know she turned my life upside down? Forever changed me... for a second time? There was no going back for either of us. *Heart to heart, soul to soul...* indeed, our *one final season.*
I sent a text.
"FB?"

She returned my text.

"Yes. Getting coffee."

I typed out my message and pressed send.

"Good having coffee together in the morning. Nice poem."

"Morning, Jake. Yes... good having coffee together. Glad you liked the poem. We listen well to one another."

"Yep, we do."

"Kathryn called late last night. Guess when the Chicago book thingy is?"

"No clue."

"The same weekend as the play... Sunday, Nov.23rd at 4 p.m. at the Palmer House. I have a room there for the weekend. Thought I might do some birthday shopping Saturday. Too bad you're busy."

"Yep, too bad. I love to shop."

"Safe, evasive answer. You're good at that."

"Years of practice."

"But what about us?"

"We'll always have Paris."

"Yes, we'll always have Paris."

The chat ended when Rose left for a dentist appointment. We left Casablanca, Ilsa, Rick, the fog, and the plane behind for another time.

The universe didn't get this one right... despite the visualizations sent out into the cosmos by both Rose... and me. I didn't know how I felt... disappointed or relieved. A little of both, I guess. Took the angst of decision-making away, but not the desire—the constant craving—to see her, to love her again.

Somehow we would make this happen.

* * * * *

A Friend Request

Woodstock, Illinois
Town Square Dinner Theater
Two weeks later

I finished applying the make-up, buffed it, pulled the Kleenex from around the white shirt collar, and put the black suit coat on. I gave myself the mirrored once-over.

Nice. Couldn't remember the last time I wore a suit before this production started. Funeral probably.

I took a couple more swallows of beer, and felt the cell phone vibrate in my pocket. I slipped it out and checked. Rose.

"Hey, you."

"Hey, back."

"Still shopping or break for dinner and a movie?"

"Took a drive after shopping. No dinner, just movie. Hey, break a leg tonight!"

"Not funny... almost fell off stage into Ben's lap Thurs night."

"Shouldn't have had that second beer before curtain call."

"How'd you know?"

"Lucky guess. Full house?"

"Yep. A few tables left in back. Full house both Thurs and Fri nights."

"Great! Beth and her family enjoy the play?"

"Seemed to. Left this morning. Tests went fine."

"Good. Got your lines down yet?"

"Sorta... kinda. Used to adlibbing. Gotta go, babe."

"K. Sending positive vibes."

"Thanks. Shutting cell off."

"Good idea. Will be close. Text later if you're not too tired. LUJ2lls."

"Will do. LU2lls."

* * * * *

225

Farming, bus driving, rehearsing, building and striking sets, and then performing made for one hectic, tiring week. I dragged my butt to bed late every night. Very little chatting or texting during play week. Rose understood.

I thought about the last time she saw me perform. It was 1969 in a university production of *The Goodbye People*. I played neurotic Arthur Korman. In the current production, I played neurotic, fastidious, hypochondriac, Felix Unger. Definitely typecast.

Hank Bailey, owner of the local Farm and Fleet, filled the role of Oscar Madison opposite me. We played well off one another, and picked up each other's lines when we forgot. Perfect odd couple.

In 1969, I stepped out on stage and there, front row center, sat Cash, Sam, Jerry, Ren, Max, Chuck, Zach, and Rose. Stoned on their asses, they tried not to laugh. Most of the cast was in the same shape, including me. I never remembered a thing after I walked out on stage. Not one damn thing. But we got great reviews the next day.

I do remember making love with Rose later... most of the night... in bed, on the floor, in the closet, on the steps. Jesus. The things you can do when you're young and stoned.

These days, I would be lucky to remember my lines after I finished one beer. What I wouldn't give for one more youthful night with a retentive memory and a hard cock.

Each play I acted in or directed over the years let me continue part of the dream, the plan I had as a younger man. It kept my head in the game during rough seasons. Thank God for small-town dinner theater.

The dressing room door opened and Pete, one of the young stagehands, poked his head in. "Curtain in ten minutes!"

I did a last-minute tie adjustment, smoothed my hair back, and chugged the rest of the beer.

Showtime.

* * * * *

The house lights blinked on and off in the lobby as I walked through the doors from the parking lot. Ten minutes until curtain.

Perfect timing. I'd made the drive from downtown Chicago to Woodstock in one hour and thirty minutes.

I traced the rose-patterned carpeting with my foot as I waited by the playhouse entrance doors. The restored, ornate lobby reminded me of the theater in Macomb where I'd seen *Moby Dick* as a child. The only thing missing... the candy counter and smell of freshly popped popcorn.

The interior lights dimmed, and I walked inside. The usher—dressed in a dark suit, white shirt and tie—escorted me to the one remaining table nestled in the far right corner of the third tier of tables and chairs.

Perfect location for keeping a low profile.

I draped my black, leather jacket over the back of the chair and sat down. I'd purposely worn the little, black-knit dress and black shoes to blend in. Good choice.

Discreetly, I checked out the renovated theater's interior. The slanting floor replaced with three, tiered platforms. Round tables and chairs, covered in crisp white tablecloths, replaced the rows of theater seats. On the floor... burgundy carpeting. I wondered how they kept the carpeting so clean. Geez... having an OCD cleaning moment. Next, I would be climbing a chair to check the chandeliers for dust. That would pretty much take care of any low-key status I hoped to maintain.

I needed a drink.

Just in the nick of time, a tall blond waiter—probably a local college student—dressed in black slacks, white shirt and black bowtie, came to my rescue.

"Good evening. My name is Scott and I'll be your waiter. Can I bring you a glass of wine, or a beer maybe?"

"Do you have white Zin?"

"We do. Would you like a glass?"

"Please."

"I'll be right back with that."

Beautiful theater, great table, nice waiter... so far, so good. Now if I could calm my nerves and not throw up, this evening would keep its "low key" status.

Anxiously, I waited for the play to begin... for Jake to walk out on stage. I knew I would be fine once the play started. But right now, things seemed a little surrealistic... like I was here, but not here. Sort of an out-of-body experience. I took a breath and silently talked myself down. Something I'd done over a lifetime.

I took the notepad and pencil out of my purse. Diversion. Something to occupy my hands and mind. Besides, I was a writer, for God's sake. Writer's are supposed to write!

Despite the diversion, my mind wandered back to Jake. I looked down toward the stage, eyes fixed on the dark burgundy curtains. Drawn curtains he now stood behind. He waited. I waited. A breath away from one another. We had not been this close in proximity since 1970. That's a long time... a very long time to wait.

My imagination wandered... I pictured Jake and I hugging and kissing our good-byes to one another years ago, as if leaving on long trips, in opposite directions. I heard myself say, "Bye, Jake. I'll see you in November 2008. I'll be in the audience. Look for me. I love you." He answered, "I'll know you're there. Wait for me to find you. I'll love you forever."

God, I was shaking.

"I need wine."

Just as the words escaped my lips, Scott arrived with the Zinfandel and a basket of pretzels and mixed nuts. He set them down on the crisp, white tablecloth in front of me. Perfect timing.

"I figured you might want something to munch on since you missed dinner."

"You figured right. Thank you."

"You're welcome. Dinner was really good. Breaded pork tenderloin and onion rings... peach cobbler and home-made ice cream for dessert."

"Sounds wonderful. I love tenderloins."

My mind drifted back to Dixie's truck stop... the first night Jake and I met. I heard his voice so clearly... "*I recommend the tenderloins. They're especially good with lots of yellow mustard. Trust me.*"

And I did. Now, I'd placed my trust in him again.

A response from Scott... my waiter... brought me back.

"Maybe next time. Can I bring you anything else?"

"No, I'm good. Thank you."

"Friends or family in the play?"

"Friend."

He hesitated... probably waiting for further information on who I was there to watch. When nothing was forthcoming, he simply said, "Well, enjoy the play."

The familiar *Odd Couple* theme music began. The house lights dimmed out as the curtains slowly opened. The spotlight picked up the actor at stage left.

Jake strode crisply to center stage.

Overwhelmed with emotion, tears welled in my eyes and trickled down my cheeks. I couldn't stop them. I reached in my purse for a Kleenex and blotted... and blotted... discreetly blowing, now and then.

Even through tears, he looked good, looked the same—though more filled out—more mature. The full graying mustache changed his look from cute to handsome. The long hair, now peppered with gray, brushed his shirt collar. I remembered running my hands up the back of his neck, through his hair, and driving him crazy. I hoped I'd get the chance to do that again... and then kiss that lovely mustache... and those sensual full lips beneath it.

I watched him move. Watched his mannerisms. Listened to his voice. The boy I once knew was now the man I watched on stage... still so familiar after all the years.

In keeping with the character of Felix Unger, he dressed in a dark suit, white shirt, and tie. He looked very handsome, and still sported the same cute butt I checked out years ago at the rehearsal barn. Sweet.

He looked hot... sexy... sensual. At a younger age... I'd never associate those adjectives with a man his age. But now, I knew firsthand of those adjectives, and more, when it came to Jake. As a young man, he'd made love to me so intensely, I remembered every detail nearly forty years later. For months now, he'd written words to me most women never hear in a lifetime. Perspectives change with the seasons. I was glad not to be that stupid, young girl anymore.

Laughter snapped me back to reality. Everyone around me... laughing. God, he was hilarious, delivering punch lines with perfect comedic timing. He made it look easy.

His fellow actor played the slovenly, recently divorced sportswriter Oscar Madison quite convincingly. They bounced lines off one another like players in a tennis match. I couldn't remember the last time I'd laughed like this. Jake used that same skillful levity with the audience as he did with me during our chats.

I saw only Jake on the stage... heard only his voice. He performed only for me. I was so proud of him for making his dream of acting a reality. He never gave up. He found a way. I loved him for that.

As I watched him play out his long-ago fantasy on stage... I realized mine was being fulfilled sitting in the audience. I visualized this months ago... replayed it over and over in my mind... and sent it out into the universe. The universe sent it back as reality.

We had to figure a way to make *our* reality happen. Visualize—do your part—leave the rest up to the energy of the universe. I hoped Jake was doing his part.

The evening went by so quickly. It seemed as though I'd just taken the first sip of wine as the curtains slowly opened, and Jake appeared on stage left. Now, I watched and listened as Felix and Oscar delivered their final lines and the audience clapped. They stood and the applause continued as the curtains slowly closed. Perfect!

I needed to exit before the curtain calls began.

I slipped my jacket on, and got Scott's attention. I paid in cash, leaving him a generous tip for the wine and friendly service.

"Thank you, Scott, for taking such good care of me."

"It's been my pleasure. Have a safe trip back to... wherever." He hesitated, and began again. "You're not from around here, are you?"

"No. I live just west of here a bit."

Flying under the radar required vague answers.

"Well, travel safely."

"Thanks."

I wove my way through tables, chairs, and people, and walked into the hallway. A couple stopped near the restrooms and exchanged conversation. She disappeared into the restroom, while he waited. I walked by, our eyes met briefly, and I sensed a familiarity about him.

Oh, shit. Ben. Ben Chapman. No wonder he looked familiar. The woman in the restroom must be Karen. Shit.

I looked straight ahead, quickened my pace, and exited through the outer doors, into the cool night air. I wanted to look back... see if he was looking at me, following me. I didn't. I kept walking. A bright, full moon illuminated the parking lot, making the black Malibu rental car easier to spot. I pressed the key fob, unlocked the door, and slid behind the wheel.

For a few tense moments, I sat in the dark, nervously waiting and watching. Did Ben recognize me in that brief moment? Follow me to the parking lot? Did he tell Karen? Oh, God... did he tell Jake? Were they all now looking for me? Oh, Jesus.

Breathe. Close your eyes. Take a breath.

I opened my eyes, looked around, and saw no one except an elderly couple ambling to their car a few rows from mine. I started the car and turned on the heat. The warmth brought relief and a feeling of safety. I decided Ben didn't make the connection... didn't recognize me. The relief triggered more tears. They ran down my cheeks and splashed onto my leather jacket.

I looked over at the lights of the dinner theater... to catch one more glimpse of the building... the building housing Jake at the moment. My heart overflowed with joy and love as I remembered the evening... and my sweet, sweet Jake.

I closed my eyes and whispered to him in the darkness, "Thanks for letting me drift away with you... one more time. I hope you felt me close to you. I love you, Jake."

I sent a text... *"I felt so close to you tonight. Take care. Night night Jake. LU2lls"* I tuned in 94.7, WLS Chicago's classic oldies station on the radio. The Beatles' "Get Back" played softly in the background as I drove out of the parking lot onto Highway 47.

Time to get back to Chicago. Get back to the hotel. And leave Jake behind... again.

* * * * *

Karen walked from the restroom over to the glass exit doors where Ben stood.

"Thanks for waiting, honey. I better head home and see how the kids are doing."

"Okay, I won't be long. Wanna talk to Jake a minute. You know the damnedest thing just happened while I waited by the restrooms."

"What?"

"This gal walked by me... nice looking, dressed well, about our age. We made brief eye contact... she immediately looked away... and hurried out the door."

"And?"

"And. She reminded me of Rose."

"Rose? Rose Allison?"

"Yep, that Rose. Looked enough like her to be her twin sister. That's why I'm standing over here. I watched her walk across the parking lot and climb into a black rental. She drove away a few minutes ago."

"Oh, my God. Do you think it *was* her? It's been almost forty years. What would she be doing in Rockton... at a play?"

They looked at one another and said, "Jake."

"It makes sense now... all the texting, the change in demeanor, his attitude. I'll bet you they've made contact again. Just don't want anyone to know. Especially us."

"Oh, shit, Ben. You could be right. I remember you told me about the texting and Jake's evasive answers over the months. People reacquaint online everyday. If it was Rose, do you think Jake knew?"

"No clue. The only thing I'm sure of is... she seemed in a hurry... didn't want to make eye contact... and she looked like Rose Allison. But I could be reading into all this."

"You could. It probably wasn't her. Just someone who looked like her. Are you going to mention this to Jake?"

"Probably not. I don't want to confront him with anything. If something is going on, I want him to tell me about it... not make me ask. I don't want you to say anything to anyone either, Karen."

"Oh, I won't say anything."

"Okay. I'll see you at home in a bit."

He kissed Karen and patted her on the butt as she walked out the door. Time to find Jake.

Chapter Fourteen

An outlined script created,
Rehearsed on the stage in his mind.
Adapted from lines that were fated,
Performed once, then left behind.
Dim the lights, raise the curtain... let the action begin.
The one act play is about to spin... again, and again, and again.

Town Square Dinner Theater
Fall 2008
Saturday night

After twenty minutes of back pats, handshakes, and conversations about the play, the weather, and the crops, the front house—packed with cast, crew, and audience members—began to thin out.

It was a big night in Small Town, U.S.A.—an event, a production, a social gathering where everyone knew everyone. Almost.

"Great job, Jake... glad we came. Food was good, too, especially the onion rings."

"Nice to see you, Bill... Sharon. Glad you could come out for the play. Good to hear about the onion rings. I'll pass it along to the kitchen crew."

Bill and Sharon Drexel—the honorable mayor and his sweet, large-bosomed wife—dyed in the wool Democrats.

"Jake, you clean up real good. Look nice in that suit, too. You could wear that to church on Sunday, you know?"

"Thanks, Reverend Roberts... Patti. I'll keep that in mind."

Fred and Patti Roberts, Reformed Evangelical Minister and choir director wife—far right Republicans.

"You did great, Mr. Richardson. Tell Dustin we said, *'Hey!'*"

Head cheerleader Becky Carlyle and best friend Alisha Williams. Politically clueless. No need.

Jesus H. Christ, could those jeans fit any tighter? Even at my age, it was difficult not to watch tight jeans and boots walking away.

"How about a beer on the way back to the dressing room? We can follow the tight jeans and boots part way."

Ben. No wonder we stayed friends through the years. Old birds of a feather.

"Yep, we can. Heading in that direction now."

"Great show, by the way. You and Hank played off each other great. Funny as hell."

"Thanks. Remembered most of our lines, and neither of us fell off the stage. A good night was had by all."

"Pretty much."

Ben and I bid the jeans farewell on a right turn, and walked back through the double doors to the dinner theater bar for a beer.

"Where's Beth and the rest of the family? Didn't see them."

"No, Beth and her family came last night because of tests on her mom today at St. Francis. She left early this morning. Won't be back until Tuesday sometime."

"That explains it. Anybody else in the audience... anybody special.. from out of town, maybe?"

"Nope. Not that I know of. All the out-of-town people came last night. Where's Karen? Thought I saw her next to you."

"You did. We drove separately. I walked her to the restroom after the first curtain call and she left. The grandkids are spending the night and one of us needed to be home. We played rock, paper, scissors earlier... she lost. Lucky for me."

"You always were lucky in the draw. Why are the grandkids back? Thought they just moved out."

"Technically they did, but Jack and Heather needed a night alone, so Karen took pity on them. She always was a soft touch when it came to Jack."

"Yep, I remember that from Parkridge days. Heather seems to be doing all right at Will's. The last couple times I stopped by, she brought the beer and never spilled a drop."

"That's good to hear. She makes damn good tips on the weekend."

"Hell, between the two of us, we're probably making a third of her and Jack's rent."

"I'm sure of it. Hey, did Frank mention anything to you about having trouble with the furnace here in the theater?"

"No. But the subject came up at the last Board of Director's meeting a few weeks back. Need to vote on a new furnace. I think Frank's hoping the bailing wire and duct tape will hold until spring."

"Well, that's the reason he's on the BOD for the dinner theater. Bank presidents are frugal... know how to stretch that dime. Anyway, it was acting up earlier. Feels okay in here now."

"Yep. Warm and toasty."

Ben and I continued talking about the furnace, Jack and Heather, and the weather for another thirty minutes or so. We finished our beers, and he headed home to Karen and the grandkids.

I dragged my tired ass back to the empty dressing room and plopped down in the swivel chair. God, I was tired. Maybe I was too old for this shit. Needed to stick with directing more and acting less.

I peeled off the suit, tie, and white shirt, hung them back on the wardrobe rack, and pulled my jeans and Illinois State T-shirt back on.

Better. Much better.

Now to get all this shit off my face. I flipped the lid open on the green, plastic baby wipes container, pulled several moist sheets out, and wiped the heavy stage make-up from my face and neck. The wipes left behind softer wrinkles that smelled fresh as a baby's butt. What a great invention.

I pulled the cell phone out of my jeans pocket, turned it back on, and found a text from Rose.

"I felt so close to you tonight. Take care. Night night, Jake. LUJ2lls."

I texted back.

"Remembered lines... didn't fall off stage. Yes, close... like you were there. Night night, Rose. LU2lls"

I slipped my insulated jean jacket on, pulled the Illinois State baseball cap snug, and dragged my tired ass home.

* * * * *

She nuzzled her face against my neck, my ear. "I love you, Jake," she whispered, brushing her soft, full lips back and forth over my cheek. I felt soft kisses across my forehead, down my cheek... trailing over to my lips. She traced them with her tongue, then kissed me so softly. I barely felt her lips on mine. I tried to press my lips more firmly against hers. Tried to work my tongue inside her mouth. She pulled back... hesitating, teasing, coaxing... and made me wait as she watched me. Anticipation. The more she made me wait, the more I wanted her. I couldn't wait any longer. I wrapped my leg over her hip and pulled her naked body tightly against mine. There was no way to mistake my desire. I kissed her mouth hard, and plunged my tongue deep inside. I heard her moan and...

The cell beeped on the nightstand. Son-of-a-bitch. I looked at the clock. Five fifteen in the morning. This better be damn important. Somebody better be on fire or dead.

"This is Jake."

"Jake, it's Frank Jensen. Sorry to wake you so early on Sunday morning, but we got problems at the theater. No heat. Pipes busted in the night. Could you call Ben and meet me down here?"

"Jesus. What a thing. Yep. Be there as soon as we can."

"Thanks, Jake."

So much for duct tape and bailing wire. I called Ben and gave him the news. He took it as well as could be expected, considering he and Karen stayed up most of the night with a puking grandson.

"I'll get dressed and meet you at the theater, Jake."

"Okay. At least you won't have to mop up anymore puke."

"I don't mop. I gag. See ya."

An hour later, I met Frank, Ben, and the rest of the theater Board of Directors in the basement to check out the antique furnace... now cold, quiet, and dead.

The pipes looked fixable. Not too much water damage. Nothing that couldn't be mopped up and dried out. The furnace, another story. Frank made a couple calls and found a good deal on a new one. With all the board members present, we voted unanimously to make the purchase. The new furnace would take a week to ten days for delivery, and another day or two for installation.

The play... officially over. The afternoon matinee... officially cancelled.

A few minutes later, I sat outside the theater in my truck... a beautiful sunrise stretched across the sky in front of me. I thought about the timing and alignment of events—the play, Rose's book signing, Beth's mom's medical tests, her extended stay—all on the same weekend. And, parent/teacher conferences Friday afternoon and all day Monday... no school.

Coincidence? I might have thought that a year ago, but not now. Instead, Rose's words whispered in my ear... *Visualize. Do your part. Leave the rest up to the universe.*

The grin on my face widened. Well, I'll be a son-of-a-bitch. There might be something to this universe thing, after all. Happy birthday!

Ben walked out of the theater and across the parking lot toward our trucks, parked side-by-side. He owed me a favor or two. Time to collect.

When he got close, I rolled the window down. "Hey, need a favor, buddy."

"Will it get me out of the house?"

"Yep. Got some business to take care of. I'm leaving around noon today... won't be home until late tomorrow or early Tuesday. Wondered if you could feed and let the dogs out."

"Business, huh? Kind of sudden. Anything wrong?"

"Nope. Nothing's wrong, just need to take care of something."

"See a man about a dog, huh?"

"Yep. Something like that."

Ben looked away, shifted his weight from one leg to the other, and focused his attention back on me, as if mulling something over.

"I meant to tell you something last night and forgot."

"Oh, what's that?"

"It was the damnedest thing. I'm in the hallway, waiting for Karen to come out of the restroom, when this woman walked by me. I caught just a glimpse of her for a few seconds."

"And?"

"And... she reminded me of Rose. About our age, and very attractive. I know it couldn't be her, but it sure as hell looked like her. Just thought I'd share that."

"Thanks for sharing. Too bad I wasn't standing in the hallway with you."

"That's what I thought."

I thought about what he said, about the woman who looked like Rose. It wasn't her. I knew where Rose was Saturday night... Chicago. Interesting. Must be a local. Maybe I'd catch a glimpse of her sometime.

"So... can you help me out or not?"

"Sure. I'll be glad to. I might even watch a game or two while I'm at your house."

"You know where I keep the key, the remote, and the beer. Help yourself."

"Yep. I know where everything is. And Jake... the offer still stands if you ever want to talk."

"I know." Jesus. It was hard to keep all of this from him.

"Well, drive safe. Shoot me a text when you head back."

"Will do... and thanks, Ben."

"You're welcome."

And with that... Ben did *his* part.

My turn. I'd visualized this happening over and over. Now, I would do my part... exchange fantasy for reality.

* * * * *

I pulled in the graveled driveway and checked the time... ten o'clock. That gave me a couple hours to shower and clean up, pack a

239

few things, grab something from the basement, and let the dogs out. I'd fill the truck up on the way out of town.

Shit. I had a list to work on.

I sent Rose a text from the truck and, by the time I reached the kitchen and let the dogs out, she replied.

"Good morning and happy birthday."

"Morning. Yes, happy birthday. Just out of shower, hair, make-up, and wardrobe."

"Wow. How's that bed?"

"Wonderful. Comfy king. Slept well."

"Room service?"

"Yes. Huge breakfast. Book club paying! LOL!"

"Good girl."

"Room 532. Ring a bell?"

"Yep. Last digits of your Parkridge phone."

"That's amazing you remembered."

"Dialed it enough. Hey, gotta go. Busy, busy today."

"Have a great matinee. Text later?"

"Yep. I'll try before your book thingy."

"K."

Room 532, huh? Good to know. I let the dogs back in and headed upstairs to the shower.

* * * * *

Chicago, Illinois
Palmer House
Sunday afternoon

I slipped into my black heels and checked my watch... three o'clock. Jake's matinee was nearly over, and my book reception started in an hour. Busy day for both of us.

I wore his favorite black-knit dress—the one that buttons down the front—with a black linen jacket and black heels. The same dress, jacket, and heels I wore last night when I experienced the close encounter with Ben.

240

Jake saw a Facebook picture of me in the dress and commented on the V-neck... but most of all... the buttons. He fantasized unbuttoning each one and discovering a pink lacy bra and matching panties underneath. I wore those, too.

Late at night, during chats and texts, we often fantasized about our first time together, after all the years. In the fantasy, we meet in a lovely hotel room, furnished with a king-size bed, and full-length mirror on the opposite wall. I wear the black-knit dress. Jake wears a button-down, white-linen shirt, over jeans. The scenario plays out the same each time...

He watches her secretly from a distance as she takes the elevator to her room.

She sends a text to him.

"Where are you?"

"I'm close... very close."

"How close?"

"Open the door."

She opens the door and he's standing in the hallway.

He walks in, takes her in his arms, and holds her. He whispers in her ear, "Easy, baby. I'm here now. I've got you. Let me hold you... just let me hold you."

She trembles... tries to catch her breath.

He tells her how beautiful she is... how soft her skin is... and how much he loves her.

She runs her hands over his body, and whispers in his ear, "And I love you. I've never stopped loving you."

They exchange passionate kisses, sensual caresses, and make love to one another on the king-sized bed. Their erotic images reflected in the mirror.

The same fantasy I visualized and sent out into the universe... again and again. I hoped this weekend in Chicago would bring us together. Apparently, my hopes still floated somewhere out in the universe.

I took my cell phone out and read our messages from last night... the one I sent from the parking lot... and his reply after arriving back at the hotel.

"I felt so close to you tonight. Take care. Night night, Jake. LUJ2lls."

"Remembered lines... didn't fall off stage. Yes, close, like you were there. Night night, Rose. LU2lls"

If he only knew how close. Someday.

I couldn't think about him now... about how much I wanted him... how much I ached for him. Another time, another place. I knew in my heart, eventually, all would align.

I checked the time on my cell. Three-thirty. Time to go. I gathered my things, pulled the door closed behind me, and walked toward the elevator.

* * * * *

I sat at the end of the bar, just behind the tinted windows overlooking the business lobby of the hotel, with a clear view of the elevators. I'd finished one beer and ordered another. I checked the time. Three-thirty. The book reception began at four. She should exit one of those elevators soon.

The waiter set the Miller bottle down and took the empty.

I laid a ten spot on the bar, took a drink, and watched the far elevator door open. Rose.

We hadn't been this close to one another in nearly four decades. Surreal.

Damn. How could she still look the same after all the years? Pretty, petite, blonde... round in all the right places. Sweet, Jesus. She wore the black-knit dress with the buttons down the front. Were the pink, lacy bra and panties underneath? The thought alone excited me... made me hard. Great.

She walked over to the poster in front of the meeting room... the one I looked at earlier. Good time for a text.

* * * * *

Just beyond the elevator downstairs, I spotted the event poster on an easel outside the meeting room.

Please join us for a special afternoon
4:00 p.m. – 6:00 p.m.
Sunday, November 23rd, 2008
Book Signing and Reception
with
Rose Allison Flynn
Meet the award-winning author of
Seasons of Rhyme and Reason

How thrilling to see my book and read the words... *award-winning*. The book had won both a local and a national writing award since publication. Tangible proof that dreams do come true.

The cell vibrated inside my jacket pocket. I checked and found a text from Jake.

"Hello."

"Play over?"

"Yep. Finished. You?"

"At 4."

"Wearing black-knit dress?"

"How'd you know?"

"Lucky guess. Pink undies?"

"Yes. Thought of you."

"Nice."

"Gotta go. Wish me luck."

"Don't need luck, remember? You have a gift."

"I do. Thanks for reminder. Text later."

"Yep. I'll be close."

I walked through the door and followed the sound of voices into the conference room. Diane Sullivan greeted me. Petite, with brown eyes and dark brown hair cascading over her shoulders, she and Kathryn worked together as pre-school teachers when their children were young.

"You must be Rose. I'm Diane Sullivan. I've heard so much about you from Kathryn. It's good to finally meet." She handed me a glass of wine.

"Nice to meet you, too, Diane. Thanks for the wine. It will help calm my nerves."

"We're a pretty friendly group. No need for nerves. Come sit. I'll introduce you soon."

Diane took her place behind the podium. I sat at a table close by, sipped my wine, and waited for the introduction. The audience—comprised of mostly women over forty-five—chatted and laughed among themselves, occasionally smiling in my direction. I smiled back. I remembered sitting where they were—smiling at a favorite author of mine—wondering what she was like. Now I was that author. Amazing.

A few minutes later, Diane stepped to the podium and began the program.

"Good evening. I'm happy to introduce the author of an award-winning collections of essays and poetry, entitled *Seasons of Rhyme and Reason*."

At nearly the same time, my cell phone vibrated. I listened to Diane while discreetly exchanging texts with Jake.

"Wine? Anyone dancing on tables yet?"

"Working on first glass. No table dancing yet. Night is young."

"Indeed. Pics please when pole dancing starts."

"K. Will text after my turn on pole."

"Have a visual on that. Later."

"You wish. ☺"

I slipped the cell back into my pocket and listened as Diane finished.

"Rose grew up in the small community of Macomb, Illinois. As a child she... Attended Western Illinois University... received her Masters Degree in Special Education at the University of Missouri... Began her teaching career... Now resides in Albuquerque, New Mexico... It's my pleasure to introduce Rose Allison Flynn."

* * * * *

The audience applauded. Rose stood and walked to the podium, book and notes tucked under her arm. At the same time, I felt a tap on my shoulder and turned toward a young, attractive redhead.

"Sir, there are a few seats up near the front if you'd like to sit down."

"No, thanks. I'm good. Don't mind standing."

"Okay... just checking."

She walked toward the front. I hated being called "sir" by young, attractive women. Made me feel like an old shit. Guess I was an old shit to her.

I moved farther to the left and positioned myself behind a couple standing in the back. Great view. Perfect for flying under the radar.

Rose began with a poem, followed by two short stories: one about finding the perfect Christmas tree when her children were little, the other about her first real crush with a boy she sat next to on the school bus in eighth grade. She followed with another poem, "Adopted By Roy Rogers." I remembered story night at Parkridge when she first read the poem to me.

In between the stories and poems, the audience commented and asked her questions... all types of questions. Were her poems and stories based on true events? Was she married? Did she have a family? What were her students like? Rose answered the questions like a seasoned veteran. I got caught up in the interaction so much, I lost track of time. Before I knew it, Diane fielded the final question of the evening.

* * * * *

"I think we have one more question in the back."

A tall, slim blonde in a gray, wool dress stood. She reminded me of Karen as a young girl, when we first moved into our apartment at Parkridge.

"Rose... you articulate the feelings of our generation. You were there and we know you were there by the stories and poems you write. Have you ever considered writing a novel? A romance novel maybe?"

"Yes, I have thought about writing romance novels. In fact, I just completed my first manuscript a few days ago. I haven't decided whether to publish. The writing's been more therapeutic than anything."

The young woman in the back continued.

"Can you tell us about the storyline?"

"It's a love story that spans four decades and involves Facebook, texting, and emails."

"Another *Fifty Shades of Gray*?"

"No, different kind of love story. I like to leave things to the imagination. Sometimes what we imagine, what we dream about, is the most sensual. It's about the thoughts, the words, the electricity that happens between two people.

"I'm basically a storyteller, a wordsmith, a dream weaver. I think everyone's life is a story, a novel, but few write it down.

"Look at your life. Look back and see it unfolding. See everything and everyone you have touched or who has touched you.

"Each story, each life—though different in content—has the ability to connect with another person in some way. It's the heart stories, the love stories, the memory stories—about friends, family, lovers, places—that connect us all.

"It's that something that can't be seen or measured or analyzed... or even explained. It can only be captured within the mind and held within the chambers of the heart.

"It's about love—about the spark, the electricity, the constancy— that creates the bond and remains forever etched on our memory pages."

The audience clapped.

* * * * *

Jesus. Who was this confident, insightful woman at the podium? How many miles had the girl from yesterday walked to arrive at this place in time?

* * * * *

"Thank you for inviting me tonight... for making me feel welcome. It's been my pleasure being here with you. I planned to close with a poem, but I'd like to share something from the manuscript, the novel, instead."

I opened the manuscript and read from the Prologue.

"Sometimes fate or providence or divine intervention or just plain luck happens, and events are set in motion, defying time and explanation. I had an opportunity to reach out to someone who became the trigger for my remembrance of something more, something left behind a long time ago.

Without a real plan for what could happen, I made an effort and reached out for a chance meeting with someone who gave me a glimpse of the color again, if only for an instant. But in that instant, I saw it. I remembered it. And I wanted it. Someone stepped back through time and into my life again... and everything routine, mundane and colorless changed.

This someone knew about my plans, my hopes, my dreams. This someone knew the person I had been when I started out. This someone knew me and because of that, I could clearly see a different path I wanted to walk down. A path filled with the colors of life once again. He had been my friend, my soul friend, a kindred spirit. He had been my lover. Forty years ago."

I closed the notebook. The audience clapped. Diane joined me at the podium.

"I don't know about you, but I hope Rose publishes the novel soon and comes back here for her first book signing! Enjoy another glass of wine and the refreshments. Rose and I will meet you at the signing table."

We walked over to the table and for the next hour or so, I signed books, chatted, answered questions, and posed for pictures.

* * * * *

I watched her close the notebook and listened to the applause. The words she read—the beginning of the love story—I recognized. The kindred spirit, the lover from forty years ago... me.

While she walked over to the signing table, I quietly slipped out the door and walked the short distance back the bar.

I was proud to know Rose Allison. Thankful to love her, and be loved by her again.

* * * * *

After signing a final book for the last person in line, I looked up and saw Diane walking back toward the table, a bottle of wine in her hand. "Rose, you must be exhausted. We'll take care of packing your books and getting them shipped off. Why don't you go up to your room and relax."

"That sounds good. I am tired. It's been a long day."

She set the wine on the table. "Have a glass of wine, relax in the tub, and watch an old romance movie."

"Sounds perfect. Thanks for making this such a special evening for me."

"You're welcome. I meant what I said about the novel."

"If I publish... I'll be back. Promise. Good night, Diane."

"Night, Rose."

I gathered my things, including the bottle of wine, and walked out the door. On my way to elevator, I passed the main hotel bar. It looked like a nice place for a drink, although crowded. Maybe next time.

I stepped into the posh elevator, pushed the fifth floor button, and waited as the doors closed. A brass railing ran along the four sides of the wood-paneled interior. Against its back wall... a tufted velvet, crimson bench. The ceiling... mirrored. Beautiful. The perfect setting for an elevator fantasy... another one shared between Jake and me. I clicked and saved two interior pictures.

I checked the cell for messages. Nothing. Maybe he and Ben were at Will's, or maybe they were striking the set since the play was over.

The elevator pinged, the doors opened. I walked down the crimson and beige carpeted hallway to Room 532. I wondered at the odds of a hotel room number matching a phone number from nearly forty years ago. Probably astronomical... but I never questioned the universe.

* * * * *

I watched her walk by the bar and glance in. Too crowded for her, I suspected. She never liked crowds.

My eyes followed her across the lobby to the elevator. She stepped inside, pushed the button, the doors closed.

* * * * *

I slid the card key into the slot, turned the knob and stepped inside. The room, bathed in a soft, amber glow from the city lights outside. The lights shimmered through countless raindrops... quietly cascading down the outside balcony windowpane. No need for other lights.

The room felt warm, comfortable, and serene—the soft patter of the rain, a soothing childhood memory—a perfect place to unwind and reflect.

I set my purse and briefcase on one of the wing chairs in front of the window, and slipped my jacket and shoes off. I walked over to the dresser, scrunching my toes in the plush, pile carpeting, and opened the bottle of wine. I filled one of the glasses from the silver tray on the dresser.

I turned the white, feather duvet down on the king-size bed, and fluffed and stacked the pillows against the headboard. I nestled into the sheets and duvet, clothes and all. I'd shower and change into my T-shirt and boxers after Jake and I texted.

I sipped my wine and reflected on the events of the past two days: the smooth, early morning flight from Albuquerque, Jake's performance in the play, being close to him, the successful book event, and the lovely hotel and room. The weekend played out like a fantasy.

Only one thing missing from this lovely fantasy... Jake.

I retrieved my phone from the nightstand and sent the elevator pictures to him.

* * * * *

"Another Miller?"

"No. Just the check."

I paid the tab and finished the beer slowly. I wanted to give her time to unwind, relax for a few minutes. This encounter would be intense for both of us.

My cell vibrated. I checked for a text and found two elevator pictures from Rose.

Time to go.

I walked to the elevator, stepped in, and pushed five. A faint scent of perfume lingered. Patchouli and sandalwood.

I noted the brass railing from the pictures and fantasized holding Rose against it, whispering softly in her ear, pressing my body into hers.

The doors opened and I stepped out into the empty hallway. I followed the faint perfume scent down the hall to the right, and found myself standing outside room 532.

The cell vibrated again. A text this time.

"Wish you were here... wine, lovely room w/view, and huge, comfy bed. You would love it."

I sent a text back.

"I would."

"Like the elevator pics I sent? Thought about you."

"Liked very much. Was just in an elevator like that... thought about you."

"You were? Where are you?"

"Close."

"How close?"

"Open the door, Rose."

Chapter Fifteen

The rain courses down now in shimmering, silver sheets,
Flooding and triggering my heart with rapid, tattooed beats.
Tangled together, intimately joined like a warm hand in a glove.
Releasing within one another's embrace, drenched in passion and love
"I loved you then, I'll love you always," soft lips sweep over mine.
Nestled closely in his arms...precious moment out of time.

Chicago, Illinois
Palmer House
Fall 2008
Sunday Afternoon

For a few surreal moments, I stood—cell phone in hand—rereading the last text.
"Open the door, Rose."
Open the door?
Oh, my God.
Was this a dream... a fantasy?
I placed the phone on the nightstand and padded across the carpeting to the door. Placing the palm of my hand against the smooth dark wood, I closed my eyes and sent a fervent, child-like prayer heavenward.
"Dear Jesus... please let Jake be standing on the other side of this door."

My hands trembled. My fingers fumbled with the lock. I grasped the knob and pulled the door open.

There in the hallway—wearing a white-linen, button-down shirt, untucked over faded, blue denim jeans, a brown leather tote in his hand—stood Jake Richardson.

His deep-blue eyes met mine... more beautiful than I remembered. His hair—long, thick, now streaked with gray and silver—brushed the collar of his shirt. A full, graying mustache lined his generous lips.

"Hello, Rose."

Overwhelming. There was no other word to describe this moment.

"Oh, my God... Jake."

I reached out to him. He stepped inside, swept me into his arms, and quietly closed the door behind us.

I nestled into him—heard the rapid tattoo of his heart—pressed my cheek against his, and held on.

* * * * *

Her body trembled beneath mine—her breath, warm and sweet against my face—and I tasted her silent, salty tears as they rolled down her cheeks, onto my lips.

I gazed down at the beautiful woman tucked in my arms, and remembered the young girl I fell so deeply in love with. Never in this lifetime, did I think I would see her, or hold her, or love her again. And yet, she was no more than a breath away... a kiss away.

I remembered words from the chat line... *"When we see each other... will you hold me in your arms, Jake... just hold me so I can feel your heart?"*

I held her—as I'd done on countless nights in dreams and fantasies—now hesitant to let go... afraid she'd slip away... drift back through time.

"Close your eyes. I've got you now. Just let me hold you."

She skimmed her lips across the hollow of my ear. "Yes, hold me. Don't let go."

"No. I won't ever let go again. I'm here for you."

I pulled her closer, entwined my fingers in her hair. She stroked the back of my neck and trailed up into my hair... the other hand rested on my chest, her long, slender fingers clutching the front of my shirt.

"How, Jake? How did this happen?"

I pressed kisses over her ear, her cheek, her temple, and wedged my thigh between her legs. She pressed back intimately against me.

"The furnace went out at the theater last night, pipes froze and busted. Matinee cancelled. That's how."

She kissed my lips, the tip of my nose. "On the same weekend as my book thingy. My God, Jake."

I returned each kiss. "I know... way outside the box for me. I stopped trying to figure it out and got in the truck. When does your plane leave?"

"Late tomorrow night... ten-fifty."

"Time is precious then."

"Yes... precious."

I kissed her and kissed her... traced her mouth with the tip of my tongue... tasted her... and tasted her again. Sweet as I remembered. She returned my kisses, traced my lips with her tongue... sucked lightly on my bottom lip, and whispered, "I remember how much I loved this pouty, bottom lip."

Jesus. Like fire and gasoline... our passion ignited.

The kisses deepened—tasting, teasing, exploring—but never deep enough. The embraces intensified—caressing, pressing, stroking—but never close enough.

Like a remembered dance—slow and sensual—I led and she followed.

Like the cadence beneath a melody—rapid and rhythmic—our breathing, our heartbeats edged the song, the dance, along.

Anticipation—that titillating rush of events yet to come—engulfed us.

"I want to lay next to you again, Jake. Feel your body against mine... please."

I cupped her face between my hands, kissed her lips harder, and stroked the side of her face with my thumbs. Her eyes sparkled, her cheeks flushed a rosy pink. I took her hand in mine and led her to the bed.

I toed my shoes off, edged onto the bed, and pulled her next to me. We lay facing one another... our bodies entwined... legs and arms tucked and draped intimately. She rested her hand against my chest. I did the same against her breast. I brushed my lips, my mustache over her mouth... she completed the kiss.

I cupped her breast in my hand, and kissed her through the black-knit fabric of her dress... first one and then the other. She stroked my face with her hand.

"You're still so beautiful... the same as when I last saw you."

She smiled and turned those dimples on me. "I'm glad I still look good to you, Jake. You look wonderful... handsome."

I kissed the palm of her hand. "Not so handsome anymore."

"You're wrong, Jake... so wrong." She traced the mustache with her index finger. "You didn't have this back then."

"No. Couldn't grow one back then."

She traced it again—this time with kisses—from one side to the other. "It's soft and sexy. Looks good on you."

Jesus. I couldn't remember the last time anyone said I was sexy.

She massaged the back of my neck with her long, slender fingers. Her touch sent the loveliest zings of electricity through my entire body. I remembered that current between us.

"I'm glad you still wear your hair long. The gray and silver are beautiful. You must have the women howling back in Rockton."

"Can't say I've heard much howling over the years."

"Do you trust me, Jake?"

"Implicitly."

"You look good, sexy, and they're howling... you just haven't been listening."

I sat up and began working my way down the front of the dress—peeling back the fabric a little farther each time a cloth-covered button popped out—until finally, the dress lay open.

There—peaking out beneath it—a pale pink, lacy bra and matching pink, lacy panties. Sweet Jesus.

I traced the outline of the lacy cups with my fingertips. "So pretty.. so soft."

She looked up at me. "For you... only for you, Jake."

I lowered my head and brushed my lips over the top of her breasts, then kissed her lips. I slipped my hand further inside the dress—gliding over warm, soft skin—coming to rest on her waist. My fingertips trailed down and over her hips, her tummy. I nuzzled my face between her breasts, turned my head and rested there. Her heart pounded rhythmically in my ear. She pulled me closer. I kissed her left breast and then her right, my tongue tracing her nipples, my lips gently sucking through the lacy pink bra. Sweet murmurs escaped her lips and floated into the amber twilight of the room.

She unbuttoned the top button on my shirt. "I want to touch you... feel your skin against mine. Would you like that?"

"Yes... please."

Yes, please, would you like that? Words and phrases from texts and chats... our late-night fantasies. Now we said them to each other in real time.

Watching her unbutton my shirt and kissing the exposed skin, grew more and more erotic, until my shirt—like her dress—lay loose and open. She used her hands, her clever fingers, to explore under my shirt.

Her lips and tongue followed the path of her fingertips. She brushed soft, sensuous, sucking kisses over one side and the other... moving to my back, my stomach, my chest. She kissed and suckled my nipples until they were taut and hard... like I'd left hers.

Jesus. I couldn't remember anything feeling this good in a very long time... if ever.

Human touch. We both missed the intimacy human touch brings.

I unhooked the front clasp of the pink, lacy bra and slowly pulled back one side and the other.

"I remember seeing your breasts for the first time and thinking how pretty and perfect they were. You took my breath away then. You take my breath away now." Her eyes glistened with tears, a slight smile formed on her lips. She stroked the side of my face. "I love you so very much."

I caressed first one, then the other in my hands... kissing, tracing the nipple with my tongue, sucking and tugging at each breast. She raked her fingers through my hair and held me to her breasts. Like a child, I lay against her, suckling first one nipple and then the other. Soothing, comforting, familiar. We lay there together enjoying one another's bodies.

Harder and faster the raindrops splashed and cascaded down. Intensifying the sensuality and eroticism playing out just inside the window from the shimmering night lights outside.

She whispered through the sounding rain, "I want to feel the weight of your body on mine, again... please."

Her words, the image of my body on hers, jolted me. The ache inside me deepened.

I rolled her onto her back and tucked her body beneath mine. I straddled her and used my knees, my thighs, to part her legs. Slowly, rhythmically, I pumped my jeans-covered hips, my erection, deeper into the sweet V between her legs. I held her head between my hands and kissed her... my tongue mimicking the movement of our entwined bodies.

"I love feeling the weight, the hardness, of your body on mine... it feels so good, so right."

"And you're so soft. I feel as if I'm sinking further into you each time I move. But if I keep pumping into that lovely, soft body much longer... we'll be playing cards the rest of the night."

A grin. "Cards aren't exactly what I had in mind."

"No, me either." I shifted my body from hers and we lay facing one another again, her leg draped over my hip, my knee between her legs.

"Love me, Jake... in every way possible. And help me love you, to know what to do."

"I will, baby. We won't miss anything this time around. We were both young, inexperienced lovers back then. Hell, I knew little, other than the basics about lovemaking or intimacy. Another regret of mine—regarding you—I've carried through the years."

"You were my first love, Jake. Everything you said or did seemed perfect to me in every way. My regrets over the years are different. I regret not sharing our youth together. I regret not having a baby with you... regret that very much. Making love and having that love become a person would have been very sweet. And I regret I'm not the one sharing your life now... spending each day and night with you."

Her list of regrets and mine... nearly the same. Our youth and the opportunity for a baby were gone. But sharing a life together... a distinct possibility. Bringing experience to our love making... I would resolve

"No more regrets for either of us. We'll change what we can, and let go of what we can't." I kissed her several times and whispered, "I never regretted loving you, Rose."

I looked into her face, and saw *love* looking back. She swept her lips back and forth over mine, and kissed me. "And I never forgot, or regretted loving you, Jake... not for one second."

I pulled her to my chest, rested my chin on her head and we held onto one another tightly. The regrets—the fears and frustrations of the past year—seemed small and insignificant. Everything important... we held tight in our arms.

Several minutes passed. She rolled onto her back. My eyes traveled down her body and back. She lay beside me in just her pink panties, her legs slightly open, one arm on her smooth tummy, the other extended on the white duvet. Her breasts, full and fair, the areolas of her nipples, large and a deep rosy pink... the nipples, hard from the cool air and my touch. I could barely breathe from wanting her.

I moved my hand over her breasts again... massaging, pulling, tweaking... then repeating each action with my lips. She watched me... my face, my hands. I played in the outfield a while longer, then edged closer to home. My hands eased between her legs... to the pink, lacy panties. Her body shuddered.

"Your panties are wet."

"It's your fault. I'm achy and wet from wanting you."

I took her hand and placed it firmly on my erection. "You have the same affect on me... achy, wet, hard... from wanting you. Those panties need to come off."

"Yes... and so do yours."

I hooked my thumbs on each side of the lace, eased them over her hips and down her legs. I helped her pull them off, then kissed my way up the inside of her thighs, in between her legs—stopping there several minutes to explore and taste that part of her I'd missed earlier—then moved on to her breasts, and back to her lips.

She held onto the back of my neck. "Closer. I need to be closer, Jake. I want to feel you against me... taste you... breathe you in. All of you."

She reached down, unbuttoned my jeans, and unzipped them. She slipped her fingers inside and ran the palm of her hand over me. Her hand crept inside my briefs and explored every firm inch. I closed my eyes and let her.

I raised my hips and she helped slide both my jeans and briefs off onto the floor. We pulled back the duvet and crawled under the covers together. I pulled her into my arms, she draped her leg over my hip, and I tucked my body into hers.

"Jesus... you feel so good, so warm and tight around me, honey."

"Oh, Jake. I feel like that young girl again, making love for the first time... the one you fell in love with so long ago."

"I never thought I'd see you again, never thought I'd hold you, or kiss you, or love you again." In between the words, we kissed, over and over.

"Neither did I."

Everything seemed to happen in lovely slow motion. Moments lingered... time waited... on us.

"My heart overflows with love for you, Jake. I don't know what to do with my emotions. What I feel for you is overwhelming."

"I'm just a farmer from Illinois, Rose. That's all I've ever been... ever will be."

"No. You're the young boy I fell in love with, the young boy no one remembered, except me. And now, I've fallen in love with the man he became... the man no one knows, except me."

Tears welled in her eyes, trickled down her cheeks, and fell onto my weathered hand. Tenderly, I brushed the tears from her cheeks with my thumb, and tasted the tears.

"I love how you taste... even your tears are sweet. No one's ever said things to me like that, only you. As a young girl, you stole my heart. Now you hold it forever."

"Tell me this is real, Jake... tell me I'm not dreaming."

"You're not dreaming, baby. I'm here. This is real."

"Then love me, Jake... make love to me. Let me love you again."

"Whatever you want, Rose. Anything. Everything. We'll make it happen."

* * * * *

We kissed, we caressed, we made love... everywhere and in every way... whispering sensual, erotic, love words to one another.

Neither held back, nor hesitated. I read her thoughts—her desires, her fantasies—and she read mine. Every one of them.

We stepped onto the pages of our own romance novel—assumed the lead roles—played every fantasy scene we'd typed out in texts and chats. Mentally, we'd made love to one another over and over... rehearsing every word, every move. It was show time.

"Look in the mirror, Rose."

I wanted her to see what I saw—the reflection of our silhouettes across from the bed—naked and kneeling—with me behind her. Her back was arched against my chest, my stomach. My hands held her breasts. My hips rocked slowly in and out, filling her with my heat. I moved my hand between her legs and touched the soft, warm folds that enveloped me.

"I wish I could be that youthful girl for you again."

"I see a beautiful woman in the mirror... and a sweet, young girl. For me, they're the same."

"That's how I see you, Jake. A handsome man who makes me tremble... and a beautiful, bell bottomed boy who took my breath away."

The image in the mirror, both beautiful and erotic, like the cover shot of a fantasy romance novel. But this was no fantasy. This was

real. She was a young man's fantasy all over again. My fantasy...
and I, hers.

* * * * *

Gently, I brushed a few wayward strands of blonde hair from her
cheek. A smile formed on her lips and she looked at me through
sleepy eyes.

"Good morning," I whispered.

"Morning," her sleepy voice, low and sexy. "I love waking up in
your arms. It reminds me of that first morning we woke up together on
the floor of my bedroom at Parkridge. Remember?"

"Of course. A short night, not much sleep... that began again the
next morning."

"Yes, a lovely night... a beautiful morning. I never forgot."

"No... me either. That memory came to mind first when I saw your
Friend request."

"Me, too, though we talked about the weather and crops and school
for weeks."

"Had to. Didn't have a plan. Still don't. Just knew I wanted back in
your life."

"Me, too. Knew I shouldn't reply to your messages, but couldn't
stop myself."

"Nope. Every word I read made me want to write and read more."

"Yes. The same for me. I remembered more... and I wanted more.
When you said you still loved me, never stopped loving me, I knew I
was in trouble."

"Yep, well. I was already there... already in trouble. I had no clue
what I was doing, and didn't care. I just wanted you back in my life."

"I know. God, I know. It wouldn't have happened with anyone but
you. The thought never crossed my mind in all my married years...
until you, Jake."

"Yep. Same here. Had plenty of opportunities over the years.
Never seemed worth the trouble for just sex. All that changed the day I
found your message."

I closed my eyes and felt the steady rhythm of her heartbeat beneath my cheek as I lay against her breasts. Being with her brought everything back—her mannerisms, her voice, her scent, her body— and especially, how much I still loved her. An image—frozen in time—trapped within my memories,

"Jake, I wanted you to be the first one to make love to me. I wanted you to be the one I gave that part of myself to. I wanted that more than anything, especially our first night together."

I listened to her words and knew she'd finally acknowledged what happened all those years ago. Did she read the words in her journal? Did Molly help her face the ugly truth? I guess it didn't matter how she remembered... but that she remembered.

I wrapped my leg over her hip, stroked the side of her face with my hand and kissed the soft upper curve of her breasts.

"Rose, in every way that mattered most, I *was* the first one to make love to you. I *was* the first one you freely gave yourself to... not anyone else... only me. I knew that then, I know it now."

I wrapped her in my arms and held her close. I brushed my lips back and forth, over her ear, her cheek, her hair.

"How did you know, Jake?"

The long ago, unfinished chapter of secrets—both hers and mine— was about to end.

"When I heard you say those words... *please don't hurt me*... I knew something was wrong. And when I asked, you weren't ready to discuss it, or confront it. Instead, I tried to make the night special, tried hard not to do anything to hurt you or make you afraid in any way. I wanted to love you, to replace the hurt with love, the only way I knew how."

"And you did, Jake. You made the night beautiful for me, sweet and tender. A night I remembered through the years."

"There's more I need to tell you."

"More? Okay... I'm listening."

"After we made love and you fell asleep. I got up and rummaged through our clothes, looking for my cigarettes. I saw your journals stacked next to the dresser and, under the guise of wanting to read more of your poetry, took a couple into the bathroom with me. I closed the door and sat in there smoking and reading for quite awhile... long enough to read the letter you wrote to your mom."

"You read my journals... about Vic?"

"Yep. I shouldn't have, but I did. I read every word you wrote about that bastard and what he did. I fucking wanted to kill him."

"You never said anything."

"No. Figured either you didn't want to talk about it or you'd blocked it out. I didn't really know what to do... so I didn't do anything. I kept quiet. I thought maybe in time you'd bring it up or remember things on your own. Another regret I carried regarding you. You needed more help than I could give. I didn't get that help for you. I let it go, like so many other things I let go back then."

"You didn't know. I didn't either. Like you said, we were young... two kids fumbling around, trying to grow up."

"Yep. Fumbling around for sure. But you remembered?"

"Yes. One late night after we finished chatting. I dug the journals out and read them. I'd read them before, but this time turned out differently. When I came to the letter, it was like reading it for the first time. I called and talked with Molly the next morning. We worked on that, along with so many other things. I'm able to see things differently... see Mom differently. I won't ever forget the past... the things that happened to me... but I've moved on with my life. I don't blame myself anymore for what happened... for events I had no control over. Children pattern early on from those closest to them, good or bad. Children learn to cope with things that happen to them... good or bad. I patterned. I coped. And this is who I am, as a result of all that happened."

"That's a good thing, Rose. Kids are seldom to blame, but always feel accountable for what they can't control... for the situations they find themselves in."

"I know that now. That's why I've always had the inner voice—the child within me—talking and advising. She's a splinter of me—a friend, confidante, protector—who evolved early on in childhood. She's still there—will probably always be there—but now I understand the *who* and *why* of her. She's a part of me and it's okay for her to be there."

"Another good thing to know... to understand about yourself. You've come such a long way, honey."

"I have. And so much of this is because of you, our conversations, after the Friend request. It was as if you came back through time, held out your hand, and let me hold it again. You remembered me. You never forgot me. And this time around, I saw things clearly enough to find help for myself. No matter what happens between us, Jake, I will always be grateful for that. "

"Not mad at me for reading your journals, invading your privacy?"

"No. I understand why you read them, and I love you even more."

She kissed my lips once, twice... and eased me onto my side to spoon against my back. A position fondly remembered. I felt her fingers creating small, circular patterns across my shoulders.

Her fingers stilled, then began again. This time, specifically tracing the tattoo—the faded red rose with green leaves—on my upper left shoulder. The *other* rose.

"When... how long have you had this?"

Silence. I had to think, to choose my words carefully. I didn't want to hurt her, make her sad for the lost time between us.

"Please. Tell me, Jake. When did you get this? You didn't have it the weekend of the rock fest. You had your shirt off all weekend. I would have seen it."

"No. I got it the weekend after we came back. I never got the chance to show it to you."

"No. I guess not."

"I always thought we'd get back together. I didn't know you would leave, that I'd never see you again."

We both sat up, my back to her, her legs wrapped around me. Again she traced the tattoo—first with her fingertips, then with her lips—kissing each petal, each leaf, oh, so softly.

I turned my head back toward her. "Do you like it?"

"Yes, very much. It's lovely."

"Kind of old school. Guys don't get flowers much anymore."

Moments passed in silence. I felt teardrops splash onto the rose tattoo. She rested her cheek against my shoulder, wrapped her arms around me, and held me.

"I know you don't want to hear this, but I'm sorry... so sorry for being such a stupid, young girl. For not listening. For not letting you explain. For running away."

I turned her in my arms, and nuzzled my head against hers.

"Hush. Stop. We've had this discussion. We both made mistakes."

"Yes, we did. But the tattoo wasn't one of them. It's beautiful. I love it and I'm glad I finally got to see it."

"Me, too. And, you know what, Rose?"

"What?"

"I've never once regretted the tattoo... the memories... or you."

I closed my eyes as she strategically placed soft, warm kisses over my eyelids, down my cheeks, and onto my lips.

"Did anyone ever ask you about it... about the rose? Did Beth?"

"Yes, she asked the first time we were naked together. I told her it was my mother's favorite flower. That was the truth. She never brought it up again. Never asked."

"Did anyone know about it back then?"

"The guys in the band... and Ben. He's probably the only one who remembers. He's never mentioned it in all the years I've known him. But he makes veiled references to you, now and then."

"He does?"

"Yep."

"Oh, my. I wonder what he would think of all this... of us?"

"I don't know. Wondered about it. Almost said something to him this morning, but changed my mind. He kept pressing me, like he knew something. I couldn't take the chance."

"No, you can't... we can't. Besides, what could he know?"

"Not a thing I know of. He mentioned seeing a woman at the play Saturday night that reminded him of you. I let the comment slide. Finally, he let it go."

"That's good... good he let it go."

"Yep. Wait here a second. I brought you something."

"You did? Corn? Tractor part?"

"Tried. Neither would fit."

I returned from rummaging through my bag and sat down on the edge of the bed. "I think this belongs to you." From behind my back, I held out the faded, fabric rose. "Happy belated birthday."

Gently she took it from my hand, inspected it, and clutched it tightly to her breasts.

"Oh, Jake, my rose. The rose you gave me when I tripped on acid with you. The one you found with all your drug stuff."

"Yep. That's the one. Thought you should have it. Wondered if I'd ever get the chance to give it back."

"This is the sweetest gift. Something tangible from our time together back then... something to go with the memories. And you did get the chance, Jake. You did."

The conversation ended when she traced and kissed the tattoo again. We made love, and slept in a little longer... the faded rose, clutched tightly in her hand.

Later we shared breakfast in bed: pancakes, sausage, scrambled eggs, and coffee.

"Still black with two sugars?"

"Yep."

I watched her hands—the long, graceful fingers—as she tore the sugar packets open and lazily stirred them into the black coffee. The same graceful fingers I licked and sucked sticky marshmallow remnants from one winter night.

"I don't remember you drinking coffee, Rose. Only Diet Shasta Cola."

"Good memory. We couldn't afford the *real thing*."

"No. We couldn't afford much of anything. That's why we shoplifted."

"*You* shoplifted."

"Okay... *I* shoplifted."

We never left the room until Monday evening. We hung the *Do Not Disturb* sign outside the door, ordered meals and wine from room service, and asked the maid to leave fresh towels and linens outside the door.

We enjoyed the honeymoon we never had, after the marriage that never took place.

Those next twenty-some hours, we enjoyed one another's company in every way possible—talking, laughing, touching, playing, loving—remembering the past, longing for a future.

We made love in the king-size bed, on the chaise lounge, and on the floor. We made love up against the shower wall. We leisurely washed each other's hair. And later, lay at opposite ends of the couch—massaging one another with lotion—slowly working our way from one end to the other. I painted her toenails *grape pop* purple, she painted mine *blush* pink.

We were no longer in a hurry to get somewhere, to do something, to see someone. What we wanted, we found in that hotel room— time and one another—both precious and finite commodities.

We held one another. We loved one another. We savored every precious moment of those dark, quiet, rainy hours in the room with a view.

Later, we sat cuddled up on the overstuffed, cream-colored sofa situated at the foot of the king-size bed. I wore her extra-large Illinois State sleep shirt over knit briefs. She wore my white linen shirt over lace panties.

We reminisced about the past—the band, the music, the drugs, the times—then focused on the *now*.

We discussed our children. She spoke lovingly of Joe and Jenna, as only a mother could. I told her about Brian and Dustin, relaying stories as a proud dad. We shared pictures of home and family and pets saved on our cell phones.

We talked and laughed, listened like long lost friends.

I asked her about her life with Paul. She shared her frustrations, her suspicions, her loneliness.

"I'm alone most of the time. Paul's gone for all intents and purposes. Hardly makes family dinners anymore. I'm pretty sure he and his secretary, Natalie, are living together at the condo in Santa Fe since he opened the branch office there. I've never said anything, but I think Joe and Jenna figured it out. They explained to the children Grandpa and Grandma live in different houses. Presumably because of Grandpa's work. So far, they haven't asked any questions, at least none I know about. I realize by doing nothing, neither of us will have a chance at happiness."

Jesus. I wanted to wrap her in my arms and never let her go, but I knew the time for us wasn't right. Not yet.

She asked about my life and I shared the daily minutia, the daily routine she already knew. She pressed for more.

"Tell me what you're really thinking, where you're at, Jake. Talk to me."

"I'm thinking how difficult it is for me to wander outside the box I've lived in my entire life. Before this weekend, I thought about being with you, in every sense of the word, until I ached. But when it came down to actually making plans, I totally stressed out."

"I understand the situation between us is stressful, frustrating. But you made this weekend happen. We're together because you stepped outside that box."

"I surprised myself. I figured with you and the universe pulling for me, even I couldn't screw it up."

She hugged me, rubbed her cheek against mine. "I love you, Jake."

"And I love you, but sometimes I'm afraid. Afraid for both of us. Afraid of screwing up what's left of our lives. Afraid of not being able to make a new life together. I have no idea how my sons would react if I asked their mother for a divorce. And who knows what Beth might do. She could make our lives miserable. I'm not sure I could start over at my age, even with your help. I worry about all of this, Rose. And I know I should have thought things through when this first began... but I couldn't think of anything except I'd found you again."

"You're not alone. I worry. I'm afraid, too. Even though our lives are different, we share common ground. I wake up in the middle of the night so stressed, I can't go back to sleep. Change is scary at any age, but especially at our age. Most choose to stay where they are, even though they're unhappy. I don't want that. I've had that."

"I kept thinking I would come up with a plan... a solution. What started out seemingly so simple, months ago, ended up complicated."

"I know. Sometimes I wish I'd never sent the Friend request... you'd never responded. I wouldn't know about you. You wouldn't know about me. We would have continued on with our lives."

"But you did send it—and I responded. Now there's no going back. Our lives are changed because of those two decisions."

"My life is better because of you, Jake. I don't want to go back to how things were."

"I can't go back either... don't want to. I'm just not sure how to move forward."

"We'll figure it out. We'll find a way. Second chances, to say and do and finish all those things left undone the first time around, are rare. I'm a dreamer, Jake. I believe in second chances, in long shots, and happy endings."

"And I've always loved that in you, Rose."

She didn't know—didn't realize—how she'd influenced me. Now I thought of possibilities outside the boundaries... dreamed of second chances, dreamed of long shots, and happy endings, because of her.

Chapter Sixteen

Lay me down and let your love wash gently over me,
And soothe me softly with that low, steady voice of reason.
Strip all the craziness away and let me just float free.
Heart to heart, soul to soul... if only for one final season.

Chicago Illinois
Palmer House
Fall 2008
Monday afternoon/evening

We sat quietly on the sofa, holding one another close, listening to the rain. *Crossroads* on Palladia music television played softly in the background... song after song. The blended voices of Alison Krauss and Robert Plant filled the room with "Killing the Blues."

I stood and held my arms out to her. "Dance with me, Rose."

She stood, took my hands in hers, and brought them to her lips, kissing them. "I've waited such a long time for you to ask again."

I took her in my arms... one hand firmly around her waist, trailing down her onto her hips, the other holding her hand against my chest. She rested her head against my chin. I led and she followed... setting one another on fire once again.

The song ended, we walked over to the bed, and crawled back into one another's arms. She brushed an errant strand of hair back from my face and lay her head and hand against my chest. I stroked her hair, kissed the top of her head, and listened to her breathing, her heart beating with mine.

For several lovely minutes, we lay together holding, kissing, petting, enjoying one another.

"Jake?"

"What?"

"I need to tell you something. Something I did out of love. Something I planned to tell you... just not this soon. I wanted another memory to tuck away in my heart."

She turned slightly and I looked at her. She tried to look away, but I saw the tears escape and trickle down her cheeks. I cupped her chin in my hand and kissed them away. I tucked her against my chest—her heart thumping beneath me—as Ben's words came to mind. *"She reminded me of Rose."*

No wonder the woman reminded him of Rose. I couldn't help but smile. She came to see the play.

"Did you enjoy the play?"

Silence. Sniffling. I reached for a Kleenex from the box on the nightstand. I held it out to Rose. "Wipe your tears and blow, please."

With child-like obedience, she wiped and blew, and placed the soggy Kleenex in my outstretched hand.

"How did you know?"

"Ben. Remember? He said he saw someone leaving the play Saturday night that looked like you. I assured him it wasn't you, because I knew you were tucked away, safe and sound in your hotel room bed, back in Chicago."

"I tucked away later. And yes, I enjoyed the play very much. You were wonderful... so damn funny. All I saw or heard was you, Jake. I couldn't be that close and not see you act."

"I understand. That's the same reasoning I used when I pulled out of the driveway today. Too close not to see." I rubbed my cheek against the side of her head and kissed her. "I'm happy you came. But damn glad I didn't know. I would have forgotten my lines and fallen off the stage for sure."

"I wanted to tell you, but I couldn't. I knew you'd tell me not to come."

"You're right. I worry inside that box I live in. You know me too well. How did you manage to pull that off?"

"I drove the rental from here and waited in the parking lot until almost curtain time, walked into the deserted lobby, and waited by the double doors for the lights to dim. I saw a corner table in the last row waiting for me. I sat down, ordered a glass of wine, watched the show, and left before the first curtain call."

"Damn slick. Is that when you had the close encounter with Ben?"

"Yes. I saw a couple standing outside the restroom, the gal went inside and I walked by the guy. I made brief eye contact, and by the time I walked by, I recognized him... Ben Chapman. I knew Karen must be in the restroom."

"Jesus. Did you freak?"

"Close. I walked straight out the door to the rental, and sat in the dark watching for Ben or Karen or both. When they didn't show, I figured I made it. That's when I sent you the text, and drove back to the hotel."

"You were damn lucky. Ben almost trailed you to the parking lot."

"Oh, my God. I'm glad he didn't. Then, I would have freaked."

"Make that four freaked out people in the parking lot. A year ago you never would have been so bold."

"No. Too afraid to move from the fringes. I look at things differently now, thanks to you. So you see, all of this is your fault. Deal with it."

"Yep. I can see it's clearly my fault... and my pleasure dealing with you."

* * * * *

We spent the rest of the afternoon rediscovering one another.

Rose wanted to see what I kept in my wallet. She wanted to know what each key on my key ring opened. I wanted to see what she carried in her purse. We looked at the pictures of our children and grandchildren again, sniffed perfume, rubbed hand lotion on one another, chewed Orbit Cinnamon gum, and shared wild cherry Tic

Tacs. I watched her carefully apply lipstick and gloss... then, not so carefully, kissed every bit of it off.

Next we moved on to luggage. She modeled every piece of lingerie and clothing she brought. I did the same with things I'd packed in the leather tote.

"I love that you wear colored briefs instead of tighty-whities. They're very sexy."

"Thank you. You have good taste in lingerie, too. Picked out exactly what I like. Especially the see-through thingies, and the lace garter belt and the thigh highs. Jesus, Rose... so hot."

She smiled and turned the dimples on me. I'd been a sucker for them since twenty. Nothing changed.

When we ran out of clothing to model... we climbed back into the big, comfy bed and explored one another... discovering details both forgotten and remembered. We made love in ways we never knew or dreamed of back in the day. And yet, with Rose, there was a sweetness, an innocence, still there... like that first time.

Nothing compared to the intimacy shared between us. Each time her body tightened and I heard her murmur, and felt the contractions deep inside, I was amazed all over again. I held her close... felt her relax against me, and kissed the little beads of perspiration from her forehead.

"Easy... I've got you now. Rest here in my arms."

She slept. I slept.

Later we moved to the jetted tub.

Rose squirted half the bottle of bubble bath into the hot, bubbling water. I set the dimmer light switch over the tub on low. She laid the bath mat in front of the tub and draped two fluffy bath towels over the back of the vanity. I helped her slip out of the white linen shirt and into the tub. When the bubbles were nearly up to her chin, I turned the water off.

"Be right back. Don't start without me."

"Promise I won't. Tired of playing alone."

That remark reminded me of a late night Facebook chat we shared regarding self-pleasure and intimacy. She and I discussed anything, everything. I shared things with her I never shared with Beth. I knew Rose did the same with me. A matter of trust between us.

I checked the cable guide and turned on the classic rock station. The Moody Blues' album, *Days of Future Past* was featured. I had that album in a box of vinyl somewhere in the basement. Probably next to the drug paraphernalia. The Moody Blues brought back trippy, drug memories—stoned, spaced-out, euphoric days and nights with Rose and the band members.

"Can you hear the music?"

"Just right. The Moody Blues are serenading me in the tub."

"Sounds crowded in there."

"Plenty of room for you."

I brought the bottle of wine from the mini refrigerator, grabbed a wine glass, and paraded into the bathroom... wearing nothing but a smile.

"I see you're wearing the same thing you wore to breakfast."

"I am. You seemed to like it?"

"Mm. Very much."

"Nice bubbles, by the way."

"Thanks. You just want me for my bubbles."

"Oh, I want more than bubbles."

I filled the wine glass and climbed in behind her, draping my legs over hers. I took a sip of wine, turned her head toward mine, and let the wine slowly trickle from my mouth into hers.

She swallowed. I repeated the process. We exchanged several deep kisses and moans of pleasure between us.

"Oh, Jake. I love when you do that. It's sensual, erotic. Makes me ache."

"I know. Has the same affect on me"

"Yes. I can feel that."

"When the warm wine runs from your mouth to mine, it reminds me of..."

Before I finished the last word of my sentence, her lips met mine. Wine slowly trickled from her mouth into mine. I swallowed and finished the kiss.

She looked at me, grinned and responded to my unfinished explanation. "I know, it reminds me of the same."

We finished sharing the glass of wine. I poured another. She settled back against my chest. I held her in my arms, our legs and feet entwined under the churning warm water and bubbles. Her skillful hands and fingers found their way between my legs. Mine toyed with her breasts beneath the bubbles.

The familiar melody and words of "Nights In White Satin" floated in, along with the memories. I could almost smell the aroma of the weed... almost hear the voices of conversation between the band members.

"I wish we had a joint. I'd loved to get wrecked with you again. Would never smoke with anyone else. Only trusted you with the drugs."

I pressed a kiss to the back of her neck. "Me, too. That song took me back. I could almost hear Jerry and Cash's voices, their laughter, smell the weed. Making love to you stoned is about the only thing missing this weekend."

"Yes. I agree. Nothing compares. We'll have to put that on our bucket list."

"Yep. That's a list I might actually enjoy working on."

She brushed her head back and forth against my chest a couple of times, then turned and kissed my chest, my nipples, moving up my neck to my lips. "I love you, Jake. I love you. I'll never tire of saying those words to you."

"And I'll never tire of hearing them." I returned the kisses and whispered into her ear. "I loved you then. I'll always love you, Rose. Always."

We leisurely toweled one another dry and applied lotion... making sure all bases and infields were covered and tended. She slipped on my green plaid, flannel shirt, buttoning only the middle button. No panties this time. I pulled on blue briefs and moved the wine and glass to the nightstand.

Rose fluffed the pillows, turned the bed down, and brought the manuscript from the table in front of the window. We slid under the covers and cuddled next to each other... propped against the fluffy pillows.

"I know this isn't the lake... but it might be the closest we get. I have the poetry book and a copy of the manuscript with me."

"Are both copies mine?"

"Yes, yours, Jake."

"Sign them for me?"

"Of course."

I handed her a pen from the nightstand, and watched as she signed the poetry book, and then the manuscript. She closed the manuscript, stacked the poetry book on top, and held both out to me.

"Wait. Will you read me what you wrote? I want to hear the words in your voice. When I'm alone, and read them again, I'll hear your voice whisper in my ear."

She pulled the books back onto her lap.

"Yes, I'll read what I wrote because I love you, and because of the words you just said to me."

She opened the poetry book, and I listened as she read.

"Jake, when you told me you still loved me... the inspiration, the memories, the love... flowed from your heart to mine and back. I couldn't write the words fast enough. Pages and pages of words... became the poetry, the stories, the book. You are and will always be my muse.—LUJ2lls"

She closed the book, and handed it to me. I pulled her close and kissed her.

"Such lovely words, Rose. Thank you."

"Welcome. They're true."

I kissed her again, and whispered next to her ear, "I know."

I put my arm around her shoulder, and she leaned against me, sliding the opened manuscript onto both our laps. I followed the words as she read to me.

"Jake, late at night or sometimes very early in the morning—while my eyes are still closed—the door opens quietly in the darkness, and you walk back inside... inside my thoughts, my heart, my memories, my arms.

I'll love you always.—Rose"

When she finished reading, I took her hand in mine, kissed the top and then the palm.

"And I'll always love you, and will remember this weekend forever."

"I know. Me, too."

For a few moments, time stood still, and we were lost in one another. Spellbound in the words, the embraces, the kisses... our love.

* * * * *

Jake refilled the wine glass, and scooted in next to me. He placed his hand on top of the book and manuscript still resting on the covers.

"I'm anxious to read these. Have you thought about a title for the novel?"

"Kind of. I came across something I wrote in my diary years ago, right after we first met. I dreamed of being a romance author, and after an evening with you, made up two imaginary book titles: *High On Love* and *Love Whispers Softly*."

"Cool. I vote for *High On Love*. Seems appropriate considering the times back then."

"It does. I'll keep that one in mind." She paused, looked at me, and continued, "I made up author names, too."

"Tell me."

"Rose Richardson. R. A. Richardson."

"I like."

I kissed her and pulled her to me. Jesus. At this moment in time, I would give nearly anything for her last name to be Richardson instead of Flynn.

"Does the story have a happy ending?"

"Of course. I believe in happy endings."

"Yes, you do."

She set the book and manuscript down on the nightstand, and slipped the one remaining button from the front of the flannel shirt. Gliding her leg over my side, my stomach... she sat straddled across my hips. I held her at the waist with my hands. She watched me as she rocked her hips into mine... once, twice... over and over again. She traced my lips with her tongue—hesitated, made me wait—then began again. Brushing and tracing my lips... making me wait. She did this several times until I thought I would explode from wanting her. Finally she pushed her tongue deep inside my mouth and set me on fire. I couldn't hold her tight enough, kiss her hard enough, press my body deep enough.

We both knew how to generate passion in the other. How to make one another *want* until we ached and moaned in desperation for relief, for release. Passion. We knew what it felt like. We generated passion in one another... like no one else could... like no one else ever had.

She brushed her lips along my cheek and whispered. "I'm going to love you... all of you... everywhere. Would you like that, Jake?"

Oh, sweet Jesus. Help me concentrate on the outfield... not sliding home.

"Yes... very much."

And she did. Everywhere. In every way.

I felt the heat, the tension, build deep inside as we rhythmically rocked our bodies together and apart.

She whimpered into my ear, "Oh, Jake..." and dug her fingertips into my shoulders.

Almost there. We were almost there.

"Let go, baby... let go."

"I will... but not without you, Jake."

"I'm right there with you, baby. Right there."

She arched against me... tensed and tightened around me, deep inside her body. I felt the contractions begin—hers and mine—together. I eased her onto her back, she wrapped her legs tightly around my waist. I pumped my hips harder and deeper into her soft core. We clung tightly to one another, and let all restraint slip away.

She shuddered and began to weep. I kissed the tears away as they fell.

"Hush. It's okay, baby. I've got you. I won't let you go. I love you Rose. I love you." The words spilled out so easily with her. Words I'd never been able to say to anyone else. Words I wanted her to hear... from only me. Words I wanted her to remember... from only me.

I shifted onto my side and tucked her next to me, facing one another. She repositioned her leg over my hips, her arm rested on my chest.

"So beautiful. So perfect. And it only happens with you, Jake. Only you. You made it happen that first time... and you made it happen again this weekend. I love you so much. I don't know what I will do without you now."

"This won't be the last time we see each other... the last time we make love. We'll figure something out. Some way to be together."

"How, Jake? How do you see that happening?"

I cupped the back of her head with my hand, kissed her, held her, and rocked her in my arms.

"I don't know yet."

* * * * *

We showered and dressed in silence, but all the while, maintaining physical contact. She skimmed my shoulder, my hips, my arms... with her hands. I brushed my chest against her breasts, her arms, her back. She kissed the back of my head, my hair. I did the same to her. We held hands.

I dressed in the same jeans and white, linen shirt I'd met her at the door in, twenty-four hours earlier. Her scent permeated the shirt. She knew that's why I wore it.

Rose wore bell-bottoms and a white, lacy peasant top. She looked as if she'd just stepped out of a page in time... our time back in Champaign, at Parkridge. Underneath the lacy top... my white ribbed, sleeveless T-shirt. She wore it for the same reason... it carried my scent.

This weekend... a game changer. Seeing one another, holding one another, talking and laughing, making love. We were no longer that fantasy—somewhere in space and time—at the end of a text, a Facebook chat, or an email. Fantasy became reality. I wanted Rose in my life... and she wanted me in hers. Again, so simple, yet so difficult.

It seemed as if I'd just swept Rose into my arms at the front door. Now we helped one another pack to leave. I watched her place the manuscript into my bag... her pink, lacy panties nestled between the middle pages. Sweet. When she thought I wasn't watching, she slipped my green, flannel shirt into her suitcase. I tucked my Illinois State baseball cap under the shirt when she looked away. Sweet, little surprises.

I tried to keep things light for as long as possible, but the tears fell anyway.

We walked to the elevator. I held her hand, carrying her bag and mine in the other. The doors closed. I set everything down and eased her back against the brass railing. I held her in my arms, pressing my body, my hips, firmly against hers. I held her head in my hands and kissed her deep and hard, sweeping my tongue inside her mouth. She leaned in, embraced me, accepting and returning my kisses.

I whispered against her cheek. "I couldn't leave without making out at least once with you in the elevator, against the brass railing."

"Mm. Glad. Future book material."

"Yep. Hot research."

We kissed and held one another through five elevator pings, until the door opened onto the lobby. We gathered our things, and walked out smiling.

Another elevator carried us down to the parking garage. She stood in front of me. I placed my hands over her shoulders, she leaned back and I pressed my lips into her hair. I needed to feel the warmth and softness of her body... remember the scent of sandalwood and patchouli... one last time.

After placing her bag into the trunk of the rental car, I tucked her behind the driver's seat, and fastened the seat belt. I stood beside the car, my hand resting on the rolled down window.

"These two days were beautiful, Jake. The best birthday since Little Phil's. Memories I'll write about. I'll carry in my heart forever."

"For me, too. I won't ever forget."

"Thanks for the baseball hat. I saw you slip it inside the suitcase from the corner of my eye. I'll wear it and think of you each morning as I walk the dogs."

"Good eyes and you're welcome. Anxious to read the manuscript." She placed her hand on top of mine. I leaned in and kissed her. "It's still raining pretty steady. Take care driving. Text me."

"I will. Text me, too."

"Yep."

"Don't text and drive."

"Nope. You either."

I leaned in and cupped the back of her head, kissing her harder, deeper. I wanted to remember the taste and feel of her mouth, her tongue on mine... and glide my fingers through her silky hair one more time.

Tears spilled down her cheeks. I kissed them, tasted them. She whispered against my cheek. "I love you. Will always love you. Don't forget me, Jake. Close your eyes each night and see us together."

"Never forgot you, Rose. Will always love you."

"In my thoughts. Forever in my heart. See you then."

"Yep... see you then."

I clenched my jaw and swallowed. Damn. I hated good-byes. They seemed so final... like the end to something... especially with her.

I stepped back. She rolled up the window and started the car... wiping tears from her cheeks with her hand. She backed out of the parking space and stopped. We looked at one another again. Her left hand formed the peace sign and she mouthed... *I love you.*

I returned both... then watched her drive to the exit, turn onto Monroe Street, and drive away. Away from me.

I picked up my bag and walked the short distance to my truck, opened the door and climbed in. I drifted back and remembered standing outside my apartment at Parkridge... watching her drive away. Away from me. I felt as empty and alone and powerless at that moment, as I did way back then.

I sat alone in the darkness, lost in thought and time, until a loud car horn jolted me back. I pulled out my cell and sent a text to Ben. "Be home in about three hours."

* * * * *

The drive from The Palmer House to Midway took nearly forty minutes in the rain and traffic. I dropped off the rental car and turned in the keys. The airport wasn't as crowded this late at night, and with only my purse and carry-on bag, I checked in and passed through security in a little less than an hour.

I had just enough time for a glass of wine before my flight. I looked around and saw Reilly's Pub not too far from my departure gate. I walked over and sat down in a booth near the back, and ordered a glass of white Zin. The bar had a retro feel... lots of black and white and chrome... with late 1960s and 1970s music playing. A perfect place to relax and reflect on the past couple of days.

Half way through the wine, Jake texted.

"Safe flight. Headed home. LU2lls."

I returned his text.

"Will do. Drive safe. LUJ2lls."

The combination of Jake's text, the wine, and flying back to Albuquerque alone, left me feeling a little tender hearted. I tucked the cell phone into my purse, leaned back against the booth, and closed my eyes. The voices of the Beatles' filled the pub with words from "Yesterday." A familiar place I traveled to and from, over the years, in my imagination.

I don't know how long I sat in the booth—eyes closed—listening to the words and music... drifting back to Jake and the hotel room on the scent of his T-shirt. I wondered if yesterday would ever come again for Jake and me... and if so, how long would it take until the next time around. We couldn't hide away for another thirty some years.

"Yesterday" ended and Percy Sledge soulfully sang, "When A Man Loves A Woman. " Oh, my... time for a little exercise or I would be sobbing into what was left of my wine. Not nearly as effective as crying in one's beer. I looked around for the restroom and saw a sign with a hand pointing toward the back of the bar. I got the waiter's attention.

"Would you bring me another white Zin and keep an eye on my jean jacket while I go to the restroom?"

"I'll be glad to. It's straight back and to the left."

"Thanks."

I walked back to the restroom, took care of business, and washed my hands. As I started back to the booth, I noticed a couple on the opposite side, sitting three booths up from mine. They looked familiar. Their voices sounded familiar. I stopped.

Paul and his secretary, Natalie Freeman.

I moved back into the shadows of the restroom and watched. Tall, thin, graying Paul, sat next to the shorter, well-built, auburn-haired, younger woman. Natalie Freeman. She had been his personal secretary for the past ten years. I always liked her. But I always suspected her.

Paul draped his right arm over her shoulder... his left hand, somewhere below the table. They kissed now and then, in between conversation. Paul always had a knack of mixing business with pleasure... just never much with me.

I watched and thought about all the weekends, over the years, he stayed away on business. I thought about the condo he now kept for business reasons. I knew a long time ago it wasn't all business, but I never wanted to confront him. I remained quiet, on the fringes, and told myself what he did away from home... didn't matter anymore.

I felt differently now. What he did, affected me. What I did, affected him. We needed to get on the same page, turn that page, and both move on to another chapter.

I said a silent prayer and hoped someone still listened.

I walked up the aisle, between the booths, and stopped next to mine. My knees shook. My mouth felt dry. I reached for the wine glass and took a sip.

At the same time, Paul and Natalie both looked in my direction. Surprise overtook their expressions.

Paul, sitting on the aisle, stood and walked the short distance to my booth. I sat down before he got there.

"Rose, what a surprise seeing you here. Natalie and I attended an ABA Convention at The Four Seasons this weekend. Are you here on business or pleasure? And are you alone?"

He flashed the lawyer face... began the interrogation. With his years of practice, he never missed a beat.

"Yes, I'm sure it is a surprise. I flew in on Saturday for a book signing at the Palmer House. And yes, I do most things on my own now."

"That's good to hear on both counts. Looks like writing's given you a new independence. How's the book doing?"

"Very well, and yes, I am much more independent now. Why don't you ask Natalie to join us. No point in her sitting alone."

Paul motioned for Natalie. She picked up her purse and coat, closed the distance, and slid in next to Paul.

"Hello, Rose. What a nice surprise."

"Yes, good to see you again, Natalie."

Paul continued. "Rose had a book signing this weekend at the Palmer House. "

"Paul told me about your poetry book. How exciting."

"Yes, and I have a friend in the theater whose off Broadway show opened. I had tickets for last night."

"Oh, I simply love Broadway shows."

"Yes. I enjoyed it very much. I'm flying back to Albuquerque tonight."

"What a coincidence, so are we. Maybe our seats are close and we can visit." Natalie's comment awkwardly hung in the air like the aroma of a burned roast for Sunday dinner.

"Yes, we're probably on the same flight."

"How nice for all of us," Paul responded dryly.

I leaned toward Paul. "Could I speak with you for just a moment?"

"Of course."

Natalie eased from the booth, and stood. "You two go ahead and talk. I need to go to the restroom." She walked quickly away.

"Paul, I'm as surprised as you are that we all ran into each other. But maybe it's for the best. I watched you and Natalie for a few minutes before I walked back to the booth. I think we both know this is more than just a business trip or business relationship. I wondered for years if there was someone else, but ignored my suspicions because of the children. But things never changed even after the children moved out. Now you've taken the condo in Santa Fe. There's really no point for pretense anymore."

I reached in my purse and pulled out a business card I'd kept for several months. Sydney Carter, a family law and divorce attorney, gave me the card after she and I talked during a cocktail party at Kathryn's. I handed it to Paul.

"Sydney is my attorney. I'll have her contact you."

"Are you sure about this, Rose. Maybe you need time to think things through."

"No, Paul. I've thought about this for a long time. I just never thought it mattered. I do now. I look at things differently than I used to."

"I'm sorry. I never meant to hurt you. We never seemed to connect except for the children. I didn't know what to do... how to reach out. After a while, I stopped trying."

"I know that, Paul. I did the best I could over the years, but I felt distant, too. We grew apart, instead of together. And for that, I'm sorry. But we did something right along the way... Joe and Jenna, and our beautiful grandchildren."

"Yes, we got that part right. Joe and Jenna have the best of both of us in them. And the grandchildren are an added bonus."

"Paul, I want us to move on and be happy with the rest of our lives, while we're still friends. Can we do that?"

"Yes. I want that, too."

The waiter came to the booth and I reached for my purse.

"I'll get this, Rose." He handed him a twenty-dollar bill. "Keep the change."

"Thank you, sir."

Paul began again. "I'm glad we bumped into each other. I can't remember the last time we had a conversation about something other than the children or the weather."

"No, me either. We needed this time to talk. I'm not much on coincidence. I believe we all ended up here tonight for this reason."

We stood, and Paul stepped to my side of the booth, held my jean jacket while I slipped it on. His hands paused on my shoulders.

"I'll always be your friend. I'll always love you, Rose." He brushed a kiss on my cheek.

"Thank you for that. I feel the same about you, Paul."

After the last exchange between us, Natalie returned to the booth and Paul helped her with her coat.

I picked up my purse and laptop bag. "Nice to see you, Natalie."

"You, too, Rose. We'll probably see each other again on the plane later."

I smiled and looked at Paul. He wasn't smiling. The lawyer face, gone. Instead, I caught a glimpse of the young man who helped me, who loved me, all those years ago. That young man... still there.

I squeezed his arm on my way out of the bar. I walked the short distance to the departure gate, and boarded. My assigned window seat, near the back of the plane, afforded a clear view of passengers boarding.

The rain continued outside. I watched it spatter against the small, oval window... watched it fall onto the wet tarmac below. I thought of Jake driving home to Rockton in the rain... back to his farm, his life. In a few short hours, I would return to my life in Albuquerque. Everything remained the same, and yet everything changed.

My heart overflowed with love and sweet memories. Words and phrases, ideas and images, swirled inside my brain. I could hardly wait to bring the laptop out. I needed to write them down, preserve them, forever.

I sent one last text to Jake.

"Close your eyes... I'm there with you. My arms around you, my lips on yours. Listen for my voice... I love you, Jake. My heart remains with you, always. This weekend... a precious moment out of time... for both of us."

I turned the cell phone off and slipped it back into my purse.

"Ladies and gentlemen, welcome onboard... with service from Chicago to Albuquerque. Please turn off all personal electronic devices including laptops and cell phones."

I closed my eyes and felt him close... holding me, kissing me, loving me. His scent remained on me, on my clothing. My body ached for him. My heart longed for him.

Jesus, help us both.

"Thank you for choosing Southwest Airlines. Enjoy your flight."

The two empty seats directly in front of me on the, otherwise full flight back to Albuquerque, remained empty. Paul and Natalie... no-shows.

* * * * *

Rockton, Illinois
Fall 2008
Monday night

Once out of Chicago proper and onto Highway 20, the traffic thinned out. I stopped at the BP in Elgin for gas, coffee, beef jerky, and to pee. When I came back out, the rain had slowed some. I climbed in the truck and sat there for a few minutes, listening to rain splat against the windshield. I checked my cell... a text from Rose.

"Close your eyes... I'm there with you. My arms around you, my lips on yours. Listen for my voice... I love you, Jake. My heart remains with you, always. This weekend... a precious moment out of time."

I turned my head slightly, pulled the shirt over my mouth, my nose... and breathed in. Her scent lingered on the linen fabric, on my skin. I remembered her soft body tensing, building, and releasing with mine that last time we made love.

My body ached to hold her, to kiss her, to love her again.

Jesus.

I texted back.

"Yes, close. Can feel you, smell you, taste you. In my thoughts. LU2lls."

I slipped the cell phone back in my jacket pocket, started the truck, and pulled back onto Highway 20. J.J. Cale rocked out to the bluesy, driving beat of "The Breeze" on the radio.

I cranked up the sound—drummed the beat on the steering wheel—and sped into the night. The miles clicked by, the rain stopped, and two and half hours later, I drove up the graveled driveway.

Home again. Home again. Jiggity-jig. A remembered sing-song rhyme my sons repeated upon returning home when they were little.

Now I typed it in texts to Rose when I returned home from bus trips, movies, late night dinners, the bar... without her. Always wondering what it would be like to have her next to me, instead of alone... instead of with Beth.

I climbed out of the truck and looked over the moonlit surroundings I'd come home to my entire life: the remodeled, century-old, two-story farmhouse... the deteriorating, unpainted outbuildings... the roofless, empty silos... the aging, abandoned feed lots... the overgrown, rusted railroad track that divided yard from farmland.

Everything looked the same as when I left yesterday. Everything *was* the same. Everything, except me. After this weekend, nothing would be the same... for either of us. Nothing.

Chapter Seventeen

Amazingly those words once shared again flow from each heart.
And somehow gently ease the pain of all those years apart.
Unspoken words their only solace, conveyed through miles and time.
Hopes and dreams, what might have been, now captured in her rhyme.

Rockton, Illinois
Fall 2008
Tuesday morning

I woke up still dressed in the white, linen shirt and black briefs from last night. Shoes, socks, and jeans shucked on the floor, beside the bed. Beer cans and cell phone on the nightstand. I reached for the cell and found two late-night texts from Rose, after she landed in Albuquerque. After I fell asleep or passed out. Not sure which.

I smiled as I read the first. *"Home again, home again. Jiggity-jig. Miss you already. LU2lls"*

I read the second. *"Under the covers, wish you were here. Began a poem on the way home from loving you. Text/chat tomorrow. Night, night, Jake. LUJ2lls."*

On the way home from loving you. A phrase from a writer to her muse.

I typed a quick text back. *"Good morning. Sweet texts. Miss U2."*

My head ached this morning and the inside of my mouth tasted like beer, beef jerky, and Rolaids. Nice combo. Bet my breath was dandy, too. The kids on the bus will love me. Might as well add coffee to the mix.

I found my Illinois State cup in the dish drainer, filled it, and trucked upstairs—showered, dressed, brushed my teeth, finished my coffee—and trucked back downstairs. I had the routine down.

Bundled up with more coffee in hand, I plodded out into the crisp, cold darkness and climbed in the truck. I cranked the heat up, defrosting the windows and warming the cab a bit, before I left. While I waited, another text came in. Beth.

"Leaving around noon. Have a few stops to make. Be home around 5. Can you pick up dry cleaning? Dinner out? Thx. B."

I returned the text.

"Yep & yep. Take care. See you then. J."

And just like that, everything in my life stayed the same.

I woke up alone. I'd fall asleep alone. In between, I'd drive the school bus, work the farm, pick up the dry cleaning, drink a few beers with Ben, and take my wife out to dinner.

Later—in between the gaps of time—I'd sit in the truck, next to the lake, and try to remember why everything changed.

I'd recall how soft she felt, how sweet she tasted, how fragrant her scent, how lovely her voice. And, as I lay alone, I'd visualize the two of us holding, kissing and loving one another.

I'd remember her words to me. *"I love you so much. I don't know what I will do without you now."*

And in the darkness, whisper my words back to her. *"This won't be the last time we see each other... the last time we make love. We'll figure something out. Some way to be together."*

Reality check. Text from Ben. "Where the hell are you?"

I texted back, "OMW," put the truck in drive, and headed down the graveled driveway... back to my life.

* * * * *

Later, after Beth and I returned from dinner, I logged in to Facebook. I typed my message from the flat, farmlands of Illinois. She replied from her home nestled in the foothills of the Sandia Mountains of New Mexico. After all, it was only geography.

"Good evening."

"Hey, you. Tell me about your day and I'll tell you about my airport adventure."

"Not so fast. Where are you? What are you wearing? Then we'll discuss our days."

"I love when you take charge. I'm on my laptop, in my bedroom, under the covers. I'm wearing another pair of pink, lacy panties like I wore under your green, plaid flannel shirt. The one I swiped while you were peeing."

"Mm. Love those pink panties, a nice bookmark... and I knew you swiped the shirt. Looked cute on you. By the way, you do *'cute' well. I have a visual now. Message on!"*

"Not so fast, plaid man. Tell me what you're wearing."

"Cold here, so more clothes than you. Plaid jammie pants and Illinois State T-shirt. Now, where were we?"

"I asked about your day."

"Good day. Forgot I had a third-grade field trip to the Burpee Museum of Natural History in Rockford. Three floors of paleontology, geology, biology, and Native American life."

"Sounds like a wonderful place for a field trip. What did you enjoy the most?"

"Lunch and napping in the bus."

"What kind of bus driver are you?"

"A old, tired one. I'm not used to twenty-four hours of physical activity with very little sleep."

"I never heard you complain. I heard you make a lot of other sounds, though."

"Mm. Yes, I did. Sat by the lake today and thought about how beautiful you are. Could only imagine until this weekend."

"Yes. I had similar thoughts of you, as well. Thoughts I don't know what to do with most of the time. I'm overwhelmed with all that happened. Just know I love you, Jake."

"I know... and I love you."

"Smiling."

"Yep, me too. All day long."

"Did you read any of the manuscript or too wiped out?"

"I read the Prologue. I liked it. Very personal. If you ever publish though, you must expect people to assume you're the female lead, so you can't be afraid for the world to see under your kimono... ☺ Just sayin'."

"Glad you liked and I understand. But there's still a great deal of fiction, too. All I have to draw on is personal experience and imagination. I weave them together. I figure that's what most authors do, but then, I'm not most authors. See under my kimono?"

"Yep... I'd like to see under your kimono. I'd buy one for you, just to take a look."

"And I'd wear it so you could."

"Indeed. I know you would. So, adventures at the airport? Make it through security without a strip-search?"

"I did. Kind of disappointing. Evidently I've lost my 1960s subversive, hippie look."

"Not sure you ever had that look working for you. More like the Midwest, small-town girl look."

"Evidently not. I found a nice retro bar and had a couple glasses of wine before I boarded."

"Nice. I always fly better after a couple of drinks. I do most things better after a couple of drinks."

"Agreed. And a Xanax works well, too."

"Yep, drugs are always good. They make things even more enjoyable, and last much longer."

"Are we still talking about flying?"

"You are."

"Do you want to hear the airport chapter, or not?"

"Yes, please."

"I had to go potty, so I left the waiter in charge of my booth... and guess who I found sitting close by when I came back from the restroom?"

"Mayor Daley?"

"Close. Paul... and his secretary, Natalie Freeman.

"No, way."

"Yes, way. Sitting three booths up from mine, on the other side. Kind of cozy."

"Define 'cozy.'"

"He had his arm draped over her shoulder... his other hand somewhere in her lap.

"Define 'somewhere.'"

"Below the salt and pepper shaker... south of the belt buckle."

"OK... got it. And?"

"And he gave her a couple of pecks on the cheek, now and then. Nothing distasteful... but friendly casual, rather than business casual."

"Got a visual on that. What did you do?"

"I stood there. They noticed me, and Paul walked over to my booth. He asked if I had business or pleasure in Chicago."

" And you said?"

"Both. I told him I had a book signing at the Palmer House, and I had tickets to a friend's off Broadway play that opened this weekend."

"I would be the friend with the off Broadway play opening?"

"Yes, you would be the friend. And I would be the author with the book signing."

"Not a stretch for you, but I'm WAY off, off Broadway. Clever though, I'll give you that."

"Thanks. I asked if I could speak with him alone. Natalie excused herself to the restroom. Paul and I talked. Probably the first real conversation in years since the kids moved out... about anything that mattered."

"And?"

"Civil, friendly, actually. I said I suspected for a long time he and Natalie were more than business associates, but looked the other way because of the kids. I told him I saw our lives differently now... separate. It was time for both of us to move on."

"For not doing confrontation... you did alright, Rose."

"I did, but under the table... trembling thighs and knocking knees."

"Never let 'em see ya' sweat, babe."

"I gave Paul a business card from Sydney Carter, a lawyer friend of Kathryn's I met at a cocktail party a few months back. I told him she represented me as my attorney and would contact him."

"Geez."

"He said he wanted to remain friends. I believed him and said the same to him. He hugged me and kissed me on the cheek when I left. Kind of sad."

"I'm sure. I understand. You shared a life together... the same as Beth and I. I wouldn't want hard feelings toward the mother of my sons. Probably how Paul feels."

"Yes. He's been a wonderful father and grandfather, and a good provider. We just started out of sync and never got in step with one another. I couldn't relate to the life I found myself in. He couldn't relate to someone as distant as I. No one's fault, really... and we managed to raise two, beautiful children. That's an accomplishment we can both be proud of."

"To be sure. Your kids are married and settled. I still worry about Brian and Dustin. Not kids. Can't read them anymore. Don't know where they'd stand on things."

"Things... as in affair?"

"Yep. Have no idea how either would react. How they'd see me."

"I understand, Jake. Kids surprise you with their intuitiveness. Just when you think they couldn't possibly get it... they do. Maybe they'd surprise you."

"Yep. They just might. So, you're going through with the divorce?"

"Yes. After the sessions with Molly, I realize I can't live in the past or stay where I am. If I want to move forward, I need to make decisions. I need to make changes. No matter how difficult."

I wondered as I read her words if she'd directed them at me. Probably not, but they sure as hell struck close to home.

"I don't know how long these things take or what's involved. I guess I should, married to a lawyer all these years. But Paul and I never shared our work. I never asked about the law practice, he never asked about school. That's why I have Sydney."

"Jesus. We've both had some universal shit happen to us in the past forty-eight hours. It started with a broken-down furnace and busted water pipes at the theater, and ended with a divorce agreement

in an airport bar." I paused, then added. "And in between all the shit, we fell in love all over again, in a room with a view."

"Yes, all of that happened after I slipped the black, knit dress—with the buttons down the front—over the pink, lacy undies, and signed a few books.

"Blame it on the buttons."

"And then I opened my hotel door... and there you were."

"Yep. You never know where a farmer and his tractor will show up."

A pause in the messages. I waited.

"I love you, Jake. Love everything about you. You're not just the boy I remember... you're the man I'll never forget."

* * * * *

On an early Saturday morning, several days later, I found a poem in an email attachment. I read the title, and remembered the text she sent from the plane, leaving Chicago... *"I love you, Jake. My heart remains with you, always. This weekend... a precious moment out of time... for both of us."*

Precious Moment Out of Time

The rain began so quietly in soft, rhythmic measures,
Splashing and filling my senses with soft, supple pleasures.
And in my ear, whispered words caressed and kissed my soul,
Washing me gently with sweet emotion, releasing my careful control.
"Close your eyes. I've got you now," soft lips sweep over mine.
Nestled closely in his arms... precious moment out of time.

The rain courses down now in shimmering, silver sheets,
Flooding and triggering my heart with rapid, tattooed beats.
Sensitive breasts, gently cupped by the hands of a once-shy boy,
Immersing me warmly in sensual wonder, triggering shudders of joy.
"You're not alone. I'm here for you," soft lips sweep over mine.
Nestled closely in his arms... precious moment out of time.

A Friend Request

The rain pounds relentlessly, in dark, deafening surges,
Trembling and shuddering my body with hard, heated urges.
Tangled together, intimately joined like a warm hand in a glove.
Releasing within one another's embrace, drenched in passion and love
"I loved you then, I'll love you always," soft lips sweep over mine.
Nestled closely in his arms... precious moment out of time.

~ Rose Allison ~

Those two days in Chicago—the rekindled love affair—would forever *be*. The love between us—invisible to the world—would survive in the words of the poem, long after Rose and I were gone.

Her gift of writing still took me by surprise. Something rare, and welcome, at this point in my life.

I finished the manuscript she'd signed for me in Chicago, while nestled closely in my arms. No getting around it. The storyline... personal. The two main characters... familiar.

She wrote of two former lovers reuniting on Facebook after a Friend request. She wrote how people, places, and events shaped two lives... two lifetimes. No doubt influenced by the sessions with Molly, repressed feelings, emotional damage, addictions, compulsions, strengths and weaknesses surfaced in the characters' personalities. She wrote of changes that transpire over time, in both people and relationships.

But mostly, Rose wrote a love story about two ordinary people, a man and a woman—kindred souls—who fell in and out of love one summer, long ago. An extraordinary love—discovered, defined, and discarded in youth—remembered, resolved, and restored years later.

I knew of the extraordinary love she wrote.

Parts of the book—passages from childhood and adolescence—I found difficult to read. I knew them to be true. Yet, some of the text/chat dialogue brought a smile and made me laugh. Again, I knew them to be true.

She moved in and out of fantasy and reality, a practiced survival skill from childhood. She invented some characters, embellished others, placing them in both real and imagined locales and situations. Some characters moved along in the storyline, others died along the way.

In the end, Prince Charming kissed and rescued the lovely princess and built her a beautiful castle to live with him... happily ever after.

Rose described the castle in great detail: a white, two-story, twin-dormered house, with a black, slate roof... trimmed in deep forest green with matching shutters and window boxes... completed by a large, front porch with a swing.

I pictured the house, the front porch, and the two of us sitting in the swing on a moonlit, Midwest evening.

She wrote the happy ending, visualized it happening, and sent it out into the universe... complete with the castle, the princess, and Prince Charming.

The words of her story—believable, relatable, and memorable—a page-turner, to be sure. But in the back of my mind, I kept hearing the infamous opening words to each episode of the Dragnet TV series: *"The story you are about to see is true. The names have been changed to protect the innocent."*

If Rose published, she needed a similar disclaimer. Perhaps, something like: *"The story you are about to read is kind of true. The names, places, and events have been changed to protect the innocent, the unaware, and the dead."*

For a first attempt at writing a novel, Rose wrote a very good one. Was it great? Would it win the Pulitzer, or take home Academy Awards? Probably not, but then that's what they said about Robert Waller's *Bridges of Madison County*, too.

Besides, what the hell did a farmer from Illinois know about love and romance?

* * * * *

A Friend Request

The days, weeks, and months following Chicago, routinely slipped by. Inevitable change—like the crunch and rustle underfoot of fall leaves along the lake, now quieted beneath a blanket of winter snow—settled into both our lives.

The divorce between Paul and Rose finalized with two signatures at the bottom of a series of legal papers. Civil. Orderly. Like the marriage. Paul kept the condo, the convertible, and his secretary. Rose kept the house, the Prius, and the dogs. She continued writing poetry, short stories, and began a sequel to the yet untitled, unpublished first manuscript... under her maiden name, Rose Allison.

Dustin followed Brian's lead and left for college. Beth and I found ourselves alone for the first time in years. She began spending more time with her mother, worked out at the gym, lost twenty-three pounds bought new clothes, and changed her hairstyle. The sleeping arrangement remained the same. I continued "hobby" farming, began rehearsal for the next play at the dinner theater, and decided this would be my last year driving school bus.

Rose and I continued our love affair through our texts, messages, and memories. I still had no plan and wondered how long we could maintain the relationship. How long could we love one another from a distance? How long could she wait for a plan, a decision?

* * * * *

This year's bitter-cold winter, again, effectively eliminated two of my three *alone* places—the lake and the unheated workshop in the barn. By process of elimination... the basement, my only choice.

This morning after another pointless, heated conversation with Beth concerning Brian and Dustin's future plans—as if I had a crystal ball—I headed to the basement, coffee cup in hand. I switched on the space heater, sat down on my grandfather's wooden workbench, and puttered among the clutter of cardboard storage boxes, cast-off furniture, old picture frames, worn boots and shoes, and miscellaneous nuts, bolts, and tools. A man alone with his junk, so to speak.

I pulled up Pandora on the cell and set it inside an old tennis shoe. Stevie Ray Vaughn plaintively sang "Life Without You." Appropriate, given the circumstances.

This winter had gotten off to a slow start, but now we were in it for the long haul until spring. The days and nights stretched long and frustrating, especially for a restless farmer. I longed for warmer temperatures, a thawed lake, and a chance to work the fields. Instead, snow, sleet, freezing rain, bitter cold, and a relentless northern wind continued to pound northern Illinois.

I remembered the winter long ago when I planned to marry Rose, but never followed through. Never even asked. I figured I had a lifetime of winters and springs. I figured wrong.

Now, I found myself in a similar position. A chance to get it right. The question, would I?

I pictured how the scene between Beth and I might play out if I brought up the subject of a separation or a divorce. I had no idea if the conversation would totally blind-side her, or if we'd grown so distant, it wouldn't come as a surprise. No way of knowing. No way to read her. A divorce could get ugly. I needed to talk to a lawyer about financial settlements, property division. Jesus. And what about Brian and Dustin? What the hell would they think of their dad having an affair... cheating on their mother? And when news of this got out in Rockton, what then? Jesus. After awhile, I could probably deal with it, but how would Rose be treated? Would we live on the farm or move away? Where the hell would we go? Jesus.

Stressful. I didn't do stress well. After a few beers, I handled it better, but then I didn't care about making any decisions. What the hell?

I thought of ways for Rose and I to meet now and then. With both boys gone, and Beth visiting her mother more, and for longer periods of time... there would be opportunities for us to meet somewhere. But is that what I wanted for us... stolen bits of time... now and then? How could I ask that of her?

No. I wanted it all. I wanted to sit by the lake with her in my arms. I wanted to take her out to dinner, share popcorn with her at a movie, toss stuff in the cart with her at the grocery store. I wanted to look out from the stage and see her sitting in the audience at my plays, without sneaking in and out. I wanted to attend book signings without hiding at the back of the room. Most of all, I wanted to spend all my last days and nights with her... loving her.

I wondered how long she'd pause, look back, and extend her hand to me.

* * * * *

Monday night's final presentation of *The Foreigner* went well, as did the cast party on Tuesday night. Each night I couldn't help but search the audience for Rose, even though I knew she wasn't there. On a Saturday night last fall, she watched me perform, unobserved from a back corner table. The following Sunday and Monday, I made love to her in Chicago, kissed her good-bye, and told her I'd come up with a plan for us to be together.

That happened six months ago.

That evening, my fellow cast members, crew, and I, shared a few beers and struck the set. In six months, another play. The plays at the dinner theater, the weather, planting and harvesting... all components of the timed routine that made up my life. A timed routine that ticked by faster and faster.

Later, I returned home and found the dogs curled up on the rug, and a note from Beth stuck to one of the upper cabinet doors. Over the years—Beth, Brian, Dustin, and I—all left notes for one another on the cabinet doors.

Already let dogs out. Leaving for Mom's early morn. Rx ready. Back porch light is still out. ☹ *B.*

Subtle. Don't wake her up, pick up shit, and fix shit. I don't remember the exact date I turned into the gopher handyman, but I think it directly followed the honeymoon.

I grabbed a couple beers, sat down at the computer, and brought up Pandora. Paul Butterfield sang "Keep On Moving," from the 1969 same-titled album. I remembered Ben playing it over and over right after returning from Vietnam. We'd smoke a joint, drink a few beers, and listen to The Paul Butterfield Blues Band. He talked of plans with Karen. I tried to forget mine with Rose.

I pulled up a favorite picture on Rose's Facebook page—a needed visual—and hit the chat button.

"Good evening."

"Hey, you. Get everything down and packed away 'til fall?"

"Yep. Many hands make light work. How was your day?"

"Good. Talked with Molly."

"How'd that go?"

"Good. Opened another door and looked inside. It's not so much about fixing as it is about accepting, understanding."

"Yep, accepting and understanding is a good thing. Not easy. We all have closed doors—demons we deal with."

"Do you have closed doors, Jake? Demons you deal with?"

"Yep. You blocked yours. I drown mine."

"I guessed that when we first started chatting, since the first profile picture you posted. I saw it in your face, your eyes. I saw your secrets."

"Yep, and I saw the distant look in yours."

"You were the only one who recognized it. That's why I felt comfortable with you, safe. I knew you wouldn't judge me."

"Nope. No reason to. I felt the same way, still do."

"Me, too. When you're alone, it's hard to open the doors and look inside. But when someone you trust is there with you... it's a little easier."

"Yep, it is."

"We're a result of our past... good or bad. I guess that's true for everyone. It's all in what we let those experiences become... boulders that crush us or stepping stones to lead us out."

"Nice choice of words. You should be a writer."

"Thanks. I think I will."

"Discuss anything else?"

"My writing. I told her I finished the novel and had begun working on a sequel. She said writing could be a powerful tool toward

accepting and understanding myself... an inlet and an outlet for my soul. Beautiful words."

"Yep. Did you happen to mention you kill people off in your book as part of your therapy?"

"I did! She laughed when I told her the husband and secretary died in a car crash along Happy Ending Road."

"Hey, it's your story. You're the writer."

"I am. She said we might have to work on the 'happy ending' scenario... not everything in life has a happy ending. That's a hard one for me. The dreamer inside needs a happy ending."

"Yep. Always the dreamer. Nothing wrong with that. Loved that about you... that and the voices."

"Thanks. I've always had someone to talk to... even alone."

"You have."

"But now I know I'm not crazy."

"I told you that."

"I know, but that worried me, considering the source."

"Thanks."

"Welcome."

"What did Molly say regarding the voices?"

"She said everyone talks to themselves—to voices—that it's healthy. The voices are more pronounced in some than others because of the purpose they serve. My inner voice is me... my inner child. She's been there in my subconscious—my dream world—for as long as I can remember. She's a friend, an advisor, a protector... my bridge between fantasy and reality."

"Makes sense."

"Yes. Better late than never, I realized there were two of me... a kind of split that happened in childhood. As time went by and my life became more difficult—harder for me to handle alone—the inner child became more pronounced, more vocal. She's still there, but quieter, and I'm comfortable with her. I'm not afraid anymore and understand it's the totality of who I am."

"Sounds reasonable."

"It does, finally."

"BRB. Dogs and I have to pee. Out of beer, too."

"K."

After fifteen minutes, give or take five, I messaged.

"Back. Temporarily lost in the backyard with the dogs. Dark."

"Need a light."

"Yep. Had a memo regarding that stuck on the cabinet door from Beth when I got home. Added it to the list."

Another pause in the messages. Rose typed back.

"Am I still on that list, Jake... your 'to do' list? How far down am I?"

Damn. She hadn't pressed the issue much since Chicago. But I knew from what she typed in texts and chats, she thought about it more and more, especially since the divorce. I did, too.

"Yep, you're still on it." I didn't answer the second question. Didn't have an answer.

"I need to talk with you about some things. I can't delete them or pretend they're not there. That's a pattern I'm trying to break. Won't do that anymore. Can't. Do you understand?"

"Yep, I do. Listening."

"I thought I could do this, Jake. Love you from a distance, from memories. When this first started, that's really all we had. I thought I'd fallen in love with a memory—a time, a place, a boy—from my past. But the better acquainted I became with the man the boy became, the more I realized I loved him, too."

"I thought the same thing at first... that I'd fallen in love with a memory, a fantasy. Someone I could never have. Chicago made you real for me."

"Chicago made it real for both of us. Once you get a taste of reality, it's hard to go back to fantasy. I want to hold you, touch you, make love to you. I know the difference between reality and fantasy. I can fantasize with you as long as I know reality is a viable end. I want a real relationship."

The exchanges stopped for a time. She typed again.

"Do you want this, or is it just me, Jake? Tell me."

"It's not just you. Don't think that. I'm still working on it, but my life is complicated. And all this is stressful. Can't come up with a plan. I think about it day and night."

"You can't continually think about a plan. You have to take some sort of action. What do you see happening between us?"

"Not sure. I know I want to see you, want us to be together."

"I want that, too. But I'm not sure we see the same end. Would you divorce Beth and begin a life with me... or do you see an ongoing affair?"

"I want a life with you. I see that, but I'm not sure I can make it happen. An affair is better than nothing."

The messages stopped again. I waited for her next message.

"You say one thing one day, and say something entirely different the next. You can see us together... and then you can't. You're working on a plan and then your life's too complicated to figure out a plan. You want to be with me, but an affair is better than nothing. And you wonder why I say what I say... ask the questions I ask. I don't want to get fucked over. I just want to love you... and be loved by you, Jake."

When Rose used the word "fuck," I knew she was upset. Damn it.

"It's not my intent to fuck you over, Rose. Sometimes I'm the one who gets fucked over."

"I don't want either of us to feel that. And I don't want to go back to the way things were before the Friend request, or before Chicago. My life is changed because of you. My world turned upside down because of you. I'm changed. I can't go back. I can't stay where I am, waiting my life away."

"Nope, me neither. And I understand what you're saying. But as hard as I try, I can't be the romantic you think I am. I can't be Prince Charming in your world of fantasy."

"Oh, Jake, you already are. You just don't realize it. You're an edgy, bastard romantic. The worst kind to be in love with. Just my luck And what if my Prince Charming world isn't fantasy? What if the dreams I hold in my heart are real... can become real? This means you can still be anything you want with me... and I with you. There are dreams still waiting to be realized for both of us. Jesus, Jake, why can't you let yourself see this? Take a chance at happiness."

"I have moments—days, like Chicago—when I think I'm there with you, but they don't last. I can't maintain when I'm back in my world... the real world."

"And I can't continue the roller coaster ride, the highs and lows, with you. Sometime I feel as if I'm dealing with two people. The person I'm chatting with now is not the person I spent the weekend with in Chicago... or the person who said he loved me then, loved me now, and would always love me. Where is he, Jake?"

When I couldn't come up with any more words or excuses, I finished my beer, and typed my reply.

"I don't know, Rose. But you are dealing with two people. The Jake you want me to be, and the Jake I am. They're not the same."

After several minutes, she messaged back.

"Tears. Can't stop the tears. You know, Jake, you're the only one who can still make me cry. The only one I care enough about, or love enough, to shed tears over. And the two Jakes? They fucking ARE the same person, except one is sober and wants to make a decision... the other is drunk and can't *make a decision."*

Jesus. I felt like I'd been slapped. She probably felt like she'd been kicked. Son-of-a-bitch. This is not where or how I wanted this conversation to go. How the hell did we end up here?

I waited for another text. Nothing. Finally, after several more minutes, I sent one. I knew I hurt her.

"Still there? Are we fighting?"

No reply. I watched the green dot next to her name disappear. For several minutes, I sat there in the computer chair, staring at her page, rereading the exchanges between us.

She stopped being tenacious, strong, and positive, because I'd returned all three with indecisiveness, weakness, and negativity.

Same shit... different day. Same prick... different decade.

* * * * *

The texts and messages from Rose stopped. The first few days, I figured I'd hurt her feelings and she needed some time. I left her alone. The fifth day, I apologized in a text and a message. No reply. By the end of a silent week, I knew I'd fucked up.

Emptiness. Loneliness. Anger. Depression. Emotions I kept in check, washed over me in waves. Some days I floated, other days, whitecaps lapped over me and sucked me under. I didn't care.

At night I typed out, *Night, Night, Rose. LU2lls,* pressed send, and waited. No reply. For a while, I continued sending the same text, my SOS signal of distress, out into the Universe.

Each morning—before I left for my route—I brought up Facebook and checked her page for posts about anything. At night—before I fell asleep or passed out—I did the same. No new posts. The first couple weeks, I sent a message nearly every day... something personal, a YouTube song video or song lyric, a picture attachment, a poem, a movie quote. No response. After awhile, I stopped sending the messages, but I never stopped checking her page.

One Sunday morning, nearly a month later, she posted a poem, a haunting picture of a woman's arm reaching upward through dark, ocean waves.

Soul, Save Me One More Time

Waves of sadness
And I am drowning.
Cannot catch my breath.
Soul, save me one more time.

Tears and brine at once
And I am slipping at sea.
Cannot see the crest anymore.

Life floats in pieces of wreckage above
And I watch with stinging eyes.
Cannot reach for a savior.

· *Beacon from shore is dark now.*
And I am ready to give.
Cannot hold on to the breath of a dream.
Soul, save me one more time.

~ Rose Allison ~

I though of both our lives... floating pieces of wreckage. Kindred spirits. Kindred souls... through the good and the bad.

Chapter Eighteen

Seasons once passed at a gentle pace,
But soon rushed by like a downhill race.
The dreams and schemes of yesterday
Now trail on the wind as legacy.

Rockton, Illinois
Spring 2009

Cooper and Teak anxiously eyed my every move as I filled their bowls and set them down on the hardwood kitchen floor. Breakfast. They woofed down every morsel in record time. I let them out the backdoor to do their duty and five minutes later they were back inside, curled up together in a sunny spot beneath the kitchen window. Naptime.

I poured a cup of coffee, walked into the den, sat down in the office chair and typed in my computer password. Brought up Facebook, typed in a password. Pulled up Pandora Radio, and typed in another password. When my memory goes, I'm screwed. It will be me and the dogs curled up on the floor in the sun.

My Pandora setting remained the same as last night when I got home from Will's... blues and jazz. John Mayall and the The Blues Breakers, Gary Moore, B.B. King, Paul Butterfield... I listened to all of them until I passed out, evidently. This morning, Roy Buchanan played and soulfully sang, "Hey, Joe."

Something about the blues moved me. Made me feel alive... in pain and pleasure. I'd had my share of both, and both changed over the years. But the blues never changed.

I moved the sound dot up just enough so the music would carry, and walked back into the kitchen. I stood in front of the sink and looked out the window. Alone with the dogs, my coffee, Roy Buchanan, and a window view of the lake. Nice day.

I don't remember going to bed last night, just waking up on top of the covers this morning, still dressed. Not the first time for that, probably not the last. Didn't matter.

I do remember sitting at the computer, drinking beer—music playing in the background and some sports program pulled up on the TV with no sound—looking at Rose's Facebook page. Still nothing since the *Save Me* poem.

I don't know how many beers I had. I counted ten cans in the wastebasket next to the computer this morning and a half-empty one still sitting on the desk. I managed to log off Facebook and the computer. Even turned off the TV. Don't remember doing any of that.

Those lapses in time—black outs—maybe were happening more than I knew. How the hell would I know? I couldn't remember them.

I checked the thermometer outside the kitchen window... forty-six degrees. Hell, four more degrees, and it would be shorts, tank tops and sandals weather. Time to drag out the lawn chairs and fishing poles. The only known cure for cabin fever in these parts. Too bad it didn't cure being a prick.

Okay. I had a plan for the day. Sit by the lake, fish, and drink beer.

Maybe Dustin would drown a few worms with me since he was home on break. Even better.

Beth and I hadn't seen much of him since he transferred to the University of Illinois from junior college. Guess he was like me in that way. I never came home much after I left Rockton for college. Busy. Found other interests. I'm sure he found the same ones. Most young men do.

Dustin and Brian... so different.

Brian, always the independent one, bull-headed and stubborn. When he set his mind to do something—he did it—good decision or bad decision. At least he made decisions. I guess he got the bull-headed and stubborn part from me, certainly not the decision making.

Dustin second-guessed himself a lot. Had a hard time deciding what to do even as a kid. Good at talking the talk, but had a really hard time walking the walk. Just like me. Of the two boys, I never thought Dustin would leave home, leave Rockton. Wrong again. He made a decision last year and, so far, never looked back.

I took another sip of coffee, looked down the graveled farm lane that ran past the lake out onto the main blacktop. Brian left college after the first year. He worked and saved his money, and bought the Harley Davidson from Ben's son, Jack. The next morning he packed the T-bags, climbed on the bike, and headed to California. I can still see him perched on the bike at that final intersection. He looked back over the farm—waved to Beth and me—and made the final turn onto the highway. Winding the Harley through the gears, he sped away... away from family and friends... away from the farm, Rockton, and the Midwest.

Jesus, that was a bad day, a bad several days, with Beth crying through most of them. She blamed me for not talking him out of going. Hell, I knew I couldn't talk him out of anything once he made a decision. Besides, what would I say? I did the same thing at his age, only on a 1971 Triumph Bonneville, now covered with a tarp in the barn.

Secretly, I hoped the same thing happened with Dustin. Maybe his plans would come together and he'd find that *someone*. I never did, but then, I couldn't make a decision. When I did, it was too late. I'd waited too long.

"Jake, will you to talk to Dustin?"

Beth? What the hell? I thought she worked today. Reality check.

She walked into the kitchen.

"I thought you worked today?"

"No. They called me off. Didn't need me. I told you that last night. Don't you remember?"

"Nope."

"No, you probably don't. You were on the computer, drinking and listening to music. You answered me."

"What did I say?"

"You said, 'okay.' But I guess you must have been elsewhere."

A given. Not sure where.

"Anyway, would you talk to Dustin today."

"About?"

She glared back at me. One of those conversations... no matter what I said, it wouldn't be the right answer. Fishing looked better all the time. Forget the warm-up to fifty degrees. Forget the shorts, tank top, and sandals. I'd wear long handles just to get out of the house sooner.

"I want you to talk to him about this girl he's mixed up with."

"What girl? Define *mixed up*."

"Well, if you'd pay attention to the comments since he's been home, you'd know."

Yep, one of those conversations.

"I'm listening. Why don't you tell me since I haven't been paying attention, and I'll decide if I'm going to talk to him about some girl he may or may not be mixed up with."

"You know, Jake... this is exactly what happened with Brian. You wouldn't talk to him either, and now he's gone."

"Drop it, Beth. Drop the shit with Brian or we're done."

I poured another cup of coffee and walked back over to the window. I leaned against the kitchen sink—hands propped on either side of the counter—and waited.

Beth pulled out a chair and sat down at the round oak dining table. She wore her favorite, pink and gray flannel pajamas—fuzzy slippers—no make-up and hair mussed from sleep. Her blue eyes sparkled. They always sparkled during the heat of battle.

I began with a peace offering.

"Do you want a cup of coffee? Toast? Scrambled eggs?"

"Just coffee, please. Black. No toast or eggs. I'm not hungry. Don't want anything to eat. Didn't sleep very well last night."

Shit. Coffee... black instead of cream and sugar. Not eating. Not sleeping.

Not good.

I poured her coffee and set it in front of her—pulled out the chair opposite her—and sat down. Might as well get this over with. I took a long sip of coffee and looked over the rim at her. "Okay. Go."

Beth drew a big breath and began.

"Dustin's leaving in a day or two. He said he's meeting a *friend* and they plan to spend time together before classes start."

I set my cup down and waited an appropriate amount of time for follow-up conversation. Nothing.

"That's it? That's all he said?"

"No, that's not all he said."

"Okay. I'm not playing twenty questions this morning."

"I asked him if the friend was a girl and he said, yes."

Again. I waited. I listened. I got up and made myself a piece of toast.

"She's from Texas or Colorado, I think. All I know is she's not from around here. Dustin said she's majoring in rhetoric or something like that. I've never even heard of that, have you? Who majors in rhetoric, and what is it?"

Right about now I could describe rhetoric to her perfectly.

The toast popped up.

"Probably communication rhetoric. Has to do with writing or journalism. Good field."

Beth returned my comment with a hard look and, "Whatever."

I spread a generous amount of peanut butter on the toast and sat back down. I started to get a feel for the direction of this conversation, and I didn't like it.

"Dustin mentioned something about transferring to a college in California next fall. They've lined up summer jobs there. I don't like where this is heading, Jake. I don't like it one bit. And I don't like her."

What the hell? Dustin wasn't thinking when he unloaded all of this on Beth. A son does not tell his mother he's leaving her for another woman without laying some groundwork. I really needed to talk to him. But first, Beth and I needed to finish this conversation... and I needed to choose my words carefully.

"Okay, let me see if I have this straight. Dustin met a girl he likes and they're planning on a few days together before spring break ends. She's not from Illinois. She's not majoring in Home Economics. There's a very good possibility they're transferring out of this winter hellhole of Illinois to attend school in warm, sunny California. You don't know this girl. Haven't met her. But don't like her. Does that cover everything?"

Beth looked at me narrowly. "You know, Jake. You can be such a prick."

"Yep. It's a gift."

"I want Dustin to stay here and marry someone we know. I want grandbabies I can hold. I don't want him moving across the country like Brian with some girl we've never met who probably doesn't even want a husband or babies. I want you to talk to him, Jake. Please."

I took a deep breath and exhaled slowly.

"Beth, we can't make Dustin stay here with us anymore than we could Brian. I can't and I won't try to persuade Dustin to do what we want, what you want for him. He has to live his own life, find his own way. For God's sake, there's a whole world outside of Rockton, Illinois—out of the Midwest—and I hope they both find what they're looking for. I want them to be happy and that may not be here in Rockton. You need to face that, Beth."

She gave me another hard look and slowly shook her head.

"Well, I guess I should have expected that from you. You never wanted to live here on the farm. I knew that early on. You wanted something else—someone else—but I never knew what or who. Sometimes I'm not sure why you married me. Was it because I was young and built like a brick shit house, or that I could drink you under the table?"

I looked over at her. So many thoughts flashed through my mind. I wanted to say... *You're right. I didn't want to be a farmer. I didn't want to live in Rockton, Illinois my entire life. I wanted to live out West—take a shot at acting or directing or writing—do something with my degree I worked my ass off to get. But most of all, I wanted that one chance back from years ago—that "do over" opportunity—to marry and share my life with someone else.*

Instead, I said, "Beth, it doesn't matter what either of us wanted all those years ago. We met, we married, and had two great sons we love, and who love us. We've shared the responsibilities of the farm and taken care of our family. That's what matters."

"I guess so. We made a life together and made it work over the years. I just wonder what we'll do now that it's just you and me. Ever think about that, Jake?"

"Every day."

"And?"

"And. I don't know."

"Well, for now, will you talk to Dustin? Can you do that, please?"

"I'll listen to Dustin if he wants to talk and will answer him honestly. That's all I can promise."

She stood, looked at me briefly, and delivered one last parting shot.

"It doesn't matter. You'll do whatever you want anyway. That's how it's always been. You've always done whatever you wanted, gotten whatever you wanted."

She picked up her cup from the table and walked into the living room. A few seconds later, I heard the din of the television.

I refocused my attention out the kitchen window... toward the lake.

I'd made my choices long ago and I lived with them... every single day. Whatever burdens or sorrows I carried, I would, most likely, carry until all my days were used up.

Quietly, I responded to no one in particular, "You're wrong. I never got anything I really wanted, except my sons."

* * * * *

Around noon, I saw Dustin's truck winding down the dirt and gravel road leading to the lake. He parked near the shelter house, grabbed a fishing pole and a small, red and white Igloo Playmate cooler from the truck bed.

I watched my youngest hike toward my fishing spot. He and Brian, both nearly six feet tall. I wondered where the height came from—not me at 5'7"—maybe a great grandfather or great uncle somewhere on the family tree. He'd bulked up some at college. Weight training, most likely. He looked good, more like a man than a boy. He had my thick unruly hair, just a little more blond than brown. The blue eyes ran in both families.

He raised his arms and smiled, fishing pole in one hand, cooler in the other.

"Hey, Dad. I made ham sandwiches with lots of yellow mustard. Found some chips and cookies, too. You got something to drink?"

"Beer."

He grinned and shook his head. Miller High Life, a given.

I unfolded the other aluminum chair from the shelter and set it next to mine. Both chairs, beat up from use.

"I hoped when I saw the cooler it was full of food and not bait."

Dustin sat down.

"Nah. I figured you'd have the beer and bait covered... just no food. Some things don't change, Dad."

"I guess you're right. I just bring the essentials. Dig the food out. I'll bait your hook."

I grabbed a beer out of my cooler, popped the top, and handed it to Dustin. I baited his pole and waited to exchange pole for sandwich. The entire process reminded me of when he and Brian were little—baiting hooks, untangling lines, setting bobbers, and repeating the process ten minutes later—in between eating, drinking, and pissing contests in the lake.

Dustin took a couple swallows, and pulled out the sandwiches. We made the trade... pole for food. I munched my sandwich and chips. Dustin cast out and rested the pole in the metal guide sticking up from the bank.

"Anything biting, Dad?"

"Bass and crappie, a little. Trying a new rig I bought at Walmart yesterday. Doesn't matter though. I'm just happy to be out here going through the motions. Good sandwiches, by the way. What kind of cookies?"

"Oreos. What other kind is there?"

"Exactly."

We polished off the sandwiches and chips, and opened the Oreos. I noticed we both still took the Oreos apart and scraped the frosting off with our front teeth. Brian probably did the same. A nice, childhood memory.

The lake sat quiet and smooth today, interrupted only by the sounds of our reeling and casting. Occasionally, a frog croaked or a Red-winged blackbird chucked at regular intervals. Peaceful. Calm. A good place to think, reflect, and talk. Father to son.

And so it began.

"I forgot how much I liked sitting here by the lake, listening to the sounds, Dad. Miss fishing. Miss skinny-dipping. Miss it all now that I'm away."

"I know. When you leave home you miss the familiar. You wonder if your life's ever going to start. And then wonder if you'll ever get it figured out. It does, and you will. The lake will always be here. You'll always have the farm to come home to."

A long silence followed. I could almost hear the wheels spinning inside Dustin's head. I waited. Always been good at waiting. Too good.

"Dad, I met a girl."

I reached down and tightened the line on my pole.

"From around here?"

"No. She's from Arizona, a sophomore majoring in rhetoric. You know, writing, journalism? She's transferring to USC next fall. More opportunities." He hesitated, and added, "She just turned eighteen. She's really smart. Graduated early like me. I saw her around campus early on, but figured she was jailbait."

"You figured right." And then added, "Legal now."

Geez. Beth hadn't gotten one thing right except the college transfer to some school in California—USC. That qualified.

Beth had poor listening skills from day one. Never improved over the years. She made assumptions, formed opinions, from what she heard. And lived her life in a black-and-white, cut-and-dried Midwest world. Nothing wrong with that, just no room for the gray areas of life.

Dustin looked over at me. Jesus. I saw it in his eyes. Love came to town.

"So, when did you decide you were in love?"

"I don't know. It just happened. I woke up next to her one morning. I knew I loved her. I always thought it would take a long time to fall in love with someone, but that's not how it happened."

Well, they were sleeping together. No surprise there. My son.

"No, that's usually not how it happens. Sometimes it doesn't take a long time. You just know. Something happens between the two of you that didn't happen with anyone else."

"You're right. It's like I've known her before. I know that sounds really weird. I didn't mean it to... it's not weird. We're such good friends, too. Like we've always been friends. It's like we're—"

"Kindred spirits?"

Dustin stared at me. "Yep. How did you know, Dad? Was it like that with you and Mom?"

I answered the first question.

"I'm familiar with the feeling, Dustin. I get it."

I didn't answer the second question.

"The chemistry is like something neither of us ever felt... like a current running between us. Can't explain that either."

"I'm familiar with the current thing, too. I wasn't always old."

"I know, Dad. I've seen your hippie pictures... the long hair and bell-bottoms. Found your Eisner's drug box in the basement. Taped it back up so you wouldn't find out."

"So, you're the one with the sloppy re-taping skills?"

"Yep, that would be me. I've looked at your motorcycle more than a few times, too—sat on it—pretended to wind it through the gears."

"So you're the butt print I kept finding on the seat?"

"Maybe. Brian sat on it a time or two. We both thought you were pretty cool for having a bike, even though you never rode it much. How come, Dad? How come you and Mom never rode?"

"I don't know. I took it out a few times over the years. Never seemed to have a reason, no place to go other than Walmart or the pub. Your mother never liked motorcycles much. Thought them dangerous."

"Yep, I remember. She never wanted Brian or me on it. Have you ever thought about selling the bike?"

"No. I'd never sell it. I figured one of you boys would probably end up with it sometime. If not, well, you can sell it after I'm gone and buy a shit load of fishing supplies."

"If I had it... I'd keep it, Dad. I'd ride it too."

"I'd like that. I'd like that a lot."

Another pause in the conversation.

I thought back on the motorcycle trip to California after college graduation. How different things might have been with Rose tucked behind me.

I looked at Dustin and saw a far away look in his eyes. His thoughts were with her... and hers most likely with him.

An all too familiar pattern. Who would have thought that at my age?

"So. What's the plan?"

"Not exactly sure. Mom doesn't like her already."

"Forget about Mom. Forget about me. What do you want, Dustin?"

He took a deep breath and slowly exhaled. "I want to be with her. I want to see where we can go together... where things might lead. When I'm with her I feel like there is so much more to me. I see possibilities. She makes me want to be more than I've ever wanted to be. She makes me feel alive inside. Does that make sense?"

"Yep. It makes a lot of sense. Besides, it only has to make sense to you two."

As a young man, I rolled those same thoughts over in my mind. And I remembered a young girl who made me want to be more than I ever thought I could be... a young girl who made *me* feel alive inside.

"I saw the Arizona plates on her VW Bug last year. She'd stopped at a traffic light and pulled into the student parking lot. When she climbed out of the car, I saw something different in her eyes, different from anyone here. I watched her for months, and decided I wanted to know her better, wanted her in my life.

Her name is Paige Reynolds. She's blonde and pretty, smart and funny, all rolled into one. She's beautiful inside and out. You'd like her, Dad. I know you would, and she'd like you, too."

"I'm sure we'd get along great."

Dustin scanned the lake, the shoreline.

"I never thought much about what I wanted to do or where I wanted to live. I've always been here, on the farm. Now, I want to see and do more. Paige and I, both. She wants to be a writer. I want to be a musician. Together, we have plans... hopes and dreams."

His choice of words sounded vaguely familiar.

"Plans are important. Hopes and dreams are what lives are built on. And it's important to find the right person to share them, to make them happen. It sounds like you've found her."

Dustin turned and looked at me. Jesus, it was like looking at myself at his age.

"I have, Dad. I found someone, and I love her."

"I see that."

"What about Mom? She's pissed already. I don't want to bring Paige here. That's why I'm going back early... to be with her. After this semester, we'll rent a place in L.A., and start classes at USC in the fall. We've already taken care of the paperwork. Oh, and you'll be getting a tuition bill that's a little higher than the one from U of I. Thought I better warn you."

He looked over at me with kind of a half smile, half grimace.

"Thanks for the warning. I'll be sure and sit down before I open it... and Dustin?"

"Yah, Dad?"

"Don't worry about Mom. I'll talk to her and take care of things on this end. I'm used to dealing with her. You should have talked to me first anyway."

"I realize that now. But I was excited and wanted to tell her about Paige. Everything kind of spilled out wrong. I didn't think she'd react that way. I thought she'd be happy."

"Well, mothers can sometimes be a little possessive with their sons, your mother especially. When you're born and raised here in Rockton, like your mother, you don't know any different. Her family is here and she's been a Midwestern, small-town girl her entire life. She always pictured you and Brian marrying local girls, living close, and having grandbabies to cuddle and spoil. Mothers count on that."

"I know. That's pretty much what she said."

"Well, those are her hopes and dreams for you. You have your own. Your mom and I will adjust to your plans, not the other way around. That's how it's supposed to be."

"Thanks, Dad. I kind of figured you'd get it."

"You did, huh? How's that?"

A very long silence ensued. We reeled in, checked the rigging, cast back out. Nothing biting. But again, it didn't matter.

"Was there someone else before Mom? You know, before you married her?"

Interesting turn in the conversation. I thought a minute, then chose my words carefully.

"There's usually someone else before you get married. Just part of it."

An Osprey swooped down—dove into the water, surfaced with a fish—and continued its flight across the lake.

"Rose. Wasn't that her name?"

I focused on the hawk... the lake. I kept my breathing steady and tried to mask the utter surprise and near panic in the pit of my stomach. How could he know about Rose? I kept her hidden away in my heart for more than forty years—never mentioned her to anyone—especially not since the Friend request. Rose and I kept our secrets between us.

I didn't respond. I didn't have a response.

"Dad, I came in late one night during a school break. I wanted to tell you about this jailbait girl I'd seen around campus. You were asleep. Well, not exactly asleep, passed out in the office chair in front of the computer."

Oh, Jesus. One of those nights.

"I pulled up the computer screen to shut it down. That's all. Just shutting it down. When the screen came up, Facebook chat came up."

Son of a bitch, here it comes.

"I saw her name, Rose Allison Flynn. She sent you a poem... a poem one lover writes to another. I know because Paige writes them to me. I didn't read it all, read some. Figured it was private, but the words I read were beautiful. I figured you'd been in love with one another for a long time—probably before Mom—and you reconnected online. It happens all the time to people. I logged off Facebook and shut down the computer. I never said anything to anyone about it. But now I know why you get what's between Paige and me. Why you understand the kindred spirit thing, the electricity, the connection. You and Rose must have had that, maybe still do. I thought it was cool you both used *letters* to say good night to one another. You called her *2lls*. She called you *J*."

An awkward silence hung between us. I mulled over a suitable response. How much did I dare say to this young man on the threshold of his entire life, standing exactly where I stood years ago? How much would he understand... this young man, my son?

I took a deep breath and hoped the words—the right words—would come.

"Thanks for shutting down the computer... for not saying anything. I must have been pretty drunk. I usually manage to shut things down before I pass out or head upstairs."

I reeled my line in and cast out again. Dustin followed suit. The brief activity cut some of the tension in the air, at least for me.

"Rose and I met in college when I was about your age, in the late sixties. We fell in love. We fell out of love. She moved away. We married different people, had children and lived separate lives. A while back we reconnected on Facebook. She's a writer."

I thought that enough information for now.

"Geez, Dad. She and Paige are both writers? That's a little more than coincidence, don't you think?"

Yes, I did think there were unknown forces at work in the universe, but I didn't say that. Instead, I responded, "Maybe."

Dustin continued. "So... have you seen her?"

As much as I hated lying... I couldn't tell him the truth. Not now, maybe not ever.

"No, we haven't seen each other since the early seventies."

"Are you still in contact with her?"

I didn't answer. Instead, I got another beer. Figured that should be enough to end the interrogation. I popped the top and glanced over at Dustin. He had the biggest, shit-eating grin across his face.

I ignored it.

"Ready for another beer?"

"No, thanks, Dad. I'm good."

He chugged the remainder of his beer, smashed the can on the ground with his foot, and tossed it back into the cooler. The boys and I had been smashing soda and beer cans and tossing them back into the cooler since they were little, and I a younger man.

Old habits. Old memories. Both hard to break. Both hard to forget.

Dustin reeled in.

"I think I've reached my limit of casting and reeling in this afternoon. The fish don't seem interested in either of your new riggings from Walmart."

"You're right. Need to speak to the department head in charge of sporting goods the next time I'm there."

"Good idea. You finished, too, Dad?"

"No. I think I'll continue the abuse awhile longer. You know me, I like going through the motions while communing with nature."

"I know."

"I'm going to head back to the house and get cleaned up. Meeting Nick and Kirk later. They're home on break, too. Probably end up here at the lake drinking a few beers later around the fire pit if that's okay?"

"Yep. Sounds good. Dry firewood in the shelter. Clean up your shit when you're done."

"Always do. You taught me well."

Like father, like son... in more ways than I ever realized until today.

I knew all of Dustin's friends. Watched them grow up and play sports together. Kirk and Nick climbed onto my bus the first day of kindergarten. When Nick turned sixteen—right after his dad died—I drove him to the DMV to get his driver's license.

That's how things work in a small town.

"Mom will want to know if we talked."

"Just give her a kiss, tell her you love her, and that Dad said we'll talk later."

"Okay. I just don't want to cause friction between you two. Don't want to make things worse than they already are."

What the hell did he mean by that? Maybe I better ask.

"What the hell do you mean by that... make things worse?"

"Well, Jesus, Dad. Brian and I aren't blind, you know. Most parents sleep in the same bedroom, or at least the parents of the friends we hung around with did. You and Mom haven't slept in the same room since we were in junior high. You don't hug or kiss much either. And when you got home, Mom goes in one direction and you go in another."

Shit. Was it that obvious? I never thought they paid attention to any of that. Guess I thought wrong.

"Yes, well, don't read too much into that. Relationships change over the years. It doesn't mean your mother and I don't love each other. It's just different."

Dustin gave me that "are you kidding me?" look.

"Well, that won't happen between Paige and me. We won't ever sleep in separate rooms."

Immediately my thoughts turned to Rose. We couldn't keep our hands off one other at that age either. And after the weekend in Chicago, nothing had changed over the years. No, Rose and I wouldn't be sleeping in separate bedrooms either. But I wasn't married to Rose. I was married to Beth.

"No, that won't happen with you and Paige. You'll probably still be chasing her around the kitchen table when you're old and gray like me."

Dustin grinned, gathered his things, and walked over to the truck. He stowed everything in the back, and slid behind the wheel.

I gave him the one finger farmer wave, and went back to fishing.

Silence. No truck engine. I waited. Still no truck engine.

"You know, Dad, there's no age limit on plans... on hopes and dreams. You have to want something bad enough... make a decision, a plan, and go for it."

I looked straight ahead at the water. Where was this coming from and what the hell did my twenty-something son know about any of this shit?

I responded. "Sometimes it can't be about you or what you want. That's part of being a responsible adult, a responsible parent."

"Maybe. All I'm saying is at some point in your life it should be about you again, not about others. Maybe the others are old enough to take care of themselves. You know? To hell with everyone else. Fuck responsibility. Did you ever think about that, Dad?"

Geez. Two beers and he sounded like me.

"Nope, never thought about it like that. Wasn't raised that way."

I lied. I thought about it every day... every day since Chicago, every day of not hearing from Rose.

"Well, maybe you should, before you're too old to do anything about it other than fish. Just sayin'. How long do you keep going through the motions? Gotta be more to life than that, Dad."

I waved him off again.

"Thank you, Dustin. I'll keep that in mind the next time I'm going through the motions."

"Welcome, Dad."

Finally... he started the truck.

"Later. Don't wait up."

"I won't."

And with that final comment, he turned the truck around, waved, and took the gravel road back home.

I watched my youngest son drive away, and wondered right out loud... "Who is that wise, young man who shared such an insightful afternoon of fishing and conversation with me?"

Today we came full circle. I gave advice, and he listened. He gave advice, and I listened. Overall, a productive afternoon of fishing on the lake, indeed.

Chapter Nineteen

Come, my love, walk beside me.
Warm me with your smile.
Take my hand in yours again.
Stay close these last few miles.

Rockton, Illinois
Spring/Summer 2009

Friday night, I stopped by Will's for a couple of beers, instead of the lake, since Dustin and friends had first dibs. Beth wouldn't be home from her mom's for a couple of days, so the "to do" list could wait. Besides, I hadn't seen or talked to Ben much, other than at the bus yard, since the Chicago weekend I called in the favor. He'd been busy with his shit. I'd been busy with mine. And winter took over. I had a feeling he wanted to talk, and it wouldn't be about the weather.

I walked in, spotted Ben at the far end of the bar, and joined him.

"Geez, it's been awhile. Busy, huh?"

"Yep. Farm, the kids, the grandkids, the store... and trying to keep from freezing. Tell me again why we decided to settle in Northern Illinois?"

"Intrinsically stupid and desperate, and free rent."

"That about covers it."

Will brought over a Miller and set it down. "Got hot wings ready, boys."

"Sure. Sounds good. Lots of Ranch dressing."

"You got it."

Ben sipped his beer and looked over at me. Shit. I knew that look. He had plenty he wanted to say.

"You and Dustin fishing this afternoon? Saw you on the way to the feed store. Thought I recognized his truck."

"Yep, he's home on break for a few days. Nice having him home. Won't have many more opportunities to fish and talk."

"The boy in love yet?"

"Yep. Got it bad. Mostly what we talked about. That and changing schools and moving to California."

"Jesus. Girl must not be from around here. Bet Beth's fit to be tied over that."

"Yep. Not setting well. His girl's name is Paige—from New Mexico—majoring in journalism. She and Dustin begin fall term at USC in LA. Won't come back for awhile."

"Brian, and now Dustin, huh? That's how it happens. Our girls left home, one by one, along with Jack... except he came back. Things worked out though. Think he and Heather are planning to get married this summer or fall. Good for both sets of kids, for sure."

"Glad to hear that. It's hard for Beth to let go of the boys. She wanted them close for future grandbabies. I told her the boys need to live their own lives, find their own hopes and dreams... and it couldn't revolve around us, or the farm. I don't want them to have regrets over decisions not made, plans not carried out. She didn't particularly want to hear any of that."

"No, I'm sure she didn't. I guess I'm lucky. Karen never looked at things that way. She wanted our kids to find someone and be happy, no matter where they ended up. Probably stems from how we met, how we started out."

"Yep. I'm sure it does."

Will brought the wings and another beer apiece. We drank and chomped the wings in silence. I recognized the heavy silence. With Ben, it usually preceded an intense conversation.

He finished another wing, washed it down with some beer, and wiped his mouth with one of the paper napkins. He cleared his throat—a familiar nervous tick of Ben's—and waded into the conversation he'd kept inside for nearly six months.

"Jake. I need to say some things to you I've had on my mind for a while now, since the play actually. All you have to do is listen. You don't have to agree or disagree, comment or not. I don't care. Just have to get them out. Okay?"

"Sure. I'm listening."

"We've been friends a hell of long time. Seen each other through good times and some really dark times. When I came back from Vietnam, I came to stay with you in Champaign. I knew you wouldn't judge me, and would help me with whatever I asked. Do you remember?"

"Yep. I do. You were messed up. Strung out on drugs and alcohol, suffering from post-traumatic stress, although I'm not sure that's what they called it back then. We both knew you couldn't go home to Rockton in that shape. Couldn't do much of anything productive."

"Nope. You joined me for a time. Right nice of you, I thought. We were both a mess."

"Yep, great influence on me. Good thing the coke and heroin made me sick. Haven't blown dope in years. Still drink though. Never had a reason to stop or even slow down. Not like you did."

"Yep. I remember waking up on the floor of your apartment late one night—between the coffee table and couch—screaming, crying. I'd flashed back to Nam. Heard sniper bullets whizzing by my head. Saw dead soldiers—my buddies—lying in the muck, covered in mud and blood. A nightly occurrence back then.

When I finally came around, and looked at all the shit on the coffee table—dope bags, pipes, syringes, spoons, straws, and razor blades—I knew it all had to go away if I wanted a life at all, especially with Karen and Jack. I just thank God, she waited."

"Yep. I remember you scared the shit out of me. Bad night to drop acid with you freaking out."

"I made a decision that night. Decided I wanted something more than the drugs... enough to quit and see a shrink about the nightmares, the flashbacks. Six months later—Karen, Jack, and I—drove home to Rockton so everyone could meet. I asked her to marry me that weekend and never looked back, never regretted the decision. But making the decision... not easy."

"Nope, but you made it. That's what counted, and what made all the difference."

"Yep. I stopped listening to the other voices, stopped making excuses, stopped being afraid. I took charge. I fought. Most things in life worth a shit are those you have to fight for the hardest. I might never have gotten a second chance with Karen."

Ben stopped talking for a moment, and directed the next remark at me. "Second chances are rare. When they come along, you need to recognize a miracle for what it is."

I didn't say anything. I didn't have to. He knew.

"Jake, the woman who walked by me on her way out of the theater the night of the play... Rose Allison. I knew it then. I know it now."

He waited for a response, but I had none.

"I saw a change in you this past year. Didn't know what to think of it. You seemed different, happier for some reason. I knew it had nothing to do with home, with Beth. I started noticing all the texts. No one texts their wife or kids that much. I thought about Jack and all the texting back and forth between he and Heather. So, I figured you had a text buddy. Someone you'd met online, maybe. Happens everyday. And then the light bulb finally came on. You've only really loved one person your entire life. I always knew that. You wouldn't take risks for just anyone. But you just might risk it all for Rose."

I didn't say anything, but our eyes met after those words.

"I saw it in your face the day you asked me for the favor. I see it in your eyes now. You, my friend, are in love again... still. Son-of-a-bitch. How lucky can one man get? For God's sake, Jake. Talk to me. It's Ben. I'm on your side, no matter what."

I thought about everything he said. I couldn't keep it from him any longer.

While Ben talked and I listened, the bar filled up with half the town of Rockton.

Not much privacy now.

I looked over at Ben. "Let's finish the conversation in the truck."

I motioned to Will for the checks. We paid in cash, and walked out together to my truck, parked next to his.

We climbed in and I told him the whole, incredible story, beginning with the Friend request.

"Rose sent a Facebook Friend request in the fall of 2007. It started out so innocently, looking for Sam McGraw. After awhile, we realized we still loved one another. Our feelings hadn't changed over the years. We began a messaging/ texting affair of sorts. That's all we could do, all we had, given our circumstances."

"Until the weekend of the play last fall?"

"Yep. Rose is an author and had a book signing at the Palmer House in Chicago that weekend. I couldn't think of a way to meet her since I had the play going on. But when the furnace broke and Frank cancelled the matinee. I figured it had to be more than coincidence. I surprised her. Showed up at her hotel door after the book signing."

"Jesus. That had to be one hell of a surprise."

"You have no idea."

"And she surprised you by coming to the play. You didn't know, did you?"

"Nope. She said she shopped for a while, saw a movie, and came back to the hotel. I didn't realize I starred in the movie she watched. When you mentioned seeing a woman who looked like Rose, I didn't think much about it, until she and I talked Sunday night. She confessed. Told me about her little scheme and how you almost foiled it."

"I sure as hell did. Should have followed my instincts, and tailed her to the parking lot."

"Glad you didn't. Too much of a shock to handle unprepared. She'd never put either of us in that situation. That's what would have happened if we'd seen one another. Rose and I aren't just old friends who can dismiss one another with a quick hug and chit-chat. I'm not that good of an actor. Seeing one another would be like opening a lovely, aged bottle of wine and not tasting it."

"You're probably right, but sometimes you need to cut to the chase."

"Sometimes. Not always. Probably afraid, too—not of seeing me—but of others seeing us and guessing the truth, like you and Karen, or my family. She took all of that into consideration and decided watching me was enough."

"Jesus, Jake. I don't know how she did it. Watched you from a distance, and left."

"That's all she could do. She took a chance, and I'm damn glad she did."

Ben and I continued talking. Well, I did most of the talking now. Ben listened. I shared my thoughts and feelings, my doubts and fears, with my old friend. The last thing I disclosed... the night I made her cry. The night she broke contact with me.

"Jesus, why didn't you talk to me sooner? I asked months back. How could you fuck this up a second time?"

"I knew you'd be sympathetic."

"Christ. You haven't heard anything since?"

"Nope. She won't answer my texts or my messages or my emails. It wouldn't matter, Ben. I still have no plan. She probably knows that. Telepathy between us, I swear."

"Okay, let's work on a plan, right now. First, you have to make some tough decisions. How bad do you want her, Jake? Bad enough to divorce Beth and maybe lose your farm, give up half your income, and have the entire town gossiping about you and Beth and Rose? Are you ready to share this with the boys... tell them the plan? Because that's the plan, Jake. That's what it looks like, but then, you already knew that. It's ugly, and it won't be easy. But like I said, most things in life worth a shit, you fight for the hardest."

I sat in the quiet, dark of the truck, thinking about all those issues he mentioned, those same issues I'd thought about barely two weeks after the Friend request.

"I know things between you and Beth have never been great. I'm surprised you both made it this long. Having the boys helped, brought you together, gave you some commonality. But I always knew, even though you settled and moved on with Beth, you never got over Rose."

He paused for a moment.

"You know what I would do, Jake. But I'm not you. I would go after her and the hell with everyone and everything else. And I hate to bring this up, but since we're getting everything out in the open, you can't and won't make a decision as long as you're drinking. I know. I've been there. When you're drinking, you're two different people—and one of them can't make decisions worth a damn."

I thought about the last words Rose messaged me... *"And the two Jakes? They fucking ARE the same person, except one is sober and wants to make a decision... the other is drunk and can't make a decision."*

"How bad do you want her, Jake? Because once you make the decision, there's no going back."

"I know. Don't want to go back. Can't. Will you help me?"

"Worst case scenario... you lose it all. Are you willing to do that for her, if that's what it takes?"

I looked Ben squarely in the face. "Yep. I can't lose her again."

"Then I'll help you."

* * * * *

Rockton, Illinois
Saturday morning

I pulled the truck up facing the lake, and rolled the window down. Still a little chilly this morning, but warming nicely. I unzipped the gray flannel sweatshirt, slid the seat back, and soaked up the rays beating through the truck windows.

I looked out across the tranquil water of the lake. Smooth as glass—scarcely a ripple—and oh, so quiet... peaceful. The sun silhouetted the distant farm buildings and trees in a soft, orange glow. The morning sky shone a clear, slate blue. Canada wild rye, growing near the bank, swayed back and forth in the wind.

I pulled the cell out of my sweatshirt pocket and snapped the picture out the truck window. I typed a short message with the image, pressed send, and forwarded both to New Mexico.

"Good morning. Nippy here, but warming nicely. In my thoughts."

I never stopped texting, just slowed. Still checked Facebook. I couldn't let go of her hand. I told her I wouldn't. She had her reasons. I understood.

Just the whisper of a breeze blew lightly through my hair, across my skin. I closed my eyes and felt her hand against my face.

Neil Young's "Heart of Gold" played on the radio. I turned it up.

Since Ben and I talked, things seemed different, clearer. I had a plan. I had hope. And gettin' old... only a state of mind.

* * * * *

Albuquerque, New Mexico
Saturday morning

After our morning walk, Henry and Sassy—my two bulldogs—frisked across the backyard patio, through the French doors, and waited by the counter for their treat. I couldn't quite remember when they worked the *biscuit after the walk* into the daily agenda. I just know they did.

I unzipped the black hoodie sweatshirt, draped it over the kitchen chair, and pulled the U of I baseball cap from my head. His scent still lingered on the hat, on my hands, my hair. When I wore it, I felt him close, as if his hand cradled the back of my head.

That morning, I'd slipped pink lacy panties and a matching bra on after I showered. Even though he had my pink panties, when I opened the drawer and saw them, I remembered Chicago, and Jake. When they touched my skin... he touched my skin. Whenever I wore them, or the black-knit dress, I felt as if I wore something from my honeymoon.

I poured a cup of coffee, walked out to the patio, and sat down in my favorite white, wicker chair. The birds sang, the fountain gurgled and splashed, and the scent of cactus and gardenia blossoms permeated the air. Ridges of puffy, white clouds—stacked one on top of the other—looked like line dancers, stepping across the bright, blue sky.

I never forgot, nor took for granted, where I'd lived as a child... and where I lived now. That alone reinforced my belief in a higher power. I felt blessed. I felt happy. I felt free.

The cell vibrated inside my jeans pocket and I heard the familiar swoosh sound from an incoming text. Even before I looked, I knew.

331

He never broke contact over the months. Never let go. Somehow he understood the silence.

I brought the image up—a peaceful, early morning lake shot—and read the text.

"Good morning. Nippy here, but warming nicely. In my thoughts."

I saved each text, message, and picture—electronic gems—from my friend, my lover. Sometimes it took every bit of resolve I had, not to respond.

I couldn't. Not yet. Even if it was tearing me apart.

Love and passion can be deafening. Decisions sometimes need to be made solely by you, in quiet thought, within the softness of your heart.

* * * * *

Rockton, Illinois
Saturday morning
Two weeks later

I let the dogs in, poured a second cup of coffee, and sat down at the table. Plans today included spraying weeds, and having a serious conversation with Beth. How long I spent spraying weeds, depended on how the conversation went.

"Morning. You came home fairly early last night. Figured you and Ben would close Will's down." Beth poured a cup of coffee and sat down at the table, still dressed in her pink-and-gray flannel pajamas and fuzzy, pink socks.

"Wasn't at the pub. Haven't been to Will's in a couple weeks."

"Give it up for Lent?"

"Something like that. Actually, Ben, Jack, and I, and a few others, worked at the theater last night. Replaced spotlights, worked on the kitchen drains, sanded down several dining tables and dropped them off at the antique store. Karen's going to refinish them for us."

"I'm surprised she can find the time. She and Ben are usually busy with sick grandkids, the store, or moving Jack in or out. Guess he's living with that waitress from Will's now. Heather. Isn't that her name?"

Jesus. Here we go. May be a rough ride ahead.

"Yep, Heather. Actually she and Jack are planning a late summer or fall wedding. Asked if they could hold the ceremony at the lake. I said, sure."

"Well, I'll believe that when I see it. Can't imagine a texting affair ending up in marriage."

Jesus. Not going there.

"I wouldn't know. Jack seems to love Heather and her kids very much, and vice versa. It's a hell of a lot of responsibility they're taking on, trying to blend two families and make a life together."

"Yes, we'll see. The kids will keep them busy for a few years, then the two of them will have to figure out what to do with the rest of their lives."

Interesting turn in the conversation. I sipped my coffee and waded in with both feet.

"So, is that what we're doing, Beth... figuring out what to do with the rest of our time, our lives?"

"I guess it is. I wondered what would happen between us after the boys left. Did you ever wonder about that, Jake?"

"Yep."

"And?"

"You brought it up. I'd like to hear your thoughts."

"Actually, I've thought about a lot of things over the past several months."

I waited for her to fill the silence.

"I want to spend more time with my mom, my sisters, in Peoria. With the boys gone, there's not much for me to do here, except work. You're busy with the farm, the lake, the theater, the pub. Seems like I'm driving back and forth more and more."

"You have family here, other interests, Beth. You have your job, your church activities, the house."

"I know, but my mom and sisters aren't here. My job and church give me something to do, but I'm not tied to either. And the farm... never really mine. Your parents left it to you, not me. It's been home to me because of our family, the boys. Now the house seems empty and I'm not so attached anymore. It's not the same with just you and I rattling around. Everything's changed. Maybe I need a change, too."

"I never knew you felt that way about any of this, Beth. And no, it's not the same since the boys left. Nothing stays the same. Time changes things... for people, for relationships. Guess it's all part of moving through life."

I paused and looked at the woman across the table from me—my wife of thirty-five years, mother of my sons—and hardly remembered either of us.

I came back to Rockton—a thirty year-old-bachelor with a college degree—set to inherit the family farm. I met twenty-one-year old Beth—a cute, spunky, former Rockton homecoming queen—and moved on with my life. Her family and mine... friends and neighbors since both sets of grandparents homesteaded in the 1800s. Our marriage was a small-town match made in heaven.

This morning, Beth didn't look cute or spunky. She looked tired and unhappy. I probably caused some of that. I wondered if she saw the same in me.

"When you say 'change,' what exactly does that mean? A change in location or something else, Beth?"

"Would it make any difference? They're pretty much the same at this point in time."

Jesus. Talk about being out of touch. She caught me totally off guard with this conversation.

"No they're not the same, and I think we need to be clear. Are you thinking about temporarily moving out? Or are you thinking along more permanent lines... a separation, a divorce? How unhappy are you?"

"I'm unhappy. Very unhappy. We barely talk anymore. We live like roommates. And even though you keep busy, I know you're unhappy, too. I see it in your face. Would that be a fair statement, Jake? Are you unhappy, too?"

Maybe it did show.

"Yep. That would be a fair statement. As for the roommate thing, you moved me out of our room and upstairs, and made it clear you weren't interested in sex anymore. I never pressed the issue."

"I won't argue that point. I'm not interested in sex anymore. It's not important to women after a certain age like it is to men. I'm not sure if it's ever as important to a woman as it is to a man. Sex is just part of being married."

Jesus. How many other women shared this view? What the hell?

"What are men supposed to do when wives don't want sex anymore?"

"Well, they find other interests. You did."

Not going there. I wanted to tell her a big part of the distance between us came from no intimacy. Sex brings intimacy to a couple. Keeps them close. When closeness stops, distance follows. It never occurred to her that someone else wanted me, saw me differently, loved me intimately and wanted that closeness.

Beth stood, poured another cup of coffee, and stared out the window, toward the lake. I'd heard the term *deafening silence*, but until today, never experienced it.

"What about a separation, Jake? You do your thing and I'll do mine, but we'll still be married."

Nope. Okay for her, but not for me.

"I don't think a legal separation would change much of anything or make either of us happy. We'll still be exactly where we are now, just in different locations."

Beth continued to stare out the window. I didn't say anything more I waited.

"Maybe you're right. It wouldn't change things. A divorce might be a better solution for both of us. Mom and I talked about this a few months ago, the weekend of her medical tests."

Well, I'll be damned. Just when you think you know someone, they go and surprise the hell out of you.

She turned to face me. "I don't want the farm, Jake. It's been in your family, not mine. Maybe someday one of the boys will decide to come home and farm. You never know. Stranger things have happened

But I've worked side-by-side with you, through the years, as a partner. I expect you to take care of me financially, and take care of me well."

"I have no problem with that. You can expect me to be fair, to take care of you financially. You should know that."

"Yes, you've always been responsible, Jake. You've always taken care of business over the years."

She looked back out at the lake. I finished my coffee and continued the conversation.

"A divorce will give both of us another chance at happiness. Are you sure about this, Beth? I want us both on the same page, no second-guessing. If we both agree to divorce, I'll call Bill Fiedler and set up an appointment. He's handled legal affairs for our family through the years. I trust him. Are you okay with him?"

Beth shifted her focus from the lake back to me.

"Yes, I'm sure about the divorce, and I'm good with Bill Fiedler, although I don't care for his secretary, Nancy. Pretty nosey."

"Well, there's bound to be gossip eventually. We live in a small town. People talk. Don't have anything else to do. We'll have to ignore it until they move on to someone or something else."

"I guess so."

A few stray tears rolled down her cheeks. I stood, grabbed a napkin from the table, and handed it to her. She wiped her eyes, blew her nose, and tucked the napkin inside her pajama pocket.

"This is hard, Jake. Things were never easy between us, but I hoped we'd grow closer over the years. That never happened. I'm sorry for that."

"No. It didn't. And this is hard. We've spent half our lives with one another. I don't think either of us need to be sorry for things done or not done. We did the best we knew how for as long as we could."

"How do you think Brian and Dustin will handle this?"

"I don't know. But they're not kids anymore. We'll just have to wait and see."

"I'll always love you, Jake. You know that, don't you?"

"Yep, I do. And I'll always love you. I want you to be happy, Beth."

"And I want you to be happy, too, Jake. I do."

I walked over and put my arms around her. She stiffened. For a few, brief moments, I held her, and she held me. The first time since... actually, it had been so long, I couldn't remember.

She pulled away, set her cup in the sink, and walked across the kitchen, pausing in the doorway. "I think I'll drive to Mom's after I shower, maybe spend the night. I'll be back before dark tomorrow."

"Okay."

Even as a young woman, I remembered Beth never liked driving after dark. When the bar closed, and our shifts finished, we'd head for a motel. She always followed closely behind my truck. Each time we pulled away, she'd say, "Don't lose me along the way, Jake."

Neither of us could have guessed the implications back then. But somewhere, somehow, we did, indeed, lose each other along the way.

* * * * *

Later around dusk—after spraying weeds all afternoon—I saw Ben's truck winding up the graveled driveway. We'd talked earlier, after Beth left, after I called Bill Fiedler.

Ben pulled in, and Karen rolled the passenger side window down.

"Hey, wassup, you two?"

"Hey, Jake. Ben and I just unloaded the refurbished tables at the theater. They look really good."

"I'm sure. You do nice work."

I leaned against the truck door and looked in, a large pizza box between them. "Pizza delivery on the list, too, Ben?"

"Nah, stopped for pizza and couldn't eat but half of it. Thought of you. Pepperoni. Always order too much. Forget we're not feeding grandkids anymore."

Karen picked up the box and handed it to me through the truck window.

"Thanks, appreciate the thought. Why don't you come in and I'll wash up. Have a cup of coffee or something."

"No, we're beat. Been a long day. Just wanted to drop off the pizza... and this." Ben held a white and blue, medium sized, Priority Mail box in his hand. "Found it on the front porch just as we were leaving to deliver the tables. Figured we drop it by with the pizza."

The thick mailer passed from his hand to Karen's... and into mine. I examined it. Ben commented.

"It's addressed to Jake Richardson—in care of Ben Chapman—from The Harmon Foundation out of Albuquerque, New Mexico. You familiar with that foundation?"

I looked over at Ben and Karen. "I am now. Pretty sure they're associated with flowers."

"Roses, maybe?" Karen asked with a smile.

"Yep. One particular species of rose."

I held the mailer up. "Thanks for bringing this by. Good or bad, it's something. More than I had yesterday."

Karen reached out and squeezed my arm. "I have a good feeling about this. Can't explain it. Just do." I watched her pretty blue eyes tear up. "You need to bring our girl home, Jake. Do whatever it takes."

I placed my hand on top of hers and squeezed back. "Working on it, Ren."

* * * * *

After a quick shower and change of clothes, I sat down at the kitchen table with a couple slices of cold pizza, a Dr. Pepper, and the Priority Mail box. I tore the tape off and opened the flap. Inside, an envelope with my name on the front, and another package wrapped in tissue paper. I opened the envelope and found a note.

Dear Jake,

You have no idea how many times I've written those words, that greeting, over the years. "Letters, bundled together and tied with ribbons... the only tangible proof of love, of relationship, or the power of the written word." Remember?

And, Jake... I never forgot, never gave up. LUJ2lls

I laid the note on the table, and removed the package from inside the box, carefully folding back the tissue paper.

Sweet Jesus. Letters.

A stack of letters bundled and tied—not with ribbons—but faded strips of paisley cloth, fashioned from the leftover fabric of my bell bottomed jeans' inserts. Tenderly, I touched the bow she'd fashioned with her hands, her fingers.

My eyes welled with tears. It had been a long time since that happened.

I thumbed through the stack of envelopes, gingerly peeking inside.. white copy paper, yellow lined legal paper, diary pages, and white, parchment stationary with pale, pink roses. Every letter addressed to me. Each with our mutual birthdate, November 23rd, written on the outside envelope, except for the most recent, dated a few weeks ago, April 23, 2009. The first one, at the bottom of the stack, dated November 23, 1971.

Jesus. Unbelievable.

How ironic she wrote letters to me over a lifetime, while I had shared John Keats's letters to Fanny Brawne with her.

I decided to start from the beginning and slipped the very last letter from the bottom... a sheet of lined paper, torn from one of her journals. Journals I'd held and read at Parkridge Apartments. Carefully, I unfolded it and a faded picture fell out—an early candid shot of Rose and me at the apartment. Her hair, not yet lightened from the sun, mine just beginning to grow long. I stood behind, holding her in my arms, as we both gazed out the apartment window. A beautiful image of a young couple in love—kindred spirits—forever captured in time. I slid the picture inside my wallet and read the letter.

November 23, 1971

Dear Jake,

You'll probably never read this, but writing my thoughts out to you in words on paper helps me through the long, lonely days and nights.

I'm sorry for the way things ended between us. I felt you betrayed my trust. Yet as time passes, I'm unsure of what happened. I've tried to remember, but like so many things from the past, the events aren't clear. So much gone from my memory. I know I made you cry, and that haunts me day and night. I'm sorry for hurting you, for leaving. But most of all, I'm sorry for not listening.

I wish I could undo things—better understand what happened—and start again. I know I can't. It seems something or someone always tells me to leave, to run away, before I'm hurt. That's all I've ever known. But this time, leaving was different. A part of me stayed behind with you... and I tucked a part of you inside my heart when I left.

I know I'm messed up—broken inside—with no idea how to repair the damage. I want to love and be loved, but I don't know if that will ever happen. Your love for me, kind, gentle, and sweet. With you, I felt love for the first time. Jake, I tried so hard to love you back.

Find someone. Someone who will love you for me, and be happy for both of us. Dream for both of us. You were the Prince Charming I'd waited for. But, I locked myself inside for so long, I didn't recognize you. Instead of embracing you, I pushed you away and ran. I know now I made a mistake I can't fix. Some things once broken, once lost, can never be fixed or found again.

I will never forget you. Never. You'll remain in my heart and be a part of me forever.

Rose with 2lls

> *Letting go is the hardest thing*
> *The human heart will ever beat through,*
> *With no way to ease the bitter sting*
> *Or numb the pain you can't undo.*

Jesus. A lifetime slipped through our fingertips like sand. How in the hell does that happen? You make decisions that affect your entire life when you have the least amount of experience or skills to make them. Who in the hell came up with that plan?

I read every word of every letter—spanning nearly four decades—then went back and reread portions of letters again.

November 23, 1974 – I've decided to write letters to you on our birthday and hide them away. Now I'll have someone to talk to—a friend—a best friend.

I live out West, Jake... just like in my dreams. I have a beautiful home in Albuquerque, New Mexico. It's not our Leave It To Beaver house, but it's very nice.

I'm doing everything I'm supposed to do. Everything seems right, but I know it's not. I can't connect with anyone, not even Paul. I have no friends. I'm alone.

Oh, Jake, do you remember me? Do you remember 2lls? A part of my heart never lets me forget.

November 23, 1979 – Three years have slipped by since I last wrote. Guess what? I'm a mother, Jake. We have a little baby boy, Joseph Paul... Joey. He's perfect in every way—blond hair and green eyes—with dimples in each cheek. His little toes look like little pink jelly beans. He's beautiful. Paul seems pleased to have a son.

Do you have children, Jake? Does someone, a little girl or boy, call you Daddy? The thought brings tears of joy to my eyes, and warms my heart. You and I are distant now and I know I must leave you in the past. But a part of me always remembers, always searches the faces in the crowd... for you.

November 23, 1981 - Sometimes I think God is punishing me for my decision years ago. Do you think God would do that, Jake? I don't think He would, but that's what some people believe. If you sin, God punishes you. If I dwell on that, I can't be the mother or wife I need to be. I couldn't live with myself or go on. And, so, I try not to. But, I'll always carry the burden of that decision. You never knew what happened after I left Parkridge. You never knew of the late night call I made to you. Sometimes it's better not knowing the truth.

I hope this was a good year for you. I picture you happy and well, surrounded by a family who loves and appreciates the good man I know you are. How lucky they are to have you.

November 23, 1991 – My life seems perfect. Perfect husband, perfect children, perfect home. And yet I struggle each and every day to stay in this life. Some days I prefer fantasy over reality. I have control over my fantasy world, and feel as if I have little control over my real world. Staying busy and focused on the details seems to be the key. I have no one to share my inner thoughts and feelings with. I struggle alone for my sanity. No one knows, except you, Jake. It's our secret.

Even after all the years, there are nights I feel you close... kind, gentle, tender, and loving. You never had an agenda. Never took from me. I gladly gave everything I could give to you. I will never forget. Remember me, Jake.

She knew. She waited. Then sent a lifetime of unspoken words from her heart to mine. Words... something tangible left behind to mark the existence of our love.

I refolded the letters and placed them back in the bundle, and drew the most recent letter from beneath the paisley bow... this one typed and printed on computer paper, probably from her office.

April 23, 2009

Dear Jake,
Tonight, I read through all the letters I've written to you over the years. The letters, alone, would make a lovely storyline for a novel. I decided you should have them now. They belong with you, not me. I never forgot you, never stopped loving you through the years, Jake.

I know Ben recognized me the night of the play, and I hope by now you've taken him into your confidence. I trust he followed his heart when the package arrived, and you are now holding the letters... reading my words.

I couldn't leave things unsaid between us and wanted to share my thoughts with you in words in a letter... one more time. Writing is what I do best. Whatever I said or did, I did out of love... always out of love for you.

A woman's heart searches a lifetime for her soul mate, her kindred spirit, her Prince Charming. Sometimes she finds him, sometimes not. But when she does, no one ever compares to him. His touch, his kiss, his love awakens all that sleeps deep within her... love, passion, and all the other possibilities they bring.

If she finds and keeps his love, they die in that love together. If she loses his love, her heart never forgets and forever longs and searches, in vain, for that same love. Jake, you are, and will always be my Prince Charming.

I've lived a lifetime on the fringes, watching others. Wondering who I was, where I fit in. I ignored things I couldn't deal with, and isolated myself out of fear. I don't want to live in that gray, shadowy area anymore. I know you don't want that either, but that's what will happen if you and I remain lovers, and nothing more. We'll spend the rest of our days stealing bits and pieces of precious time to be together And no matter how much more I want, because I love you, I might settle for those stolen moments, and come to you. This was my mother's life, and I'm not my mother.

If you love me, Jake, you won't ask this of me.

Even as I write these words, I fear it might be too late to save my heart a second time. Don't you see, Jake... if I hold on to your hand, I'll die alone of a broken heart. If I let go, I may die alone of a broken heart, anyway.

The texts and messages create a constant craving—maddening—with no way to satisfy, to placate. You are like a drug to me, and I am addicted. I can't text or chat or see you briefly, without wanting more. There can never be enough "more" in an affair.

I've come so far in understanding myself over the past months. I've discovered so many scattered puzzle pieces, and places where they fit. Part of this with Molly's help... part with yours. I'm not afraid to step from the fringes.

No matter how much I love you, I can't be just an affair. I can't be the invisible woman in your life. I thought I could at first. I thought that would be enough. It's not, can never be. Maintaining an affair requires living part of your life in fantasy. I've done that. I know the difference between reality and fantasy. I can write fantasy, but I need reality in my life.

I want it all, Jake... Prince Charming, the kiss, the white horse, the happily ever after. Is that what you want? It's your decision now.

You will always be my kindred spirit, my soul mate, my muse. My heart will always remember and long for only you. Because of you, because of your love, I'm forever changed inside, a second time. You've helped me find my strength and courage and confidence again. There's no going back. Not sure I can go forward without you, but I must try, and you must understand.

When you hear something, feel something—a whisper that hushes and lightly touches you—it's me, Jake. It will always be me... waiting.

LUJ, Rose

I slipped the stack of letters back inside the strips of paisley cloth, tucked the note and tissue paper inside the mailer, and carried them upstairs. I slid the mailer inside the nightstand drawer, turned off the lamp, and sat on the edge of the bed, holding the letters in my hand, staring out the window into the darkness.

The images from the words of each letter, burned inside me. I ached for her, body and soul. It took everything I had not to climb in the truck and drive to Albuquerque.

I picked up my cell and sent a text out into the night.

"Trust me, Rose. I want it all, too. LU2lls."

I stripped down to my black knit briefs and crawled under the sheet. Mentally and physically exhausted, yet my mind raced. I closed my eyes and drifted. In the quiet, darkness of my room, I held her. I kissed her. I felt her heart beating against mine. My mind quieted.

Several minutes later, the light and sound of an incoming text on my cell.

Rose.

"I've always trusted you. Waiting. LUJ2lls."

Chapter Twenty

When bare feet scampered over dew-covered grass
And lazy summer nights were so very slow to pass.
Endless possibilities, our lives had just begun.
Twilights long ago, when you and I were young.

Albuquerque, New Mexico
A few weeks later
Saturday evening

B.B. King and U2 were belting out "When Love Comes To Town" on the radio as I pulled in front of the tan, stucco, Southwest-style house—20415 Cactus Wren Drive—a black Chevy truck and white Prius parked in the driveway. In the front yard, situated amid the cactus, yuccas, and rocks... a for sale/sold sign.

Rose never mentioned anything to me about selling the house or moving. Of course, we hadn't communicated in months, so how could I know her plans? She certainly had no way of knowing my intentions, or that I even had formulated a plan. But I knew better than to ignore the feeling gnawing my gut this past week whenever I thought of her.

I wondered how this unannounced visit would be received. It didn't matter. No more second-guessing or indecisiveness. For the first time—in a very long time—I was confident about my intentions. Somehow, I would make this work.

I opened the truck door and stepped out. It felt good to finally stretch my legs and walk around a bit. The twenty-hour drive from

Rockton was a long haul. I walked up the driveway and through the open, double garage door. I wound my way through the stacked moving boxes... and knocked at the back door. No response. I knocked again. Nothing.

I poked my head inside. "Anybody home?"

From another room, a woman's voice. "Step inside. I'll be right there."

Not Rose.

Whoever the voice belonged to must be expecting someone. I stepped inside the kitchen and waited. A pretty, silver-haired woman, in her early fifties—no taller than five feet and probably all of one hundred pounds soaking wet—walked from the adjoining hallway.

* * * * *

I stopped when I saw *him*. Our eyes met. Rose's descriptive words from her writing immediately came to mind.

Handsome. Rugged. Weathered. He wore a white linen, button-down shirt, untucked over faded, blue denim jeans. His hair—long, thick, streaked with gray and silver—brushed the collar of his shirt. A full graying mustache lined his generous lips. His eyes, deep blue.

The only difference today, a blue chambray shirt.

Oh. My. God.

Oh, my God!

How could he know of all the thoughts and prayers I'd sent out into the universe over the last few days? He couldn't. This was a miracle and an all-time universe response record for me.

I closed my eyes and silently said to anyone and everyone listening, "Thank you. Thank you, God. Thank you, Jesus. Thank you, Supreme Being. Thank you for listening."

* * * *

"I didn't mean to barge in, but no one came to the door." Before I could get one more word out, she responded.

"You're Jake, Jake Richardson, aren't you?"

346

"Yep, that would be me. And you are?"

"Kathryn—Kathryn Harmon—Rose's editor. Kind of a shock seeing you here. I thought maybe the moving guys finally arrived with the storage units. But you were the last person I thought I would see in the doorway of this house. A genuine surprise."

She walked over, put her arms around my neck, and hugged me. Really hugged me. I didn't quite know what to do. When she pulled away, her eyes brimmed with tears.

"I'm glad you're here. I wanted to call, but I wasn't sure what to do."

Those words brought a sinking feeling to my gut. "Where's Rose and what's wrong?"

"She's in the hospital, Jake."

"Oh, Jesus. I knew something was wrong all week. I felt it. What happened? Why is she in the hospital?"

"Come sit down and I'll fill you in over a cup of coffee. Black?"

"Yep, black. Two sugars, please."

She poured two cups of coffee, handed one to me, and we walked into the adjoining family room... one of the rooms not yet packed. This room, like the kitchen, looked familiar from the pictures Rose texted over the past two years.

A dark-brown leather couch and matching love seat—separated by an antique dry sink, end table, and lamp—formed an L-shaped sitting area. A large, wooden coffee table, with a vase of fresh sunflowers, sat angled in front of the couches. The room was filled with comfortable furniture, antique tables, fringed lamps, an assortment of clocks, family photos, and a variety of green plants. Homey. Rose's taste, more Midwest than Southwest.

Kathryn sat across from me on the love seat. I sat on the leather couch.

I took a long swallow of the coffee, and looked over at her. "Okay. Let's have it."

"Rose spoke at a local women's club Thursday night. The evening went well and she seemed happier than I'd seen her in months."

Kathryn averted her eyes as she finished that last sentence. Shit. I had a sinking feeling I was part, if not *the* reason, for Rose's unhappiness these past months.

Kathryn continued.

"Rose chatted and signed books for the last few in line at the table. When she finished, she stood and started to walk away. But after taking only a few steps, she collapsed. It happened so fast, no one could catch her or break the fall. She hit her head especially hard on the tile floor."

"Christ." Kathryn's words seemed unbelievable to me, made my head swim. "Were you close when she fell?"

"Not more than a few steps behind her. I didn't realize what was happening until she hit the floor. I couldn't do anything except watch her fall. God, it was awful. Luckily, a nurse in the women's group—Jennifer Carlson—saw her fall, and immediately took charge. She folded her sweater and placed it under Rose's head, while I called 911, and Joe and Jenna. We stayed with her, talked to her, and tried to wake her, but she didn't respond.

The paramedics arrived about ten minutes later, checked her vitals, stabilized her, and rushed her to the hospital. Joe met us there, along with Doctor Webb, a neurological specialist, and family friend. He ordered all the initial tests and scans. No broken bones, no spinal injury, just a huge, goose egg-size knot on the back of her head. She's been unconscious since.

"Jesus. What a thing to happen. Is she in intensive care?"

"No, a private room. She seemed to come around yesterday, moaned, and even fluttered her eyes a couple of times. But nothing since. It's like she's asleep. The doctor said, for now, it's a watch and wait."

Shit. I didn't like the sound of that. How long do they watch and wait before the tubes go in?

"What about family... her kids, Paul? Is someone with her?"

"It's been Jenna or Joe or me. Paul and Natalie spent some time with her last night, but drove back to Santa Fe this morning."

The room grew quiet. I took another swallow of coffee and thought about the events of Thursday night.

"Why would Rose collapse? Too much wine? Has she been sick? Is something else wrong?"

Kathryn took a sip of coffee, placed the cup back on the table, pursed her lips, and looked over at me. She seemed hesitant.

"Let's have it all, Kathryn. What's been going on the past few months? I need to know."

She drew a deep breath and exhaled.

"First of all, you need to know, even though Rose and I are friends, she is guarded about what, and how much, she says to me. She lets me in... up to a point."

How like Rose. After all the years, she still kept people at a distance, even Kathryn, who considered her a close friend. Old habits, indeed, die hard.

"I'm familiar with that... understand."

"You're probably the only one, besides Rose, who does. Having said that, I only found out a few weeks ago that you and she were no longer communicating. I knew something was terribly wrong, but I didn't know what."

"Why did you think something was wrong?"

"Rose lost weight over the past few months. Too much. When I asked her about it, she said she'd lost her appetite. I noticed the last few times we ate lunch together, she picked at her food, hardly ate anything."

"What else?"

"I noticed dark circles under her eyes. She seemed tired and stressed. When I asked her, she attributed it to allergies, but added she wasn't sleeping well, either."

Son-of-a-bitch. Not eating, not sleeping, and stressed out. Hell, no wonder she collapsed. I caused this stress in her life and I knew it. But I was damn well determined to alleviate it, as well. Jesus, give me the chance to fix this... to make things right with her.

I continued fishing for information from Kathryn.

"I was surprised by the Realtor sign in the yard when I drove up. What's up with that? Do you know why she's selling?"

"I know of two reasons—down-sizing for one, too much house for her to maintain alone. She also told me she wanted to live in a home of *her* choice. I guess every place before, Paul chose. She talked of buying a condo here in Albuquerque or maybe Las Cruses. She even talked of moving back to her hometown of Macomb, maybe trying to purchase her grandparents' home, and restore it. She hadn't made a decision yet. When the house sold and closed so quickly, she decided to put things in storage and stay with me until something felt right to her. I think her exact words were, 'I'm hoping a plan will come together.'"

Again, how like Rose. She kept moving forward, just like she'd always done. She'd decided to sell and move somewhere that made her happy. A decision, made independently of me. I knew she loved me. I knew she wanted to be with me. But she would make no compromises. She would not come to me again. If I wanted a life with her, I'd better saddle up with a plan, and ride in on the damn, white horse.

Well-played.

"I need to see her, Kathryn."

"I know. We'll go together as soon as the storage units arrive. You can drive. Presbyterian hospital is only fifteen minutes from here."

"Okay. I'm not quite sure how to explain to her family who I am or why I want to see her. I don't think anyone knows about me, other than you, and Molly."

"Yes. We're it."

"Well, it might be time to let things play out. I didn't drive for twenty hours not to see her."

"Did you drive straight through?"

"Yep. Left yesterday morning."

"Are you staying anywhere?"

"Nope. Drove here first."

"Rose would want you here. Bring your things in from the truck and put them in one of the extra bedrooms down the hall."

"Sounds good."

"Make yourself at home. I packed linens earlier today, but I think the sheets, and pillowcases are near the top of one of the boxes in the hallway. The pillows and blankets are somewhere in the bottom. You'll have to dig for them. Not much left in the fridge... water, cheese sticks, and some yogurt. There's more coffee... no wine or beer, though."

"Coffee's good. Gave the rest up for Lent."

"Lent, huh?" She paused, looked at me, and smiled. "Good for you." She knew. "I need to back out my car and Rose's truck, and park them on the street."

"I'll help you with that, then bring my things in."

Kathryn got up, rummaged through her purse, and handed me Rose's truck keys.

"You know, it's weird. I had a gut feeling something wasn't right all week."

"Not weird at all considering how close you are with Rose. I didn't quite know what to do when this happened. I wanted to call you Thursday night, right after I called Joe and Jenna, but didn't want to cause problems."

"No problems. That's the main reason I'm here. I wanted to tell Rose I finally had a plan."

"Well, it's pretty amazing how events play out sometimes. I've sent a lot of thoughts and prayers out into the universe this week. Some real long shots."

"Get anything back?"

She reached over and squeezed my hand. "Yes, Jake. You're one of the long shots."

"Well, I'll be damned. I've never been anyone's long shot." A comfortable silence hung between us for a few moments. "Kathryn. I'm grateful for everything you've done... for being here with Rose when I couldn't be."

"She's like a sister. I love her, too. We'd both be lost without her. Now, she needs a reason to wake up."

"Another long shot?"

"Maybe. But the odds seem much better now that you're here."

"I know that's why I'm here... why I had that gut feeling."

"Yes, me, too. She's waiting for you."

* * * * *

Kathryn and I finished backing out the vehicles just as the moving company arrived. I parked Rose's truck behind mine and watched them unload the two large, white metal storage units onto the driveway. As I sat there behind the wheel, I noticed a beaded, leather dream-catcher suspended from her rearview mirror, feathers hanging from either side. A dream-catcher for the dreamer. She helped me believe in dreams... twice. As a young man, I watched them slip away. I wasn't going to let that happen a second time.

I brought my things in from the truck and laid them on the antique, four-poster bed in the guest room. Rose had texted pictures of it from an estate sale one Saturday morning. I told her I thought they belonged in a farmhouse bedroom. I had just the bedroom in mind.

I never imagined my twenty-hour trek from Illinois to New Mexico ending like this. Instead of holding Rose—discussing future plans—I'd sit at her bedside, and hope something I said or did might bring her back.

In a heartbeat, the plan had changed. The priority shifted. Just when you think you're in control... you're not.

* * * * *

Presbyterian Hospital
Saturday night

Kathryn and I arrived at the hospital a little after eight, and rode one of the stainless, sterile elevators to the fourth floor. She brought Rose's favorite purple violet from the desk in her office... the one she named "Violet." I brought the package carted with me from Illinois.

We stepped out of the elevator and walked down the shiny, ceramic-tiled corridor past the nurses' station. Hospital patient floors never seem quite as hectic at night as during the day. I remembered from visiting my dad during his battle with cancer. Jesus, I hated hospitals. I hated how they looked, how they smelled. I hoped I died at the lake or fell off my tractor into a field. Let me die anywhere other than in a hospital. Rose and I chatted about this one late night. She felt the same.

352

The desk nurse glanced up, smiled, and went back to her paperwork. I followed Kathryn to the end of the hallway, last room on the right, room 415. The patient name placard read: Rose Allison, Dr. John Webb.

I opened the door for Kathryn, just as a pretty, salt-and-pepper-haired nurse, probably in her late fifties, exited. Her nametag read, Nurse Day.

She stopped and spoke to us. "You just missed her son. He left about ten minutes ago."

"How's she doing? Any change?"

"She's fine. No change, though. Pretty purple violet."

Nurse Day shifted her focus to me. " More family? Rose's brother?"

"Nope. I'm just a friend from out of town."

Kathryn added, "A very *close* friend who drove twenty hours from Illinois."

The nurse studied me a moment, nodding her head slightly. "You know, sometimes a very close friend is the best medicine of all."

"Jake and I are counting on that. It may be a late night in room 415."

Nurse Day smiled and winked. "No problem as long as you keep the loud music and dancing down. Ring if you need anything. My shift ends at midnight."

She continued out the door and down the hallway, toward the nurses' station. I drew a deep breath, and followed Kathryn into the room, setting the package on a nearby metal chair.

I walked to the foot of the bed, and gently grasped Rose's feet through the thin, white, waffle-weave blanket. They felt warm. I thought this a good sign, but what the hell did I know? She looked very thin and pale against the stark, white hospital sheets and cold, metal bed frame. I saw the dark circles under her eyes. The light, blue hospital gown, too large for her small frame, drooped over her right shoulder, an IV inserted farther down her right arm.

In that one moment, I wanted to scoop her into my arms, tell her how much I loved her, and that I would make everything all right. I wanted to take back every wasted, indecisive bit of time over the past two years. Jesus. Give me a chance to make this right.

While I stood wallowing and doing penance, Kathryn found a place for Violet on the metal nightstand... amid a yellow, plastic water pitcher, a box of Kleenex, a coordinating aqua-encased thermometer and barf pan. She scooted on the bed, next to Rose, held her hand, and began talking.

"Rose, it's Kathryn. How are you? The nurse said Joe left a few minutes ago. I noticed your grandchildren sent more drawings and notes today. They're quite the budding artists... authors. I brought Violet from your office and set her on the nightstand. She's loaded with velvety, purple blossoms. You have such a green thumb. I packed more boxes this morning, and the moving guys finally came with two, huge metal storage units. You'll hate them. Your house looks like Honey Boo-Boo's family moved in. I'm sorry. It's only temporary."

I watched Rose's face as Kathryn spoke. Nothing. I swallowed hard, and fought back emotions of anger, helplessness, and regret. None of those would help. She needed my strength and stubbornness.

"Rose, I brought someone with me. He drove all the way from Illinois to see you. I want you to listen to every word he says."

Kathryn released her hand, and we exchanged places.

Now, I sat on the edge of the bed, held her hand in mine, and stroked her cheek, her hair, with the other. I leaned in and whispered next to her ear, "It's Jake, baby. Can you hear me? I'm sitting next to you. Listen to my voice. I'm right here. You're not alone. Wherever you are, I'm going to help you get back. I won't leave without you."

I brushed my lips over her cheek, kissed her forehead, her temple, and continued talking.

"I woke up Thursday in the middle of the night. Something didn't feel right. I packed a bag, climbed in the truck, and left. It took just a little over twenty hours to drive from my door in Rockton to yours here in Albuquerque. I thought about you the entire way. Pictured us driving the scenic route back to Illinois... stopping in a small town for lunch... rummaging antique stores on our way out. We could find a nice family-owned motel, or maybe, a bed and breakfast to spend the night."

I stroked her arms and gently massaged her shoulders. She seemed smaller beneath my hands, more delicate than I remembered from Chicago.

"I'm staying in your guest room. See what happens when you leave for a few days? Squatters show up. I sat on the antique, four-poster bed this afternoon. Very nice and comfortable, but I missed having you beside me." I leaned closer. "Do you remember what I told you when this first began, Rose... after the Friend request? I said I loved you then, loved you now, and I'd always love you. I meant every word."

* * * * *

For the next two hours, Jake continued his one-sided conversation. Now and then, he pressed a kiss against her cheek, her temple, or trailed his fingers through her hair.

I sat quietly in the corner... mesmerized. I felt as if a romance novel opened in front of me. I walked into the story, sat down on the wordless border of the book—feet dangling over the edge—and watched a beautiful love scene unfold on the pages.

Jake Richardson. Gentle, soft-spoken, humble. I understood why Rose loved him. I felt his love for her, just sitting near him. Remarkable.

He didn't fit the mold of a tall, dark, handsome Hollywood lead, nor a corporate power broker. Just an ordinary man—a farmer, a bus driver, and someone's dad—living out his life on a farm in Illinois.

Yet, I knew from conversing with Rose—from reading her words—how extraordinary he was. She wrote a romance novel, created a lead character, based on him.

His love, passion, and desire for her, kindled a love affair that smoldered over a lifetime. He made love to her so intensely, she remembered it nearly forty years later. He kept her safe at his side through campus riots, and danced for her—across a sea of faces at a rock concert—one hot, summer long ago. He quoted Keats... whispered words of love in the night, most women only dream of hearing... and made love to her in ways most women only read about in romance novels.

I'd never been much of a romantic until Rose... until Jake. But they made a believer out of me.

Ordinary people *can* become extraordinary in their lover's eyes. Love has the capacity to elevate one to another level. You truly can become more than you ever dreamed... when someone believes in you and loves you.

* * * * *

"Jake, I'm going down to the cafeteria for coffee. Would you like me to bring a cup back?"

"Please."

She smiled and walked out the door. I stood, stretched my legs, and checked out the view from Rose's window. A beautiful night view of Albuquerque, unfortunately, a hospital view. Jesus. What the hell were we doing here? The night seemed surrealistic, a dark place we all needed to come back from.

I glanced back at Rose. Except for her breathing, the room held absolute quiet. Too much quiet. I took out my cell phone, brought up Pandora, and programmed several late 1960s groups and songs. Music had always played an important part in her life. Maybe a familiar voice, or song, would reach her—catch her attention—turn her thoughts homeward.

I sat next to her again, and held the cell close. "Blackbird," by The Beatles began playing. "Homeward Bound," by Simon and Garfunkel played next, followed by "Guinnevere," by Crosby, Stills & Nash.

The songs played, one after the other. I watched. I waited. Then I noticed something... a change in her breathing. A deliberate change in the rhythm. Jesus. Not much, but something.

"We listened to these songs over and over. We made love to these songs in the upstairs bedroom of your apartment at Parkridge. Do you remember, Rose? We'll do that again, under the moonlight, next to the lake. We chatted and texted about this. Now, I'm going to make that happen."

I turned up the music a bit. Another Crosby, Stills and Nash tune played, "Lady of the Island."

"You're my Lady of the Island, Rose. The day you sent the Friend request, this song played on Pandora. I listened to the words and remembered tracing all the places on your body where the sun didn't go... with my fingers, my lips. I want to do that to you again. Would you like that?"

I leaned closer. "Where have you wandered, Rose? What can I do or say to bring you back to me? Listen to the music... come toward the sound. I'm here for you... reaching out to you. You're not alone, baby."

* * * * *

My head ached. Somewhere in this quiet, dark place... music played. I wanted to stay and sleep and drift in the darkness, but a voice kept waking me, bringing me back. The voice, low and steady, soothing.

"Where have you wandered, Rose? What can I do or say to bring you back to me? Listen to the music... come toward the sound. I'm here for you... reaching out to you. You're not alone, baby."

I drifted toward the sound... toward the music... toward the voice. Whose voice?

* * * * *

Led Zeppelin sang "Stairway to Heaven." I continued watching her closely as I reached for the package on the chair.

"I brought a present for you. Feel it?"

I took her hand in mine and moved it slowly over the plastic horse—the head, legs, body, and tail—then, over the rider—the hat, his body, his legs and arms, the guns and saddle.

"It's Roy Rogers and Trigger. Remember them? I think they're identical to the ones you described. Karen found them at an antique store in Wisconsin a few weeks ago."

I continued guiding her hand over the horse and rider... reassuring her with my voice, my words.

"Ben and Karen know about us. I needed someone to talk to and I figured you'd understand. Ben guessed anyway. He recognized you the night of the play, nearly followed you to the parking lot. They can't wait to see you. Do you know what Karen said to me when they brought the letters? 'You need to bring our girl home, Jake. Do whatever it takes.' That's my plan. I'm doing whatever it takes."

* * * * *

This time I heard another voice—a still, small voice from childhood—I remembered well. Her voice whispered, "Rose, you don't belong alone in this quiet, dark place. I'll take you to the warm, sunny place in the West, where we traveled back and forth as children. You can stay there for a time with our friends. They'll help you. I'll help you. It's time to leave the darkness and remember the feeling you get when you look to the West."

Yes, I remembered—off in the West, the white buildings of the ranch—familiar faces and surroundings from childhood.

Drifting toward the light... toward the west... toward the music.

Almost there.

"Can you hear me, Rose? It's Roy. What a nice surprise to see you. It's been a while. What happened? Did you fall and bump your head? You should have worn your purple helmet."

Purple helmet? I remembered something about a purple helmet... space junk.

"Yes, Roy, I can hear you. I think I fell and hit my head. I can't quite remember. I've been alone in a dark place... sleeping. But today, I heard her voice again, like when I was little. She brought me here."

"You let her bring you here, Rose. That's a good girl. You've always been a good girl." He held my hand as he spoke. "And you're always welcome here, no matter how old. Stay until you're rested and

ready to go home. But remember, Rose, someone else is waiting for you. Did you hear his voice, too?"

"Someone else? Yes, I think I heard another voice. He said I'm not alone."

"No, you're not alone. We're all close. We'll stay and help you get back. Rest and listen. Rest and listen."

* * * * *

I tucked the horse and rider next to her hip—on top of the blanket—and placed her hand over them.

"Rose, so much happened since our last chat on Facebook... since the prick conversation. I understood why you stopped communication. I needed a wake-up call. It forced me to take a hard look at myself, make decisions I'd avoided for years. Are you listening, baby? I don't want an affair. I want you in my life permanently.

I want to wrap you in my arms at night, and wake up next to you each morning. Sit beside you at the lake and watch the sun rise and set. I want you to write under the name R. A. Richardson, the name you wrote in your diary as a young girl. Do you remember writing that?"

I stroked and kissed the top of her hand. Rubbed her palm over my stubbly cheek, my chin.

"Should have shaved, huh? Probably feel like a prickly cactus against your soft hands. Can you hear me? I'm here waiting. It's Jake. I want to take you home, baby."

Her expression changed... a smile. A soft moan. Not my imagination. Jesus.

"Good girl. I hear you. I know you're trying. You're so close, I can feel it. Look around. Where are you? You don't belong there. I know you're tired, but you need to leave. You need to come back. Be strong. We have so much to do. I need you here with me. I can't do it alone."

She moved her head from side to side, and moaned again.

* * * * *

His familiar voice, so soothing.

Prickly cactus. His words made me smile. Jake. I knew that name. He waited for me. Could he hear me, too?

"I'm here. Can you hear me, Jake?"

"Yes, I'm a good girl. I always tried to be a good girl."

I heard Roy's voice again. "Almost time to go, Rose. Are you ready?"

"Yes, I'm ready to go back now."

"Would you like to hear the story about the beautiful princess and handsome Prince Charming before you leave?"

"Yes... please. I love that story."

* * * * *

Jesus. What else could I do... what could I say? I thought about all the words between us... the texts, the messages, the emails, the letters.... tangible proof of love, of relationship. Letters. I remembered that last letter she wrote... one particular part of that letter.

"Story time, Rose. Listen to my voice, the words, and shut out everything around you. This is a special story... just for you."

I took her hand in mine, leaned closer, and let the words flow. I would use all of my acting abilities and experience to breathe real life into this fairy tale.

"Once upon a time there lived a beautiful, little princess—smart and sweet and innocent—loved and adored by her father and mother. Like most little girls, she dreamed of a happy life, and her heart searched for true love.

"One terrible day, her father died suddenly and her world turned upside down. Her mother forever grieved—searching throughout the kingdom—for the lost true love of her life. The constant searching finally took her life. The little princess—left behind and forgotten— had no one to love or protect her from wickedness within the kingdom.

"Time passed and bad things happened to the little princess, because of the wickedness around her. She lost innocence, confidence, and trust. Though not her fault, she saw herself differently and lived in fear on the shadowed fringes within the kingdom.

"Deep within her soul—unknown to the princess—lived another little girl whose still, small voice whispered words of love, comfort, strength, and warning. During wicked, frightful times, she whisked the princess away to lovely, imaginary safe places. There, inside the safe places, the princess held on to her hopes and dreams... and waited for true love.

"One day, a handsome prince rode through the kingdom in search of true love. Because of his kind, gentle, and honest character, the little girl inside allowed him to find the beautiful princess... sleeping among the shadowed fringes.

"'How shall I wake her from this deep sleep?' asked the prince.

"A still, small voice whispered to him. 'Wake her with the kiss of true love.'

"The prince sat next to her, leaned down, and brushed a kiss across her soft, full lips. Her green eyes fluttered, then opened. She looked into his face, and saw love looking back.

"The prince whispered, 'I love you. I'll always love you.'

"And the princess answered. 'I waited for you.'

"He took her small hands in his and lifted her up onto his white stallion, as though she weighed nothing, and mounted behind her. He took the reins, held her tightly, and they rode off as one, to find their hopes and dreams... and to live happily ever after."

I leaned down, pressed a kiss against Rose's lips, and whispered, "It seems I've loved you forever. Maybe I am your Prince Charming, after all."

Another soft, sweet moan... and another.

Gently, I cushioned her in my arms, and lay my head against her breasts. I closed my eyes and listened to her breathe, listened to her heart beating beneath mine... and visualized her waking up in my arms

A minute passed, two minutes, maybe more. Time didn't matter. I'd hold her and wait for as long as it took.

Like the whisper of a gentle breeze, I felt her soft hand on the side of my face.

Rose.

I opened my eyes, took her hand in mine, and looked into her face. Her eyes fluttered, once, twice... and opened. She never looked more beautiful.

"Hello, Princess. Welcome back."

"Jake..."

I scooped her into my arms and rocked her back and forth like a baby. She cuddled against me and pressed the sweetest kiss against my stubbly cheek.

* * * * *

While I waited for coffee to brew in the cafeteria, I returned a client call—an author I was currently editing—for clarification on a pivotal passage in his novel. After nearly twenty minutes of conversation, we ended the call. I propped my feet up on a nearby chair and closed my eyes for just a few minutes. Right.

Twenty minutes later, I woke up to the smell of coffee. I filled two Styrofoam cups, drank one, and returned to the fourth floor with the other cup—filled with hot, black coffee and two sugars—for Jake.

I stopped at the nurses' station on my way back down the corridor.

"Wild party started yet?"

Nurse Day. I liked her.

"Not yet. I'll keep you posted, though."

"Hope it starts soon. I'll be looking for my glass slipper and heading home in about thirty minutes. Party on!"

Just then, a light on the callboard next to her lit and sounded. She smiled, winked at me, and responded to the call. I smiled back, and continued down the hall, back to room 415.

Holding the coffee with one hand, I pushed the door open with the other, and stepped inside the dimly lit room. I wasn't prepared for the scene I walked in on. Jake held Rose in his arms, rocking back and forth with her, as she kissed the side of his face. Her eyes open and focused on him.

Thank you. Thank you for another long shot.

I stood quietly, watching and waiting. I didn't think either of them saw or heard me, but then, her gaze turned to me.

She smiled. "Kathryn."

I returned her smile. "Hello, my friend. It's good to have you back. I think I'd better tell Nurse Day."

Jake turned and looked at me through glistening, moist eyes, and simply nodded.

I walked back through the door, toward the nurses' station, coffee cup still in hand. I couldn't wait to find Nurse Day and tell her the party was in full swing!

* * * * *

The next week passed in a blur of activity... continuing progress on a long, awaited plan.

Dr. Webb—not surprised by Rose's recovery, but at the rate—gave a clean bill of health the next morning and released her. While waiting on the doctor and the paperwork, I met Rose's son, Joe, and daughter, Jenna.

My apprehension at meeting them quickly faded when she introduced me as a very dear, old friend, no other explanation seemed needed. They both understood.

Joe took me off to the side and asked my intentions concerning their mother. Above all, he and Jenna wanted her to be happy. I assured him, our intentions were the same. Like Dustin and Brian, Rose's son and daughter saw the change in relationship, over time, between their mother and dad. A good thing—for both Rose and me—to be blessed with smart, intuitive offspring.

Over the next few days, Joe, Jenna, Kathryn, and I helped Rose finish packing storage units and closing up the house. Somewhere during those days of shared Chinese take-out, fast food hamburgers, pizza delivery, and one leisurely dinner alone at a nearby restaurant—Rose's appetite returned. At the end of each day, nestled securely in my arms, Rose slept.

On Monday—two days before the end of the month—the moving company loaded the units, and scheduled a two-week delivery date in

Rockton, Illinois. The antique, four-poster bed headed off to a farmhouse bedroom where it belonged.

* * * * *

Bright and early Tuesday morning, Kathryn, Rose's children, and the grandkids, hugged, kissed and said their good-byes to us. We bantered about the idea of fishing on the lake with kids and grandkids as a real possibility in the near future.

Paul had sent a text earlier. True to form... brief and to the point. "Drive safe. Be happy. I wish you well. P."

With both trucks packed—mine with mostly personal items, and hers with Henry, Sassy, and Violet—Rose and I pulled out of the driveway, and traveled the scenic route back home to Rockton, Illinois.

Bringing Rose back home with me to Illinois would complete the circle, bring us back to the unfinished life we left behind so long ago.

* * * * *

Late Friday afternoon—before sunset—we wound down the graveled road, past the now-harvested corn and bean fields, toward the lake. I pulled next to the shelter and Rose parked next to me. I stepped out, opened the back door of the Black Silverado, and watched Sassy and Henry eagerly jump from seat to floor to ground. They hesitantly explored and sniffed, then marked and claimed their new territory.

I opened Rose's door. She turned her body, resting her feet on the sideboard of the open door. I moved in between her knees, tilted her head with my hand, and kissed her several times. She wrapped her hands around my neck and returned each kiss.

"Welcome home, Rose... welcome back."

"It's been a long time. Thank you for bringing me home, Jake. "

"Welcome." I stepped back, took her hands in mine, and helped her from the truck.

We walked hand-in-hand down near the bank.

Stalks of brown, spent cattails rustled among the weathered Canada wild rye. The rippling water glistened in the setting sun, reflecting shades of pink, purple, and blue from the western sky.

We stopped near the dock and watched a pair of Smiling Mallards paddle by. I stood behind her, my arms wrapped around her. A gentle breeze moved across the surface of the lake, swept over us, and continued on.

"I'm glad we stopped here first. It's so beautiful... calm and peaceful... just as I pictured. Being here with you, feels like a dream, like make-believe. I keep waiting to wake up... to step back into reality."

I turned her in my arms, framed her face with my hands, and kissed her. "Baby, this is reality, not fantasy anymore. I love you... never stopped loving you. I brought you to the lake—my favorite place—for a reason.

"I wanted to marry you years ago and I let the chance slip away. I won't make that mistake twice."

I took her hand in mine, and looked into her face. A face as lovely today as when she first caught my eye on rehearsal night. "Rose Allison, will you marry me? Will you be my wife?"

She squeezed my hand tighter, and blinked back tears of joy.

"I loved you as only a young girl falling in love for the first time, could love. Today, I love you even more. Who would have thought we'd get a second chance? Yes, Jake Richardson, I'll marry you and be your wife. Nothing would make me happier or prouder."

We held one another close. Two kindred souls. Two kindred spirits Time travelers in the universe... together once again.

* * * * *

Rockton, Illinois
November 23, 2009

The unseasonably, mild weather continued through late November. The crisp, cool, autumn temperatures swept away the lingering summer heat. Tufts of cottony, white clouds drifting in a sea of blue, reflected on the lake's surface, now sprinkled with orange and yellow falling leaves. Still and serene.

Picture postcard perfect.

The perfect place... the perfect day... for a wedding.

The four of us—Ben, I, Rose and Karen—stood side by side in front of the local Justice of the Peace, Will Jayson... owner of Will's Sports Bar and Grill.

Rose looked stunning in a white, gauzy, lace peasant dress... sprigs of baby's breath in her hair... white, strappy sandals on her tanned feet. She carried a simple bouquet of wildflowers, tied with strips of paisley cloth.

I wore her favorite white linen, button-down shirt, over faded, blue denim jeans... leather sandals on my tanned feet.

Karen, her long salt and pepper hair pulled back and tied with a blue, satin ribbon... looked beautiful in a similar lacy, peasant dress in denim blue... and sandals.

Ben wore his favorite, denim jeans with a blue-denim, button-down shirt... and his well-worn, brown, leather boots.

I squeezed Rose's hand and whispered, "You look stunning, baby. Happy?"

She squeezed back and whispered, "Very. And you take my breath away."

Will smiled at the four of us, and began the ceremony.

"As we gather here today—in this beautiful lake setting—to join Jake and Rose, in marriage. It is fitting Ben and Karen are here to witness and participate in their wedding... for the ideals, the understanding, and the mutual respect they bring to their marriage... have their roots in lasting love and friendship.

"Jake and Rose, please face each other and join hands.

"The hand offered by each of you... an extension of yourself, as is your mutual love. Cherish the touch, for you touch not only your own, but another life, as well.

"Jake Richardson, do you commit yourself to Rose Allison, as your wife, accepting her for all the risings and settings of the sun... pledging your faithful love and encouragement, as long as time is yours?"

I looked across at the beautiful woman standing in front of me... the woman I'd loved for as long as I could remember.

"I do."

"Rose Allison, do you commit yourself to Jake Richardson, as your husband, accepting him for all the risings and settings of the sun... pledging your faithful love and encouragement, as long as time is yours?"

She gazed at me as if she could see all the love I held for her deep within my soul.

"I do."

Ben slipped the ring from his pocket and placed it in my hand. Karen took the other ring from her pocket and placed it in Rose's hand.

"A circle is the symbol of the sun and the earth, and of the universe It is a symbol of wholeness, perfection, and peace. The rings you give and receive this day, are symbols of the circle of shared love into which you enter together as husband and wife."

I took her soft, graceful hand in mine, focused on her face, her eyes and recited the words from memory.

"Rose, I give this ring, in token and pledge of my constant faith and abiding love for you."

I slipped the wide, silver band on her finger... brought her hand to my lips.

Rose took my hand—her beautiful green eyes met mine—and I listened to her sweet voice reciting the same words back to me.

"Jake, I give this ring, in token and pledge of my constant faith and abiding love for you."

She slipped the matching silver band over my finger... and brought my hand to her lips. I held both her hands in mine and spoke from my heart... to her heart.

"Rose, when you sent the Friend request, you changed my life, for a second time. You gave me a reason to get up each morning, a reason to look forward, a reason to be. You took a chance on me again, loved me again, let me dream again. I know I'm not perfect, and I'm going to make mistakes, lots of them. But you can always count on my love for you. I'll always be here. I'll never let you go again, Rose."

I brushed the teardrops from her cheeks with my thumbs. She swallowed hard, took a deep breath, and I listened to her words..

"Jake, I'll always be a work in progress... always be the dreamer, thinking outside the box... always hear the voice. It's who I am. And I know who you are. You're the one person who touched my life, my heart, with kindness and tenderness. Because of you, I learned to trust, to love. You showed me how it feels to love, and be loved. Your love is priceless to me. And I'll never let go, Jake."

Will smiled at Rose and me... and then at Ben and Karen.

"Now you will feel not the rain, for each will shelter the other. Now you will feel not the cold, for each will warm the other. Now you will feel not solitude, for each will accompany the other. Now you are two persons, but both will lead one life.

With every season comes change... around us and within us. These days of autumn are gentle and pensive, brilliant and spectacular. They allow us to recall familiar melodies, while giving us the opportunity to dance to new songs, yet unwritten.

Today, we celebrate two kindred spirits who have loved one another over a lifetime... once in spring and now, again, in autumn.

Jake and Rose, you recited promises, exchanged signs of love and commitment, and shared words of love, one to another. From this day forward, you will dance to a new song, as you begin a life together.

Now, in the presence of these witnesses, it gives me great pleasure to declare Jake Richardson and Rose Allison are now, and forever... husband and wife. Jake, you may kiss Rose."

I took her in my arms and kissed her once, and again. I trailed my lips to her ear and whispered, "I loved you then, I love you now, I'll always love you. Happy Birthday, Rose."

She kissed my cheek and whispered back, "I know. I've always known... and I'll love you forever. Happy Birthday, Jake."

Epilogue

As ageless winds gently sweep the passing of time and season,
You'll feel my touch upon your face and know beyond all reason
That every life, yours and mine, becomes a unique, entwined endeavor.
Leaving memories as eternal reminders... that life goes on forever.

Rockton, Illinois
Spring 2010

*T*he cool grays of early morning slowly faded, replaced with warm beams of sunlight filtering through the drawn shades of the upstairs bedroom windows. The light and warmth edged across the aged, oak floors, and inched up the bedcovers.

I turned on my side, fluffed and bunched the pillows, and watched her sleep. Some mornings, I'd wake, and find her watching me... a lovely smile on her face. We'd both forgotten how good it felt waking up next to someone you loved... someone who loved you. Each new morning together, sweet and tender, for both of us.

She lay on her back—snuggled in a plush pile of quilts and sheets and feather pillows—across the big brass bed. The same brass bed I kissed her and tucked her in one cold, winter night, long ago.

Her hair tumbled around her head, tousled and messy from sleep and from making love last night. The disheveled covers exposed a sexy peek-a-boo of sun-tanned legs and arms, creamy white hips and breasts, and lovely rose-colored nipples.

A beautiful girl then. A beautiful woman now. I thought myself one lucky bastard to love them both during a lifetime.

Bob Dylan's edgy voice crooned "Lay, Lady, Lay" in the background. Somewhere early on, Bob must have had a similar brass-bed experience with a beautiful woman.

I reached for her, drawing her closer. She nuzzled into me—resting her head against my chest—her arm and leg draped over me like a warm, sensuous blanket. Skin against skin. Nothing compared to the softness, the smoothness, of a women's body. Nothing.

She stretched against me and moaned, reminding me of the love words whispered between us in the night. The words penetrated our senses and spilled over us like a rhythmic rush of naughtiness... sexual, erotic, explicit.

Nothing changed. We couldn't get enough. Needed too much. Ached too much.

Last night, I lifted her, drew her leg to my hip and tucked deep inside the soft folds of her body. I rocked gently in and out of her, my hands tightly on her hips, her knees pressed against mine... fingers clutching my shoulders. We moved rhythmically as one—consumed in love and passion—lost in pleasure that ended in a sweet, mutual release, deep inside.

In our youth, we made love all night, over and over. Just the thought of kissing and touching and loving one another, made us ache with desire and burn with passion. Now, the lovemaking—more deliberate, measured, unhurried—remained no less intense. Our bodies and minds existed in a different place now, not just older, but more experienced, more appreciative, more forgiving.

Now we both marvel at the human body we took for granted in youth... so perfectly created to give and receive pleasure. Gone, that urgency to cross an imaginary finish line, or hurry toward a self-imposed completion. Instead, each embrace, kiss, and caress, became a meandering, scenic overlook to stop and explore—to savor and enjoy—before traveling on.

Who would have thought this, back then? Who would have thought love adjusts to the time of the season? Certainly not me.

I brushed her hair back from her face, and tucked a wayward strand behind her ear. A smile formed on her lips. She looked at me through sleepy, green eyes.

"Good morning."

"Morning," her sleepy voice, low and sexy.

We settled back into the soft, warm nest of the bed, and held one another. She looked and felt different early in the morning... her scent unique. The same held true after a shower, or at the end of the day, or after making love. I loved the subtle differences, and never noticed this about women, until Rose.

She wrapped her hand, her long fingers, around the back of my neck, massaged the muscles, and trailed up through my hair. I leaned into the movement. Each touch, stroke, and caress... intense, sensuous, and soothing. A soft moan escaped my lips and floated out into the room. She still had the same affect on me... made me moan, made me whimper.

I cupped her cheeks, and skimmed my lips lightly over hers, pressing kisses along her jaw to her ear. I clenched her hips with my legs and we cuddled closer. The combined warmth of our bodies... sensual and fiery.

That initial electricity still remained.

"You still make me ache, baby."

She trailed little, sucking kisses from my lips to my ear. "And you send chills down my spine. I can barely breathe from wanting you."

"I like hearing that. I like that very much."

"Mm... me, too."

I looked over at Roy and Trigger on the nightstand. "Seems we always have an audience. Good thing I don't suffer from performance anxiety."

She grinned. "Good thing for both of us."

I reached over, picked them up. "I remember the night you described them to me in great detail—the same night you shared the poem about a frightened little girl who hid under her blankets. I never forgot the horse and rider, or the frightened little girl. Everything came to memory when Karen and Ben brought them over. I couldn't wait to give them to you."

Her eyes brimmed with tears.

I wrapped her and Roy and Trigger in my arms. "Talk to me... tell me your thoughts, baby."

The plastic model passed from my hands into hers. She tinkered with them—like a child—trailing her fingers over Trigger's mane and tail... removing and replacing Roy's hat and guns.

"Whenever I see them standing vigil on the nightstand, I'm reminded of all the times you've made love to me... then and now. Each time, a frightening, childhood memory slipped farther and farther away... and got replaced by a sweet, new one. You remembered everything about me, Jake. You never forgot."

Her words brought a smile and warmed me to the core.

"You always thought of me as a good listener, thought I remembered things well. But the truth is—after the first night we met in the rehearsal barn—you stayed in my thoughts, my head. I couldn't stop thinking about you. From then on, my heart listened only to your heart. I remembered you, because I couldn't forget you."

She saddled Roy back up, and placed him and Trigger back on the nightstand. I reached on the opposite side and grabbed a Kleenex from the box on the dresser.

"Tissue?"

"Yes, please."

She blotted the tears, blew her nose, and placed the soggy Kleenex in my outstretched hand.

"Thank you."

"Welcome."

She settled back into the crook of my arm, and I pulled her close, resting my head against hers. I looked down at our silver wedding bands. Talk about a long shot. Sometimes there's no logical explanation for how or why certain things happen. We're all just passing through, along for the ride, hoping to stay in the saddle as long as possible.

I traced her ring with my finger. "I guess you never dreamed you'd find Prince Charming at the intersection of Gravel Road A and Gravel Road B, next to a big, brown cow, and a green tractor."

"No, and I never thought Prince Charming would arrive on the scene disguised as a long-haired, hippie, war activist... or much later, as a plaid-flannelled farmer."

I grinned and raised my eyebrows up and down. "It's the actor in me. I like theatrics... like to make an entrance."

"Yes, you do. I'm just glad you finally showed up. I'd been waiting a long time. It would have been much simpler if you'd asked me to marry you that winter weekend, years ago."

"Yep, I know, but I didn't realize I'd been cast as Prince Charming back then. Didn't have the script yet... didn't know my lines."

"No, I guess not. Good thing I cued you with the Friend request so you knew when to finally ride in on your white horse. Make that a green tractor."

"Yep. Good thing I still had my trusty tractor."

"Good thing, since this play ran long... really long."

"Just because a play runs long, doesn't mean there isn't a happy ending written in the storyline."

"No, I guess not. Maybe the longer the play, the more time to believe in fairy tales and happy endings."

"Do you believe, Rose?"

"Yes. I've always believed... in fairy tales, in happy endings. And I've always believed in you, Jake. Do you believe?"

"Yep. All of my nearly forgotten hopes, dreams, and possibilities for happy endings came floating back to me one morning with a Friend request. I realized when love happens, especially a second-chance love, anything in the universe was possible."

"Thank you for still being there, for reaching out, for accepting my Friend request. I love you with all my heart, Jake Richardson."

"Welcome. I love you, Rose Allison Richardson. Will love you forever, 2lls."

I held her. I kissed her. I loved her... while Roy and Trigger stood watch on the nightstand.

The End

373

CL Gillmore

The Letters

The words began so long ago,
It's hard to remember when
She hadn't shared her hopes, her fears,
In late-night words to him.
A mother's sins, buried and born,
Purged on notes in silence,
To the patient friend—tender lover—the keeper of confidence.

Year after year, two lives played out,
Actors on distant stages.
Linked forever from seasons ago,
On secretly written pages.
Private letters, bundled and tied,
Written in quiet despair,
To the gentle man—kindred spirit—the long ago love affair.

The Letters

Year after year, their lives played out,
Two actors on distant stages.
Linked forever from seasons ago,
On secretly written pages.

November 23, 1971

Dear Jake,
You'll probably never read this, but writing my thoughts out to you in words on paper helps me through the long and lonely days and nights.
I'm sorry for the way things ended between us. I felt you betrayed my trust. Yet as time passes, I'm unsure of what happened. I've tried to remember, but like so many things from the past, the events aren't clear. So much gone from my memory. I know I made you cry, and that haunts me day and night. I'm sorry for hurting you, for leaving. But most of all, I'm sorry for not listening.
I wish I could undo things—better understand what happened— and start again. I know I can't. It seems something or someone always tells me to leave, to run away, before I'm hurt. That's all I've ever known. But this time, leaving was different. A part of me stayed behind with you... and I tucked a part of you inside my heart when I left.
I know I'm messed up—broken inside—with no idea how to repair the damage. I want to love and be loved, but I don't know if that will ever happen. Your love for me, kind, gentle, and sweet. With you, I felt love for the first time. Jake, I tried so hard to love you back.
Find someone. Someone who will love you for me, and be happy for both of us. Dream for both of us. You were the Prince Charming I'd waited for. But, I locked myself inside for so long, I didn't recognize you. Instead of embracing you, I pushed you away and ran. I know now I made a mistake I can't fix. Some things once broken, once lost, can never be fixed or found again.

CL Gillmore

I will never forget you. Never. You'll remain in my heart and be a part of me forever.

Rose with 2lls

Letting go is the hardest thing
The human heart will ever beat through,
With no way to ease the bitter sting
Or numb the pain you cant undo.

November 23, 1974

Dear Jake,

I've decided to write letters to you on our birthday and hide them away. Now I'll have someone to talk to—a friend—a best friend.

I live out West, Jake... just like in my dreams. I have a beautiful home in Albuquerque, New Mexico. It's not our Leave It To Beaver house, but it's very nice. I'm a good housekeeper and a good cook. You would be proud of me. This spring, I planted flowers in the backyard... tulips, iris, lilies of the valley, and sweat peas. Grandma and Grandpa Allison would love them. I think of them so often and wish they could see where I live and what I'm doing. I still use the pink and yellow Howdy Doody glasses. Do you remember them? Remember donut day? I never forgot.

I'm doing everything I'm supposed to do. Everything seems right, but I know it's not. I can't connect with anyone, not even Paul, my husband. I have no real friends. No one to talk to, or laugh with, like we used to. I'm alone... alone in a crowd of familiar faces. If it weren't for the voice inside, I'd never talk to anyone. What is wrong with me? There must be something.

I lie in bed at night, after Paul's asleep, and wonder where you are, if you still think of me. Sometimes I wish I could call you, hear your voice. But I have no idea where you are, or how to reach you. And what would I say to you, or you to me? No, none of this can ever happen. I know that deep inside, but I dream of it anyway. I keep my dreams to myself, but now I can share them with you. I can share anything with you, can't I?

Oh, Jake, do you remember me? Do you remember 2lls? A part of my heart never lets me forget.

Be well and take care, my secret friend. I'll write again soon.

Love and happy birthday,
Rose with 2lls

November 23, 1976

Dear Jake,

I graduated from college this past year. Can you believe that? No one in my family ever thought about going to college. I changed my major from PE to Special Education. You were right. I was never cut out to be a jock, too small, not assertive enough. The only thing I was good at was dance and synchronized swimming. I nearly flunked golf! Who flunks golf?

I love the little special ed. kids. They see my heart, my soul... and I see theirs. I let them in. I connect with them. I love them. Isn't that something? For the first time I can remember, I have purpose.

I jotted down a few lines of poetry last night after observing a student yesterday. She sat against the hallway wall in her wheelchair as students and teachers passed by. See what you think.

I watch as you walk by me
Looking, but not really seeing.
I listen as you talk around me
Speaking, but not really conversing.
I can feel your touch on me
Patting, but not really connecting.
Do you know I'm in here?

I understand. Sometimes I wonder if anyone knows I'm in here. Me. Maybe lots of people feel that way. Do you feel that way, Jake?

I picture you at Parkridge, but you've probably graduated by now, too, and moved on. Are you married? Are you happy? I wish I knew. No, I don't want to know. If you're with someone else, I couldn't still come to you in dreams at night. It wouldn't be right.

Happy Birthday, Jake. You're still older than me... and probably wiser, too. Hope you had a great day with cake and candles and presents. Did you celebrate with friends, a special friend? Did you go to Little Phil's? I remember sharing our birthday there together. Such a sweet memory.

Here's to another year, my friend.

Love, Rose

November 23, 1979

Dear Jake,
Three years have slipped by since I last wrote. Guess what? I'm a mother, Jake. We have a little baby boy, Joseph Paul... Joey. He's perfect in every way—blond hair and green eyes—with dimples in each cheek. His little toes look like little pink jelly beans. He's beautiful. Paul seems pleased to have a son.

I'm overcome with the responsibility of another person. I'm not sure I know how to be a mother, not sure what a mother does. I watch other mothers and try to do what they do. Trying my very best to get this right. But some days I feel so overwhelmed, so afraid I won't.

I've always fought depression, but now it seems worse. Why would I be depressed? I have so much to be thankful and happy for. Late at night, when Paul and Joey are asleep, I slip into the shower, and let my tears merge with the warm water. I don't want to be like my mother Is it inevitable? Jesus, I hope not.

I keep these thoughts to myself... hide as much as I can. I've always been good at hiding things... at pretending. I don't want to be a pretend mother. I want to be a real mother.

Do you have children, Jake? Does someone, a little girl or boy, call you Daddy? The thought brings tears of joy to my eyes, and warms my heart. You and I are distant now and I know I must leave you in the past. But a part of me always remembers, always searches the faces in the crowd... for you.

Did you think of me when you celebrated this year? I always think of you and wonder where you are, who you're with, if you're happy. I wish you only good things and send you my love, Jake.

Happy Birthday,
Rose with 2lls

November 23, 1981

Dear Jake,

Hello, my friend. Another two years and another baby. This time, a little girl. We named her Jenna Allison, after Grandpa and Grandma Allison. A second C-section didn't go well for either of us. A very rough time. We almost lost her. I'm so thankful she's alive and healthy. Her hair is blonde, her eyes blue like Paul's, and she has my dimples. She's a very good baby, just like Joey. She will be our last. Paul wanted more children, but I can't give him more.

Sometimes I think God is punishing me for my decision years ago. Do you think God would do that, Jake? I don't think He would, but that's what some people believe. If you sin, God punishes you. If I dwell on that, I can't be the mother or wife I need to be. I couldn't live with myself or go on. And, so, I try not to. But, I'll always carry the burden of that decision. You never knew what happened after I left Parkridge. You never knew of the late night call I made to you. Sometimes it's better not knowing the truth.

I thought of you and how very careful you were with me, always taking every precaution when we made love. Now and then I wonder what would have happened if we'd had a baby together. Again, I try not to go there, and tuck the memories of us deep inside my heart. Thank you for not being careless with me, or my feelings—for not taking me for granted—for never being in a hurry. Because of this, I remember and treasure our time together.

I hope this was a good year for you. I picture you happy and well, surrounded by a family who loves and appreciates the good man I know you are. How lucky they are to have you.

Love and Happy Birthday,
Rose

November 23, 1982

Dear Jake,

I've decided to try my hand at writing a novel. I have so many thoughts inside my head, day and night. Maybe writing them down, creating a story, would give me an outlet, and maybe a chance to find a little of me again. There's not a lot of time with two babies, but I can write at night when the house is quiet and asleep.

It's a romance novel and I will write a happy ending. What else would I write? I named my two lead characters, Nick and Jessie. Nick is fashioned after you. Jessie, after me. I don't know anyone else well enough to write about. When I closed my eyes and heard Nick speak... your voice came out. When I watched him with Jessie... I saw you and me. I wonder if that's how all authors write stories?

I wrote the outline and two chapters in one of my notebooks and keep it stashed in the piano bench. I'm the only one who ever looks there. It felt good to write again—to see my thoughts, my words, on paper. Maybe you'll read one of my novels someday and recognize the two of us.

Are you still acting, or directing, maybe? Last fall, a local theater group performed "The Goodbye People." I almost asked Paul to take me, but then decided not to. Watching someone else play Arthur Korman wouldn't be the same. Nor would watching it straight, rather than stoned. I always thought you were a born actor... clever, quick, animated, with impeccable timing.

Are you still taking pictures with the Nikon? I remember the beautiful black and white photographs hanging on the apartment wall at Parkridge. Maybe you're a photographer. I guess it doesn't matter. All that matters is that you're happy. Are you, Jake? Are you happy?

Funny how life plays out. I dreamed of being a writer, you dreamed of being an actor. How long do we wait for a dream to come true?

Happy Birthday, Jake.

Love,
Rose

CL Gillmore

November 23, 1984

Dear Jake,

It's late. Everyone's asleep but me. I thought maybe if I wrote to you, talked with you, my mind would calm and I could fall asleep. Happy Birthday. We celebrated at home tonight. I fixed a roast with potatoes and carrots, and baked a chocolate cake. Lots of candles this year... a good thing I had help blowing them out. Hard to believe we're both pushing forty, isn't it? How quickly time passes the older you get. Remember when we were kids? The summers seemed endless and the next school year so far away.

Joey started kindergarten and Jenna is in preschool. Paul's very busy with his law practice. We moved into a bigger house this year. It's lovely and I've been busy landscaping the backyard. I planted more tulips, iris, lilies of the valley, sweat peas, and a peach tree last spring, all reminders of Illinois. I keep the patio filled with flowers... pink and red geraniums; white alyssum; yellow and pink hibiscus; purple and blue hydrangeas; and white, fragrant gardenias. Much like Grandma and Grandpa Allison's yard, the patio and backyard are my sanctuary... a place to get away, to be alone.

I don't mind being alone. Alone has always been easier for me than being surrounded by people. It's getting harder and harder for me to find a quiet time or place. I go to the guest room after Paul falls asleep and lie there in the silence and solitude. It's soothing and quiet in the shower, too. Tonight I'm sitting out on the patio, wrapped in a quilt, looking at the Milky Way stretched across the night sky. There must be a zillion stars out tonight, and every so often, a satellite speeds among them.

Are you someplace tonight watching the same stars, the satellites, the same Milky Way? I believe you are out there somewhere, because some nights I feel you close to me.

Star light, star bright,
First satellite I see tonight,
I wish I may, I wish I might,
Have this wish I wish tonight.

A Friend Request

I wish you love and happiness wherever you are tonight, Jake. I wish we could see each other, hold one another, one more time.

Love, Rose

November 23, 1988

Dear Jake,

It's been awhile since my last letter. My life is busy, busy. Filled with details... wife details, mother details, household details, life details. I'm good at this, at details and order. Not so good at other things most mothers and wives are good at. It's hard for me to show my emotions or be physical with Paul or the children. It's difficult for me to talk about anything personal with anyone. I try, but all I can do is go through the motions. For the most part, my words remain locked inside. I can write them, but I can't say them. Nothing changes.

Life is born of endless details, and other dreams just simply die
A painless and unnoticed death. No time to mourn or cry.

I went back to teaching when the children both started school. Paul wanted me to stay home, but I needed the connection with those special children again. I can't explain the bond I have with them. It's just there. I feel it. They keep me focused, grounded, and fulfill a need others can't fill. I jotted down a few lines as I watched the children playing the other day.

A place where wheelchairs can come and go,
And fragile friends can swing to and fro.
A place to explore on hand and knee,
With things to touch when eyes cannot see.
Where trickling waters and fine white sands
Sift and flow over stiff, small hands.

I'm thankful for Paul. He's a good father, Jake... affectionate, loving, and able to verbally and physically communicate his feelings. Something I can't do, no matter how hard I try. The words are there, and I know what I should do, but neither seems to find a way out. Our roles have kind of reversed. He mothers and I attend to the daily routine. Somehow it works.

I wonder if he realizes or regrets the person he married. He had no way of knowing. I didn't know, but as each year passes, I realize how difficult it is for me to bond, to trust, to show affection, to love. I think you might have sensed this, but didn't know what to do. Maybe it's a good thing I left, that we never married. A good thing for you.

I find myself writing pieces of poems and saving them. Something I haven't done much of over the years. I think of the children. I think of you. I write of the children. I write of you. I can love them from a distance. And I can continue to love you from a distance. You are my secret friend, my secret love.

Happy Birthday, Jake.

Love,
Rose with 2lls

CL Gillmore

November 23, 1990

Dear Jake,

The saddest thing happened since I last wrote. Sam called from California to tell me Cash died of congestive heart failure. I felt as if a part of me—a part of all of us died with him—along with the hopes and dreams we held together back then. We were all so young. I never thought we'd grow old... we'd die. How naïve of me. How like me to live the fantasy, rather than face the reality.

I needed someone to tell me things would be all right, to hold me that night. Instead, Paul seemed irritated the call came in the middle of the night and woke him. He didn't get it. How could he not get it? One of my dearest friends died. I didn't get to tell Cash how much I missed him over the years, how much I loved him as a friend, but most of all, I didn't get to tell him goodbye.

Later that night in the guest room, I thought of the night I sang with Cash, the night you danced with Sam and me at the Library... the same night you and I roasted marshmallows together in my apartment. Do you remember? The fire flickered—the shadows danced—and we lay wrapped within one another's arms inside your sleeping bags. You kissed me softly and passionately, until my eyes closed. And I drifted in and out of the loveliest dreams until morning.

Do you dream of me? I still dream of you from time to time. How can that be after all these years? My memories of others fade, but my memories of you never fade. I wonder if you and I will ever get the chance to say goodbye.

Happy Birthday, Jake.

Love,
Rose

November 23, 1994

Dear Jake,

My life seems perfect. Perfect husband, perfect children, perfect home. And yet I struggle each and every day to stay in this life. Some days I prefer fantasy over reality. I have control over my fantasy world and feel as if I have little control over my real world.

Staying busy and focused on the details seems to be the key. I have no one to share my inner thoughts and feelings with. I struggle alone for my sanity. No one knows, except you, Jake. It's our secret.

When I think of you, I remember a time when I might have been healed. I might have been whole again. And yet, I realize more and more, some things—once broken—can never be fixed or made whole again. Some hurts—deep wounds—never heal, no matter how much time goes by.

I know I can't live in the past, in the "what ifs," and yet I'm more comfortable there. When I'm alone, that's where I choose to go.

I remembered one summer evening, I left Parkridge, and headed for a party somewhere. I'd had too much to drink before I left and made an improper left hand turn at an intersection near the college. A guy in a truck clipped my fender. You happened by shortly after and made sure I was okay. You noticed a drink sitting in between my legs. Without saying a word, you picked it up and took it with you just as the police arrived. To this day, I can't figure out why we weren't together.. why I was going to a party without you. You saved me that night, Jake.

You've saved my life more than once over the years. Nights when I wanted to sleep—and not wake to another day—you came to me in dreams. Both of us, young again. I felt you reaching out, felt you there. You took my hand and whispered, "Trust me, Rose. You can do this a while longer. You're the strongest person I've ever known." Feeling you close, hearing your voice, gave me strength. I woke to another morning and went on.

CL Gillmore

Even after all the years, there are nights I feel you close... kind, gentle, tender, and loving. You never had an agenda. Never took from me. I gladly gave everything I could give to you. I will never forget. Remember me, Jake.

Love and Happy Birthday,
Rose

November 23, 1997

Dear Jake,

Hello. How are you? It's been awhile since my last letter. Time just seems to slip away... a year, five years, ten, twenty. Lots of gray hair mingled within the blonde, but then, I am the mother of two teenagers. I've managed to stay fairly sane. Well, about the same, actually. Just better at handling it.

Jake, I want to tell you about my kids. I'm so proud of them. They're turning out really well and it's amazing to watch.

Joey is a senior this year. He wants to be a police officer or a paramedic. Not sure that's what Paul had in mind for him, but Joey's not much of a desk guy. I hope he opts for the paramedic job. I won't worry as much. He's a fine, young man, kind-hearted and thoughtful. You'd like him. He has a quick, witty sense of humor with a way of putting people at ease. He plays basketball and golf, and was editor of the school newspaper this year. He and Jenna both help with my students on field trips.

Jenna's a sophomore—turned sixteen this year—and now drives. She and Paul had several white-knuckle driving sessions together. She's a very good driver. It's the bad drivers sharing the roads, who worry me. She's pretty, smart, and creative. She wants to be a teacher, so far. She'd rather play sports than cheer them, and is a sucker for stray animals. She found an injured, abandoned, golden lab a year ago on her way home from school. We named her Goldie Hawn, and she pals with our two stray cats, Elton and Elvis.

Paul's practice is thriving and he's away on business more and more. I take care of things at home and he takes care of things away from home. It works out okay. You know me. If reality isn't quite what it's cracked up to be, there's always fantasyland.

I think back on the band—to Parkridge—and wonder where everyone ended up. What do long-haired Hippie, pot-smoking, war activists grow up to be? Here I am, married to a lawyer, teaching school. Who would have thought?

Where are you, Jake? What did you grow up to be? An English teacher or college professor? A photographer with your pictures

in a gallery somewhere? Maybe you're a cinematographer on a
soap opera.

*Whenever I think of you, I picture you living on that beautiful,
family farm in Rockton, a pretty wife at your side, and lots of kids...
and maybe a dog or two. Do you have teenagers, too? I've wondered
about that off and on over the years. I'll bet you're a great dad.*

*I hope we get the chance to find out someday. I've never forgotten
you. Never really gotten over you. Maybe it's that 'first love' thing, but
I'd like to think it's more than that. We made a special connection, a
special bond, didn't we? To this day, I still feel it. Maybe you do, too.*

*I'll probably always love you. Can't explain it. Just happened one
fall evening long ago. Happy Birthday, Jake.*

Love,
Rose

November 23, 2001

Dear Jake,

We lost our sweet dog, Goldie, this year. She'd been less and less active for several months. I thought maybe it was just old age since we never really knew how old she was when Jenna brought her home. But finally, she wouldn't eat or play, and had a hard time going outside to potty. Very sad to watch.

One Saturday morning, I took her to the vet. Paul was gone on business, and Joe and Jenna both away at college... so I was alone. Dr Sadler checked her over, took X-rays showing several tumors in her lungs and liver. The tumors were inoperable and she was in pain.

I held her and kissed her—whispered in her ear how much we all loved her and would miss her—until I felt her go limp in my arms. I sat alone in the small examining room with her and cried until no tears remained. I came home—her collar and leash tucked in my purse—and called Paul and Joe first, and then Jenna. She cried... and I cried with her.

A few days later, I picked up Goldie's ashes. I've kept them in my dresser drawer since. Not sure what to do with them. Maybe I'll wait for a beautiful, warm morning, and scatter them where she loved to lay—among the tulips, iris, lilies of the valley, and sweet peas—shaded by the peach tree. Goldie can rest within my sanctuary.

Such a bittersweet birthday this year. One I think you'd understand Tonight, as I sit alone on the patio—writing and sipping a glass of wine—I'm thinking of you and how you could always make me smile, make me laugh. I've missed that over the years. I've missed you, my friend.

Cheers to us, Jake. May we both find peace though the coming years.

Love,
Rose

November 23, 2004

Dear Jake,

Once again I find myself alone, sipping a glass of wine, thinking of you, writing to you. It's become a habit over the years. One I've never wanted to break.

Paul and I are officially empty nesters. Joe and Jenna are both married and starting families of their own. Joe lives here in Albuquerque, while Jenna moved to Santa Fe. Oh, she's a pharmacist. Thought for sure she'd end up teaching.

As the children moved away from us, Paul and I moved farther away from one another. He's gone more on business than he's home. But, he does make sure he's home for family dinners, family celebrations. I appreciate that. But mostly, he's gone. I've decided it's not a good thing or a bad thing. It just is, what it is. My life stays the same whether he's here or not.

We never had much in common to begin with, but establishing a home and raising children gives you common ground, a common purpose, for a good part of your marriage. After that, there's no manual, no rulebook to follow. You both just make adjustments. I guess every marriage navigates through this or it ends. I'm not sure where we are at this point. It doesn't seem to matter.

I've wondered over the years if Paul has someone else. Makes sense if your husband prefers to be somewhere else, rather than at home with you. I've grown indifferent to whether he's having an affair or not. It doesn't affect me. So... again, it doesn't seem to matter.

I now have two rescue bulldogs, Sassy and Henry, to keep me company. They are a joy to have around and I'd be lost without them. They take me for long walks through the desert morning and night... and keep me on a strict schedule of activity.

I'm still teaching special education, and still enjoying getting up each day and going to work. I'm so glad I changed majors in college. My life would have been empty without these special kiddos, their parents, and my colleagues. I look forward to each new school year. The work is physically demanding and I rely more and more on my assistants for help. One of these days I'll have to think about retirement. Now, that word makes me feel really old. I guess we are old, Jake.

I wish I knew how you are, where you are. Something. Anything. But then, I'm not sure what I would do if I did know. Your memories and my memories are probably not the same. I still think of you, remember you, as that young man I left behind years ago.

It's his arms that hold me on lonely nights, his lips that brush softly across mine, his hard body I feel the weight of on mine. Would I love the man you've become in that same way? I wonder.

I must truly be crazy to still think of you... still dream of you. But then, I've heard and talked to a voice in my head for years, since I was a young child. I remember we talked about this—you and I—and you assured me I wasn't crazy. I believed you then, I'd believe you now if you walked through my door.

Happy Birthday, Jake. Here's to all the crazy people in the universe, like me, and maybe, like you.

Peace and love,
Rose with 2lls

CL Gillmore

November 23, 2007

Dear Jake,
I am elated! I have found you!! You are still there. You remember me.

A month or so ago, I sent Facebook friend requests to three Jake Richardson's. As I pressed the send key, I told myself it was okay because I was looking for Sam, who I lost touch with after Cash passed. But I knew down deep inside, I was looking for you. Still searching, after all these years, for my friend.

A few days later, I received a reply. Your reply, Jake.

Oh, my God. I'm not sure what to do at this point. I am happy and hopeful and apprehensive. I am all of these.

Today you sent birthday wishes to me in a Facebook message, and asked if I knew when your birthday was. If you only knew how many times I'd written that date over the years. How many birthday wishes, birthday letters, I've written to you. I won't tell you. I can't. Not yet.

Tomorrow I'll send my reply and you'll know I still remember you, too.

Happy Birthday, Jake Richardson. Happy Birthday to you... and to me. Finding you is the loveliest birthday gift I could ever ask for.

Love,
Rose Allison with 2lls

April 23, 2009

Dear Jake,

Tonight, I read through all the letters I've written to you over the years. The letters, alone, would make a lovely storyline for a novel. I decided you should have them now. They belong with you, not me. I never forgot you, never stopped loving you through the years, Jake.

I know Ben recognized me the night of the play, and I hope by now you've taken him into your confidence. I trust he followed his heart when the package arrived, and you are now holding the letters... reading my words.

I couldn't leave things unsaid between us and wanted to share my thoughts with you in words in a letter... one more time. Writing is what I do best. Whatever I said or did, I did out of love... always out of love for you.

A woman's heart searches a lifetime for her soul mate, her kindred spirit, her Prince Charming. Sometimes she finds him, sometimes not. But when she does, no one ever compares to him. His touch, his kiss, his love awakens all that sleeps deep within her... love, passion, and all the other possibilities they bring.

If she finds and keeps his love, they die in that love together. If she loses his love, her heart never forgets and forever longs and searches, in vain, for that same love. Jake, you are, and will always be my Prince Charming.

I've lived a lifetime on the fringes, watching others. Wondering who I was, where I fit in. I ignored things I couldn't deal with, and isolated myself out of fear. I don't want to live in that gray, shadowy area anymore. I know you don't want that either, but that's what will happen if you and I remain lovers, and nothing more. We'll spend the rest of our days stealing bits and pieces of precious time to be together And no matter how much more I want, because I love you, I might settle for those stolen moments, and come to you. This was my mother's life, and I'm not my mother.

If you love me, Jake, you won't ask this of me.

Even as I write these words, I fear it might be too late to save my heart a second time. Don't you see, Jake... if I hold on to your hand,

I'll die alone of a broken heart. If I let go, I may die alone of a broken heart, anyway.

The texts and messages create a constant craving—maddening—with no way to satisfy, to placate. You are like a drug to me, and I am addicted. I can't text or chat or see you briefly, without wanting more. There can never be enough "more" in an affair.

I've come so far in understanding myself over the past months. I've discovered so many scattered puzzle pieces, and places where they fit. Part of this with Molly's help... part with yours. I'm not afraid to step from the fringes.

No matter how much I love you, I can't be just an affair. I can't be the invisible woman in your life. I thought I could at first. I thought that would be enough. It's not, can never be. Maintaining an affair requires living part of your life in fantasy. I've done that. I know the difference between reality and fantasy. I can write fantasy, but I need reality in my life.

I want it all, Jake... Prince Charming, the kiss, the white horse, the happily ever after. Is that what you want? It's your decision now.

You will always be my kindred spirit, my soul mate, my muse. My heart will always remember and long for only you. Because of you, because of your love, I'm forever changed inside, a second time. You've helped me find my strength and courage and confidence again. There's no going back. Not sure I can go forward without you, but I must try, and you must understand.

When you hear something, feel something—a whisper that hushes and lightly touches you—it's me, Jake. It will always be me... waiting.

LUJ, Rose

A Friend Request

November 23, 2009

Dear Jake,

Tonight, while you lay sleeping, I slipped this letter in with the bundle of others you keep in your dresser drawer. I wrote this one as I watched you drift off, after making love to me. Even now, your scent lingers on my skin... your taste on my lips.

I hardly know what to do with my emotions for you, my love for you. Even the happy ending dreamer inside me can hardly believe all that transpired over these past months to bring us together.

Today, I married my soul mate, my lover, my best friend.

Today... I, Rose Allison married you, Jake Richardson.

You took me in your arms and kissed me once, and again. You trailed your lips to my ear and whispered, "I loved you then, I love you now, I'll always love you. Happy Birthday, Rose."

And I kissed your cheek and whispered back, "I know. I've always known... and I'll love you forever. Happy Birthday, Jake."

Happy Birthday to us.

I love you,
Rose with 2lls

A page turned... new chapters begin.
The sequel yet to unfold.
Never forgotten and never to end.
Images etched on each soul.

A Friend Request Playlist

Enjoy all the music from Jake and Rose's story
by accessing the book's play list on my Web site.

http://www.clgillmore.com

About C. L. Gillmore

Iowa native, C. L. Gillmore lived most of her childhood in Muscatine, a small, picturesque town nestled along the banks of the Mississippi River. Her heartfelt poetry and detailed story lines often reflect her Midwestern roots.

"I weave the details of what I know best into my writing. I remember hot summer nights along the Mississippi and crisp autumn mornings waiting for the school bus; small-town football games, Homecoming dances, and the smell of mum corsages; former teachers and students, friends, and lovers; local bands, music, rock festivals, and drugs; campus riots, assassinations, and war protests. These day-to-day, remembered details, breathe life into a character, and lend credibility to setting and storyline."

Gillmore retired after twenty-five years in education to pursue writing full time. Other interests include reading, gardening, decorating, and garage sales. She and her husband live in Surprise, Arizona, with French bulldog Pitty Pat. Two married sons and six grandchildren live nearby.

Find out more at clgillmore.com.